out of focus

Love in LA Series
Book Three

cristina santos

For all my fellow neurospicy pals.
You deserve to be known, understood and loved.
By others and yourself.

playlist

1. So Long, London - Taylor Swift
2. La La Land - Bryce Vine
3. GOOSEBUMPS - Ross Harris
4. Midnight Rain - Taylor Swift
5. Fortnight - Taylor Swift, Post Malone
6. 24/7, 365 - elijah woods
7. Wave of You - Surfaces
8. Risk - Gracie Abrams
9. Hey Girl - Stephen Sanchez
10. Nobody Gets Me - SZA
11. Like No One Does - Jake Scott
12. All Of The Girls You Loved Before - Taylor Swift
13. Can I Be Him - James Arthur
14. Cornelia Street - Taylor Swift
15. Softest Touch - Khalid
16. Coração Vagabundo - Gal Costa, Caetano Veloso
17. Floating - Alina Baraz, filous, Khalid
18. ILYSB (Stripped) - LANY
19. Electric - Alina Baraz, Khalid
20. Mine - Bazzi
21. hate to be lame - Lizzy McAlpine, FINNEAS
22. Best Part - Daniel Caesar, H.E.R.

23. on purpose - Ni/Co

24. Favorite T-Shirt (Acoustic) - Jake Scott

25. Off My Face - Justin Bieber

26. SAY IT BACK - Ross Harris

27. ilu - elijah woods

28. Your Bones - Chelsea Cutler

29. Só Tinha De Ser Com Você - Elis Regina, Antônio Carlos Jobim

Get the playlist here!

a little note...

first of all, thank you!

It will never get old, knowing you picked up *my* book and thought, "Yeah, I want to read that." A million times, thank you. I hope you love these two silly rabbits.

That being said, parts of this book may be triggering to you. I always want you to go into my stories knowing what to expect, but if you don't have any particular triggers and don't want any potential (*minor*) spoilers, skip the 'Content Warnings' page.

This is an 'open door' book, and that means that my characters have sex on the page, and things are described in detail. If that's not for you (or you're related to me), the chapters you should skip are in the 'Dicktionary'.

I hope you see yourself in one of these characters and see how loveable you are!

xoxo,
-Cristina

dicktionary

Whether you want to skip it, or skip *to* it, here's where you can find the spice and whose POV it's in:

Enjoy! (Or don't…)

content warnings

Please note that this book contains the following:

- Main character with autism and ADHD
- Main character with ADHD
- Mention of adoption
- Mention of pregnancy and childbirth
- Character goes into anaphylactic shock on page
- Open door scenes of the couple being intimate (in 8 chapters as mentioned on previous page)

Reading this book should make you feel things, yes, but I never want to trigger negative thoughts or feelings, so please be kind to yourself.

1 /
ouch. that's going to leave a mark.

charlie

now

"STOP CALLING ME, Robert. I'm not your girlfriend. I never was. You made that perfectly clear." I breathe in a lungful of the warm Los Angeles air and immediately regret it. I came outside to clear my head. To go for a walk and forget about London and Robert for a bit. And now, I'm acutely aware of everything around me yet again.

What is that smell? And why does the bottom of my shoe feel sticky?

"You said you needed space. How much more space could you need? We're on opposite sides of the planet!" His words instantly make my temples throb.

"You know that's not what I meant. We agreed that you would give me time." I huff out a breath, unsure of how many more ways I can find to tell him that I need him to leave me alone.

"Charlotte, stop acting like a petulant child. Come home."

A few weeks ago, I would have.

I would have said I was a shoo-in for CFO at the company Robert and I work for. Worked for? I haven't formally quit, but the thought has crossed my mind more than a handful of times in the seven months since my last visit to LA. I've earned this hypothetical promotion, though, and that's why I haven't handed in my resignation. As their VP of Finance, I helped Robert Thorpe, the current CFO, and voice at the end of the line, reduce costs and address operational inefficiencies. A job he has proven to be completely inept at. Now, Robert's father is stepping down as CEO, and he's gunning for the job. Instead of staying and fighting for my place as the company's first female with a C-level executive position in its seventy-three-year lifespan, I asked for a leave of absence. Effective immediately. And then I got on a plane to LA. Again.

"Charlotte? Are you even listening to me?" Ugh. I hate that he keeps calling me by my full name. My mother calls me that. Well, my mother *and* Robert, who refuses to be called anything else. The Thorpes only do full names or obnoxious nicknames. There's no in-between. My thoughts are slipping away again, so I know what the answer to his question is.

Nope. So not listening.

Squinting against the harsh sunlight, I realize that I forgot my sunglasses yet again on my way out the door. The sunglasses that are sitting on the kitchen counter, next to my to-do list, which includes a reminder to change my phone plan while I'm here because, this time, I am staying. This won't be like last time when I only stayed for a few days before running back to Robert and whatever emergency he was feigning.

I wonder how much this call is costing me. And did I close the balcony door before I left?

I take a breath and decide that it's fine. I'll tackle the list later, and it's okay if the door was left open. The flat is on the seventh floor, so it's not like anyone can break in, and it rarely rains here, anyway.

Despite the circumstances, I couldn't have come to LA at a better time. It's been two weeks since I told my twin, Maeve, that I was finally ready for the change I claimed to need all those months ago. Last time I was here, she had just accidentally married the love of her life and then decided to officially adopt the baby who had been placed in her husband's care. Owen's gone through a lot, and a drunken Vegas wedding was apparently what they both needed to start their lives together.

Since then, both Maeve and our best friend Elaina announced pregnancies just weeks apart. Elaina and Adam had their baby girl on New Year's Day, just two years and a day after they met. I've missed so much over the years, and it feels good to be here and witness all of the joy in Maeve and Elaina's lives. They're the two most important people in my world, and while they've been falling in love and growing babies, I've been living a monotonous routine of work, take-out, and a standing three-night-a-week date with my vibrator. I'm not jealous of what they have because I'm truly so happy they have found such joy, but I'm tired of hearing about everything over phone calls while I feel stuck living a life that isn't exciting anymore. I want more for myself, and I know I deserve it.

Between our mum's latest man drama and the announcement at the firm, I was being suffocated in London. I've always loved the city, but lately, everything there has felt wrong. Including Robert. Maybe, especially him. And that's why I'm here. I need space, clarity, and to make sense of my life.

Thanks to my twin's endless connections in Los Angeles, I was able to sublet a furnished place as soon as I got here. Maeve and Elaina have lived in LA since we graduated from NYU eight years ago. They asked me to come then, too, but the thought of living in another strange city just four years after moving from London to New York was completely overwhelming to me. Once I got the scholarship to Oxford for my master's degree, it was time to head back to England and eventually back to London after I graduated.

LA made sense for them. They were pursuing jobs in Hollywood, and they've both made names for themselves in their respective careers. I'm immensely proud of them. I suppose I've done the same, just in London and in a career I'm not entirely sure suits me anymore. A career I picked because it seemed like the right thing to do. It was safe. Predictable, yet challenging. It seemed so perfect. And I'm so damn good at my job, but is all of that enough?

I must make some sort of noise because Robert sighs and continues. "Oh, good. You're still there. Charlotte, you've got to come back. My father won't step down until I prove I've settled down. We've talked about this. We're the dream team. CEO and CFO power couple. Please, Lottie." He's the one sounding like a petulant child now. A spoiled rich boy who's always gotten his way, and that has unfortunately included with me as well. Right down to the fact that I let him call me that ridiculous nickname, which he reserves for when he wants something from me.

He latched on to me the moment I started impressing our professors at Oxford. I caught his attention, intriguing him with my brain. My mistake was thinking he'd be interested in other parts of my body, but all he's ever done is allude to the fact that he's not ready to take that step yet. He loves to tell me how someday we'll be the ultimate power couple, married and running the company his great-grandfather founded. Once he's done enjoying being a bachelor, that is, because he'd hate to resent the woman he spends his life with. And I've understood it.

We met at twenty-two, and I didn't want to get married then, either. I wanted to focus on school and my career. So when Robert said he wanted to wait until we were both ready for that final commitment, it made sense to me. And it made me feel like I had a safety net ready to catch me. I figured marrying the right man was worth the wait. And despite his many faults, Robert mostly understands me and accepts me as I am.

We decided years ago that an open relationship was the best thing for us. We knew we wanted to eventually fully commit to one another. Robert wanted to make sure we both got dating other people well out of our systems before we became exclusive.

Maeve doesn't understand it, but for me, it always made perfect sense. I got the security of knowing I'd found my person, and I could choose to date other people if and when I wanted to. Though for the past couple of years, I haven't wanted to, and Robert and I have spent almost no time together as a couple.

"Lottie. Babe. I'm ready now. What do I have to say to make you believe me?" His whiny voice cuts through the noise, and I shake my head, attempting to focus.

"Nothing. I've already told you I need a break. That's why I'm taking this leave of absence. I need you to respect that this time." My voice is firm, even if inside, I'm completely falling apart. "Two months ago you said that we're not in a relationship. Now you want me to commit to being with you permanently because your dad is giving you an ultimatum?" My heart is racing, and my nerves are completely shot. Have I just left behind my one chance at the two things I've always wanted? A top position in my field and a husband. Those are the next goals to be achieved.

A husband.

Something both my best friend and sister have now. Well, Elaina will soon. She's been engaged to Adam for over a year, but her pregnancy was so rough on her that she couldn't bring herself to plan a wedding at the same time.

"Well, yes, Charlotte. I'm ready now because the CEO position is ready now. We both said we wanted to meet career goals before committing. We both agreed. We've waited years for this, and you know you're the only one I could ever marry." This fact is what had kept me going. Kept me waiting. I always thought Robert was a good guy for not pressuring me into a relationship when I wasn't ready. He once told me that he knew the first time I smiled at him that I was the one. I don't even remember the moment. Don't remember the smile since it was probably fake. Likely because I was trying so hard to look like I belonged in the room, rather than fighting off the urge to put on headphones or leave and quiet my mind with a book or a walk. I had my mask on when I gave him that smile, but he doesn't know that. Most people don't.

"How long?" Robert's voice barely registers among all the noise. In my head. Out here. I need to find somewhere quiet.

"What?" I ask, not even sure what he's going on about.

"How long do you need?" His tone's changed from cajoling to slightly annoyed.

"I'm not sure. Perhaps until Lainey and Adam are married? Once Maeve gives birth? I don't know. I need space, Robert. I need space from *you*." There. I said it. It might feel as though my heart is about to gallop out of my chest, but I said the words.

Robert clears his throat. "Oh. I didn't realize. All these years, I thought, well, I thought you wanted this. Me."

"I did. I…" I can't force myself to say I do because I'm not sure that's true any longer. "I did. I still might. But I can't figure that out when you tell me we're not together and then two weeks later decide you want to marry me because your dad has a position ready for you. Where am I in all of this? When do my feelings start to count?" I take an exasperated breath. "We made this decision years ago when neither of us were ready, and I'm still not sure that I am. I need to see for myself what the best thing for me is. Personally and professionally. And my sister might need me here. It's a delicate time. There's so much going on. I don't want to miss it all." My temples throb as the words pour out of me.

"I'm trying to understand, Lottie." This time, when I hear the nickname that only he uses, my muscles relax. The familiarity is soothing. This is the conundrum I always find myself in with him. One moment he overwhelms me, and the next, he's the familiar presence I need to calm down. But it never lasts with Robert. One way or the other.

"Thank you. Are you all right?" The words stick in my throat. I know I need to do this, but Robert has been a constant in my life for years. Other than Maeve and Elaina, he's the person who knows me best. Who mostly understands my need to get away; my difficulty with sensory overwhelm. It's hard to simply let a person like that go, especially when I'm not very good at letting people in.

"Yeah. Fine." His voice is a bit harder again, and I'm back on the Robert roller coaster. Is it too much to ask for to simply be understood? Fully? "Is this you trying to get back at me? Because we agreed to an open relationship until we were married, Charlotte. It's not my fault you chose to stop dating other people, and I didn't. But if what you need is for us to be broken up so you can shag some LA boys before you come home to me, then fine. Get it out of your system." He's completely serious, too.

It's never bothered him to think of me with other people. I thought it was sort of progressive, even if it did always feel like a bit of red flag hanging limply between us. Now that red flag is practically glowing, waving aggressively and warning me to stay away.

He's partially right, though. It's not his fault I chose to stop dating, but now, I feel completely unprepared for the possibility of a permanent relationship. With anyone.

"I should go. I'll call you when I'm ready, all right?" I'm

about to say goodbye when I hear the telltale sound of the call ending. He hung up. I keep the phone to my ear, embarrassed.

Do the people around me know I was just hung up on? Can they tell? I say goodbye, pretending that didn't happen and willing the burning sensation in my cheeks away.

It doesn't work. The whole interaction throws me off, and I end up pacing back and forth on the sidewalk for several minutes. My phone is clutched to my chest like a security blanket as I dwell on every single word we just said to one another. My heart rate is still accelerated, the whooshing sound loud in my ears. Sweat is trickling down the back of my neck, making me itchy. Tears sting my eyes, but I can't let them fall. There are too many people, and I can sense their eyes on me, so I start walking.

What am I doing here? I should have stayed in London. What if I go back and they don't want me? I won't have a job. How will I make money?

I should have moved to LA a long time ago. I haven't been happy in London for ages. Have I ever been happy? Why don't I know the answer to that? What is wrong with me?

What if working in finance is my entire purpose, and I've just messed it up? I should go back. But what if I hate it? Do I have to do it for the next several decades?

I owe it to myself to figure this out. That's why I'm here. But what if I don't? Do I have to suffer through living in this limbo forever?

Why am I so indecisive that I can't just pick something and someone and live a happy life? Why am I so stupid and unable to handle simple things like everyone else can?

When I find myself in front of a small park, I spot a woman running, and I remember the reason I left the apartment to begin with: to escape. While the world of finance is where I've always excelled, writing is what brings me home.

On my walks, I often get lost in the characters I'm reading

or writing about. What started as a hobby, quickly turned into a hyper-fixation, and has now morphed into an all-consuming, secret side hustle. I write the love stories I wish I lived myself. I write the happy endings I hope everyone gets to have. The one I never saw my mum get because she was so selfish and always seemed to pick unavailable men. I live in both worlds, but this one that I've created, with flawed but beautiful characters, I get to keep to myself. I get to control it.

I tuck my phone into the pocket of my pants and take in my surroundings. The relief is almost immediate as the thoughts fall away, and I focus on my breathing and the movement of my legs.

Soon, my thoughts trail to the characters I'm writing. I get lost in the mental planning of the settings, the mood, and how I want things to feel. I let myself get lost in getting to know these people.

I walk for so long that my legs are almost numb, but I can't stop now. Not when my mind finally clears. I need to hang on to this feeling.

I close my eyes for a second. Just a second. And my body comes in full contact with a wall. Then, the pavement. I open my eyes just in time to feel my elbow hit the sidewalk.

Ouch. That's going to leave a mark.

I lay my head back on the floor and drape one arm over my face to hide from the embarrassment of walking with my eyes closed. I'm acutely aware of the shooting pain in my other elbow and the soreness in my lower back since I landed mostly on it. Words are leaving my mouth, but I couldn't tell you what they are. And is someone talking to me?

"Can you tell me where you're hurt?" The voice is soothing and sounds a little closer now.

"I think it's mostly my ego if I'm honest. I'm so very sorry. I was just getting into this groove, and I closed my eyes for only a second, I swear—"

"So, you *did* have your eyes closed." My whole body

tenses. Recognition hits me harder than the pavement beneath me. I know the sass in that tone. I can practically see the arrogant smirk painted on the face of the jerk it belongs to.

Rafael Machado.

You have got to be bloody joking me.

2 /
i read a lot of romance novels. like a lot.

charlie

three years ago

I MISS THE RAIN. Why is the sun so bloody bright in LA all the time?

My now-famous sister is presenting an award at an event, and I'm her plus-one. She hates taking dates to these things, so it felt like the perfect excuse to come for a visit and have some quality time with my favorite people. And I brought some of her favorite snacks to surprise her with, which I'm about to unpack so she sees them as soon as she's home. We don't get to be together nearly enough anymore.

Gone are the days when things were simpler. In university, I lived with my sister and best friend. I knew my role as a student well. I could control so much of my life because we lived in this bubble, even in a city the size of New York. We'd eat pizza in the middle of the night, and I'd listen to Maeve and Elaina tell me about the boys they'd gone on dates with. It helped me so much, having them as my guides for how to interact out in the world.

Things are so different now. Maeve needs a bodyguard to

attend events with her because she's had some majorly creepy things happen lately. The guard assigned to her sounds like he might actually be perfect, though. She says he's hilarious and doesn't make it feel like he's a security guard following her everywhere but feels more like an overprotective friend. Plus, Lainey already knew him, so it feels good to know we can trust this man whose entire job is keeping my sister safe.

I've arrived early, as a small surprise for her, and I'm waiting for her in her kitchen when I hear a deep voice outside the window.

"Well, maybe I can show you tonight just how sorry I am that I couldn't make it to our date last night. I can show you with my hands, with my tongue, with my co—"

"Ahh!" I walk backward and stumble on a pair of shoes Maeve left on the floor, making a giant crashing sound as I fall flat on my bottom. Who leaves shoes in the kitchen?

"What the fuck?" The deep voice is now inside the house. I can't see who it belongs to because I'm currently all kinds of twisted up on the floor, but large hands wrap around my arms and lift me effortlessly. My eyes travel up a set of abs— visible even through the crisp, white dress shirt Mister Dirty Talker is wearing—to a wide chest with clearly hard pecs, to a perfectly chiseled jaw, and finally to the darkest, deepest brown eyes I've ever seen. Yes, he does indeed look like he belongs on the cover of a romance novel. All the breath leaves my lungs when his face breaks out into a bright smile. Two deep dimples appear on his right cheek, and I cannot tear my eyes away from them.

"Hey, red. See something you like?" His voice is smooth, too smooth.

"N-no." I narrow my eyes at him. "And my name's not red." I step away from his grasp, feeling strangely unsettled by this beautiful man. The heat of his hands sears my skin even through my shirt, even though he's no longer touching me.

"All right, Ginger Spice." He smiles, and again, I find myself staring at the bloody dimples. "Care to tell me what you're doing in here? Your sister thought you were arriving later tonight."

"My sis—how do you know who my sister is? Who are you?"

"It's my job to know, honey bun. Not to mention that other than you have red hair and a much bigger rack, you and Maeve look pretty much the same." He lifts an amused brow at my wide eyes when he mentions my breasts.

"Who the bloody hell are you?" I shift uneasily on my feet, crossing my arms over my chest.

"Rafael Machado, but my friends call me Raf." He steps closer and takes my hand in his pornographically large one. "You can call me whatever you want, though, carrot cake." He winks, lifts my hand to his lips, and kisses my knuckles. My eyes widen again, and my breath hitches. I don't know how to respond to this.

Deep breaths, Charlie. Deep breaths.

"I'm Charlo—you can call me Charlie." I quickly remove my hand from his, doing my best to ignore the tingles running all the way up my arm. "I'm not a fan of nicknames, and you don't know me, so I'd appreciate it if you'd stop that."

He chuckles, and it's a deep, rumbly sound. "Oh, I'm sorry, Chuck. Maybe I can show you how sorry I am with my hands, or with my tongue, or—"

"All right, funny guy. You think you can rattle me by talking about your probably very mediocre, below-average cock? I think not." All the blood in my body rushes to my cheeks. I don't normally engage with strangers like this, but something about this guy thinking he can get a reaction out of me has my skin on fire. The feeling is nearly unbearable. As someone whose sexual experiences have been as exciting as watching paint dry, some might think this would shake me up. But I read a lot of romance novels. Like *a lot*. So I know how this goes. I'm supposed to clap back, right? At least the lack of filter between my brain and mouth helps in this situation.

The beautiful man has the audacity to chuckle again, and that rattles me. It's a wonderful sound. Sexy, deep, rich. But then he opens his mouth to speak again and ruins the effect. "Maevey was right. You are the interesting twin, aren't you?"

I hear the pitter-patter of footsteps, and Maeve strolls in. "Raf, I told you to go easy on her!" She hops over to me and throws her arms around me. "Charlieeeeee! I'm so happy you're here. I thought you were coming later tonight." She's squeezing me tightly, and it calms my nerves a bit as I give the smiling, dimpled man in front of me a death stare. "I see you've met Raffy, my loudmouth friend and bodyguard."

I tear my murderous gaze away from the beautiful bronze god and take in my sister's face. "I wanted to surprise you. Looks like I'm the one who got a surprise." I wave my hand toward Rafael without looking at him. "*This* is your body-guard, Mae? Really? Do you have any idea what this man was just saying to someone on the phone just now? To me? How can you trust someone like this with your safety?" I'm incredulous. This can't be the same person she speaks so highly of.

"Char. Rafael is one of the very best. I promise you. He's just a giant flirt who talks a big game. And I may have told him you're likely the only woman on earth other than me and Elaina who wouldn't fall for his muscles and those sinful dimples." She looks over at him and shakes a finger at him. "I warned you she wouldn't think your antics were funny, Raffy."

"Funny? *Funny*? Is that what you were trying to be, you big-chested wanker? Because I do not find it funny that you just propositioned me. And how about the fact that you're my sister's bodyguard, and you didn't even know I was in here."

My face must be as red as a tomato. I can feel it. The anger is burning me from the inside.

He scoffs. "Aw, come on, red, that's not fair. You had the code for the gate *and* the front door. It's not like you broke in, and I failed to stop you." I hate that he has a point. He knows it, too. That stupid smug smirk on his face tells me so.

"What?" I screech. "This is your entire job, how—"

"Why don't we have something to drink and catch up, Char? I've missed you!" Maeve cuts me off before I can pick an even bigger fight with the bronze wall of muscle in front of me. She's right, though. I would much rather catch up with my twin than bicker with a stranger.

"You ladies enjoy. I'll be out of your way." He shoots us a salute and walks out the same way he came in. I inhale my first full breath since the moment I first heard his voice.

———

I'M NOT sure why I've agreed to come to this with Maeve. I don't like big events with so many people and all these photographers around, but she insisted I be her date tonight. Her bodyguard is also here, but he's been quite professional so far, and we haven't said a word to one another since we met a few days ago.

Unfortunately, I have eyeballs, so of course I noticed just how good Rafael looks in his charcoal suit, white shirt, and black tie. His hair is a little longer on top than the sides, and there's a bit of a curl to the nearly black locks. I flex my fingers, pushing away the need sparking at my fingertips to feel how soft those curls must be.

I've been hiding in the bathroom of the green room Maeve had been waiting in. There were so many people around, all moving so quickly, and I started to feel dizzy from the commotion. Maeve was pulled away briefly, and Rafael went with her. Left on my own, I suddenly felt itchy with the need to get away from it all, but they should be back any moment.

I've just finished washing my hands to give myself something to do when voices carry through from the main room.

"I just think you can make more of an effort to be friendly to her, Raf. She's introverted." Maeve is talking to him about me? Why?

"So are you, and we've never had an issue." That's his rebuttal? I'm certain he wasn't caught nearly having phone sex with a woman when he met Maeve.

"You know it's different. We met under different circumstances, and you weren't purposely trying to make me squirm. Plus, I know how to deal with pretty boys like you who are far too used to women throwing themselves at them." Maeve doesn't completely clam up when new people speak to her. *Not like me.*

"Chuck just needs to loosen up. I thought maybe I could help her do that, but she's too... I don't know... stuck up to even talk to me." Ugh, I hate that he calls me Chuck. No one has ever called me that before, and my temples throb in anger. And stuck up? I am not stuck up! "You know I would never make a move on your sister, Maevey. I was just goofing around when I met her. Obviously, I made a mistake thinking she could take it. But she can't. I can tell by the death glares she shoots me every time I've walked in the same room as her these past couple of days."

He clears his throat, and I have the urge to do the same as a cluster of unnamable feelings become lodged in there. But the need to keep listening to Rafael's opinion of me is far too strong, and I definitely don't want to be caught.

I wish I could see his face. All I picture is him looking arrogant as he proclaims his obvious distaste for me. Thank goodness the feeling is mutual. Still, the rejection stings more than I want it to. I press a hand to my chest to suppress the ache. It always comes when I know I haven't met someone's standards. I don't want to date Rafael, but hearing him say he would never want *me*? It hurts. I lean on the wall for support as the embarrassment engulfs every inch of my skin. The burning sensation starts at my toes and climbs all the way to the tips of my ears.

"I just wish you two could be friendlier. She's my sister, and you're one of my closest friends. Can you just go easy on her, please? Charlie is… delicate. If you got to know her better, you'd understand." I don't like my sister imploring her friend and bodyguard to be nice to me. I hate that she's dancing around my symptoms, but I love her so much for not sharing more of the details.

"Maybe if she gets that giant stick out of her ass, sure. I'm perfectly civil. She's the one openly scowling and calling me names. My hands are tied here, M. Why don't you set her up with one of your pretty-boy co-stars? Maybe getting laid will help her prickly personality." What a total jerk! As if *he* gets to have any opinion on *my* sex life! He really is disgusting.

I hear a distant knock on the door, and a few seconds later, it opens. A third voice comes into the room. "Miss Howard, we're ready for you now."

"All right. Let me just send this text quickly. I need to let my sister know to meet us back here." I check quickly that my phone is, indeed, on silent, not only because we're at an award ceremony, but sometimes, all it takes is a ring or the ping of a text to send me over the edge. I let out a sigh of relief, knowing I won't get caught listening in. "Okay. Ready. Come on, my fearless protector." Maeve lets out a little laugh, and I hear Rafael's deep chuckle. I close my eyes as the goose-bumps rise on my arms and tell myself it's because I hate the sound of his stupid laughter so much. Despite my body's reaction to him, he is not someone I want to befriend.

3 /
may i touch you?

rafael

now

"IF YOU THINK you can do it better, why don't you?" Her voice cracked on the last word, telling him everything he needed to know. She was nervous.

"Is that what you really want?" He stepped closer as he asked the question. His eyes drifted away from hers for only a moment and landed on her lush, red lips. She nodded and swallowed. "Words, beautiful. I need your words." Another step closer.

"Yes, that's what I want. I want you to—"

"Whoa!" I see a flash of bright red hair, and then a body crashes into mine and promptly lands on the pavement in front of me. *Were her eyes closed?*

"Ouch. That's going to leave a mark." She lays her head back on the sidewalk, apparently not giving a shit that people have to walk around her. Her arm lands over her face as she lets out a noise somewhere between a growl and a whimper. I didn't even know that was possible. "Crikey. It really bloody hurts."

"Where? Where are you hurt?" I take her in from head to toe and fail miserably at not noticing her thick thighs or how her baggy T-shirt has ridden up her torso to reveal a sliver of creamy white skin, and damn! This girl's body is bangin'. I can't see where she's hurt herself, and she still hasn't answered me, so I crouch down, pause the book I had been listening to—which was just getting to the good stuff— and ask her again. "Can you tell me where you're hurt?"

"I think it's mostly my ego if I'm honest. I'm so very sorry. I was just getting into this groove, and I closed my eyes for only a second, I swear—" She's still covering her face when I interrupt her, smiling at her comment and cute British accent.

"So, you *did* have your eyes closed," I tease with a smirk now firmly planted on my face, and her whole body goes rigid. I think she even stops breathing.

"Please, no. No, no, no," she whispers as she finally exhales. Slowly, she starts to move her arm. Her face is all scrunched up, eyes shut tightly, and as her fingers move over her face, she whispers a final *please*. I lean forward, not wanting to wait to see the face of this angel who just walked right into me, and when her eyes open to reveal the brightest blue I've ever seen, a bolt of lightning hits me square in the chest, and I rear back, nearly falling on my ass as well.

"Chuck?"

"Bloody hell." She brings both hands to her face, and I see the not-small scrape she's got on her elbow and forearm. "Ow, ow, ow."

"Yeah, you are a little bloody. Can I help you up?" I extend a hand toward her, and her mouth twists up into an even more severe scowl.

"Oh, you've got jokes, have you, Rafael? Brilliant, really." She attempts to pull herself up, but she's clearly sore from the fall and a little disoriented. I reach out again, and she swats at my arm, flailing about as she tries to stand. I could sit back and watch, but I don't want her to hurt herself any further, so I reach out and grab her under her arms, pulling us both up.

With the momentum of it all, her body ends up plastered directly on mine, and it hits me that I have only been this close to Charlie once before. I freeze. My hands are still holding her, my thumbs most definitely digging into the sides of her breasts. Not gonna focus on *that* right now.

She tips her head up to look at me, a look of pure shock on her face. She has so many freckles on her nose and cheeks. I've never been able to see them like this before. My fingers itch to connect those dots, to wipe the hair that's clung to her forehead, to feel how warm her rosy cheeks are.

"You can let me go now." Her voice cracks, and she clears her throat. I've rattled her. Fuck, I love that feeling. And when I realize she's gripping my bicep even tighter than I am her, I know just what to say.

"You're gonna have to let me go, too, red." I smirk and loosen my hold on her, but don't let go. She drops her hand quickly as if the realization that she's touching me causes her physical pain. She takes a forceful step back and stumbles, and I lower my hold to her waist to steady her. Frustrated, she huffs out a breath, more at herself than at me, I think.

"I'm good. Please let me go so I can go drown in a tub of ice cream and forget this ever happened." She winces as she curls her left arm around herself, and blood smears onto her shirt.

"I live around the corner. Let me clean this up for you so you don't get blood everywhere, yeah?" My heart beats violently inside my chest, and I'm not sure if it's from being this close to her or the idea of having her in my house. If I know her, she's going to fight me on this. She fights me on *everything*.

Sure enough, she shakes her head. "It's all right. I'm staying… actually, I don't really know where I am." Her eyebrows furrow, and her cheeks turn a delicious shade of cherry red. "I'm fine, though, really, I—" She stops as she takes in the blood marks on her shirt and the scratches running along her forearm. Her eyes widen again, and her once-flushed cheeks pale.

"I got you, Ginger Spice. Come with me." I extend my arm, knowing she won't take it. She doesn't. I point in the direction we're going to be walking in and turn, giving her a moment to gather herself. It feels like she needs it.

A couple of minutes later, I hear her take in a deep breath. "What were you listening to?" Her voice is so quiet I almost don't hear her. I chance a look back at her and find her looking up at me. Some of the color is back on her face, and she's cradling her arm close to her body.

I slow my pace so I can walk next to her, rather than ahead. "Uh, it was an audiobook. I usually listen to them on my runs." I shrug, swallowing down the unsaid words, the reason I usually listen to books rather than read them.

"What book?" Her eyebrows shoot up, and I revel in her sudden curiosity in anything that has to do with me. She's never asked me anything about myself before.

"It's a romance novel. The last in this series, actually, which really sucks because it's really, really good." When I look at her again, she cocks her head to the side, silently asking again the question I haven't yet answered. "It's called *Flirting with Fate* by C.M. Howe. Have you heard of it?" It's very likely she has. Elaina got me onto this series, and she's working with Adam on the movie adaptations of the books.

"Mm-hmm. Yep. I know it." She rolls her lips between her teeth, almost like she wants to say more. Maybe she thinks it's weird a guy is reading smutty romance books, but I've never cared about that. "Do you run often?" She changes the subject, and given her current state, I don't push to talk about what she thinks of the book.

"Every day, yeah. You?" Fuck, I swear I'm usually a better conversationalist than this, but Charlie always gets me in a fucking state. Like all my good, working brain cells leave my body when she's around. It's probably why I made a horrible first impression when we met. Probably why we still don't get along.

She shrugs and winces as her scraped arm rubs against her shirt. "Not running, no. Walking. I do it as often as I can. It helps me clear my head. It's why I don't usually listen to anything when I go for walks, though. There's enough noise up here, you know?" Using her uninjured arm, she taps her temple with her index finger. When she drops her arm again, her eyebrows furrow, and she shakes her head lightly. "Sorry. TMI. I go for daily walks, but since getting to California, I haven't had much of a chance. I don't know Santa Monica well, so that complicates things, I suppose."

"You're staying here? In Santa Monica? Not with Maeve?" The surprised tone slips out, and that little crease makes a comeback between Charlie's brows. "Sorry, you don't have to answer that." I clear my throat and look ahead, putting a bit of distance between us.

"I'm staying here. In Taylor's flat. He moved in with his partner, so he's letting me sublet it. For as long as I need." Her voice wobbles at that last word, which tells me this is an obviously sensitive topic for her. But the thought of Charlie being here is oddly exhilarating. We only see one another a few times a year, and I'm always greedy for more. More of calling her by her nicknames. More of her blushes. More of the eye rolls she loves to throw my way.

I connect the dots after a few seconds of silence. "Taylor's place is just down the street from me. We're practically neighbors." I smile at the thought and look down to catch her scowl, which only makes me smile wider. "I could show you a few of my routes around here. It's a safe neighborhood, but, uh, don't go for walks at night, yeah?"

"Yeah. Thanks." I'm not sure whether she's agreeing to let me show her the routes or not going for walks at night, but we arrive at my place, and I direct her toward the gate. "Whoa. This is nice." I note the surprise in her tone but choose not to address it.

"Thank you," I respond jovially. Rather than taking her inside, I head to the backyard. "Have a seat. I'll grab a first aid kit real quick." She nods and pulls out a chair at the outdoor dining table, still clutching her arm close to her body.

I take the few minutes inside to gather myself. It's weird having Charlie here. This whole interaction has been strange. We're almost never alone; we haven't talked this much since that first New Year's Eve, and seeing her hurt is making me squirmy. I'm gonna need to go for a run to recover from this run.

When I walk out with gauze, peroxide, and a couple of bandages, she's sitting with her head thrown back. The sun is shining on her body, but her face is perfectly shielded in the shade. I stupidly let the door slam behind me, and she jolts, sitting up and flinching when her forearm hits the side of the table. *Damn it. I'm an idiot.* "Sorry, I didn't mean to startle you."

She eyes the contents in my hands and swallows nervously. Great. Now I'm nervous too. I set everything on the table and pull out a chair so I can face her. I hold out my hand to look at her arm, and she sucks in a sharp breath. "Oh. I can do this. It's all right, you don't have to."

Fuck, this is so fucking awkward. "It'll be hard for you to see from this angle. I really don't mind." Her gaze locks in on my hand, still out in front of her. "May I touch you?" When she blinks again, her eyes meet mine for a brief moment.

She nods. "Yes, you may." Another swallow. "Thank you for asking," she whispers and moves her injured arm toward me.

"I'm sorry I didn't ask earlier. When you fell. I should

have." My stomach turns with the realization that I touched her so easily, as if we're not almost strangers to one another. Though to me, she doesn't feel like a stranger at all, I would imagine that to Charlie, that's exactly what I am. She hardly looks at me while I'm always watching her. Every chance I get.

I get to work on cleaning up her arm, focused on the task at hand rather than on the person I'm currently touching. Thankfully, none of her scratches are deep, but she hisses when I wipe them with the peroxide.

I'm careful not to get any of the sticky parts of the bandages on the broken skin, and with a final caress of my thumb over the adhesive strip, I finally look up at her face again. "All set, carrot cake." Her name is on the tip of my tongue, but I don't let myself say it. Call it a defense mechanism, cowardice, whatever. It's one of the small ways I keep some semblance of emotional distance from Charlie. Saying her name out loud, especially after years of nothing but nicknames, which started as a joke, would feel so intimate. And we aren't that. *Ever.*

Our heads are so close I can feel her breath on my cheek. In an instant, the soft look on her face disappears, and she rears back, furrowed brows firmly in place.

"Ugh. Are you ever going to call me by my actual name?" She pulls her arm away from my hands, and I miss the contact immediately.

"You really want me to call you Charlo—"

"No! Forget it. Never mind." With a shake of her head, she pushes her chair back and rises. "I'm going to go home now." She starts to walk toward the gate, and I stand and go after her.

"Do you want me to walk you home? Do you know how to get back?" I do my best to keep the minor panic out of my voice.

"I'm fine, thanks. I looked up the directions when you

were inside, and it's very close. An eight-minute walk." She gets to the gate and turns her head, not making eye contact.

I nod dumbly. She can't see me, but it doesn't matter because she's gone.

It's always like this with Charlie. Even when I get a small piece of her, it slips through my fingers.

4 /
i thought he looked more like a ken doll.

charlie

two years ago - the first new year's eve

MY LIPS TINGLE, and I'm giggling. I don't giggle. Ever. It's a telltale sign of having too much alcohol, but I told myself I'd have a good night tonight, and I am. Even if *he's* here. Ugh, just the sight of him is enough to make me want to drink until I blackout, and I hardly ever drink.

Rafael is dancing with someone I've never met, and she's throwing her head back, laughing like she's having the time of her life. I'm not a jealous person, but I'm jealous of her. And of him, too. Just once, I'd like to know what it's like to live the easygoing life Rafael seems to. I certainly would like to have someone to make me feel like that woman probably feels. Beautiful. Sexy. Wanted.

I want someone to make me laugh like that.

Robert. It should be Robert making me laugh like that.

Not *him*, though.

I could sit here and watch them, use their joy as inspiration for my next book, but the thought of watching Rafael makes me nauseous. I'd much rather look at someone else to give me a little inspiration.

A tall blond man making aggressive eye contact with me interrupts my thoughts. He's walking over here. *Oh dear.*

"Hey." Yes, that's all he says as he looks me up and down, about as subtle as a punch in the face. In an effort not to roll my eyes, I take a sip of my drink.

"Hi there," I bite out as he walks closer. He has hazel eyes, a visibly fake tan and there's a lot of product in his hair, which makes it look shiny, like one of my old Ken dolls I played with as a kid. I have the urge to touch it, but I am also scared I'll lose my hand in there or that the sticky mess will end up all over me.

"You having a good night, beautiful?"

I could do without the generic question and calling me beautiful, but sure. Let's go with this. I'll give Ken a chance. If nothing else, for the book content. And the possibility of an orgasm. Thank goodness small talk comes a little more easily with the help of alcohol.

"I am now," I whisper to him, and the loser falls for the bait. His eyes sparkle with the idea that he is actually enticing enough to make me interested in him. I'm about to step closer and put my hand on his forearm when I feel a massive warm body beside mine and then a matching massive hand on my lower back.

"Chuck. There you are. I need to talk to you." I turn my head and deep, dark eyes are staring me down. "Right now, please." He doesn't even acknowledge Ken; he just guides me away from my potential one-night-stand, and I'm so stunned that I let him. His hand never leaves my back, fingers wrapping around one side of my waist. It's the kind of intimate touch I'm completely unfamiliar with.

We make it to a quiet area of the garden, and I come to my senses. "What do you think you're doing, Machado?" I step away from his scorching, fiery touch and stumble forward, only to be caught around the waist. I hardly have time to process the warmth in my lower belly before my back is up against a tree, and I nearly smash my face against Rafael's massive chest.

"What am I doing? Oh, that's rich. You're completely wasted and were about to get sloppy with that department store mannequin, but yeah, ask *me* what I'm doing."

His hands are on his hips and I'm pretty sure I've never taken notice of just how good he smells before. Fresh and citrusy. Probably because we've never been this physically close before. Probably because we don't like each other.

"I thought he looked more like a Ken doll, but mannequin works, too." I lean against the tree, letting my head fall back so I can look him in the eyes briefly. "And I was trying to get laid, in case it wasn't obvious. Thanks for ruining that for me." His breath warms my cheek, and the heat in his eyes is almost too much for me to bear. "Now, if you'll excuse me." I make a move to swerve around him, but he stops me with a giant palm landing on my forehead, pushing me back against the tree. "Owww!"

"Not tonight, Ginger Spice. You've had way too much to drink to be going home with anyone, let alone that leather-skinned dumbass out there." He lowers his hand, and I stay put, once again shocked by the physical contact and the sheer size of him.

"Oh, stop. You're not on duty, Machado. And you're not my bloody bodyguard." Heat rushes to my cheeks as it always does when I get into a tiff with Rafael. "What's it to you, anyway? You shag a different girl every other night. What happened to the one that was just hanging off you? It's positively appalling how you—"

"Are you about to slut shame me? Because I thought you were better than that." He crosses his insanely tanned and tattooed arms, and the way his muscles bunch up only distracts me for a moment.

"What? No! Of course not. I don't care about your sex life enough to bother trying to shame you for it. But why do *you* get to sleep around, and when I try to get busy with a guy *one time* you think you can stop me?" With my arms over my chest, mimicking his stance, I do my best to stand up straight, but I can feel my upper body swaying. I'm so bloody wankered.

"Get busy? You don't *get busy*." He air quotes annoyingly. "I know you." I'm hit with a waft of his cologne again, and I hold my breath to keep myself from breathing in deeper.

"You know nothing about me." My voice is shaky, and suddenly, I don't feel like I've had nearly enough drinks to be this close to him.

"Oh no? But you know so much about me that you can talk about who I sleep with?" He quirks up an eyebrow, and I want to drop-kick it. I want to smack that eyebrow right off his unreasonably handsome face.

"I know enough."

He steps forward, and the air becomes instantly thicker. Hotter. It's hard to breathe, move, think.

"Is that so?" He smirks, and I scowl up at him. It's a look I know he's used to seeing from me. "Why do you fight with me so much? What is it you think you know about me that makes you hate me?"

"I don't… I never said that I…" I can't look at him now, but I can feel his gaze is steady on me.

"You don't have to say it, red. You avoid every room I'm in. When you see me, you scowl. Every time I smile at you, you roll your eyes and walk the other way." He leans in closer and pulls my chin up, so I have to look at him. "Is it because you're the proper British girl who's never had a real man make her scream his name before? Or is it that you're so attracted to me that you get jealous of the women who take me to their beds?" The flush hits my cheeks before he even finishes the question. The jerk chuckles. "So that's it then. You want to know what all the fuss is about. Want to find out for yourself if you'd melt in my hands, too." It's not even a question, and the pompous jerk raises one eyebrow with all the confidence in the world. "How did I do, Princess Charlotte?"

Anger rises from my chest to my temples. I push my hands as hard as I can against his chest, but he doesn't budge. "Screw you, Machado. And don't ever call me that again. You really want to know what I think about you?"

He licks his lips and lowers his chin, urging me on. I keep my eyes locked on his nose, avoiding his eyes while refusing to be distracted by the lip-licking. If it weren't for the fact that I've thought about these words before, I would be frozen right now, completely unable to retort. But I've defended myself against his picture-perfect smile laced with taunts in the comfort of my own mind before. I'm ready now.

"You probably peaked in high school, and that's why you feel you need to keep up this little charade now. Let me guess… you were some sort of sports star who got away with doing bugger all, not having to actually try at anything. Your little girlfriends probably did all your homework for you because you were too dense to figure it out yourself, and all that charm that oozes out of your pores allowed you to get away with it. You wear your conquests like a badge of honor because you have nothing else to be proud of." I'm panting as the words I've thought about so many times explode out of me. "How did I do, big guy?"

I look up long enough to notice that the glimmer in his eyes is gone, and his jaw is clenched. I should feel guilty about what I said, but I'm too drunk and angry to care, and still far too unsettled by him calling me out on my curiosity about his sexual prowess—because damn it, I *am* curious.

He steps back, and if I hadn't been staring at him unblinkingly, I might have missed it. He looks down at his shoes before looking back up at me. "You got it, Chuck. You got it just right."

But I don't feel like I got anything right. I feel like I got it all wrong, but I can't take anything back now because before I can apologize, I'm throwing up into a bush. And it is violent. Maeve is going to throw a wobbler when she finds out about this.

5 /
the story is about my sad, dehydrated vagina.

charlie

now

"YOU CAN DO THIS," I mumble to myself as I try to prevent myself from throwing my laptop out a window for the seventh time this writing session. "Think about kissing. What do you feel when you kiss someone for the first time? Come on, then. Think about the anticipation. The tingly feelings in your... wait... where is one supposed to feel tingly when kissing? Aaaah!"

A weird pang in my chest hits me as I think about the book I've started writing. Things don't feel as clear as they did before, and I'm really struggling with writing any of the romantic scenes. Don't even get me started on having to write about sex. Sure, I've had sex before, and, of course, I know what an orgasm feels like. I'm thirty, and I'm not dead.

I've never felt the passion I read or write about in romance novels, and now that I'm writing my tenth one, I feel like I should really have more experience in the field. That, and the pressure from Robert for us to officially be in a monogamous relationship with one another, has me wondering how I can prepare myself for true intimacy with someone if I've never experienced it.

While he's been actively dating in London for years, I've been writing about it. My personal experience with relationships is… well… I don't have any. It makes me feel very inadequate and unprepared, and I'm not comfortable being either of those things. It's messing with my writing and my head.

Feeling like I'm about to crawl out of my skin, I plop myself down on my bed, careful not to hit my still-sore arm, and scream into the pillow so loudly I hardly register the buzzing of my phone. I roll over and read the screen before picking up with a groan.

"Char, are you all right?" My twin's tone is concerned.

"I'm fine," I respond. "Ugh, no, I'm not!" There's no use in lying to Maeve. She may have asked if I'm all right, but my greeting by way of a groan gave me away already.

"Oh, what is it, love?" I can practically feel her firm touch on my back as I come up for air. "Maybe I can help."

My sister is one of my favorite people for many reasons, one of them being how well she can help me settle down. I sometimes feel so out of control, and when I do, Maeve is the one who can get me through it. She knows I write. I've done it since we were kids, but she has no idea I've ever published anything. Still, she treats this "hobby" of mine as seriously as anything else I've ever done because she knows how important it is to me. Like screaming into a pillow, writing is a way I can express the emotions I don't know how to articulate out loud.

"I think this whole situation with Robert is throwing me off my writing game." I have more time than I usually need to write, and I wanted to use this sabbatical from work to get most of it done, but it's not working. Nothing is. I always find myself thinking about life in London—and about Robert— who weirdly hasn't called or texted since our last conversation.

Should I be thankful or worried that he's giving me space?

"What were you writing about? Talk it out with me." Her steady tone and genuine interest put me at ease.

"It was… I don't even know. This couple has already been in a relationship for a while, and I have no idea what that looks like, so I'm stuck."

"All right. What's happening with the characters?" Her voice remains calm as I hear her shuffling about on her end.

"They've been together for years, and they've become complacent, I suppose. Now, they're finding their way back to one another. I'm struggling with the everyday stuff. The mundane. That and the intimacy that comes from two people knowing one another so well. I don't actually know what that looks like." My tone turns frantic again, and I take a deep breath to calm myself down. "This isn't normal, is it? At least not for a romance writer, right?"

"Everyone struggles sometimes. Why do you think you're having such a hard time with this?" Of course she's not just giving me a fix to my problem. I swear this sister of mine should have been a therapist rather than an actress. Then again, she's exceptionally good at what she does, so perhaps it's okay that Elaina and I are the only two who reap the benefits of her counseling.

"I think it's because I don't want to just write the words for the sake of it. I need them to really mean something, and in order for that to happen, I have to draw from personal experience. Something I am seriously lacking at the moment when it comes to sex or any other kind of relationship." My cheeks burn as I say it aloud. It's Maeve, the person who knows me best, but it's still embarrassing to admit.

"Hmm. So, what you're saying is you need a good shag." She doesn't ask. That fact does not escape me.

"Is your answer to everything to go out and get laid?" She laughs then, and I can't help it; I do, too. Few people can make me laugh like this—so genuinely—but with Maeve and Elaina, it's natural. Easy, even.

"Pretty much! And I think, in this case, it's the only answer. At the very least, you need to go on dates. Connect with someone. Push yourself out of your comfort zone." A scowl overtakes my face as that final word. "Don't scowl at me, Charlie Mae!"

"Right. Because dating in LA is just the easiest thing in the world!" I roll my eyes, knowing full well how much harder it used to be for her to find anyone to date because she can't go anywhere without being recognized. "And it's not like I haven't tried. I have triiiiiied!"

Ugh, how I've tried. Over the years, I've dated them all. The famous ones who had egos so big I felt like I was competing for the oxygen in the room. The rich ones who were obsessed with their portfolios and cars. One time, I nearly fell asleep on a date as he tried to explain the stock market to me. My degree is in business and accounting. I did not need the mansplanation. In fact, he got several things wrong, and I nearly chewed the inside of my lip raw from holding back my thoughts. Friends have set me up, and I've done the dating apps. I've dated in London, and New York. I have never met a man who sent shivers up my spine or tingles on my skin. I've written about it. I've daydreamed about it. I've heard about it from Elaina, who is so in love with Adam that it makes me believe the fairy tales can actually be real. I've seen it play out with my sister and Owen. It's why I write romance novels. I wholeheartedly believe in fairy tales, in love that lasts forever, and people choosing one another day after day. I've just never experienced it myself, and sometimes, I question if it's possible for me and the kind of brain I have. It's probably why I agreed to this arrangement with Robert years ago. It was a guarantee that I would get my happy ending. Like I had some control over it.

I used to wonder if my autism diagnosis was the thing

that would keep me from ever feeling real love. I believed that until I realized that despite what doctors and psychologists had told me, I connected with someone outside of my family. Elaina is like a sister to me, but I didn't meet her until I was eighteen. I had recently been told that friendships and relationships of any kind would always be difficult for me, but somehow, with her, it wasn't. And so, she gave me hope. Hope that I would one day meet a man who would send shivers down my spine. Who would see me for who I am and accept me. Just like she did. Just as my twin—who couldn't be more different from me—always has.

Robert is attractive. He paid attention to me. He listened to me, seemed genuinely happy to spend time with me, and never pressured me into anything. But I've never experienced the kind of admiration, intimacy and friendship that I write about with him. And I want to believe those things are possible. For anyone.

Something else I haven't experienced? The steamy, toe-curling, all-consuming sex I have also read/written/heard about. Not once. I've had sex. I've had orgasms. When a man was involved, I had to work very hard for those orgasms, whether that be with my hands or with a toy once they'd left. But my imagination has always been pretty exceptional, so I've been able to write about it all convincingly if my fan base, publisher, and upcoming movie deals are anything to go by. But suddenly? I'm coming up dry. Literally.

I could write a book about all kinds of bad dates. It would be a horror story about a woman who goes on one horrible date after another. A woman who, at thirty years of age, has never been in love. A woman who's become so jaded and numb to the male species that she can't even make up stories about love anymore. Her creativity has run as dry as her minge. In case it wasn't obvious, I'm the woman. She is me. The story is about my sad, dehydrated vagina.

Maeve goes on despite my mental tangent. "Is the issue just with writing?"

I shouldn't be surprised that she knows that's not all there is to it. I shake my head and look down at my lap. "I think I've realized that my life in London was making me numb. I knew what to expect from my job, from the city, from Robert, from everything. And yes, that can be boring, but it can also be comforting. As if nothing would ever change. Then, Robert went and offered me the one thing I thought I wanted most, and I started thinking that maybe I didn't want that life as much as I once did. Maybe I don't want him as much as I used to." Maeve lets out a little grunt at the mention of the man I've told her is who I'll end up with. "I'm feeling a little out of control here, Mae. This move—it's what I needed, but change is more than just difficult for me, even if this isn't permanent. You know that. It's the real reason I didn't stay last time. Because when Robert called me back, I was happy to fall back into the safety of my routine. A routine I'm trying really hard to let go of and forget about. I'm trying really hard to push myself to feel. Everything." My voice cracks, and there's this desperate feeling in my chest that I don't know what to do with.

In a near whisper, she asks, "What are you feeling in your body right now, this very moment?"

I take a deep breath and close my eyes. "Warm. A little calmer, maybe. *Heard.*" I don't have my fight or flight system activated because I feel safe with my sister. She knows better than anyone what it feels like in my head, in my body, even if she doesn't share my diagnosis.

"See? You're not numb, Char. I think maybe you need to experience safety with someone who isn't just Lainey or me. And perhaps also someone to hump you into remembering what an orgasm from someone other than yourself feels like." We both burst out laughing, and it feels good. So, so good.

"I'm sorry I don't have the answers for you, sissy, but can

I say one last thing?" I hum in agreement, feeling in my bones that I will not like whatever this *one last thing* is. "Look for the places and people in your life that evoke powerful feelings in you. Even negative ones. Maybe especially those. Start there. Don't push yourself too hard, but look for the people and things that make you feel something. Anything."

"Why do I think you have an exact person or place in mind, and you're just not saying it?" Dread clings to my chest as I wait for her response.

"Love and hate aren't that different from one another, Charlie. I thought I hated Owen for years, when, in fact, I never stopped loving him. I blamed him for all of my emotional outbursts, thinking they came from resentment, but that's not all it was. I had to be honest with myself about what I was feeling." She pauses, and I know the blow is about to be delivered. "I can only think of one person you dislike enough to make you have big, potent emotions. No one else gets you worked up quite like him. It's always *him*."

It's always him. Ugh, if she only knew how many hours I've spent thinking about the man who makes the blood boil inside my veins. The one who inspired the villain in my last book. The one whose words I can't ever forget, no matter how hard I try.

Stick up her ass. Prickly personality. You're the proper British girl who's never had a real man make her scream his name before. You're so attracted to me that you get jealous of the women who take me to their beds.

"I'm not sure how this comparison between how you felt about Owen, a man you've always loved, and Rafael, a man I have only ever barely tolerated, makes sense. But I hear you on being honest with my feelings." My last conversation with Robert comes to mind, and my stomach lurches at the thought of bringing him up. Maeve can't stand the guy. "I talked to Robert the other day. He wants me back in London. He keeps insisting that he's ready now."

"Ready? For what? To stop dicking you around?" The protectiveness in her tone is the same one she always takes on when we discuss him.

"It seems so, yes. His father is stepping down, and Robert wants the CEO position. He wants me as CFO, and says he's ready for our relationship to move forward—"

"Your *relationship*?" Maeve drags out the word, her voice going up an octave or two. "What relationship? He's been promising you the world for years while he sleeps with anything that will open its legs to him. Except you, that is." I wince at the description, accurate as it may be. "Fuck. I'm sorry, Char. That was too harsh, I just—"

"I know. I know. You want more for me." I blow out a long breath. "I think I want more for me too. I think that's why it's been so difficult to write anything. I used to be able to pretend that these happily ever afters were Robert and me. That one day, we'd end up like my characters. But it's getting harder and harder to imagine that life. And now that he's offering it to me, I keep thinking that maybe…" Can I say it? Can I be really honest with myself and with my sister?

"Maybe what, sissy?" Her gentle voice is hopeful for what's next.

"Maybe there's more for me than being a CFO in London. Maybe being married to Robert isn't where I'm supposed to end up. I don't know. I've had my whole life laid out in one clear path for a long time, and suddenly, it feels like there's a fork in the road, and that fork leads to another and another and another. It feels like…" I'm not sure what.

"Like you have endless options? Because you do, Charlie. You can do anything you want to do." I nod because I know she's right. I've told her the same thing countless times.

"I'm just not sure what it is I really want anymore." The admission feels bitter on my tongue, laced with this sour, rotten truth that I'm forced to swallow. Because it is true. I don't know, and the unknown has never been a place of comfort for me. I plan, I execute, I achieve, and I move on to the next thing. My life has been a series of boxes neatly ticked off, but now, as I'm being handed a shiny new marker to tick off the husband box with, I'm ringed with doubt. Not in myself, but in the option I've been presented with.

"I'm here for you. Always. Regardless of what or whom you choose." Without a doubt, my sister is biting her tongue on the other end of the line, holding back the part where she says she hopes it isn't Robert. The fact that she doesn't say it, though, that she remains steady in her decision to support me despite her own personal feelings, makes my love for her grow even stronger. A feat I didn't realize was possible.

"I know, Mae. Thank you. And I'm sorry." I press on my forehead as if the motion will wipe away the tension there. "I didn't even ask how you're doing. How Julia is. How you're feeling." I have no idea what being pregnant is like, and I hope I never find out, but I love living vicariously through my sister and Elaina as they experience motherhood.

"I'm fine. Jules is great. Everything is okay. You don't need to be sorry. I'm happy I called and we got to talk about this. I knew something deeper was going on when you decided to come to Cali, and I feel much better now that I know." Guilt pours over me for causing my sister to worry at such a precarious time in her own life. "Really, Char, I'm so glad you told me."

"I know. Love you most, sissy," I say as I need to end this conversation and release some pent-up energy.

"Love you most, Char. See you Sunday."

We hang up, and I throw my trainers on, heading out the door for a walk.

6 /
like several inferior versions of ross geller.

rafael

one year ago - the second nye

I'VE ALWAYS LOVED New Year's Eve. Not because of the parties or the ball drops or fireworks or whatever. But because I love how hopeful people are at this time of year. December is full of anticipation, and January is full of promise.

I should be happier today. My best friend and the girl I love like a little sister just got engaged. They're ridiculously happy and in love, and yet something just isn't sitting right. It has nothing to do with them. It has everything to do with me. And my memories of this day a year ago.

Charlie doesn't like me; I already knew that. I knew she had a hard time being near me, and I thought teasing her about it would get us to clear the air a little. Maybe I pushed it too far that night, but I didn't think she'd go off on me like that. Somehow, she hit on all my insecurities without even trying. The words stung like rubbing alcohol on an open wound.

You probably peaked in high school. Your little girlfriends prob-

ably did your homework for you because you were too dense to figure it out yourself. You wear your conquests like a badge of honor because you have nothing else to be proud of.

I've thought about Charlie's heated words countless times this year. At first, I kept my distance from her and made myself scarce whenever she was around. I know she's the kind of person who sees people for what and who they are, so the fact that she saw that in me really fucking sucks. I'm told I'm a pretty optimistic and easygoing guy, even if it doesn't always feel that way inside my body, so I've done my best to let it go, or at least make it look like I did. I'm not even sure Charlie remembers the conversation, so it seems better to pretend it never happened.

We went back to our normal banter, eventually. I still really like seeing the blush creep across her neck and cheeks whenever I call her Chuck or make any mention of her having a secret crush on me. Maybe I even like it too much. Charlotte Howard would never in a million years go for a guy like me, though, and that's always been just fine with me.

Yeah, keep telling yourself that, bro.

Elaina's approaching smiling face momentarily distracts me away from thoughts of Charlie, and I'm grateful for it. Lainey's only a couple of years younger than me, and ever since I met her while serving in the Marines with her brother Owen, she's been like a sister to me, too. And now, all these years later, she's marrying my best friend. I reach out to her and twirl her around to the beat of the music. She squeals, and it makes me laugh, which feels good.

"Okay, okay. That's enough spinning, Raf. I gotta sit down." Elaina hugs me quickly and plops onto a nearby chair. I look up to see Charlie scowling at me from the bar. She quickly looks away, but I don't.

"What is it with you two?" Elaina glances over at Charlie and back at me as she catches her breath. Of course she noticed. "Hasn't this little hating game gone on long enough?"

"Go over there and ask Chuck that. I don't have a problem with her." Elaina narrows her eyes and frowns at me, but it's quickly replaced with a smile as Adam, her fiancé, comes to stand next to her.

"Raffy. Be serious. What's the deal with you and Charlie? We've been watching you practically at each other's throats since you met, and it's only gotten worse this past year." She and Adam casually shift around so he's sitting on the chair, and she's on his lap. My best friend doesn't even look at me. He knows Charlie is a sore subject.

"Baby girl, I promise I have nothing against her. I just like riling her up." Elaina looks thoughtful while Adam mutters something under his breath that I can't quite make out. "What was that, my very loyal and non-judgmental best friend?"

"I just said maybe you like it a little too much. You're not like this with anyone else. It's always her." Leave it to my best friend to call me out. He's right, of course, but I don't need to admit that right now. *It's always her.* He's also the only person who knows about what happened between me and Charlie last year. But he doesn't know everything she said. No one does. "Have you ever tried to talk about it? When one of you isn't blackout drunk?" He also knows the answer to that.

"Nah. It's more fun to watch her face get as red as her hair every time I hit her with a nickname she hates." Adam and Elaina shake their heads at me, and when I see Elaina scooting a little closer to him, I decide it's my cue to leave. I scan the party for someone else to talk to. I've got to get away from these lovebirds. Maybe focus on who I'm leaving this party with tonight.

I look around for a woman I can flirt with. Maybe my midnight kiss, maybe more. It never takes much work. I see a blonde looking my way, and when our eyes meet, she licks her lips in a way so suggestive it would make a porn star blush. She's objectively hot, but my dick doesn't seem to care, so I quickly look away toward the bar, and my gaze lands on a pair of wide blue eyes that surprise me. Charlie's. Being the glutton for punishment that I am, I walk over to her.

"Not going for a repeat performance of last year, are you, Chuck?" I take her in as she rolls her eyes at me. She's wearing a very short black skirt and a loose white top tucked into the front of it. She has flat shoes on, because she never wears heels. Her hair is that same bright orange-red, but it's straight tonight. She almost doesn't look like herself without the wild waves and curls.

"Not that it's any of your business, but no. I don't plan on getting so drunk I forget nearly everything." She looks past me as if she's looking for someone. "What about you? I don't see a scantily-clad woman hanging off your giant body tonight. Are you all right?"

Fuck, she really thinks so little of me.

My brain chooses to focus on the fact that she just said she doesn't remember a lot of last New Year's Eve. We hardly ever talk, so this isn't something that would have come up in conversation.

"What exactly *do* you remember from last year, pumpkin?" I can't help my curiosity.

She takes a sip of her water and scrunches up her face. "Talking to a Thor look-alike. You taking me away from him." She shoots me a death stare, but it never reaches my eyes. "Me waking up with a massive headache. Thank goodness Maeve took pity on me and left me with Gatorade and aspirin. It was a rough New Year's Day."

"Hmm. Is that all you remember?" I narrow my eyes at her, trying to see if she's just omitting our entire conversation, but she just shrugs, nodding at me. If there's one thing Charlie isn't, it's a liar. "What about that bush over there you got real up-close and personal with?"

She looks over to where I just pointed with my thumb,

and her look of confusion is quickly replaced with shock. Her eyes go wide and when she looks up at me, her cheeks are flushed, and she nearly spits her water out.

"Oh no. I spilled my guts all over those bushes, didn't I?" I feel my lips jerk up into a smile at the look of horror on her face. She really doesn't remember.

"Uh-huh." I laugh, and I love how her eyes shut as she takes a deep breath, like she's trying to calm herself down. Charlie wears all her emotions on the surface, though she tries her damndest to hide them as well as her sister does. They're always right there, though. In her eyes, her body language, the deepening blush of her skin. I've watched them all play out for over two years now, even if most of the time, the feelings are annoyance, anger, and frustration; all pointed directly and exclusively at me.

I heard her laugh once. I couldn't see her face, but I remember the sound vividly. It plays like a radio commercial jingle in my head, on a loop, over and over and over. I rub my forehead to wipe away the memory and an annoying headache as Charlie opens her eyes.

"Well, I'm sure you took great pleasure seeing me in such a compromising and humiliating situation. I'm surprised you haven't brought it up sooner or used it to embarrass me in front of our friends." Her lips are set in a straight line. She is waiting for me to make fun of her, but I won't.

I haven't.

I wouldn't.

"It gave me no pleasure to see you hurting and not feeling well. So, I don't need to bring it up or embarrass you. No one knows." Her eyes grow even wider at my statement, then immediately narrow again, which tells me she doesn't believe me. "All right, so Maeve knows because she's Maeve." I didn't even tell Adam that she was sick in the bushes, just that she drank too much. And I refuse to tell Charlie that it

wasn't Maeve who got her to bed and set her up with elec-
trolytes and aspirin.

She swallows and looks back up at me. "Thank you," she
whispers.

"Wow, that was hard for you, huh, carrot cake?" I chuckle
to lighten the mood and she goes back to slightly narrowed
eyes, shaking her head at me. Back to the Charlie I know. I'm
opening my mouth to say something, anything that isn't an
insult or a stupid nickname, when the goddamn walking
mannequin from last year comes to stand next to us.

"Well, what are the chances I'd see you again, beautiful?"
He smiles widely, a Cheshire-cat smile if I've ever seen one,
and his unnaturally white teeth are bright enough to light up
the entire yard. I look at Charlie, but she doesn't have an
ounce of recognition in her eyes.

"Hello. I'm sorry, have we met?" She looks at me for less
than a second and goes back to the severely tanned man who
smells like the body spray aisle at the drugstore. I like that she
doesn't bother smiling at him. Charlie doesn't do pleasantries,
especially not with people she doesn't know.

Dude scoffs but keeps smiling. "Yeah, babe. In this very
spot last year, don't you remember? We were having a
pleasant chat until your friend here took you away, and then,
I couldn't find you for the rest of the night."

Charlie seems to put it together, and when she looks my
way again, her expression is horrified. I can almost hear her
pleading with me not to leave her with this douche. I love
watching her squirm, so I clap him on the shoulder and smile
brightly. "Well, I'll leave you two to finish what you started.
Have fun!" I have no intention of taking my eyes off this
asshole, but Chuck doesn't know that. I wink at Charlie and
walk past her; then I feel the warmth of her slender fingers
wrap around my forearm. She has never intentionally
touched me before.

"Oh, honey, you're hilarious!" She looks up at me, and

there's almost a smile on her face. "Always full of jokes, this one." She grips my arm tighter. "I'm sorry, but my boyfriend and I were actually just leaving." I nearly choke on air when she says *boyfriend*. She smacks me on the back harder than necessary, and I smile through my coughing fit. *Well, this is fun.*

She practically drags me by the arm, and the mannequin man is left at the bar looking thoroughly confused. She stops in front of a tree, and I can't believe the overwhelming sense of déjà vu I'm feeling. It's the same spot as last year.

Charlie rolls her head back to the tree, and the feeling gets stronger. "*That* was the guy I nearly went home with last year?" I raise my eyebrows in confirmation. "Do you think anyone has told him his leather pants, fake tan, and startlingly white teeth make him look like several inferior versions of Ross Geller all rolled into one?" I laugh at her *Friends* reference and how accurate it is. Charlie is funny.

"Last year, you said he looked like a Ken doll. Today, you said Thor. I insisted he was more of a walking mannequin." Her lips quirk up ever so slightly, and it might be the closest Charlie has ever come to smiling directly at me.

"I think all of those work, to be honest." She looks down at her feet and licks her lips. I'm immediately aware that Charlie licking her lips gets my dick's attention, very much unlike the blonde from earlier. "Sorry about grabbing you like that. I didn't want to talk to him." She looks back up at me, and her eyes are so bright, reflecting every light out here. "Thanks. Again." She holds eye contact for a few seconds, then looks away. It's the longest we've ever looked at one another, and my brain starts to turn to mush at the realization. Good thing I recover quickly.

"Two thank yous in one night, *and* you drag me back to the scene of the crime." She looks around, taking in the garden and the bushes next to us. I click my tongue before I continue. "Careful, Chuck. I might start to think you don't actually hate me as much as you let on."

Her eyes shoot back up to mine but quickly veer elsewhere on my face. In a whisper, she says, "I don't... I've never... Rafael, I don't *actually* hate you." She shakes her head lightly, and the air between us suddenly feels thick. Something tugs inside my chest, and between that and the half boner her mouth just gave me, I know I can't stay around her much longer. Not when I'm hyper-aware of every move she makes, every fleck of light reflecting in her eyes and the way her hands felt on me just minutes ago. I rub my forearm, urging my skin forget the way her slender fingers gripped me so tightly.

It's my turn to look down at my feet now, and when I look back up at her, those blue eyes are dark and cloudy. I swallow down the lump in my throat, my mouth suddenly dry. I'm not sure what to say, and my mouth decides for me before my brain gets any say in the matter. "I didn't know you liked *Friends* too."

The fuck? That's the best you can do? Really?

Her lips turn up in what I can safely say is definitely a small smile. "I love it. The girls and I watched it all the time at NYU. I wouldn't have pegged you for a fan, though."

"Are you kidding me? Joey's my man." I smile at the memories of Adam and me watching the show with my aunt. "Adam and I used to watch it whenever he came to my house. My aunt got us into it when she taught us the alternate hand gesture for flipping someone off. We were just kids, but we thought it was hilarious, and now it's sort of a..." I realize too late that I'm talking too much, but I don't know how to undo the damage.

"A comfort show. It's safe." She finishes the sentence for me, and without knowing, I hold my breath from the sheer shock that Charlie and I have something in common.

"Yeah," I let out, along with the breath I was holding.

Charlie nods, that hint of a smile still playing on her lips. "I guess I don't know you very well at all."

And dammit, at this moment, I want to be the bigger person. I want to agree or say something witty and let it go, but I can't. Her words from this very spot last year flash in front of me like a goddamn neon sign, and I feel my smile falter, the blood in my veins run a little colder, and the compulsive need to keep my distance from her is back. "That's not what you said last year, Ginger Spice." I swallow down hard again, watching her tiny smile fully slip away. Something like confusion forms on her face, so I look down at my feet. "Anyway, I'll let you get back to the party. Enjoy the rest of your night." I nod and turn on my heels, feeling too many things to be standing still. Too many things to look at her face for a second longer. Too many things that put me right back in a place I don't want to go to.

7 /
a kiss that's all lust and tongues.

charlie

one year ago - the second nye

I NEVER WOULD HAVE PEGGED Rafael Machado for a *Friends* fan. When I made that Ross Geller reference, I thought for sure it had gone over his head, but he laughed, that beautiful sound hitting me smack in the ribcage. He lit up when he told me about how he and Adam used to watch it. The same way he does when he's talking to Adam or Lainey or Maeve. He shared something about his life with me. We've never done that before. We've never just talked. And it was nice, but something shifted when I told him I didn't know him very well. And now, I'm sitting here wondering what exactly happened.

I close my eyes and lean my head back on the tree. I hear his words again. *That's not what you said last year, Ginger Spice.* In a flash, it all comes back to me. What I said about him being a dumb jock, not having anything to be proud of. Oh no. I really said those horrible things, didn't I?

You probably peaked in high school. Your little girlfriends probably did your homework for you because you were too dense to figure it out yourself. You wear your conquests like a badge of honor because you have nothing else to be proud of.

I feel like I'm going to be sick all over again. My breathing speeds up, and I open my eyes to see Maeve walking toward me with her brows furrowed.

"Char. You all right?" She places a firm hand on my arm, and my mouth feels dry. I'm still breathing fast, thinking about how mean I was to someone who obviously didn't deserve it. I'm not that girl. Why did I say those things? I had thought them in a moment of fury, had said them out loud to myself, but I never intended to say any of it to him. "Charlie Mae. Look at me. Did you have too much to drink again? Please don't throw up in my bushes two years in a row."

That brings me back to the moment. "No. No, I'm not drunk." I blink my eyes a few times to get her face to come into focus. "Just how drunk was I last year, exactly?"

Maeve giggles a little, eyebrows shooting up to her hairline. "I've never seen you that drunk before or since. Raffy nearly had to carry you to your bed."

She keeps talking, but I can't hear the words. She just said Rafael nearly carried me to my bed? My head is spinning, and for a moment, it does feel like I might be drunk, except I have had no alcohol tonight.

"Charlie, are you listening to me?" Her look of concern does nothing to ease the tightness in my chest.

"No. Sorry." I shake my head and wave my hand in front of me. "Go back for a second. You said Rafael took me to my room. I thought you had done that. You even left me a Gatorade and painkillers."

"No, that was all Raffy. He took your shoes off, got you into bed, and left everything on the nightstand for you. When I walked in, he was sitting on the floor, watching you. He was worried you might throw up again, and he didn't want you to be alone." Her eyes soften as she retells the memory, and my chest pangs again. "It was quite sweet, actually, the way he took care of you. But that's Raf."

"Oh, no." I shut my eyes tightly in complete disbelief at what I'm hearing. He helped me when I threw up in the bushes, then stayed with me to make sure I was okay? Ugh. Why did he have to be so nice to me that night? Especially after I was so awful to him?

"Char, are you sure you haven't had too much to drink?" I feel the soothing presence of her hand still on my arm and place my other hand on top of hers, giving it a light squeeze.

"I'm sure. I feel awful that he was so nice to me that night when I wasn't very nice to him." My throat tightens again, thinking about him sitting on my bedroom floor.

"I've been telling you for years that he's the nicest bloke!" Her eyes widen again as she gives me that *I told you so* look.

"I know. I know. You're right. I'm going to apologize to him, and then I promise I'll be nicer." Her whole face lights up at my words, and I can't help but smile.

"Really? Is this the end of your feud, then?" She squeezes my arm, eyes still bright as a wide grin spreads across her face.

"I guess so." I shrug, though inside, I am reeling.

How am I going to apologize? When?

She lets out a little squeal as she bounces on the balls of her feet. "I'm just going to take another minute here if you don't mind. But I promise, I'll tell him I'm sorry and thank him for what he did."

"All right, sissy." Her smile softens, and she tilts her head to the side. "I'm proud of you."

I smile back at her. "Thanks, Mae." I squeeze her hand one last time, and she lets me go. "Now get back to being the perfect hostess you are and enjoy your party."

She blows me a kiss as she walks backward, then she turns and someone grabs her attention as soon as she's back in the light again. I take several deep breaths, trying to think about how I can even begin to tell Rafael that I'm grateful but, most importantly, that I am sorry.

After a few minutes of trying to psych myself up, I smooth my hands over my skirt and look up. My whole body stiffens, and I freeze as I watch Rafael place his hand on a blonde girl's waist. She whispers something in his ear, and he laughs. The sound travels over to me, and it might as well be a physical blow with the way I tense at the impact. The very leggy, very beautiful woman runs her fingers up his arm until they tangle in his curly hair. She pulls his face down to hers, and their lips meet in a kiss that's all lust and tongues. My cheeks heat as I stand there, unable to look away. When they shift, Rafael's eyes open and lock with mine, and I swear his lips lift into a smile. I jolt back, a grimace taking over my face as I shake my head and remember that Rafael may have done something nice for me once. I may have said some things I didn't mean while blackout drunk, but he's still the same guy, just looking for the next woman to conquer.

Well, not this one.

I will never ever fall for his charm, and that's just the reminder I needed. Rafael Machado is the same disgusting pig he was the day I met him, and regardless of the fact that I should apologize, it's not happening today.

I walk out of the darkened spot in the garden and head straight inside. Maybe this is a good time to write. I certainly won't be writing any love scenes, but perhaps I can write about a beautiful womanizing man. Perhaps said beautiful man ends up castrated. Perhaps I can get as descriptive as possible with exactly how such a tragic thing might happen. Seems like a great way to end the year.

8 /
somebody get her that popcorn.

charlie

now

I SLAM the door behind me as I walk into Maeve's house and wince, hoping Julia's not asleep. We're meeting here for an early morning chat before we all go to Elaina and Adam's place, where the guys are making us a Sunday brunch.

Rather than looking for a route this morning, I walked to the Santa Monica Pier and back to Taylor's apartment. Just over five miles later, and I still don't feel any better about the fact that I'm going to see Rafael today after I walked into him, and he patched up my arm.

I walk into the kitchen and am met with one pair of wide blue eyes and one pair of even wider green ones, Maeve and Elaina, respectively. I send my sister an apologetic look.

"Don't worry, Julia is out with Owen," Maeve says, reading the look on my face.

"And this one can sleep through just about anything," Elaina says, laying a gentle kiss on Agnes's head. She looks so at ease, holding this two-week-old baby on her chest like this is what she was made to do. "Why don't you sit with us,

Char?" Elaina's sweet voice cracks a bit when she asks me to sit, and I immediately feel guilty. Again. I felt guilty all week. For I don't know what, but it definitely wasn't for not thanking Rafael properly for bandaging me up. Nope. That definitely wasn't what I felt guilty about. And I didn't once think about how I never thanked him for that New Year's Eve, either.

I take the cup of tea and sit at the kitchen island with them. Elaina's head tips to the side, and when she looks at me with those bright green eyes of hers, I feel myself soften, even if only slightly. "Ugh. What is happening to me? I just slammed a door. Do you know when the last time I slammed a door was?"

Maeve and Elaina give me matching blank looks before they both respond with, "Never?"

"Exactly! I'm not like this." I've spent most of my life keeping my emotions in check. I've been called sensitive and irrational too many times. So, I wear my suit of armor. I do it to protect myself, yes, but also to protect the world from my emotions. It's easier not to express any feelings. I lay my head down on the counter in front of me, letting out a muffled groan.

My sister's warm hand comes to rest on my shoulder with a squeeze. "Oh, Char." She doesn't need to say anything else. She knows as well as I do that growing up with our mother didn't do either of us any favors. Maeve was always told she'd amount to nothing, that she wasn't smart enough, while I was told to do something exceptional with my brain, but to act more like my sister. I was always told to be less myself and more like her, but only on the outside. Maeve grew up thinking her only value was on the exterior because she was broken inside. Twins, destined at birth to be pitted against one another, and yet here we are. Best of friends.

I inhale a deep breath. "It's fine. I'll be fine. It's just been a weird week." Looking up, I feel rather than see Maeve's heated gaze on me. I made the mistake of telling her how Rafael helped me after I walked right into him. She's silent, but it's like I can hear her thoughts.

You didn't thank Raf, did you? she asks silently.

No. And he's still a complete wanker, so...

We eye each other as we sip our tea, the silent conversation somehow seeming too loud inside my head.

"You know what I'm gonna say before I even say it, so I'm not gonna say it, but if you don't say it, I'm gonna have to say it." Maeve's face is deadpan, but Elaina's is the reflection of delight.

"Oh, please say it," Elaina whispers. All the girl is missing is some popcorn as she watches this ridiculous mostly silent showdown happening between me and my twin.

I let out a loud sigh and look away from my sister's judgy eyes. "I know, Mae. I said I'd thank him. But then I remembered every other interaction I've had with the guy, and I knew that he'd always be the same wanker I've known him to be since day one."

"Thank who? Or is it whom? Thank whom, or whatever. And what for?" Elaina's eyes are frantic, bouncing between me and Maeve. I made the mistake of texting my sister to tell her I'd gotten hurt, but that I was fine, and that Rafael helped me, but I hadn't told Elaina. She's been busy getting to know her newborn daughter, so it didn't seem right to bother her with this.

"I thought Charlie came to her senses this week about what a nice guy Raffy is since he helped her with something, but it seems like she wants to keep going with this annoying game they've been playing. This is just like New Year's Eve when you said you'd apologize to him, but then you didn't." Maeve rolls her eyes at me so hard I think they might get stuck in the back of her head.

"Can we please not talk about him?" I take a deep breath, saying a silent prayer that we can stop this now. I'd rather not have the focus on me at all right now, given how uneasy I'm still feeling about coming to LA and leaving the comfort and predictability of London behind. At least, for now. Being here, having this new proximity to Rafael makes my whole body feel tense from replaying every interaction we've had over the last three years.

"Char, why don't you tell us about Robert or what you're writing about?" Dear, sweet Elaina is clearly trying to make me feel better, not knowing that the only other things I don't want to talk about are Robert and writing.

The breath that comes out of me is far louder than I intend, more of a growl than a puff of air.

"Robert says he's ready to commit, but now Charlie's not sure that's what she wants. And the lack of intimacy with him or anyone means she's struggling to write. She wants to feel all the big feelings, but she's not sure how to do that." Maeve is addressing Elaina, essentially ignoring me as she fills our best friend in on our conversation and how she recommended I put myself in more situations that cause me to feel "all the big feelings." As if she can read my mind—which I swear, sometimes she can—she turns to me with a knowing smile.

Elaina's mouth opens, then closes. It opens again and closes again until, finally, she speaks. "Have you ever thought that maybe Raf could help?" I raise my eyebrows at that, not quite sure what she's getting at. "I just mean that, yes, he makes you feel things like anger and frustration, but also, he would be the guy to ask about feelings in general. The guy wears his heart on his sleeve. And he has a *lot* of experience with the intimacy side of things if you know what I mean." It's her turn to wiggle her eyebrows up and down now.

"Ew, Lainey. No. I am not going to ask him to help me write smut. Not happening. Not ever. That's not what I need help with, anyway." Just the thought of it makes my stomach tighten. Sure, he knows far more than I do about getting busy in the sheets, but that does not mean I would ever ask him for help. "And what makes you think he would even be willing to help me, anyway?" Besides the fact that he's proven to have a few moments in which he's capable of acting like a half-decent human being, I don't think his idea of fun is spending time with me.

"Because he's the *nicest guy*, Char. And if ever there was an emotionally intelligent man, Rafael is it. Trust me. And he wouldn't think twice about helping you." Lainey looks down at her baby and then scoops her into her car seat on the counter, rocking it gently back and forth as Agnes continues to sleep.

"Well, I'm sure you and Maeve would also be well-equipped to help me now that you're happily receiving multiple orgasms from your hotter-than-hot husbands and their perfect dicks, no?" Maeve scoffs loudly, and Elaina coughs, spattering tea on the countertop. "And are they not also emotionally intelligent?"

"First of all, not even Adam's perfect dick is coming near my lady bits for at least another month. Oh, and ew, Owen is my brother!" She makes a gagging sound and does a full-body shiver. "At least give us a little warning next time!" Maeve chuckles as Lainey wipes the tea with a paper towel.

"I'm just trying to make a point here. Rafael isn't the only qualified person I know when it comes to hot, sensual, mind-numbing sex."

Uh-oh. Mistake. I know it immediately. There's no way they're going to overlook this.

Maeve slaps a hand on her lap; the unsaid *ah-ha* is heard loud and clear with the motion. Elaina wiggles in her seat.

"I thought this wasn't only about sex. And how do you know sex with Raf is hot, sensual, and mind-numbing, Char?" The question comes from Maeve. Because, of course it does. Lainey sips her tea and watches quietly, a small smile playing on her face. Somebody get her that popcorn.

"Oh, shut up. You've seen the man. He is sex on legs with

that perfect brown skin and all those muscles everywhere. And the tattoos. And those stupid dimples on one cheek. Never has asymmetry worked so well."

What is happening to me? I feel personally attacked by the loose-ness of my lips and their willingness to reveal my secrets. I have never talked about Rafael like this. Not to anyone.

"Is that so? Sex on legs, you say?"

Nope. Not falling for it. I'm keeping my mouth shut so it can't betray me again by saying something else that could be used against my plan to forever detest Rafael.

"Elaina, why didn't you correct me when I said you both had husbands? Normally, you'd give me the *we're not married yet* spiel." Deflect, deflect, deflect. It doesn't always work, but given the sheepish look on Elaina's face right now, it is.

She looks back and forth between me and Maeve a few times before blurting out her next words. "Okay, fine, I have a secret!" Tears immediately spring in her eyes, and Maeve looks at me, slightly panicked. "Oh, it's nothing bad. But we're married. Adam and I are married. Fuck, it feels good to say that out loud."

"What?" my sister and I hiss simultaneously. It comes out more like *wot* because we are extra British when we're surprised / excited / nervous.

"We wanted to be married before Agnes was born, but with how sick I'd been the whole pregnancy, I didn't think we would. I was feeling great those last couple of weeks, but I was super hormonal and broke down crying one night because I just wanted to be married already, so Adam worked some things out, and we got married on New Year's Eve and didn't tell anyone. And then, I immediately went into labor." Two tears slide down her cheeks, and she quickly wipes them away. "I'm so sorry I didn't tell you sooner. We're still going to have a celebration and do the whole party or whatever with everybody. Probably. Maybe. *Fuck.* I don't know. I don't really care for parties that much, and I honestly can't imagine planning anything that isn't a nap right now." Our sweet best friend looks so defeated.

With our twintuition firmly in place, Maeve and I surround Lainey and hug her tightly. "You're married," I say into her hair that always smells of coconut and honey. "To your soul mate."

"Yeah," she sobs. "I am."

"Oh, Bon, this is wonderful." Maeve sniffles as she hugs us a little tighter. "I'm so happy for you."

"We both are," I add.

"So, you're not mad?" Lainey shimmies out of the hug, looking at us both as we shake our heads.

"Not even a little. I totally get the appeal of a private ceremony." Maeve winks and gives a watery laugh, and eventually, all three of us are laughing, crying tears of joy for our growing little family.

"We'll tell everyone at brunch. I mean, I guess it's just Raf and Owen left anyway." Elaina shrugs and wipes away her remaining tears as we go back to our seats.

"I have a secret, too," Maeve announces quietly. She wrings her fingers together over her belly. "I slept with Owen years ago." She shuts her eyes tightly, likely expecting a big reaction out of Elaina.

I wait for it too. But it doesn't come.

"Yeah, he, um, he sort of told me already." Her shoulders lift in a shrug. "When I asked him how he knew he was in love with you, he told me about your conversation after Dad's funeral. You know, before you fucked on the beach." She smacks Maeve on the arm lightly, then bursts with laughter.

"That man cannot keep a damn secret." Maeve sighs. "I love him." My sister's hand lands on my forearm. "All right, sissy. Your turn. Have any secrets you wanna spill?"

Before I can give it any thought, I say the words I've

thought about saying to my sister and best friend for months. "I'm C.M. Howe."

Elaina gasps and brings her hand to her mouth to stifle the sound. Maeve's jaw drops to the floor. "You know, the author of all the romance novels Lainey reads and Maeve has no interest in?" No one says anything. "Someone say something, please." My face twists into a grimace as I look down at the countertop.

Elaina starts sobbing. Hard. She's the crier out of the three of us, but I did not expect body-shaking sobs. I freeze for a moment, and just when I'm about to say sorry or hug her, she moves her hand. "I'm… s-so… h-h-happy." I place a hand over hers, squeezing gently.

I turn to look at Meave to find she has tears running down her face. "I'm so proud of you, Char." Great, now I'm crying, too.

"I'm sorry I didn't tell you." I sniffle and feel Maeve's hand squeeze my shoulder.

"We understand."

"Yeah, we do." Elaina looks up, wiping her face with a napkin. "And we're going to have to talk about this in much more detail. I have so many questions. I need the inside scoop." My biggest fan and best friend smiles hopefully at me.

"We will. I promise. Maybe another time?" I'm so not prepared to dig into this right now. "Maybe you could tell us about your wedding instead? Because I think it's safe to say we will never be asking for details about Maeve's secret," I deadpan, but we all laugh.

"Not fucking ever," Elaina says. "But yeah, I can tell you about our ceremony."

As I listen to her recall the details of their special day, I keep running over what I would like that to look like for myself. Robert will want a lavish wedding, full of people neither of us really know but who would be important to the company and the growth of the business. It would have to be fancy. He would want me to wear a puffy dress and heels.

Blimey, that sounds awful, doesn't it? I want the marriage without the big wedding. I want what Maeve and Elaina have. The loyalty and love of their most treasured person. Being seen, known, wanted, and chosen every day for forever. I want safety without complacency.

I suppose if the price to pay for that is one day of discomfort and social anxiety, it might be worth it.

Right?

9 /
what the fuck alternate universe have i entered?

rafael

I WAKE up with a headache and the weird, tight feeling in the middle of my chest that hasn't left me since Charlie walked away from me in my own backyard. Glancing at my watch, I see it's still early and decide I have time for a quick run before I head to Elaina and Adam's place for brunch. My movements are practiced, almost robotic—I've done this every day since I was a teenager. Running and exercising have always been necessary for me. I need to let out pent-up energy and clear my thoughts.

After getting my five miles in, I shower, grab the ingredients I need for brunch, and head out.

Adam is outside with a big smile before I even get out of my car. Frankie, their dog, is hiding behind Adam's legs as he pulls me into a hug, patting my back. "Hey, man." When he pulls back, he takes one look at my face and his eyebrows furrow. "I wasn't gonna make mimosas, but I'll pop open some bubbly for you if you want. You look like you need it."

"No, dude. I'm good." I laugh, thankful for the light-hearted comment that also tells me he noticed I'm not quite myself. "Just didn't get a lot of sleep last night." I grab the bags from the backseat and follow him into the house. "Smells like Lainey made some coffee though; I'll take some of that."

"How do you know I didn't make it?" He turns back with a quirked eyebrow.

"Because it smells good. I can tell it was made properly and not like the weak-ass shit you like to brew."

It's his turn to laugh. "Yeah, you're right. Lainey's way better at coffee than I am. She made it before heading to Maeve and Owen's with Agnes." Once inside, he pours us both a cup—mine black, and his loaded with cream. It's one of the many ways his fiancée has influenced him since they met. He takes a sip of his coffee and smiles like it's not totally fucking disgusting how much cream he just poured into it. "So. How's your new neighbor?" He pauses, looking up at me, doing that waiting thing he and Elaina do.

"I don't know. I haven't seen her since she walked into me." Frankie walks toward me, and I scratch behind his ear before he runs away again. He still takes his time warming up to me, but I'll take it since the dog doesn't normally go anywhere near men—unless it's Adam. He's always loved Adam.

"I know Lainey talked to you about this, too. Have you given it any more thought?" *Only every waking minute since that conversation*, I want to say. They asked me to try to make things less awkward with Charlie. Something about the bickering not being a good example for the kids, but I know they just want us to be nice to each other. "I know you two have this weird tension or whatever it is, but it would really mean a lot to her. To us." He says all of this like I don't already know.

"Yeah. I know. I'll talk to her today. I just always feel like such a fucking dumbass around her."

"Raf. No." He pins me with a look that I know all too well. "You know what I'm going to say, don't you?"

I smile because, as my oldest friend, he knows more about me than anyone. We met as young kids, and despite not always being in the same city, we've been like brothers since day one. He was the only friend who kept in touch when I was a Marine, and he's the type of guy who shares his feelings openly. I've always admired that about him. So, I know exactly what he's going to say because I've been hearing it for years.

Still, as if he knows I need the words said out loud, he goes on. "You've already come so far, Raf. I'm so fucking proud of every single thing you've done since the day I met you. From the kind of brother and friend you've always been, to your commitment to the Marine Corps, to starting a business and moving into this shared CEO role with Owen. You're one of the most capable people I've ever met, so I'm not gonna tell you what to do, but I am going to tell you that I believe in you. I always have, and I always will. Being nice to Charlie isn't going to come close to the shit you've already been through. You know this."

My best friend, ladies and gentlemen. And he's marrying the girl who bakes muffins and makes my favorite soup when I'm sick. Can you believe that? Somehow, they found each other. It'd be sickening, really, if it hadn't happened to two of the greatest people I've ever known.

Yet again, I know he's right. I tend to be the guy who defaults to *it could always be worse*, despite the fact that my life hasn't been all rainbows. Sure, I was adopted by an amazing family, but I still have to deal with the emotions that come from not being wanted by my biological parents. No, I wasn't taken hostage and nearly killed like Owen while I was a Marine, but I've still seen some shit most people can't even imagine. And no, I haven't experienced heartbreak in a romantic sense, but I also have never known what it's like to fall in love in my nearly thirty-three years.

I smile at him, feeling the warmth of gratitude taking over the feelings of anxiety and uncertainty, though those certainly still linger.

"You got this. Just talk to her. Not like she's better than you or thinks less of you. Not like you're trying to annoy the ever-living shit out of her. *Really* talk to her. Let her see the real you." I nod my head while the fear of Charlie seeing me for who I really am grips me so tightly it's hard to breathe. The girl is some kind of genius. Maeve mentioned once that she has a double degree in Math and Economics from NYU, and then she went on to get a master's in Financial Economics from Oxford. I'd be intimidated if I wasn't so fucking impressed. And what am I?

Not answering that question is what I am.

"All right, man, moving on. Let's get this brunch going before those hungry girls show up and we have nothing ready." He chuckles and makes his way to the fridge, getting more ingredients out, and we both get started on our dishes. My pão de queijo is always a hit, and Adam has some sort of cinnamon roll concoction going.

By the time the girls walk into the kitchen an hour later, we've got music going, I've made fresh coffee, and the table is set.

"Morning, boys! It smells fantastic in here!" Maeve strides in with her nose in the air and a happy grin as she rubs her round belly with both hands. "I'm chuffed to bits. This is impressive!"

Lainey makes her way to Adam, giving him a quick kiss. He takes the car seat from her and pulls it closer to his face, smiling at his sleeping daughter as they both watch her as though it's for the first time.

Looking away from their private family moment, I walk over to Maeve, and she spreads her arms wide, pulling me into a hug. "Yes, can you believe men actually managed to cook a whole meal all by themselves?" I ask. She laughs, smacking me lightly on the shoulder.

"I can believe *these* men did, yes. Now, where's that handsome husband of mine?" Before she finishes the question, Owen turns the corner with a big, cheesy smile as he strides toward his wife.

"Right here, sunshine. Jules is sleeping, finally." He wraps an arm around her waist, hands resting on the underside of her belly, and kisses her neck. "You hungry?"

I ignore the tone in his voice that makes me believe he's asking her about more than brunch. I'm happy for my friends, I really am, but everything feels different now. They each have their person to go to when they walk into a room, when they go home, and when they go to sleep at night. And what do I have? A long list of failed dates and near-relationships.

I want what they have. I want it so fucking badly, and I've been looking for it for a long time, but no one has fit as well as they seem to with their significant others. It's starting to become a little frustrating, this wild goose chase to find the person I can fully belong with. Belong to. All while watching my best friends have it all. I'm feeling a little redundant here. Like it wouldn't matter if I weren't in the room. And that's not some self-deprecating, self-pitying bullshit—it's just how it feels now.

My friends are like my family. That's what we are to each other, and I'm so lucky to have them. I know I belong in this group as much as anyone else, but something still feels incomplete. Like there's another unit I'm meant to be a part of. I want to belong with and to someone who's just mine at the end of the day. And I want to be *only* theirs.

There's a weird sense of security in that for me. It's not something I've ever had before. I'm one of six siblings, so the mantra *sharing is caring* got thrown around a lot in our house.

As the only adopted kid, I was sort of thrust upon my family, and sure, they chose me as a baby, but I want to be chosen *now*. As I am. With all my mistakes and faults and insecurities out in the open.

I rub at my chest, hoping it helps ease the pressure that tends to build there when I think too much about this shit. Then, addressing no one in particular, I shout, "Teapot's full of peppermint tea. I just brewed some coffee, too, and there's iced coffee in the fridge."

I look around for Charlie. I know she doesn't drink hot coffee, so I made sure to have some waiting in the fridge for when the girls arrived. I spot her on the other side of the kitchen, and she looks up when I mention the coffee, nodding once in acknowledgment. She seems as quietly out of place as I do right now, making me feel a strange sense of camaraderie with the unlikeliest person.

Adam takes the last of the food over to the table, and we all sit to eat. The conversation is light and easy, like it usually is when we're all together. When Lainey apologetically announces that she and Adam got married just before Agnes was born, Owen and I seem to be the only two people surprised, but we're also both genuinely so happy for them. We all take turns holding Agnes, and it feels natural, this new dynamic in our little family; though there's some new tension in the room no one but me seems to notice.

And now Charlie is here. I don't know for how long, and I don't know why, but it's different this time. It's not just a quick visit. The thought makes my whole body tingle, the way it gets when your leg falls asleep, then you move it, and it's like pins and needles everywhere. You want to move, want to get away from that feeling, but that only makes it worse. You just have to sit still, waiting for it to pass. But I can't, so when brunch is over, and everyone heads into the living room with the babies, I walk back into the kitchen quietly, hoping cleaning up is enough to occupy my mind and hands.

I'm just about to start washing the pots and pans when I hear a cup being set on the countertop. I turn, and my eyes widen in surprise, seeing Charlie a few feet away from me. Suddenly, I feel like I'm standing on top of a mountain. The air is thinner, harder to pull into my lungs. Just looking at her scrambles my brain cells.

She clears her throat before parting her lips. "Thank you so much for cooking. Those little cheesy bread things you made were perfect." She's looking at me, but not in the eyes.

What do I have to do to get her to look at me? To see me?

"I'm glad you enjoyed them." A long moment passes without either of us saying anything. I'm about to turn back to the dishes when she speaks again.

"I'll load the dishwasher. You shouldn't have to clean up alone after cooking." She starts moving toward the dishes stacked next to the sink, and I breathe in too quickly, the scent of her shampoo filling my nostrils. *Roses.* She always smells like roses.

It's my turn to clear my throat now since I've let the silence linger too long as it is. "Thanks."

Yep. You are a great conversationalist. Fucking idiot.

We work in silence for a few minutes, me washing the pots in the sink, and her loading the dishwasher. She's been chewing on her lower lip the entire time, looking deep in thought about something.

We both start speaking at the same time.

"I need to say something—"

"So, listen, I was wondering—"

We stop simultaneously.

"Sorry, go ahead."

"You go first."

In an effort not to have this go on any longer, I stop talking, simply nodding at her to continue what she was saying.

"All right, I'll go first." She clears her throat, eyes on me. "Thank you for helping me the other day. I didn't say it then, but that was really nice of you."

That's not what I was expecting. Actually, I wasn't expecting anything. "I thought you did. And it was the least I could do after being the cause of your fall." All right, so the cause of her fall was her walking with her eyes closed, but if I wasn't there, she might not have fallen at all, so it's sort of my fault.

"I'm not finished." She stops her movements and looks down at her feet, pulling that lower lip into her mouth one more time. "I'd like your help with something."

I scoff. Loudly, too. Not because I don't want to help her, but because I am shocked as hell at the sentence that just came out of her mouth. Regret hits me like a bag of bricks to the gut when I see her brows furrow as she takes a step back.

"Never mind. This was a terrible idea." She shakes her head and walks to the other sink to wash her hands.

Fuck.

"No, Chuck. Wait." I walk toward her and reach for her arm but think better of it and pull my hand back. She doesn't seem to like being touched, or maybe it's just being touched by me. Either way, I'm not about to make her uncomfortable. "I was just surprised. I'm sorry. I actually need to ask you something, too." She turns her head, so I can see her profile. Her brows have relaxed a bit. "Can we please start over?"

She turns, and I hand her a tea towel to dry her hands. Our fingers brush in the process, and she flinches at the contact. We'll think about that another time. I need to focus on easing this awkwardness between us.

"Want me to go first?" I ask. She nods, keeping her eyes on her hands. I take a deep breath and just go for it. "I'd like us to spend some time together. Get to know one another. I know I'm not related to anyone here, but these people are my family, too, and neither of us is going anywhere. It's not fair to them for us to keep doing whatever this is. We owe it to them to learn how to be nice to one another." She looks up at my face, never reaching my eyes but taking in my features like she's studying me.

"Is this a joke?" Her brows furrow as she continues to watch me.

"What? No, of course not." I keep my tone light, hoping she can hear my sincerity. "I thought maybe we could go for walks together, and I guess if you need my help with something, we can work on that too. What do you need my help with, anyway?" I can't imagine how I could possibly help her, but I'm curious.

"Writing." She takes a breath in and releases it slowly. "And something else." This is obviously hard for her, but I need her to tell me what else, so I wait. "I'm just having a hard time describing the relationships my characters have with each other, whether romantic or otherwise." When she breaks off this time, she doesn't seem to have much more to add.

"I'm not sure I understand." I really don't know what I could do to help her write. And write what? She works in finance.

"I'm struggling with writing about emotions. This next series I'm writing is very heavy on family and romance, and I don't have a ton of personal experience in either of those fields. I'm struggling to find inspiration. Writing sex scenes or any kind of intimacy is nearly impossible. That's where you come in." This isn't making any sense.

My eyes are as big as dinner plates; I can feel it.

Did she just ask me for help writing sex scenes?

She looks up, and her own eyes widen as she realizes what she's just said. "And where I lack experience, you have it in bulk. I just need you to help me with writing about it, not with having it myself. I don't need help with that. I mean, I could probably use it, but not from *you*. I just need to use your vast experience as inspiration." Nothing about her face or her body language indicates this is an elaborate joke. She actually looks a bit nervous, she keeps biting the side of her lip and wringing her hands together. She's 100 percent serious. My brain is melting inside my skull, trying to process what she's just said.

She just said she needs help with having sex. And she wants me to share my experiences for her book. What the fuck alternate universe have I entered?

"Ginger Spice, let me get this straight. You want me to tell you about my own experiences with having sex to inspire a novel. Is that it?" I'm not sure I'll ever truly process the sentence that came out of my mouth.

"Yes!" She looks up, and for the briefest moment, her eyes meet mine. As fast as it happens, though, it's gone. Those big blue eyes are scanning my face again. "You got it. Should be simple enough, no?"

"Um. Sure. Yeah. I'll help you write sex scenes. That makes sense." Will she pick up on my sarcasm? Because this is the craziest shit I have ever heard.

"Is that sarcasm?" Her eyebrows are scrunched together on her forehead, and her cheeks are slightly flushed. She seems embarrassed. *Fuck.* "Are you making fun of me?"

"No, Chuck. I'm just in complete fucking shock right now. You're writing a book?" I have so many questions, but I don't want to overwhelm her.

"Oh, I suppose I failed to mention that. Yes. It's something I've done for a long time. Writing helps me be creative. Keeps my overactive brain busy and all that. I like to write stories as a way to process my own emotions, but I'm struggling. Things have been… anyway, it's just been hard." She's very matter-of-fact about it all, but it feels like some part of this story is missing.

"Why are you asking *me*? You kind of despise me." Maybe I'm fishing for her to say something nice here, sue me.

"You want honesty?" She stares down at her hands as her breathing picks up. Fuck, she's so fucking beautiful, especially up close.

"Always, red." Her wild, fiery waves are pulled back in a messy bun on top of her head, and I make my hands into fists at the sudden urge to undo it and watch her hair cascade below her shoulders.

She sighs before looking up, but nowhere further north of my chin. "Because I don't trust people easily. Maeve and Lainey told me I can trust you, and I believe them. Also, the thought of talking about this to a stranger is actually even less appealing than talking to you about it." She takes a breath, and her cheeks turn a delicious shade of pink. "And because I'm kind of tired of this stupid little game we play all the time. Fighting with you when you happen to be friends with my best friend and my sister takes far too much energy."

I can't help but chuckle at the way she rolls her eyes as she finishes talking. Finally, her eyes move up, but only as far as my lips. "Thanks for the honesty, carrot cake."

"You're welcome. Why did you suddenly decide to be nice to me? The real reason." She squints her eyes as I consider a sarcastic remark, but decide against it since Charlie doesn't seem to be a fan of those.

"Well, Lainey and Adam sort of encouraged me to." It's a simple truth.

"And if I had said no?" Her arms are now crossed, and I will my eyes to stay on her face and not to move down to where I know they want to go.

"I took a risk. It was worth it." I pause, opting for a bit of humor. "That and Maeve's been asking me to be nice to you for a long time, and she's kind of hard to say no to these days."

She swallows, and the scowl I'm so used to seeing on her face makes a comeback. "Right. Well then, if we're all done with our bonding session, I really must be going. We can get together soon. I'll be in touch." Her eyes are icy cold as she slaps the tea towel on the countertop and walks away faster than I've ever seen her move.

I guess now I wait. And try not to lose my shit over the fact that Charlie is about to become someone I spend time with. Someone I talk to about romance, sex, intimacy, and whatever else she needs help with.

What the fuck have I gotten myself into?

10 /
totally fine. i'm totally fine.

charlie

TWO WEEKS GO BY, and I don't hear a word from Rafael. We haven't seen one another because I have intentionally avoided going for walks in the direction of his house. Not that I've gone out much. I've spent hours in front of my laptop at home, at coffee shops, at the beach—that was an unpleasant sensory experience—and it's useless. Nothing is coming out. I'm just leaving a coffee shop, which serves mediocre coffee at best, after staring at a blank screen for ninety minutes when my phone rings.

"Hi, Robert," I answer. I don't know why I'm still taking his calls. Though he's been mostly silent, this is the third time in three weeks.

"Lottie. How are you, babe? Listen, I've just emailed you something. Could you take a look at it for me? Dad needs the file by end of day tomorrow." He didn't even wait for me to answer his questions. Rather, he just bulldozed through to get to whatever he needed from me. So typical.

"Uh-huh." I give a non-committal answer to keep myself from saying what I'm really feeling. It's not worth getting into it with him right now.

"You're the best. So, when will you be back? We miss you around here. You know, I never realized how much you were doing. Jack isn't nearly as proficient as you are with budgeting strategies." He chuckles at his stupid commentary, and I take a deep breath, reminding myself that Robert is at work, so he's saying he misses me in a professional capacity because there might be someone around him. Of course, he's just being professional. Still, I wish he'd miss me in other ways. Does he miss nothing else about me other than my ability to do my job *and* his?

I hear his muffled voice, and without even giving me a chance to speak, he continues, "I've got to go, Charlotte. But I'll call again soon, okay? Take a look at that email for me? Tootles." He hangs up.

Did I even say anything, or did he just have a whole conversation with himself?

As I stare at my phone, a text comes in from Maeve, so I open it right away. Better not to dwell on whatever that just was anyway.

MAEVE:

> Charlotte Maeve Howard you haven't called Raffy yet?

Shit. She used my full name. She never does that. It's always the short form, Charlie Mae. It makes me sound like I'm a Southern belle, but it's less harsh than my actual full name.

MAEVE:

> He told me you said you'd be in touch. And you haven't been.

Bollocks. I did say that, didn't I? I hate being wrong. And forgetting details. Or making mistakes. And I made a mistake.

MAEVE:

Char. Please get in touch with him, will you?

ME:

I'll text him. I promise.

My response makes me feel small, like a scolded child, though I know my sister's intentions are nothing but loving.

ME:

Give my niece a big squeeze for me.

Love you most.

MAEVE:

I love you most, sissy. Speak soon, all right?

I know I just need to get this over with before I talk myself out of it. Rafael and I have had each other's numbers for a while. He insisted on it when he was Maeve's bodyguard, in case anything happened. I pull up his name and start typing, deleting the message at least four times before hitting send.

ME:

Hi. I'm sorry I didn't reach out sooner.

Would you like to have our first meeting soon?

The three little dots appear almost instantly, and I nearly drop my bag as I fumble with my phone in my hands.

RAFAEL:

How's tonight?

Tonight? Oh. It's Friday night. Doesn't he have a date to go on or something? And what if I had plans? *As if.* Of course I don't, but he doesn't know that!

RAFAEL:

> Unless you already have plans. Maybe tomorrow?

Yeah, maybe I do have plans.
Except, I don't.

ME:

> Tonight's fine.

My heart is hammering, and I cannot explain why.

Probably because you haven't even talked to another human being other than the barista at the coffee shop down the road for approximately three days.

Ugh. Shut up.

RAFAEL:

> Come over at 7. I'll have dinner ready.

Dinner? How is he so casual about all of this? He sends his address next as if I won't remember the house I've been avoiding going near for weeks, and I don't respond. He doesn't send any other messages, so I guess it's settled. I'm going to Rafael's house tonight. We're going to eat dinner, and he's going to help me sort out my future love life under the pretense that I need help with writing. Which I do, but that's not all this is about.

It's fine.

He doesn't need to know.

Totally fine. I'm totally fine.

11 /
are you propositioning me, carrot cake?

charlie

THE HOURS TICK BY, and I end up spending the afternoon cleaning up my flat, then having a shower early enough that my hair isn't soaking wet by the time I need to leave. I attempt to tame the loose curls but end up giving up, reminding myself that this is just a meeting between two people who barely even tolerate one another.

Despite the slow pace of my walk, I arrive seven minutes early. I'm always either early or late for things. On time? I'm not familiar with that concept. Now, I don't know what to do with myself. I don't want to seem too eager, so I pace around the front of his house until my phone vibrates in my back pocket.

RAFAEL:

I can see you pacing on the sidewalk. Come in before my neighbor calls the cops on you. Front door's unlocked.

Crikey! This is embarrassing already. I look up and see Rafael's profile as he stands at the kitchen counter. He's bobbing his head to music I can't hear, and he lifts his hand, waving me in without looking out at where I now stand perfectly motionless.

I take a couple of deep breaths and walk to his front door, finding it unlocked as he promised. I'm expecting to be greeted with loud music, but the moment I step in, it's the smell that hits me first. Garlic, basil, and something else. The music ends up being quite low, a song I haven't heard before, with acoustic guitars coming through the speakers.

"Hello?" I call out. I can't see the kitchen from here, so I walk around the corner toward the delicious scent in the air. As I round the corner, his colossal frame comes into view. I should have been ready to see him in his white T-shirt and jeans since I saw him from the sidewalk. Up close, however, the sight of him in a perfectly fitted white shirt, low-slung jeans, and bare feet, with a tea towel thrown over his shoulder is making me a little weak in the knees. I freeze on the spot yet again, my gaze traveling back up his body slowly. *Too slowly.* By the time I make it to his face, his grin is so wide that I gasp.

"Did you want me to do a little spin, red? Give you all the angles?" I shake my head, and some sort of sound leaves my throat, but no actual words. *What the hell is happening?* His smile grows impossibly wider, and those twin dimples impossibly deeper. "I made pasta. I hope that's okay." He looks at me over his shoulder as he walks away and points to the breakfast nook, where he has two place settings. "What can I get you to drink?"

He's annoyingly casual about this whole thing. But then again, I suppose that's far more normal than my speechlessness. Rafael and I have known one another for over three years; we've eaten many meals at the same table and even celebrated holidays together. This shouldn't feel so strange, and yet I have to work hard to remind myself that this is exactly why I asked him for help. I don't need to make small talk. There's no awkward getting-to-know-you phase; it *should* feel easy. He's not a stranger I'm putting a mask on for. He's seen me remove myself from social situations and knows I'm introverted. Though it's not the whole truth, those facts stabilize my rickety emotions.

It hits me that I've gone too long without answering his question when I catch him cocking his head to the side, eyebrows raised, but without a hint of irritation. He's just waiting for me. "Um water, please." He nods and turns toward the fridge. I take the opportunity to remove my jumper since it's inexplicably hot in here. I also take a moment to toss my hair up in a bun. I can't enjoy a meal with hair around my face.

"You ready to eat?" I feel his eyes travel up my body as he sets the glass of water down, but he looks away so quickly I almost miss it.

"Mmhm." I down half of my glass as Rafael takes a seat in front of me, setting our pasta bowls on the table. It's spaghetti bolognese, which I absolutely love. It smells divine, and I'm reminded of the fact that I didn't eat lunch before my cleaning spree today.

"Dig in," he says with another deadly smile, so I do. As the perfect sauce hits my taste buds, I close my eyes, and I'm almost certain I moan as I chew. Hearing Rafael's choking sounds, I drop my fork, causing a loud clanging noise as he takes several gulps of his water.

"Are you all right?" I've never seen his face so red before, but at least he seems to recover quickly. He gives me a thumbs up, and I take that as my cue to stop staring at him and get back to my delicious dinner. It might be the best spaghetti I've ever eaten. "You have to tell me what's in this sauce. This is incredible."

He has fully recovered, and now he's the one watching me with a small, dimple-free smile. "Glad you like it. I can give you my recipe." He looks back down at his plate and resumes eating.

"Thank you. I'd appreciate that. I'm not a great cook. I absolutely need recipes to follow; otherwise, it's just chaos, and everything tastes rubbish." He watches me intently as I talk, and I find that kind of attention from him a little overwhelming. Not uncomfortable, but new.

We finish our bowls in an oddly comfortable silence. I offer to clean up, but he makes quick work of tossing everything in the dishwasher and sends me to sit in the living room instead. I take in his space for the first time, appreciating how clean and tidy it is.

The furnishing is minimal but warm, with a few unique handmade pieces mixed in. He has colorful artwork on the walls and a few family photos on the massive bookshelf. "Do you live alone?" I nearly shout, hoping he'll hear me in the kitchen.

His deep chuckle catches me off-guard as he's standing closer than I expected. "I do." I widen my eyes while he rounds the couch, setting two glasses of water on the coffee table. "You seem surprised by that."

"Not surprised, per se, just pleased I don't have to spend the evening in some bachelor pigsty." He laughs softly, and I move around the coffee table to take a seat. "You haven't shagged on this sofa, have you?" The question pops out because I hate the idea of touching someone else's bodily fluids, but of course, that's not how he takes it.

"Are you propositioning me, carrot cake?" His smirk causes his dimples to pop, and I glare at him, waiting for him to answer the question. "No, red. I haven't fucked anyone on this couch. I don't bring women here." He says it so matter-of-factly, so easily, that every instinct tells me he's being truthful.

"Like ever?" I ask incredulously, despite his sincerity.

"Like ever," he answers simply. "I know you think I'm some kind of fuckboy based on how we met, but that's not really who I am." He shrugs as if to diminish the statement that I've pegged him all wrong all this time.

As I lower myself to the couch, the words slip out of my mouth, my curiosity getting the better of me. "Then tell me who you are, Rafael Machado."

"I'm… I'm not that guy you met who says crude things on the phone. I mean, I am, but only when I know someone likes it. And that particular person liked it. She told me so." He eyes me intently, and he must see the question written on my face because he blows out a breath and continues, "I don't know why I said it back to you that day. I guess I liked the reaction I got, and Maeve had told me you were a bit more serious, so I pushed. I know I pushed too far. I do that some-times, and I'm sorry for it." Again, I don't hear any dishon-esty. His body language hasn't changed. He's still sitting up, still looking at me with those unwavering chocolate eyes.

If I'm very honest with myself, I liked hearing him say those words the day we met. It was hot. No one had ever spoken to me like that before, and I wondered what it was like to be on the receiving end. But it was much easier to be repulsed by it than to admit that I wish it had been me he had been talking to. Not even necessarily him, just someone. Anyone.

Now, I have no idea what to say. I struggle with reacting to things like this, and being surprised only mars my ability to show emotion. I feel my mouth moving, but it's not until the words have left my mouth that I realize what I'm saying.

"I'm autistic," I quite literally blurt out. "And I have ADHD." I can hear my heart beating. I have never flat-out told anyone else this. I'm not even sure 'I'm autistic' is a sentence I've ever said out loud before.

The people who know are my family, Elaina, and, of course, every doctor or teacher I've had since I was seventeen. And Robert, because I asked him once if he thought I fit the description of an autistic person, and he laughed and said no.

When I revealed to him that I'm an AuDHD'er—a person with both autism and ADHD—he was disbelieving, saying he thought I was "just one of those really smart people who acted a little weird sometimes." Those were his actual words.

Rafael hasn't reacted to my revelation. Once again, he's simply waiting for me. "That's why this is all so hard for me. It's why I've always struggled to talk to you or literally anyone else I come in contact with. It's why I sometimes don't understand if you're being sarcastic and why I don't always look you in the eyes. Not just you, of course."

I look up, and while I don't dare meet his eyes, I know they are steady on me. I can feel them. He doesn't say anything though, and the lack of words being said is making my skin itchy, so I keep talking. "Sometimes, it feels like autism and ADHD are in a fight with one another inside my body. Sometimes, I feel one more strongly than the other. Mostly though, it's just a lot of pretending and learning what society deems as acceptable behavior and then just doing that instead of being myself."

"Is eye contact difficult for you?" Rafael's question catches me off-guard. Considering I was mostly expecting him to dismiss my outburst or laugh about it, this is truly shocking.

Is it shocking, or is that what I keep telling myself because I've learned to expect the worst from him?

After many seconds of silence, I find him patiently waiting. "Sort of. I find it a bit uncomfortable, sometimes distracting, and it doesn't come naturally to me. It's easier to focus on what someone is saying when I can look at their whole face, their body language, or simply whatever's around me so I don't have to focus on them at all."

Rafael nods and links his fingers together as he leans in, elbows resting on his thighs. "I need to say something to you, but I'd really like it if you could look at me when I say it." I suck in a sharp inhale as his words sink in. "Just for a few seconds, can you try to look at me? Please?"

I shut my eyes tightly, wanting to say no, but something about *the way* he just asked makes me want to say yes. The vulnerability in his voice is brand new to me. I nod, but my eyes remain closed.

"Take your time," he urges.

And again, the softness in his voice stirs something so deep in my chest that I can't help but look up. And up and up until my eyes meet a pair of brown ones filled with emotions I couldn't possibly name. It lasts half a second before my eyes move over the rest of his face, noticing the thickness of his lashes and how one of his eyebrows has a scar through it. I've looked at Rafael dozens of times, but never this openly.

"I'm sorry, Charlie." My eyes flit back to his again, and this time, I can't look away. His coffee-colored eyes have me transfixed. He said my name; he's never said it before. Not to me, anyway. There's an erratic fluttering in my chest that I need to shoo away, but it's also weirdly pleasant. I don't have time to process it before he continues, "I'm so, so sorry. I never would have said or done so many things if I had known. And that's not an excuse, I just want to apologize. And thank you for telling me. For trusting me."

When I blink, I look away, focusing on a random spot on the floor. I feel two hot tears travel quickly down my cheeks. I don't wipe them away, and before I can retreat into myself, I hear the whisper of my voice. "I'm sorry, too." I don't say what for. My throat suddenly feels tight, and I can't get any other words out. I close my eyes again and hastily swipe the tears off my cheeks. "Do you think we could pick this up again tomorrow, or perhaps another day? I'd like to go home. I'm feeling quite tired."

There's no hesitation in his response. "Of course. Yeah."

your place or mine?

rafael

I'M PACKING leftovers in the kitchen, feeling like a complete asshole. I thought I could play it cool. I invited Charlie here, hoping she'd be comfortable and not have to worry about me coming into her space. I made spaghetti, knowing it's a dish she likes because I've seen her eat it before. I didn't force conversation, knowing she needed time to warm up, and she's not much of a talker, anyway. I thought it was all going so well.

Fuck. I have never felt more like a total loser in my life than I did when she started to explain the things she struggles with. All the things I had judged her for. All the things I thought made her stuck up and difficult. Meanwhile, she was just doing her best to act in a way that people expected her to. That *I* expected her to.

Having those sky-blue eyes locked on mine nearly knocked all the air out of my lungs. It stirred a feeling I'm not sure I've felt before—like we were tethered by something much more substantial than eye contact.

So, it doesn't surprise me now when she asks to go home. That was a lot for me, so I'd imagine it feels several times more exhausting for her, which is why I opt to give her a minute alone.

I've just finished packing some leftovers for her as she walks into the kitchen with her empty glass. "Thank you for this," she says as she sets the glass down. "For dinner, I mean."

"Oh, no sweat. I love to cook, so anytime." The words slip out easily. Too easily. When I look up at her, she's biting her bottom lip, looking down at her feet.

"Right. I'm gonna go." She throws her thumb over her shoulder and then starts to walk toward the front door.

I follow her there, but I notice her eyebrows scrunch up on her face as she eyes me putting my shoes on. "Are you going somewhere?" I smile at her question and nod. "Oh. All right." Her lips turn into a frown, but as much as I love messing with her, now's not the time.

"I'm walking you home, red." My smile remains on my face as her eyebrows scrunch impossibly closer together on her face.

"No. You don't have to do that." She shakes her head lightly, still not looking up at me.

"I know. But I'd feel a lot better if I did. It's dark. You don't even have to talk to me or walk with me. I just want to make sure you get home okay." I do my best to keep my voice quiet. I have so much more to learn about this girl, and I already know I'm about to come home to spend several hours on my laptop doing more autism research, maybe even if autism and ADHD present differently in women.

"Well, who's going to make sure *you* get home all right?" *Ahhh, there she is.* I chuckle, and a sense of relief washes over me as her face visibly softens.

"I'm a six foot one, two hundred and fifteen pound former Marine. I think I'll be all right." She rolls her eyes, and the world seems to right itself once again. She walks out first, and

I follow, pushing the button on my door to lock it as we step out.

We walk in comfortable silence for the first few minutes. I stay beside her, and it doesn't seem to bother her.

"So, what's in that?" She points to the paper bag in my hand.

"I packed you some leftovers."

Her eyes go wide as she eyes the bag and looks up at my face. "You didn't have to do that. Why did you do that?"

You'd think Charlie wasn't used to people doing nice things for her, but I know her twin and best friend very well, so I know that's not true.

"I made enough pasta for like eight people. You'd be doing me a favor if you took this. Seriously." That seems to appease her. I've always known that coming off too strong doesn't work with her. It's the whole reason she kind of detests me in the first place.

"Oh. Well, thank you." We cross a road, and her shoulders seem to relax a bit more. She's a tough nut to crack, this one. "Should we get together again soon? I'd prefer to have a plan than do anything too last minute."

I smile, thankful for the information she's giving me so freely about herself. "Yeah. Let's do that. I'm a little busy with family stuff this weekend, but I don't have to be in the office on Monday. Would that work for you?"

She takes a few moments to think and then nods. "Monday is fine. One o'clock, okay?"

"That's perfect. Your place or mine?" My question throws her off; I can see it immediately in the way she stiffens, though I had no intention for it to come out sounding like that.

"Um, yours." She stops so abruptly that I have to take a couple of steps back so I'm standing in front of her. I didn't realize we'd already reached her building. Her eyes go to the bag in my hand, and I carefully pass it to her without our hands touching. There's relief in her posture when she takes it.

"Sweet. See you Monday, then. Night, Chuck." I move my hand over my head in a super awkward salute/wave combination. My dorky move amuses her, and she pulls her lips between her teeth as she steps toward her apartment building.

"Night, Machado."

I speed walk back home, thinking of all the things I'm going to Google while I eat leftover spaghetti.

13 /
you are not an idiot.

rafael

IT'S safe to say I understand Charlie a little better now. Sure, I don't know which of the things I learned about apply to her specifically, but I'm happy to have researched as much as I did about the spectrum, and I feel like I've learned a lot about autism in adult women.

Between helping my grandma with her garden and hanging out with my family all weekend, I read more articles. I wanted to ask my brother some things since he has way more experience with autism than I do, but I know he'd ask me why I'm asking, and that's not a road I wanted to go down when my nosey-as-fuck family is together. And it's not my place to talk about Charlie that way. So, I've taken notes, read threads about how adults on the spectrum respond to different things, and now, I'm hoping this makes things a little easier. As someone who's dealt with a fair share of people not understanding my brain, I want to know everything about Charlie's.

· · ·

IT'S NEARLY ONE O'CLOCK, and when I look out the window, Charlie is standing on the sidewalk, chewing on her fingernail. I laugh, remembering her pacing the other night. That was cute.

Cute? When have you ever found a woman cute in your life?

I brush away my thoughts by opening the front door, watching as her eyes dart up to where I'm standing in the doorway.

"Come on in, Ginger Spice. No need to wait out here." I smile in the hopes that she feels more at ease. As she walks up with an almost smile on her face, I say, "I guess you're a little like your sister in some ways. Always early." Immediately, her face falls, her lips in a tight line.

What the fuck did I say?

"I have a hard time with time management. I'm often late, so I tend to err on the side of caution and end up being too early." I nod, storing away that extra bit of information about her. She walks in, takes off her shoes, and heads for the kitchen table.

"You can keep your shoes on, if you want, red. I just don't enjoy wearing them, but it's fine if you want to." I walk to the kitchen, grabbing a couple of glasses to give my hands something to do. I feel weirdly nervous now, like I've already fucked this up.

"I don't like shoes either." I turn toward her to find her looking somewhere in the vicinity of my face.

"Cool. Water?" I raise an empty glass in offering, and she nods. "Ice?"

"No, thank you." She's already busying herself with her laptop, a notebook, and some highlighters. She's so official.

I set down our water and join her, knowing she's about to jump right into it.

"Before we get into anything, I'd like us to have some sort of agreement for how we're going to work together." Wow. Yep. She's just getting right into this.

"Like a contract?" I ask incredulously, but she lights up, nodding.

"Yes! Exactly like that." She doesn't flinch, just continues to write on the notebook that is facing away from me. "I've started with a few key points already. Here. Take a look." She turns the notebook so that the words are no longer upside down for me.

The thrumming in my head is instant. My normally steady breathing quickens, and I feel like a little kid again, being asked to read aloud in class, ready to be laughed at. Except Charlie laughing at me would probably hurt a lot more than a bunch of snotty little kids doing it.

"Why don't we try getting to know each other a little more before we get into a contract?" I try to keep my voice light, even if my palms are already starting to sweat a little.

She pushes the notebook closer to me, eyebrows scrunched as she pulls something up on her laptop. "What? No. Contract first, so we know exactly where we stand. I've thought about this, Machado. I need us to be on the same page before we move forward." Her face softens as she blows out a breath. "Sorry. I just… I would like us to both understand how this is going to work so that no one's feelings are hurt. Is that okay?"

I feel like an asshole. She's doing this because she needs it to feel comfortable and safe, and here I am trying to stop her. I nod and take the notebook, pulling it to the edge of the table. She keeps typing as I start to look at the words on the page.

Taking a deep breath, I hold it for a few seconds and quietly release it, hoping my heart will settle and I can calm myself enough to make sense of her handwriting. It doesn't work. I look up and see she is still concentrating on whatever has her attention on the screen. The letters scramble on the page in front of me, and my eyes start to hurt as I do everything I can to focus on the shapes that should be familiar. It's no use. I'm nervous, anxious, even, and it's making every-thing worse.

Charlie stops typing and pushes her laptop a few inches away from her body. I can feel her looking at me, but I keep my eyes on the page. She clears her throat, and I imagine a giant hole opening in the ground to swallow me whole.

"Umm, is it that bad? We can work on it together, I just thought this was a good start and would give you a better idea of where I stand." I don't respond. I can't. It's like all I can do is focus on my breathing and the heavy feeling in my stomach. I'm gonna have to tell her. "Is there something in particular you don't like? You can just tell me. I'd rather know." She pulls her hands onto her lap, squeezing her fingers so tightly I see her knuckles turning white. Still, my vocal chords have decided to stop functioning. Every ounce of embarrassment I ever felt as a kid, as a teenager, and as a young adult are sitting on my sternum right now, suffocating me. "You know what, it's okay. You don't want to do this. It's fine. I can leave." She pushes the laptop screen down and starts to stand.

No!

I place my hand over hers, stopping her movements and simultaneously blurt out, "I'm dyslexic. I can't read this." She sits back down and regret slams into me like a thunderclap. I go to move my hand away from hers, but she flips hers over and wraps her slender fingers around mine so the tips are resting over my knuckles. When I look up from our point of contact, her eyes are glued to our joined hands. We sit like this for several seconds, both processing the moment.

After a hard swallow, her lips part, but her eyes remain on our hands. "I'm sorry. I didn't know. I wouldn't have—"

"You don't need to apologize." I hate to interrupt her, but I also won't have her apologizing for something that's not her fault. "You're right, you didn't know. It's not your fault."

Charlie's chin lifts, and she looks at me, her eyes moving

over my face as they do whenever we're together. "It's not yours, either." She squeezes my hand and begins to slide it away from mine. It takes superhuman strength to allow her to break our connection.

Touching Charlie is new to me, to us, but every time it happens, I find myself wishing for more of it. Just a few extra seconds. A little bit more time so I can memorize the feel of her skin. But it's always over too soon.

"Would it help if I typed this out?" She places both hands on her laptop, ready to fix the awkwardness. "I could do that now; I just sometimes prefer to write on paper," she says as her hands shake slightly. "I could—"

"Could you read it to me?" I interrupt again because I can't stand to see her become anxious over something completely out of her control. "We can work on it together if you don't mind reading it out loud." Pushing down the feelings of inferiority and the fear that she now thinks I'm even more of an idiot than before, I flip the notebook back toward her.

She doesn't answer, just gingerly pulls it toward herself and licks her bottom lip before starting. "Charlie and Rafael's friendship contract. Number one: We promise to be honest and transparent with one another in a kind and respectful manner." She looks up at me, and I nod, forcing a smile to appear on my face so she can see that I agree. "Number two: No sarcasm." At that I find a real smile pulling at my lips. I know that one is for me. "I don't always pick up on it, even if I am pretty good at reading body language. Sarcasm is just hard."

"Got it," I say, fighting the instinct to wink because I'm not sure if she would take that as sarcasm.

"Number three: We don't talk about what we're doing with other people, including our mutual friends. *Especially* our mutual friends," she emphasizes with an eyebrow raised.

"*Fight Club* rules. Understood." My smile widens as she frowns, eyes still on the notebook.

"Absolutely not. We *will* be keeping our shirts on." The smallest of smiles tugs at her lips, and a surprised laugh spills out of me, making my chest feel lighter. I love it when she says these hilarious things with a completely serious face. Charlie simply continues reading. "This is to ensure that we can build trust with one another. Also, it's none of their business, and we both know they'll pry."

I chuckle as she finishes, and my shoulders relax. "You wanna keep me a secret, pumpkin?"

She rolls her eyes, and my dick has the audacity to twitch.

Charlie rolling her eyes? Really? That's what's doing it for me these days?

"It's not a secret. They're the ones who pushed for this to begin with, which also means they're highly invested. I think not knowing will annoy them, which I'm fine with, but it'll also give us the security of knowing there aren't four other people involved." She doodles something on the corner of the page and then covers it up by scribbling all over it. "Does that make sense?" She scrunches her face up as she draws a square around the doodle, coloring that in more carefully.

"Yeah, carrot cake, that makes sense. Do we need to sign this thing? Make it official?" I keep my tone light, thankful she's moved on from my outburst, and my nerves have, too.

"Uh, no? I mean, we can just have a verbal agreement, right?" She sits back, shoulders stiffening.

I keep fucking this up. "Yeah. Yes. Of course. Sorry. I was joking. It was stupid. I make stupid jokes sometimes. I'm sorry. But please don't put anything in there about not being able to make jokes because, I swear, I can't help it. It's a factory setting that can't be toggled off, you know? Shit. There I go again. That was a joke. Jesus. Fuck. I gotta stop. I'm sorry. Dumb things just come out of my mouth sometimes, and then they just keep coming. I'll try harder not to be such an idiot."

I feel the sweat build on my palms and rub my hands on my thighs as I try to calm down. Apparently, the anxiety from before hasn't fully left my body yet.

"I'm going to add a number four in here. We will ask for what we need, and the other person will respect it, period, no questions asked," she says as she writes quickly. "I need some time and space to process. And if I had to guess, since I've never seen you this flustered before, I would say you need them, too." She sets the pen down. "Am I right?"

It feels like there's jet fuel running through my veins right now. "Yeah. You're right." I need to go for a long run. A very long run.

"Right. I'll go, then." Charlie stands, and I do the same. I watch as she packs her things back into a bag. She takes off in the direction of the front door, and I follow. "We can text and sort out our next meeting," she says as she walks away. She slips her shoes on and adjusts her bag on her shoulder. "And Rafael?"

"Yeah?" I look up at her face, finally, finding her slightly flushed.

"You are not an idiot." The way she says this like she's stating a fact as true as the color of the sky, has me swaying on the spot. "I'll see you later."

And just like that, she walks out of my house.

I don't bother putting shoes on. I rip off my socks and walk to the backyard, where the skipping rope is hanging.

And I skip.

I skip until I can't catch my breath. Until the bottoms of my feet hurt. Until I'm too tired to think of anything other than my exhaustion. Until I can wipe her words clean from my brain.

14 /
you actually like something about me?

rafael

CHARLIE:

Hi. Can I ask some questions about your dyslexia?

I'm sorry if that's rude.

I just haven't been able to stop thinking about it, and the research I'm doing isn't exactly clear since this seems to be a little different depending on the person.

It's been six hours since Charlie left my house. After skipping, I worked out for nearly an hour, then ate enough food to feed a family of four, and still, my brain has not stopped replaying the last five words she said to me. This seems to be a recurring theme in my life since meeting Charlie—the words that she says stick to me like they're feathers, and I'm covered in Elmer's Glue.

CHARLIE:

Okay. That was rude.

I'm sorry.

> You don't have to answer me.

> But can you also not ignore me?

> Because it's hard for me to deal with rejection, and being ignored feels like rejection.

> It's an ADHD thing. You can look it up if you want.

> Rejection Sensitive Dysphoria.

I look at the time stamp and notice the first couple of texts were sent over three hours ago. Shit.

ME:

> Sorry, I didn't have my phone on me. You can ask whatever you want.

> And I know about RSD. I have ADHD, too.

Before I've even hit send on that second message, three little dots appear on the screen.

CHARLIE:

> Is reading these text messages difficult for you?

> Because I'll stop texting if this is frustrating or whatever.

> You have ADHD, too????

> I should have seen the signs, but without context, reading people can be hard. Thanks, autism.

> And I know it can present differently in men vs women.

ME:

No. Texting is fine, and if I'm tired, I just have my phone dictate it to me so I don't have to read it. Or I'll send back voice notes, if that's okay.

Handwriting is tricky because the letters are different and inconsistent. Things sort of blur together, and it's hard to make sense of it all. Even my own handwriting is awful and makes no sense.

CHARLIE:

Okay. That's good to know.

Is that why you listen to books?

ME:

I read them sometimes, but I prefer listening to them, and I also like to read and listen at the same time.

But since I like to move around a lot, listening while running is a way for me to multitask two things I like.

CHARLIE:

Ohhhh.

Yeah, I don't have the hyperactivity thing.

Not physically, anyway.

Just mentally.

Do you have any questions for me?

I feel like I'm asking for a lot of information here.

ME:

Ummm I can't think of anything right now. Even though there are probably a hundred things I could ask.

I guess I want to be careful with you. I don't want to make you uncomfortable. I've done that enough already in the past, and I feel kind of sick about it.

CHARLIE:

Oh.

ME:

Sorry. That obviously made you uncomfortable. See? I'm no good at this.

CHARLIE:

It didn't.

It's fine. You're fine.

No one has ever told me they want to be careful with me before.

Don't walk on eggshells around me just because you know I'm autistic.

It's nice that you want to be sensitive to that, but it's worse if you start acting the way you think I need you to act. I can't be myself if you're not yourself, too.

Does that make sense?

ME:

Yeah. That makes perfect sense, actually.

Can I just ask for one thing, then?

CHARLIE:

Sure.

Yes.

Sorry, sure can sometimes seem standoffish.

Please, go ahead.

ME:

> Can you let me know if I do or say something that makes you feel uncomfortable? Even if it's not right away, can you just at some point let me know so I can stop doing it?

CHARLIE:

> Yeah. Okay.

> I'll add that to the contract.

> And I'll send you a document so you can have a copy, too.

> But yeah. It's part of being honest with each other, right?

ME:

> Yeah, red. That sounds great.

> Also, I really dig the fact that you send so many messages all in a row. My phone is blowing up, and it's kind of awesome.

CHARLIE:

> You actually like something about me?

> And here I thought you were committed to just barely tolerating me.

ME:

> I like a lot of things about you, Chuck.

The three dots appear and then disappear a few times before they're gone completely. Why did I say that? I mean, it's true. *I like her*. I like her more than I think I should. More than I want to like her, even. But I like all of my friends. I like most people, actually. But I don't like most people the way I like Charlie. I don't think I've ever liked anyone the way I like her.

ME:

Was that weird? I'm sorry. I just don't want you to think I don't like you. I've never not liked you. We just somehow ended up bickering all the time.

CHARLIE:

I just needed a moment to process.

I think that maybe I've held on to a grudge since meeting you.

I've had this idea that you're a perfect guy with a perfect life, and nothing has ever been difficult for you.

And maybe I resented that.

No, I definitely resented that.

And I should apologize to you for this.

In person.

ME:

It's okay. You don't have to.

CHARLIE:

Yes, I do.

I want to.

It's part of pushing myself to feel things and deal with them appropriately.

ME:

All right. But it's okay if you don't.

You know, I always thought you were the one with the pretty perfect life. You're smart and beautiful. You always seem to go after what you want unapologetically. I've always thought that there was nothing you couldn't do. I still do think that, but now I also respect the fuck out of you for doing it all while trying to fit into a world that doesn't understand or always accept neurodivergent people.

CHARLIE:

Well, then, you should also respect the fuck out of yourself for doing the same.

Also, thanks.

I guess we just needed to find some common ground and let go of those misconstrued images we had of one another.

ME:

Haha yeah. That's all.

Shit. Sorry. That was sarcasm.

All I'm saying is you're right.

CHARLIE:

Relax. I got it.

Okay. Well, I should get some sleep.

Talk soon, Machado.

ME:

Later, Ginger Spice.

15 /
this guy rubs his own meat.

rafael

IT'S A TYPICAL TUESDAY AFTERNOON, and I'm about to reach my parents' house in Siesta. I've been listening to a romantasy novel on the way here, but I'm gonna have to listen to all of these chapters again because I'm still distracted by yesterday's text conversation with Charlie.

I'm wondering if maybe it's easier for her to text than to have conversations that deep in person. Probably. I mean, she might not get to see body language, but it's probably easier for her to respond without any prolonged silences or anything.

Sometimes, that's easier for me because I either feel the need to interrupt someone so I don't lose my train of thought, or I end up not hearing what they're saying because I'm trying to hold on to my thought.

The knowledge that there are things like this that Charlie and I have in common is messing with my mind. I never thought we'd have anything in common.

· · ·

AS I PULL into the long driveway, I see no other cars and feel slightly relieved. There isn't usually anyone here during the day since both of my parents still work full-time, but occasionally, my mom will take an afternoon off. I'm glad today isn't one of those days.

I love my parents. I really do. I just love my grandmother more than anything, and getting to spend time with her since retiring from the Marine Corps has been one of the best things to happen to me.

I exit the car, knowing she's expecting me, and a smile forms at the thought. This has been our thing for a while now, these Tuesday hangs.

As I open the front door, the smell of coffee immediately hits my nostrils. I walk to the back of the house and take in the sight before making my presence known.

"I heard you come in, Rafa. I may be old, but I'm not deaf yet," she says in Portuguese with her back still to me. I chuckle and wait for her to turn.

"Bença, vó," I say in greeting, asking for her blessing as I walk toward her, laying a kiss on her knuckles. It's a tradition my dad insisted on since he grew up doing this with his grandparents in Brazil.

"Deus te abençoe, meu filho." God bless you, my son. She pulls me in for a hug, and my body instantly relaxes. She's getting up there in age, but her hugs are strong, always ending with a few pats to the cheek. No, not pats, per se. More like subtle slaps. Eva, Owen and Elaina's mom, gives gentle cheek pats. My grandmother gives slaps. And I love it. She always takes a moment to look into my eyes when she does it, her eyes and cheeks crinkling with a smile.

"Café?" she asks, but it's not really a question. She knows I'm going to sit and have her afternoon coffee with her. There's fresh bread already on the table with butter, mortadella, sliced cheese, and a few cookies next to it. "Senta." She points to the chair closest to me. "Tell me, how's my boy?" she asks in Portuguese. I know better than to ask her how she's doing first. This is our routine now.

Ana Maria, at eighty-seven years old, refuses to speak English with us, though she certainly can. She claims it's the only way any of her grandchildren speak Portuguese fluently, and she takes full credit for this feat with all six of us. I'm pretty sure my parents would have handled it. They mostly speak Portuguese around us, but Vó made sure that never changed with my siblings and me, even as we got older and started speaking English with one another.

I take a seat, waiting for her to sit next to me before answering. "Everything's fine, Vó. I just saw you two days ago." I smile as she scowls at me, ready to reprimand me in the way she always does.

"Yes, well, you were all so busy wrestling with one another that I barely got to talk to you. Something seems different. What is it, Rafa?" She butters a piece of bread as she speaks and passes it to me. She won't rest until I eat, and that's never been a problem for me, so I take it.

I grapple with her words for a moment, busying myself with the mortadella and cheese to buy myself time. I feel different. Ever since Charlie became someone I see on a semi-regular basis, I'm not the same. Every time I talk to her, I feel like I'm being turned inside out. Like everything I try to keep shoved away is on display. Like she sees every part of me. And the weirdest part? I'm not sure that makes me as uncomfortable as I thought it might. A common thing when it comes to the woman who occupies nearly all the space in my head these days.

"Ah, it's nothing. I'm just not sleeping well." Vó's eyes flick up from the cheese she's placing on her plate, and I mentally kick myself for the error I've just made.

"Are you having headaches? Maybe I should make you some tea instead." She braces her hands on the table to stand, and I place a gentle hand on her shoulder to stop her.

"I'm feeling great. I promise." At least physically, I am. It's not a lie. She doesn't need to know about the tornado of emotions twisting in my chest. "No headaches lately. Not since I had one a few weeks ago when I was here. And you took such good care of me that I haven't had another." I wish they were just headaches, but my migraines, when they decide to hit, hit real hard. Like throwing up, can't open my eyes, everything hurts kind of hard. I've had them nearly my whole life, and because the prescription medication makes me so loopy, I tend to avoid taking it. Vó knows that I need the right mix of caffeine, sleep, and not to move for a few hours to make it go away.

She sits back in her chair, narrowing her eyes at me. "Menino," she scolds. "A grandmother always knows when her grandbabies are going through something. But, fine, if you're not going to tell me now, keep it to yourself. I'll be here when you're ready." She takes a bite of her cheese and waves a hand over to me, urging me to do the same.

As I chew on my afternoon snack, I also chew on her words. *I'll be here when you're ready.* It always hits me hardest when she says things like that. She's healthy, yes. Spry as fuck and could probably still handle a long workday better than most people in their thirties. But still, it always feels like time is running out, and the pressure to spend as much time as I can with her, to make the most of every moment, is always there. If I let it, the anxiety I feel over lost time will consume me. It was that anxiety that prompted me to have these Tuesdays with her, to make sure that a part of her legacy was left here for us. For *me.*

"What are we cooking today?" I change the subject, and she doesn't protest.

"Strogonoff." After a sip of her coffee, she smiles up at me. It's my favorite dish. One I usually request when I need comfort food. She really did know I needed a little extra love today.

. . .

AFTER WE FINISH OUR COFFEES, I wash the dishes, and Vó puts the remaining food away. She always puts way too much out, and not even I—being the bottomless pit that I am—can eat it all.

"So, what are we replacing the mushrooms with this time?" I move to where she is at the large island and start to help her tie her apron. She swats my hand away, and I laugh. Fiercely independent, this woman.

"I thought we could try leeks. I didn't like how the tofu crumbled last time, and zucchini is too watery." Vó takes the vegetables from the fridge, and I tie my apron, shaking my head at the design on the one she picked for me. It says, "This guy rubs his own meat," with big arrows pointing to my face. Yeah, my grandmother has the most inappropriate kind of humor, and she is unapologetic about it.

"All right, Vózinha. Let's do this!" I rub my hands together, already feeling the tension in my shoulders melt away as I get lost in the comfort of cooking.

WHEN WE FINISH, the kitchen smells fantastic. The leeks seem to hold up well in the dish, and it tastes great, too, as we come to find out when we do a quick taste test. Vó pulls a container to pack some of the food so I can take it home with me but struggles with getting the lid on and spills some of the stroganoff on the counter.

"Merda!" She slams the container down, her hands shaking slightly, and I calmly stand next to her, taking one of those life-giving hands into my own and bringing it to my lips. I place a kiss on top of her right hand, noticing that the skin there feels even more paper-thin than the last time I paid attention to this detail about her. "These old hands don't want to cooperate. Can you pack this up while I clean up my mess?"

We work silently. I know she's proud and won't want me to mention this incident to anyone. We finish up, and she waves a hand at my phone sitting on the counter. "Don't forget to type into your phone that we used three leeks, bottoms only, cut into slices. Not too thin. I'll write it into the notebook when my fingers decide to be useful again."

"Not too thin. Is that the actual size?" I smirk, hoping she'll do the same. Her arthritis is getting worse, and she sees it as losing bits of her independence. "Or should we be more vague?" I chuckle as she twists the tea towel on her shoulder and whips it at me, hitting me right on the nipple with sniper-like precision.

Her husky laughter fills the room as I yelp, dropping my phone to the countertop with a loud clank. "Any other questions?" she asks through a fit of giggles.

"None at the moment, thank you. Ow. That one got me good, Vó." I rub at the spot on my chest that is going to be sore for the next several minutes and hold in my own laughter. Picking my phone back up, I finish typing in her modifications, eyeing the closed notebook. "I'd really like to keep the notebook going, but I don't think we'll be able to. I don't want you doing this, knowing it's painful for you."

It sucks because this is actually really important to me. Cooking has been the most visceral connection I have to who I am and where I'm from. It's something I can share with my friends and my family; it brings joy, it helps me keep my hands occupied, and it calms me. Cooking, like running or exercising, is vital.

When Vó and I started this book a few months ago, the goal was to include everyone's favorite dishes along with traditional Brazilian ones. All the things she's made for us over the years without a recipe book, without measurements. Now, I'm taking care to get specific quantities—even if they're not always as accurate as I'd like—so that any of us can recreate her dishes. I've asked her not to tell anyone we're working on this. Selfishly, I want this handwritten version to be just for me, even if I can't really read it. I'll have this typed up by someone, at some point, and create something I can read and print multiples of to gift to everyone.

She looks at me with sad eyes, and the guilt I'm all too familiar with smacks me in the chest harder than the towel she just whipped me with. "I'm sorry. I know how important this is to you. It's important to me, too." Her eyes fill with tears, and the need to diffuse this situation is all-consuming. If she cries, I will not be able to hold it together. That's already difficult for me on a good day. Thankfully, she shakes it off. "Maybe we can get someone to help us? Or you can do that thing where you talk to your phone, and it types for you. We can figure this out." She pats my forearm and shifts over to hang a tea towel.

Just the thought of having to focus on cooking, getting measurements, and getting the recipe correctly onto a document is enough to overwhelm me. I can multitask things like listening to a book and running. One is mental, is the other physical. But with cooking, there's already a lot involved, and I know I'd struggle to add one more thing. I already do most of the prepping so that Vó doesn't have to use a knife to chop anything or do anything else that will cause more pain. That's why she writes the recipes down.

I don't even know why it's so important to me to have this handwritten version. Maybe because it's physical proof of what we're doing together. Of this time we get to have. Some pages end up stained with oils or sauces, and when I flip through them, they look like little pieces of art.

As someone whose genetic family history starts and ends with myself, this matters to me. The only history I have is the one I'm actively creating, thanks to the Machado family. My parents didn't want me. They chose to give me up in a closed adoption. This family chose to have me, and they continue to choose me every day.

I have to find a way to make this happen.

With my car smelling of my favorite meal, I drive in silence, letting my thoughts become as chaotic as they want. I just want to get home and snuggle my cat.

As I pull into my driveway, my phone vibrates.

CHARLIE:

Is tomorrow okay for us to get together?

Maybe go for a walk?

Anytime is fine.

I fight the urge to mark the messages as unread and respond to them later, knowing that Charlie might assume that I'm ignoring her again. I know she'd probably understand if I told her that sometimes I open messages before I'm mentally prepared to respond to them. But I haven't explained that to her yet, so it's not fair to just expect her to know this about me.

ME:

Tomorrow is great. I'm going to be at the office until around two o'clock for a meeting, but I'll be home before three for sure. I can come by your place, and we can go from there? I'll text when I'm on my way.

I read the text back twice before hitting send. Her response is immediate, as usual.

CHARLIE:

Great.

See you then.

All right, then.

what is this feeling?

charlie

MY CONFIDENCE WAS HIGH, until I reached the main door of the apartment building. My heart nearly skipped out of my chest when I spotted him leaning on a palm tree. He's wearing dark jeans and a black Henley, his hair disheveled in a way that makes me think he either spent a lot of time styling it, or he lets his curls do whatever they want. I think it's the latter.

It surprises me to see he's not on his phone, either scrolling aimlessly, texting someone, or whatever people do when they're out in public and need to busy themselves with something other than simply existing in the world. He's just standing there, looking out at the road as traffic rolls past. He looks up at the palm trees swaying in the wind and smiles. He actually bloody smiles! At the bloody trees! When he looks down and spots me, the smile remains, and I fight twin urges to either keep my expression at whatever it currently is, which is probably my resting bitch face, or smile back at him because that's what I've learned you're supposed to do.

I get it; I'm not a naturally chipper person like specimen A in front of me. But telling me to smile is like telling someone having an emotional breakdown to calm down. It's not going to work.

I let my face do whatever it wants and walk toward him. His smile actually widens as he pushes off the tree trunk. This man gives out smiles freely, constantly. I don't understand him. It must be exhausting.

"Hey there, strawberry shortcake. How was your day?" Rafael is so naturally friendly. It would be annoying if it weren't slightly endearing. The nicknames, however, I find mostly annoying. This one is brand new, though, and I think I might like it.

Wait, what?

"Um, fine, thanks." I should ask him how his day was, too. It's not that I'm not interested in how his day was; I just find small talk and pleasantries so laborious. "How was yours?"

"Great. Better now that I'm not in a budget meeting that most definitely could have been an email." He grimaces after he finishes. "Ugh. Sorry. That wasn't very nice. The meeting wasn't even that bad. But the coffee was, which means I haven't had my afternoon coffee yet, and maybe it's making me a little grumpy."

"Ha!" I cover up my mouth at my sudden outburst. Rafael watches me with widened eyes, and I clear my throat to recover. "Sorry, it's just that if this is you grumpy, I'm scared to know what you look like when you're blissfully happy. You're like the human version of Olaf, only with really good hair and muscles everywhere. I mean, blimey, you were just smiling at trees like you're a literal Disney character." I point to where he was looking earlier, but my gaze quickly jumps back to his face as his laughter booms out of him. I've heard Rafael laugh countless times. It comes as naturally to him as smiling, which is as natural to him as blinking. I don't even think he knows he's doing it.

But *I've* just made him laugh. Really laugh. Without even

trying. So much so, he's clutching his chest and bending at the waist.

"You got jokes, Chuck!" He lets out another small chuckle as if what I said is still affecting him. "Olaf, that's a good one." With a final shake of his head, he stops laughing and sets his eyes on me. "Wanna walk to Smitty's and grab a coffee with me? They have all kinds of iced coffee. My treat."

"Yeah. Sure." My stomach feels tight, almost like the feeling you get when you're starting to get hungry, but I just ate, so that's not it. Must be the mention of iced coffee, a detail about me that Rafael has picked up on with our time together over the years. Hot coffee isn't my thing. I never get to drink it at the temperature it's supposed to be, and there's a massive difference between drinking cold coffee, which was meant to be hot, and iced coffee. Once I discovered iced coffee, my relationship with the drink went to the next level. We're besties now.

Rafael starts to walk in the direction of this unknown-to-me coffee place, and I notice that he slows to match my pace. I don't like walking fast unless I absolutely have to.

"So, why don't you tell me a little more about what you need my help with?" Rafael's gaze remains on the sidewalk ahead of us as he speaks.

"All right. Well, I write romance. I know that may be surprising for someone who has a hard time understanding emotions, but it's different when I'm making the characters up." I pause and notice that he tips his face toward me, but only for a second.

"That makes sense, though. You're in control," he says matter-of-factly.

"Y-yeah. Exactly." I watch him nod as he looks around us. "Anyway, lately, it doesn't feel like I have control of the characters anymore. I actually don't feel like I have any control over myself, either, and that's terrifying." I catch the movement of his head in my peripheral a few times as he glances at me, but it never lasts long. I like this. Just like with texting, there's no pressure on me to make eye contact, and I don't feel like I'm being watched.

"My therapist warned me that shutting myself off from the world wouldn't be helpful, but that it's also okay to need time alone. She said I need to make sure I have my safe people, the ones I don't need to mask with. The problem is that those people are Maeve and Elaina, which isn't great when I live in London, and they live here." I pause as Rafael looks thoughtful. I assume it's thoughtful because I've seen him look like this—brows furrowed and mouth pulled to the left side of his face—whenever he plays board games with the guys and he's figuring out his next move.

"There's no one in London?" He does look at me a little longer then, the question hanging between us.

"Um, there is… someone. The other reason I've recently decided that I need to get a better hold on my life and my feelings. Robert and I have known one another for years, and though we had been in an open relationship, it was much more open on his side, if you know what I mean." I widen my eyes, though he can't see me. It's slightly awkward to discuss my relationship status. I chance a look at him, and note the tightness in his jaw, the way his lips are set in a thin line. A brand-new expression I'm not sure how to translate.

"Anyway, I don't know if these things are related—my sudden inability to write, wanting to find people who accept me as I am, and needing to sort out whether I'm prepared for a committed relationship—but since turning thirty, I've started to get honest with myself about my life. I can admit that my bubble in London wasn't making me as happy as I thought. I told Maeve to go after her joy, and I think I need to take my own advice. And figure out exactly what that is for me." We cross the road and turn. He shuffles behind me and moves over so he's walking closest to the road.

"Red, I think it's really amazing that you're pushing yourself out of that bubble. That's not an easy thing to do. Can I ask a question?" I hum my response, and he pulls in a long breath. "How exactly am I going to help you?" His tone is curious yet uncertain. It's as if he doesn't believe he's the right person for the job.

I've thought a lot about this, so I have the answer, but it still makes me a little jittery having to say it out loud. My nose scrunches as the words take wing inside my throat. "Well, the first way is you'll help me sort out the things with my characters. You read romance, so maybe we can talk through some of that." Can I just come right out and tell him what I need? I'm not sure. This feels a bit more palatable for now. "And the second is that you'll maybe become another safe person on my roster, or at least help me figure out what I need to do to find safe people. I know we have our—whatever this is with us—but I trust my sister and Elaina implicitly. And they trust you. I'm leaning on their guidance with this since I can't seem to trust myself with big decisions lately."

He stops in front of a bright yellow shop and turns to face me. I tip my head up so I can see his face. Yep. He's smiling. But it's a small smile. A shy smile? "Charlie, I would really like to be a safe person for you. I want you to know that I'm taking this very seriously, and I'm honored that you're choosing to try to trust me." He swallows hard, and his brows furrow again, then slowly, the almost pained expression fades away. "Thanks for telling me all that," he finally says, but the sentence feels unfinished. I nod once, and his smile returns. "Ready for the best iced coffee of your life?"

"That's very presumptuous of you, Machado. You have no idea how much iced coffee I've had." His hearty laughter garners a few looks from people around us, who all smile when they see the joy painted so clearly on his face.

"You haven't had Smitty's coffee. I'm about to change your life, pumpkin." He wiggles his eyebrows and opens the front door to the establishment, holding it for me. I don't know why, but I honest to goodness believe his last statement.

The smell of coffee and caramel is strong as I step inside. It's wonderful. A middle-aged man with thick, clear-framed glasses stands behind the counter, and when he sees Rafael, he extends his arms in the air, a wide smile taking over his tanned, wrinkled face. "Raf! How's my buddy doing?"

Rafael lifts a hand in greeting. "Hey, Smitty. I'm doing well, how are you? How was your visit with your family?" The two men chat, and I tune them out as I take in the menu above Smitty's head. There are so many options. And a lot of drinks with their homemade caramel sauce. It's completely overwhelming, and I have no idea how I'm going to choose a drink anytime in the next century, let alone within the next few minutes. I like to look at a menu before I go somewhere for the first time. I like knowing what I'm going to have. I like having my first choice, and if that's not available, being prepared with a second and third option. I'm looking at the menu, but it's hard to focus with the way my palms are starting to sweat and how my clothes are starting to suffocate me.

The conversation stops, and I realize one of them likely asked me a question. I look to Rafael, and he smiles at me. Shocking, right? "This is my friend, Charlie." Fact: This is now the third time he has said my name. "She only drinks iced coffee, and I've promised her yours is the best, so you better not make me look bad, Schmidt." He points a finger at his friend behind the counter, who clutches his chest in response.

Looking back at me, the older man waves a hand in the air. "Nice to meet you, Charlie. I'm Smitty—or sometimes Schmidt to your friend here—owner of this fine establishment with the insane menu. Can I ask some questions about your drink preferences?" My body sags in relief, and I nod my head enthusiastically, which earns me a chuckle from both men. "Well, we know you like your coffee iced, but are you like this one who doesn't like milk or cream?" Immediately, I shake my head. "Any preference for which kind of milk?"

"Um, no?" I've never given much thought to the skimmed milk versus whole thing. I don't actually care.

"Good, good. If you had to choose a flavor, would you choose chocolate, vanilla, raspberry, caramel, or a mix?" Smitty eyes me intently, not only listening carefully to my responses but watching the way I respond.

"Just caramel, and not too much." I don't even need to think about this answer. Based on the smell in here alone, I'd choose something with caramel. "My taste buds don't like too many flavors together, so just one is more than enough."

"I was hoping you'd pick the caramel. We just whipped up a fresh batch." Smitty claps and takes a plastic to-go cup from the stack to his right. "All right. It'll just be a few minutes, then." He turns away from us, seemingly getting to work, though I don't know what on.

"Wait. What am I getting?"

Smitty exchanges a look I can't decipher with the wall of muscle next to me, who has the decency to shrug. Anxiety begins to claw its way from the tips of my fingers to my neck.

"Smitty likes to guess drinks for anyone who's a first-timer," Rafael says with one eyebrow raised.

"Guess? It's an art, what I do. I've only been wrong once, and that was because I was still a little out of it from my painkillers after surgery. It doesn't count." Smitty keeps working, hands moving quickly and his head tipping back toward us on the words *once* and *count*, as if he needs to punctuate them to make his point.

I squeeze my hands together, linking my fingers and focusing on the pressure there, focusing on keeping my breathing even. I crane my neck to see what's going into my drink, but I'm not tall enough. I can't see.

Rafael comes to stand between me and the counter as if he's shielding me from what's happening behind it. "Hey, Pumpkin. You all right?" His brows furrow in concern, and I know mine are doing the same.

"I don't like surprises. I'm particular about what I eat or drink." My voice comes out clipped, but I don't have it in me to care at the moment.

"Yeah, I know. Schmidt never gets it wrong, though. And if he does, you get as much coffee as you want for free for a whole year. That's his guarantee." His hands move up as if he's about to touch me, then he fists them and releases them back at his sides. "May I touch you?" God, my stomach tightens and twists as he whispers those words to me, his minty breath landing on my cheek.

What is this feeling? Why can't I name it? Why is my body having so many reactions to him?

Not wanting to make the moment more awkward than it needs to be, I respond with a *yes* and his hands slowly move up until one is squeezing my shoulder and the other lands on my chin, tipping my face up to look at him.

"I guess this is an exercise in trust. I know I'm asking a lot, but I promise you, if you don't like what he makes, we can sit here and try every single coffee, milk, and syrup combination on that ridiculous menu until we find one you like." His gaze is unwavering, even when I don't meet it directly. "How does that sound?" He keeps his voice low, and though there are no other patrons near us and this isn't necessarily a private conversation, I appreciate that this normally boisterous and loud man is making an effort to be so quiet for me.

"Yeah. Okay." As soon as the words leave my mouth, a wide smile spreads across his face, accentuating the perfectly lopsided dimples in his cheek. His hand slides down from my chin to my shoulder, giving a final reassuring squeeze before he releases me and steps away, leaving behind a lingering warmth.

"All right." With a resounding clap, Smitty brings his hands together once more. His eyes, bright and shining like stars in the night sky, scan over us with eager anticipation. "One Caramel Cloud Brew and one plain old black coffee that's about to be doused in more sugar than anyone needs. Thankfully, he only does this with his afternoon coffee, right?" He rolls his eyes as he finishes his sentence, and I stare at the cold drink next to the bright yellow paper cup filled with steaming coffee. It looks amazing. The top is creamy white and foamy, the bottom is the color of caramel itself, and there's not too much ice in it.

I break away from my thoughts and look at Smitty, who is still smiling hopefully. I don't like attention on me, and rather than reaching for my drink, I find myself frozen on the spot.

"Let me pay for this while Charlie decides whether or not you know what you're doing, old man." Rafael walks away, reaching back into his pocket for his phone to pay for our drinks.

When I see both men are focused on their conversation and not on me, I pull the cup closer to me and lift it to my mouth. I taste the creamy cold foam first. It's sweet, but not too sweet, with a hint of vanilla. When the coffee hits my tongue, I make a sound that's somewhere between a groan and a moan and slap my hand against the countertop. Loudly.

My eyes widen in embarrassment, but I can't find it in me to care about that. I need another sip of this magical drink. It's not often that I'm pleasantly surprised by anything, so this is wonderful.

I pick up Rafael's drink and walk the few steps to where they're still watching me. "This might be the best thing I've ever tasted," I say as I hand the cup of hot coffee to Rafael. "What exactly is it, and how did you know I would like it?"

The older man in front of us puffs out his chest, clearly proud of his work. He should be. It's a masterpiece. "Well," he begins, "I used cold brew instead of espresso, a mix of cream and milk for the, well, creaminess, and topped it off with cold foam that has just the tiniest bit of vanilla. I know you said one flavor only, but I took a chance."

"If I were the type of person who hugged strangers, I would be climbing over this counter to get to you right now, Smitty." Both men burst into happy laughter, and in my periphery, I see other customers' eyes turn toward us, making my cheeks heat.

"I like you, Charlie. I hope you'll come back." Smitty's sincerity washes away the embarrassment I felt over potentially saying something inappropriate.

"Good luck getting rid of me after a taste of this. I don't know how I'll ever drink anything else ever again." And I mean it. I'm not sure I can go back to other iced coffees after tasting this one. The minute I find something I like—food, drinks, clothing, TV shows, songs—I become fixated on them. Usually, for a very long time, if not forever.

Still grinning, Smitty hands Rafael one of those glass sugar dispensers you often see in diners, and he turns it upside down for one, two, three, oh my goodness, four, five seconds.

"You don't have a family history of diabetes, do you?" My question slips out, that impulsive curiosity getting the best of me as it always does. Rafael's smile falters, and he focuses on stirring his coffee and putting a lid on the cup. He doesn't answer me, and the coffee in my stomach sours.

17 /
your feelings
matter.

charlie

"RAFAEL?" I stupidly press on.

"No. Um, I don't know." He runs a hand down the front of his face. "I mean, I only have sugar with my afternoon coffee, so I think I'm all right." He smiles, but it's different. It's not happy like all the other ones. It's like when I force myself to smile and it comes out more like a grimace. I am the queen of the Chandler Bing smile. Awful, incomprehensibly awkward. So I know one when I see one.

My question bothered him. But why? I think back on everything I know about him. He's got several siblings, both parents are alive, a grandmother... What did I miss? What nerve did I hit with my question?

I lose myself enough in my thoughts that I don't hear what Rafael is saying, but clearly, he's said his goodbyes because he's turning toward the door. "Thank you for this," I say to the coffee magician. "I'll see you soon."

"Great to meet you, Charlie. I look forward to it." Smitty smiles kindly, then greets the customer who's just walked up to the counter.

I turn hastily to catch up to Rafael who is waiting at the

door, holding it open for me to exit through. Again, he walks on the side closest to the road, but he doesn't say anything. The energy between us feels off now. Stunted. Stiff.

"Are you upset with me?" I either run completely away from confrontation or slam head-first into it. I guess I'm picking the latter today because I need to know what just happened. His pause is too long. I'm impatient. "I don't know what I did, so I'm going to need you to tell me."

He takes a slow sip of his sugary coffee and shakes his head. "It's nothing, red. I'm good. Why don't you tell me about your books?" I've never heard his voice so flat, and he's changing the subject, avoiding telling me what I did. But I *need* to know.

I scoff. "It may be difficult for me to read people's emotions, but even I can see when a ray of sunshine is covered by a cloud of doom. And we're not changing the subject." His lips twitch, but no smile comes. Crikey, this is bad. "Number one. Honesty and transparency, remember?"

He sighs and looks up at the sky as if he's looking for an answer there. "I remember." He looks down at the sidewalk ahead of us. "I'm adopted." My eyes fly up to his face, his gaze locked on the ground. "So, I don't actually know my family history. My biological parents didn't want me, and it was a really messed-up situation. There are no medical records, so I don't know. I don't know if I'm prone to diabetes or which one of them had ADHD and potentially passed it down to me. That's the honest and transparent answer."

He doesn't look at me, doesn't move anything other than his legs to continue walking.

For a while, neither of us says anything. He drinks his coffee wordlessly, and I walk while my thoughts bounce around in my brain like a bunch of preschoolers on a sugar high. When I take a breath and try to focus, one thing feels incredibly clear: I should apologize. I want to. I've wanted to before, but this time, I need to.

There's a small alleyway to my right, and I take hold of Rafael's wrist, pulling him into it with me. I set my coffee down on the ground next to my feet and roll my shoulders back, physically preparing myself. I look up into his face and find his eyes already studying me.

"I'm sorry," I say while I look at the tip of his nose.

"That I'm adopted?" His head tips to the side like a dog when they're confused about what you're saying.

"What? No." I shut my eyes tightly and open them again, making full contact with his chocolate eyes, noticing in the sunlight that the little flecks look more like the color of caramel. "I'm sorry I made you uncomfortable and perhaps a little sad by my question. I'm sorry that I pushed you to answer me when you clearly didn't want to." Now that I've started, I can't stop. It's like the dam I had built to keep all of this inside me finally burst, and my desire to be a compulsive truth teller has taken over. "I'm sorry I called you dumb and that I said you have nothing to be proud of. I'm sorry I probably threw up on you and that you had to take care of me. I'm sorry I never thanked you for that, even after my sister told me it was you and not her who helped me. I'm sorry I'm always so surly with you and that I've let my completely incorrect impressions of you obscure the goodness behind them."

My hands are shaking, and I try to stop the movement from traveling to the rest of my body by wrapping my arms around myself. If Maeve were here, I'd ask her to hug me. The heavy pressure of a tight hug can help activate the parasympathetic nervous system, settling me back into my skin when I feel like I'm ready to fly out of it. This kind of confrontation leaves me tired, wired, and feeling like I'm simultaneously coming down from a high and climbing back up.

I break our eye contact and close my eyes again, trying to control my breathing, pulling air in for four seconds, holding for six, breathing out for eight. I'm still shaking, fighting the urge to stim, pace, and do something to soothe the fight-or-flight instinct at war inside me right now.

Rafael's gentle voice breaks through my counting. "Do you need a hug?"

I keep my eyes closed, tears immediately gathering behind my eyelids, and nod as I hold my breath. His strong arms wrap around me, and the side of my face meets his warm chest. My arms are now locked between us, which is perfect. I remain stiff, and his hold tightens, making me relax into him.

"Is this okay?" I feel his words reverberate in his chest as his chin comes to rest on my head. He doesn't rub my back, doesn't loosen his grip. He remains steady in his hold.

"Yes," I whisper. But what I want to say is *This is perfect. This might be the best hug I've ever received. It would only be better if you rocked me a little.* And as if he can hear my thoughts, Rafael releases a long breath and starts to sway gently from side to side. I could fall asleep like this, standing in the middle of this dirty, empty alley, listening to his strong and steady heartbeat.

Rafael doesn't pull away first like my mother always did when I asked her for hugs as a child. He doesn't ask if he can let go, either. He just waits. He waits for me to decide when I'm finished with his embrace, and though my breathing is back to normal and I know my shaking hands are now steady, I selfishly want to stay in his arms.

He smells good, and I hadn't expected it, but we fit together quite naturally, with the way my head rests on his chest, and his arms wrap around me. *I like it.* I like being held like this. I like being held by *him*, even if it is a very new experience. One I didn't think I'd get with anyone other than Robert once we took that next step.

With that sobering thought, I lift my head and step back. Rafael lowers his arms to his sides, and I notice his coffee cup on its side, a few feet away from where we stand, coffee spilling from the open lid. "Oh no, your coffee, it's—"

"I don't care about the coffee. Are you okay?" I flinch, noticing his voice has taken on a harder edge. My thoughts take flight, wondering if he's upset with me for asking about the coffee or maybe he's annoyed by my rant of an apology. He must notice my reaction as he huffs out a breath. "I just, I don't like seeing you upset. That," he points to the discarded drink, "is nothing. You're a person. With feelings. And your feelings matter far more to me than a cup of coffee. Even if it's the best cup of coffee in LA County."

I chance a look at him and find his eyebrows are angled downward. He has such an expressive face, and I wish I knew what all of them mean. I think he's trying to lighten the mood with the joke about the coffee being the best in the county, though it's not a joke at all. I'm certain it is the best. My brain snags on three words. *Your feelings matter.*

The turmoil in my body slowly starts up again. I've been so wrong about this man. For three and a half years, I've chosen to only see the worst in him. I've chosen to ignore any of the good that has so easily poured out of him. I bring a hand to my stomach as it tumbles with the guilt of my actions.

What else can I have been wrong about?

"Hey." His hand reaches for mine, but he pulls back just before his fingers make contact. For a moment, I wish he would feel comfortable enough to touch me freely. That our relationship, or whatever this is, wasn't so strained that he needed to ask for permission to do so. "Talk to me. Don't worry about getting it right; just say whatever is on your mind." He takes a step closer, not touching me, but definitely in my space. It feels safe here, in this circle of trust we're slowly building around ourselves.

"I've been horrible to you, and that realization is eating at me. Maeve and Elaina have been telling me for years that you're the nicest person they know. I told myself it was an act because my gut feeling is almost never wrong. I've spent years honing this internal algorithm that hasn't led me astray. Or at least I thought it hadn't. It was a survival mechanism for people who seldom let their true intentions be known. I told myself I could see the real you when they couldn't. I was wrong, Rafael. I don't like being wrong, so I'm feeling... something I can't name. That along with guilt and maybe embarrassment over this little breakdown happening in an alley." I take a couple of breaths and gather my next words. "How did you know to hug me like that?" I can't help it. The curiosity takes over. It always does. And where I would normally hold back my questions, I remind myself that I'm trying to be more me without the mask I've always worn, and I'm starting to feel like that's okay to do with Rafael.

He tucks his hands into the pockets of his jeans, and looks down at our feet, nearly touching. "At first, I really just wanted to. Hug you that is. But then I also thought of my niece. She's uh... she's on the spectrum. She's only five and newly diagnosed, but she really likes it when I hug her like that and rock her a bit when she gets upset."

I remain silent, letting the words sink in. Rafael has someone in his life with autism. Someone *else*. And he wanted to hug me. I must stay quiet for too long because he rocks back on his heels and continues talking.

"I'm sorry. I shouldn't have assumed that it's what you'd need. I just didn't know what else to do, and you had this look in your eyes, like you were about to cry, and, fuck, if you cried, I'd cry too, and that's never helpful, so I just—"

"It was perfect. You were... Your hug was perfect. Thank you." We stand, both unmoving, as the world seems to buzz around us.

Eventually he shuffles his feet. "Thank you for everything you said earlier. I don't blame you for thinking whatever you've thought of me all this time. I was a bit of a jackass to you when we met." He mutters something under his breath that sounds faintly like *if, by a bit, you mean a complete and utter asshole of the greatest magnitude known to man.*

A chuckle slips through my lips, forcing my muscles to relax into a smile. After this type of intense interaction, I'd normally feel tired enough for a nap. And I'm sure I could fall asleep if the opportunity presented itself, but I also don't want to miss what's next. Not when he seamlessly manages to make me smile after I've just been in tears.

When I look up, Rafael's eyes are locked on my lips. The expression is another I've never seen. His cheeks take on a pink tinge I didn't know was possible for him.

"You're smiling at me."

18 /
date me up, machado.

rafael

AS SOON AS the words leave my lips, the smile leaves hers.

Fuck.

I shouldn't have said anything. I should have taken more time to watch the way her cupid's bow stretches when she smiles. The way her eyes squint a little and how her freckles seem to dance over her crinkled nose. I missed the chance to savor it.

Charlie chews on her bottom lip, and I find I can't tear my eyes away from that, either. It's when she clears her throat that I finally look elsewhere, taking in the rosy cheeks and her lowered gaze, intent on the coffee cup at her feet.

"Thank you for saying all of that. I didn't expect it, but I appreciate it all the same. I think it'd be nice if we could maybe forget all that shit in the past. Otherwise, I feel like we're going to keep getting stuck in this uncomfortable place where we keep saying sorry to each other, you know?" I massage the back of my neck, aware of the tension building there, knowing all too well that if I let it, it'll keep building until I can't take it anymore. It's been a while since I've had a migraine, so part of me feels like I'm due for one, and when this kind of tension builds, it's a pretty safe way to guarantee I'll have one. Like the last one. When things with Dad and Arthur really went to shit. Probably best not to think about that now, though.

"Yeah. I think you're right." She gives a tight-lipped smile. Twenty minutes ago, I would have been beside myself at seeing any kind of smile on her face, but this isn't a real smile. Not like the one she just gifted me with a minute ago.

"All right, then let's move on." I crouch down, pick up her iced coffee, and extend it to her. It feels like a peace offering of sorts, a way to mark this new start to whatever the fuck this is. "Shall we?"

Charlie takes the coffee, her fingertips brushing over my knuckles in the process. She brings the cup to her lips, then abruptly lowers it again. "Wait. Do you want this? I mean, yours is gone, and you really seemed to want coffee before we walked here, so it only seems fair."

I chuckle at her offer because while she's audibly offering me her coffee, she's also clutching the cup with both hands against her chest, clearly wrestling with letting it go. "I'm good, Ginger Spice. That one is all yours." She gives me a skeptical eyebrow raise. "I drank most of mine anyway. It wouldn't be fair to take yours. I'm fine."

"All right then." She barely gets out as she tilts the cup to her lips, and that sound comes out of her once again, alerting every nerve ending in my body to the fact that she makes extremely sexual noises when she tastes something she likes.

Fuck. Me.

It's time to change the subject.

"All right, so how do you want to start tackling this? If you want to feel more comfortable with people, you gotta meet new ones, right?" I shuffle my feet so we're facing the sidewalk again, and she steps in the direction we'd been walking in before.

"Yeah. I think so. Maybe go on a date? I've been out of the dating pool for so long, I think I'm going to need a pool noodle to help me stay afloat." She's serious, but I smile at the image she's painted.

Charlie hanging onto a pool noodle.

Charlie in a bathing suit.

Charlie all wet, coming out of a pool.

Just… *Charlie*.

Goddamn it, am I really this far gone for this woman?

I'm not laughing anymore.

I clear my throat. "A date. Yeah. We'll get you back in that pool in no time." I think about a plan for a moment as she sips her coffee, thankfully without any more erotic noises. "Maybe I could be your wingman. If things aren't feeling right, you can do what Lainey always did and tug on your left ear. I'll come and create a reason for you to leave." I shrug, feeling pretty good about my little plan. "I think that could work; what do you think?"

When I look down at her, she's gripping her coffee cup tightly, letting out a slow breath. "I might be nervous knowing you were watching me. Maybe I could text you if I need an out?"

"Yeah. Of course. Would dinner at a small restaurant work? Maybe being set up with someone the girls already know, so it's not a random person?" I sure as hell don't know anyone I'd be willing to watch Charlie go on a date with.

"Right. Okay. That might be nice. But if we're trying to keep them out of this, maybe we don't ask them for suggestions on a potential date. I'm sure you know someone, right?" Well, I guess I'm about to find someone for her to date. She sips her coffee again, visibly relaxed, which is both comforting and not because I'm so very uncomfortable with her going on a date with someone. *Anyone*. "And you can help me prep? Help me pick an outfit and coach me on what to do?"

I quickly reign in my thoughts and try to match her nonchalance. "Oh yeah, Pumpkin. I can coach you. I am *very* good at all of the date things," I tease, smiling at her with wide eyes. "But, I'm a very hands-on instructor."

"Bollocks! I should have known you wouldn't make this easy on me." She huffs out a breath. "Your ego is enormous, you know that? And don't you dare say anything about it not being the only enormous thing about you because I will turn and walk the other way. And I won't come back."

My smile is a full-fledged grin now because that is *exactly* how I would have responded to that. A small laugh leaves Charlie, and I find myself laughing as well. It feels big, this moment. Because before whatever our new arrangement is, there wouldn't be this lightheartedness. It's nice.

"What does a first date usually feel like for you? Do you get nervous? Excited? Turned on?" I quirk an eyebrow, and the heat rushes to her cheeks.

"Mostly nervous because I don't enjoy meeting new people, and I know I don't always make the best first impression." My mind immediately goes to the day we met, and I think she knows it based on the way her lip twitches.

"Hmm. And where had you been meeting guys previously?"

"Usually just dating apps." She shrugs, but my eyebrows pull together at her answer.

"You go out with complete strangers you swipe right on in an app?" My voice lowers and she nods her response. "Not anymore, red."

Fuck. That. Shit.

"What? Why not? I don't see what the big deal is, considering millions of people do this." She thinks she's got me, but in my line of work, I know too much.

"I've seen that shit go sideways way too many times. So, you won't be going on any more of those. Your dates will be vetted, got it?" I know I sound like a complete caveman. A scoff escapes her as her blush rises from her chest all the way to the apples of her cheeks. Whether it's irritation or something else, I don't know, but I don't care. I'm not taking chances with her.

"Sure." She tilts her head to one side and continues, "And you'll be helping me by giving me pointers? Telling me what to giggle at and when to play footsie under the table?"

"Yeah, Chuck. I'll help you with all the details, from dressing sexy but not slutty, to when to touch a man to let him know you're interested. Is that what you want?" Ugh. I fucking hate this.

"Yep. That'll do it. For now." She unlocks her phone and opens the calendar app. "When can we get started?"

I groan inwardly, knowing this is going to completely suck, but also knowing that if this is what she wants, I'll do it. "I'll see what I can do to make something happen on Saturday. Are you free, then?"

She quickly adds in *First date. Man TBD* to her calendar and locks her phone. "As a bird. Date me up, Machado." She wears a triumphant expression, and I laugh, though it's completely forced.

"I'll text some guys. I'm sure it won't be a hard sell." I throw her a wink, and her breath catches, eyes darting away as she bites her lip to hold back a smile. *Fuck, yeah.* "So, other than a restaurant, where do you like to go on dates? We should make sure you get to go somewhere you feel comfortable."

"I feel comfortable on my couch in nothing but my old uni jumper, my favorite pair of panties, and long socks." I choke on absolutely fucking nothing as Charlie keeps talking. "But since that's not exactly ideal for a first date, I could settle for a quiet restaurant. Nothing too big. Somewhere where we can hear one another talk without having to yell."

"Noted." Wait, what did she say? I'm not sure anything made it into my brain after socks. "Anything else?"

"No. I like it when the guy puts in some sort of effort, but that's hard to do when we've never met before, so I'll keep expectations pretty low." She shrugs again as I feel my face twist into a scowl.

"We're gonna work on raising your expectations, carrot cake." Her apartment building comes into view, and I'm kind of glad for it. I'm not sure how much more of this conversation I can take before I take over and show her exactly what effort looks like.

Standing in the same spot we were in a couple of hours ago, before emotional apologies and spilled coffee; I take in Charlie for likely the last time before I have to her set up on a date. She looks at ease, and the realization is comforting. I want that. I want her comfort and her unfiltered comments.

"Thanks for the walk. And the coffee. It was amazing." She shakes her now-empty cup, save for a couple of ice cubes. "Text me when you have more details for Saturday?"

"Yeah, I'll do that."

"Great. Oh, and if you think of anything I could help you with, just let me know." Right, because we're friends now? She's light as feather on her feet, waving as she walks away. "See you soon, Machado."

When she's out of sight, I look up at the sky, but there's no smile on my face this time. Just a gigantic fucking boulder sitting in the pit of my stomach.

19 /
wait, we never said anything about getting freaky.

rafael

I SENT a text to a few of the guys I know to be pretty decent and who aren't away on assignment for Aegis. A couple of them got back to me saying they'd be down. I definitely sold it by mentioning that Charlie is gorgeous and British, so I send Charlie a text with the news.

ME:

> Got you a date for Saturday, Chuck. His name is Zach. He works for me, loves to surf, loves his mama (in that very Southern way of his), and he's good looking enough. See?

I attach a picture of Zach that I asked him to send me. He's obviously trying to impress Charlie already because he sent a picture of himself at what must have been a wedding. He's wearing a three-piece suit and a big smile. He's squinting, so it's hard to see that he has brown eyes, but I don't think Charlie will care about that.

CHARLIE:

> Would it be weird to say I'm impressed by your set-up skills?

I type back quickly.

> ME:
>
> Oh, red, I have many skills. I just happen to know you like the clean-cut, preppy boys.

> CHARLIE:
>
> Oh, you think you know me so well, do you?

> ME:
>
> Uh-huh

> CHARLIE:
>
> And you think Zach could put his preppiness aside and get freaky in the sheets with me?

Wait, we never said anything about getting freaky.

> ME:
>
> I mean, I don't know him well enough to know what he's like in bed. How freaky are we talking here, red?

Fuck, I really want her to answer me, and I also hope she doesn't. What the hell am I supposed to do with this kind of knowledge about Charlie?

> CHARLIE:
>
> My requirements are simple: He has to be willing to try all the things I've read about in romance novels.

> ME:
>
> I read romance too, Chuck. ALL the things?

> CHARLIE:
>
> Aye.

> ME:
>
> Even the stuff from C.M. Howe's third book?

CHARLIE:

> I'd like to know what being tied up feels like, yes. But I wouldn't do that unless I was with someone I completely trusted.

> Have you ever tied someone up in bed before?

Jeeeeeeesus. What. The. Fuck.

Charlie wants to be tied up. I need to digest that information for a minute.

No, wait, that's a bad idea. Just answer her.

ME:

> I have.

Honesty and all that…

CHARLIE:

> And? You've got to give me more than that, Machado.

ME:

> With the right person, it can be pretty hot. But it means giving up a lot of control. You up for that?

CHARLIE:

> Like you said, with the right person.

> Maybe Zach will be the man to tie my hands above my head, blindfold me, and fuck me until I see stars.

I think I just blacked out.

Fuck me until I see stars.

Hands tied above her head.

Don't picture it. Don't picture it. Don't picture it.

Goddamn it. I'm picturing it.

ME:

Damn, Chuck. Blindfold too?

CHARLIE:

I told you. I want to try it all.

I'm not sure I'll survive this.

I think I blushed a little, and I'm not a man who blushes. At all. Ever.

And sure, Zach might be the guy to make that happen for her, but there's a significant part of me that doesn't want him to be. I don't know him that well. He's worked for Aegis for a little over a year, and he's always been decent. Goes back to visit his mom often, so I know family is important to him. He's never given me trouble. But does that mean I want to see him with Charlie?

Fuck, I didn't think this through well enough.

ME:

Should we get together on Saturday before your date to prepare? You two are meeting for dinner at 7, so I can come over at 4. That should give us plenty of time.

CHARLIE:

Yes, please.

4 is fine.

Apartment 712.

See you then.

I smile as my phone vibrates four times in quick succession.

And just like that, the conversation is over.

I need to go for a run.

———

I CALL Charlie to buzz me in at 3:53 p.m. on Saturday afternoon and am knocking on her door by 3:54 p.m. She opens it, and the first thing I notice is the way her glossy red hair cascades over her shoulders and down her back in one perfect smooth line. Her hair is nearly straight, shining in the sunlight. Damn, she's pretty.

"Hey. Sorry, I'm a few minutes early. I hope that's okay." I smile at her, taking in the soft makeup she has on and how bright her blue eyes look. Showing up early was intentional. I want her to feel comfortable with me, and a big part of that is being a little early or a little late for things without it being a big deal.

"Of course. Please come in." I like that her shoulders relax as I walk in. "This isn't what I'm wearing on the date, by the way," she adds in quickly.

I chuckle, eyes roaming over her gray leggings and cream oversized sweater. "You look great, red." *Oops.* Didn't mean to say that. I catch the adorable flush of her cheeks, but I pretend not to notice. Today is about building her confidence and making sure she feels good about herself for this date. She walks toward the living room, sitting on the lounge chair I assume is her favorite spot based on the blanket draped over its side and the paperback sitting on the table next to it.

"Thanks for doing this. Where shall we start?" Her legs are crossed in front of her, elbows propped on her knees, and her chin resting on her fists. She's so fucking cute, and for a second, I forget what we're even here for.

To get her ready for a date. Not with you.

Right.

"I can tell you a little more about Zach if you want?" I have a feeling she wants to be prepared for this.

"Yes, tell me about Mr. Southern Boy. What's he like?" she asks curiously, no doubt hoping for some juicy details. You'd expect just about anyone to deliver that line with a smile, but not Charlie. Seeing one of her smiles is like seeing a shooting star. It's a rare and kind of magical thing.

"Well," I begin, "he's been at Aegis for a year, loves to surf, and has a big fluffy dog who goes everywhere with him."

"Sounds like a catch," she quips. "Did you write his Tinder profile for him?"

My eyebrows shoot up in surprise before I burst out laughing. Even Charlie can't resist cracking a smile, her eyes twinkling with amusement as she settles back into her chair.

20 /
so... so naked!

charlie

IT SOUNDS like Rafael actually put some thought into setting me up with Zach. As he talked about the man I'm about to go on a date with, several thoughts ran through my mind.

Wow, I can't believe he actually chose someone who sounds so great.

Why are you surprised? He's nice, remember?

I wonder if Zach dates a lot and if he's expecting anything from tonight.

It's been a couple of years since I've gone on a date. Do I still remember what to do?

"Do you think Zach's expecting me to sleep with him?" The next question in my brain comes out of my mouth, but he takes it in stride.

"Who the fuck cares what his expectations are? You—and only you—get to make that decision, red." His shiny, chocolate eyes focus on me, and then he swallows. "Is that... is that what you want?"

I shake my head. "No. It's not."

Wait. It's not?

"I mean, I don't know. I haven't even met the guy. But I'm not planning on sleeping with him. I'm also not planning on *not* sleeping with him." Maeve was very encouraging when I mentioned I was going on a date and reminded me to make sure to pack a condom or two in my bag. I already have them in there, in a zipped compartment so they don't accidentally fall out if I drop my bag, or something. I want to be prepared, but I also want to know I can trust the person I'm with, and that's not happening after one date.

"Right. Yeah. Makes sense." Rafael swallows again. "So, he's taking you to an Italian place tonight. It's the one Elaina and Adam always talk about, Bella's. Want to take a look at their menu?" He passes me his phone, with the menu already on the screen.

It's thoughtful, this small action. He's looking out for me and making sure I don't get overwhelmed like I did in the coffee shop. I briefly wonder if it wouldn't be better to just go on this date with Rafael instead of Zach, but I shake that idea out of my head before it can take root. When I take his phone, he stands and walks to the balcony doors, looking out at the sunny view below.

I make my three selections, picking two desserts, just in case, and take a look at their wine list, though I probably won't drink anything tonight.

Rafael is outside, arms leaning on the railing, and I realize he's left me in here alone. With his unlocked phone. It feels like a monumental thing. I have access to all of his conversations with this device. And he's not even looking back to see if I'm scrolling through anything.

I walk out to stand next to him and hand him the device. "You weren't worried I'd go through your messages or photos?"

Rather than taking the phone back, he turns his body toward mine and chuckles. "Go ahead."

I scowl, picturing a series of flirty texts and pictures of all the beautiful women he dates. "No, thanks. I'd rather not know what your flavor-of -the-week texts you or how many pictures of boobs are in your camera roll."

He laughs again. Nothing rocks this guy. "No flavor-of-the-week. Or of the month, even. And my camera roll is mostly pictures of my family, food, and my cat."

"You have a cat?" I shriek in shock. "How did I not know this?"

He laughs again.

"I do. She's very temperamental, so when I can get pictures of her, I take like a hundred. I think she hates me though. She always wants to be alone." He sighs, seeming genuinely upset by the possibility. "I just wanna snuggle her, you know? But she doesn't like to let me. When I try, she pushes her little paws out and runs away. I swear I can see her shake her head every time I walk into the room, like she's telling me *go hug someone else*."

"Maybe your cat is autistic." I shrug and watch as his face pales and his eyes widen to the point that they're comical. The sight has me bursting into laughter. "You should… see your… face," I manage, my eyes squinting with the force of my laughter. Despite my eyes being nearly closed, I don't miss the slow smile that blooms on his face or the way his warm gaze drifts over every part of my face, collecting on my lips.

"You have a fucked-up sense of humor, red." The dimples on his cheek hold all of my attention. "I like it," he adds before I can misconstrue his words as something negative. "Now, let's go inside and see what you're wearing on this date, yeah?"

"Yeah," I answer. I have four outfits ready. I walk through the flat, heading to my room, but when I don't feel him behind me, I whip around. "Are you coming?"

"To your bedroom?" His voice raises at the end.

"Yes, Machado. My room. Where the clothes are laid out

on the bed so you can see them." I roll my eyes, a habit my sister and I share.

"Uh, why don't you try them on and show me?" Is he serious? No, thanks.

"Because that sounds like an absolute nightmare, and I'm not trying on multiple outfits." I don't understand his hesitation. It's just a bedroom. "Can we stop this yelly conversation with me in the hall and you in the living room? Just get in here."

I hear his footsteps and smile to myself, walking toward my bed before he can see me.

"All right, so I have a dress I actually like and feel comfortable in. Jeans and this sort of ruffly top. A silky skirt with a light sweater—Elaina picked this one. And finally, the leather-looking leggings with a long jumper. I'm worried I'll be too hot in that one, though, because it's always too warm inside restaurants." I blow out a breath, taking in the clothing on my bed as he stands silently. I look up at Rafael, waiting for his opinion.

He drops his phone on my nightstand and scratches the back of his neck. He must hate all of these options. My shoulders come in on themselves as I deflate a little.

"You'd look amazing in all of these, carrot cake." His eyes stay down, scanning the items as his tongue moves back and forth across his lower lip. "I'm gonna say we cut the leather pants, which is too bad, because your ass would look great in those. But you should be comfortable." He waves a hand at the items, as if dismissing them. My stomach summersaults as his compliments land. "The jeans might seem too casual, even though I bet that shirt would look really pretty with your hair." He smiles as he says the words, then runs a finger along the silk skirt, finally looking up at me. "So, now the question is, which one do you feel better in? The dress or the skirt?"

I glance at him, then back to his hand on my skirt, still

absentmindedly stroking, and instantly, I decide I won't be able to wear that without thinking about his hands on it. While it's on my body. And I'm about to go on a date with... Zach! Right!

"I think I'll go with the dress, then." I silently beg him not to touch the dress, or I'll be going on this date naked. Ugh. No. Do not think about being naked.

He claps, startling me out of my chaotic thoughts, his lips curling up into that irresistible, easy smile. I shake myself out of whatever this is and pick the dress up, walking toward the bathroom attached to my bedroom.

"I'll be right back," I mumble and scurry to the bathroom, shutting the door and leaning against it as I catch my breath. From what? I don't know.

I undress quickly and look at the dress on the hanger. It's a deep green with sleeves that flutter over my arms. It wraps in the front, and the hem sits just below my knees, but there's enough cleavage to make this a little sexy. I look down and realize the bra I have on will not work with this dress, so I remove it. Except now I don't have a bra on, and I definitely need one with these generous D-cups. I don't hear any sounds coming through the door, so I open it enough that I can peek into the bedroom. He's gone.

I walk toward my dresser, and the moment I take the first few steps, Rafael appears at my bedroom door, reaching for something on my nightstand. When he turns, his eyes are locked on my very, very naked breasts.

"Shhhhhhhhhhhhhiiiiiiiiiiiiiiiiit!" Without blinking, his eyes scan the rest of my body. The black boy shorts I have on, my bare legs, and when his gaze starts to move back up to where I am most naked, my arms finally shoot up and wrap around my chest, my hardened nipples poking into my forearms.

"Get out!" I shout, and he rears back, nearly falling on his bum.

"I'm sorry. I'm so sorry! I thought you were in the bathroom," he yells from the hallway.

"And I thought you left the room," I yell back as I find the bra I need.

"I did. I forgot my phone. I didn't think you'd come out so… so naked! I'm sorry." I can hear him pacing, his voice sounding closer than farther away as we have another shouting conversation. I hope the walls in this building aren't too thin.

"Well, I didn't have the right bra." I wave it in the air, forgetting he can't see me. "I'm going to go put this and the dress on now. I will come back out fully dressed." I slam the bathroom door a little too hard as I step in. If I thought I was out of breath before, all of the breath has definitely left me now. He just saw me as close to naked as anyone has seen me in two years.

I cannot think about this. We have to just be adults and move past it. And we will. This is fine. He's seen plenty of breasts before.

Oh God, he's seen so many breasts before. So many probably perky, perfect ones that are nothing like mine. What if he thought mine were gross and weird?

Ugh, who cares? You're not going out with him. Ever. It makes no difference what he thinks. He's probably already forgotten all about them anyway.

I slip the dress on, tying the bow at the side with slightly shaky hands. I check my makeup in the mirror, smooth down my hair, which I can easily straighten here thanks to the lack of humidity, and open the bathroom door.

The bedroom is empty. I walk to the door, seeing that the hallway is also empty. Peeking into the living room, there's no sign of Rafael. I hear mumbling and walk to the kitchen. There he is. Holding a glass of water, whispering something to it.

"Am I interrupting?"

He whips around, nearly dropping the glass. His eyes land on me for half a second before he looks down at the floor.

"No. Sorry. Thirsty. Sorry." He clears his throat, eyebrows furrowing as he shakes his head.

"All right, well, I need you to actually look at me now and not make this weird." I put my hands on my hips, feigning annoyance. "They're just breasts. Let's move on?" I'm mostly terrified he's never going to be able to look at me again.

He closes his eyes and then looks up, blowing out a breath that comes out sounding like, "Phooooooo-oh-wow." He swallows and motions with his finger for me to spin, and for completely mysterious-to-me reasons, I do. Well, they're not that mysterious. It's the little glimmer in his eyes when he took me in, the way he stood a little straighter, and how his lips relaxed, parting just slightly. That's why I don't hesitate. Because Rafael makes me feel beautiful with nothing but a look. "Damn, pumpkin. You are wearing the fuck out of that dress." His expression gives nothing away and now I feel confused.

"I don't know what that means," I say, fighting the urge to run back to my room.

"It means you look beautiful." With his gaze steady on me, he continues, "You're going to have a great time, Chuck. You're ready for this." He sets the glass of water in the sink. "Text me if you need anything, yeah?"

Before I get the chance to say thank you, ask him what I should talk about tonight, or even say goodbye, he's gone.

I spend the rest of my time before the date wondering what he's thinking. Wondering if this date even matters.

If my goal is to explore big feelings, to prepare myself for my only long-term relationship, and to find my way back to writing meaningful relationships, then going on a date with a stranger might not be the thing that propels me in that direction. Because what are the chances this date will lead to more?

That Zach and I have a good enough connection for me to let him into my life?

I also find myself wondering who Rafael dates and what the women he spends time with are like. Does he let them take his phone? Does he have deep, meaningful conversations with them? Does he call them beautiful?

Probably. Right?

Fifteen minutes before the scheduled meeting time with Zach, I'm in my ride-share and strongly considering asking them to turn back and take me home. The way Rafael left isn't helping the lack of confidence I'm feeling, either. I'm blowing out a long breath as my final attempt to calm down when my phone vibrates in my hands.

RAFAEL:

> I'm sorry about how I left, Chuck. I was being weird about the thing that happened that we most definitely don't have to ever talk about like ever. But if you want to, we can, or I can forget about it. Whatever you want.

> Fuck. I'm still being weird. I'm sorry.

I feel a smile form as a giggle builds in my chest. For someone who always appears so confident, he's actually a little insecure, and it's nice to see this side of him. Like a new layer is being peeled back, and I'm seeing the real him the way he's been seeing the real me.

RAFAEL:

> Have a great time tonight. Just be yourself. Any guy who gets to spend even ten minutes with you should consider himself lucky, and if he doesn't, he's an absolute idiot. I'll be here if you need me.

Butterflies take flight in my stomach, and I clutch my abdomen in an effort to calm them. I read the message over and over and realize that the fluttering feelings increase with every read.

I should respond to him. I know I should, but then the car comes to a stop in front of the restaurant, and I thank the lovely lavender-haired driver—who I'll most definitely give five stars for having the temperature well-controlled and the music nice and low.

I gather my bag and exit the vehicle, and when I look up, there's a very handsome man smiling at me. *Zach.* He's dressed in navy pants and a white buttoned shirt that looks well-ironed. His brown shoes are clean, and as I walk closer to him, his smile widens just a touch.

"Charlie?" He takes a step forward and I nod. "Hi, I'm Zach," he says as he extends his hand toward me.

We're shaking hands, then. All right.

His grip is firm without crushing my fingers. "It's really nice to meet you. I'm glad I showed up early so you didn't have to wait for me."

Oh. That's nice. I hadn't even thought about the fact that he was even earlier than me. I should say something. I haven't said anything.

Come on, Charlie. Words.

"It's nice to meet you, too. Did Rafael warn you about my terrible time management?" Why am I bringing him up? Why is Rafael the first thing I'm choosing to talk about? Bollocks.

"Nah. He actually didn't tell me much about you other than that you're beautiful, smart, and funny as hell. Pretty sure those were his exact words." He shrugs, still smiling.

"Oh." Is my brain even attached to my skull? I can feel my mask slipping on—the cute, smart, flirty one who will live up to the girl this guy was promised.

"Should we get inside?" He gestures to the front door, and I walk in front of him. He doesn't put his hand on me, which I'm thankful for. He's respectful, but not handsy. Maybe this won't be so bad.

We're seated by the window, at a table not too close to any others. It feels private and quiet. I would have hated sitting in the middle of this busy restaurant, surrounded by people.

"Wow, Rafael reserved a great table," Zach says casually as he takes a seat.

"What do you mean?" I ask.

"Oh, he insisted on reserving the table to make sure we got a good one. Nice of him, huh?" He picks up the drink menu and looks it over as he speaks.

"Yeah. Nice." He picked this place. This table. Knowing I like pasta. Knowing I wouldn't want a table in the middle of the room. I'm so thankful I don't need to look at the menu because I'm not sure I'd be able to retain any of the information.

Our server comes and takes our drink orders—I stick to water while he gets a beer—and Zach orders Bruschetta as an appetizer without asking me if that's what I'd like. He's lucky I'd never say no to deliciously toasted bread, or tomatoes, or basil.

"So, Charlie, how long have you been in LA?" Zach takes a piece of bread and breaks it over his plate. When he looks up at me, I notice that his brown eyes don't have any traces of caramel swirling in them.

Nineteen days, I want to say, but that's far too precise, and I know people think it's strange when I know that kind of information. "Almost three weeks," I say instead. "How long have you lived here?"

"Over a year now. I love it here." No follow-up question. Hmm. Great, now I need to think of something else to say or ask. Uncomfortable silences are never great on a first date. Pretty sure I've read that in every magazine since I was in my teens.

"You're from Texas, right?" I did hear a bit of a Southern drawl in his voice earlier, plus Rafael told me…

"That's right. Let's go Cowboys!" He smiles widely at me. Not one dimple in sight, let alone two, side by side.

"That's American football, yeah?" I couldn't care less about the sport, but obviously, he does.

"It's just football here, sweetheart." The nickname doesn't land. It doesn't feel condescending, but it doesn't feel good either. I force a small smile on my face. "Anyway, tell me about you. Do you have any siblings? What do you like to do for fun? What kind of music do you like? I want to know you."

Wow. So many questions, but at least he's interested in me, I suppose.

I let myself indulge in the conversation, in looking at this rather attractive bloke, in letting someone know more about me. And I keep thoughts of Rafael mostly out of my mind. Mostly.

you can be a little spicy sometimes.

rafael

ZACH:

She's a little thicker than I usually go for, but damn... great tits

I don't respond. Fuck, Zach. That's bullshit. Charlie's body is perfect. Also, fuck him for making me think about her tits when I was finally starting to get them out of my mind.

I'm a fucking liar. I haven't stopped thinking about them since I saw them. The image is burned into my retinas, and I hope that shit is permanent.

ZACH:

Do you think the carpet matches the drapes?
I bet it does.

Why the fuck is he texting me and not paying attention to Charlie? And is he for real?

ZACH:

Might find out tonight.

Abso-fucking-lutely not. Nope. No way.

My fingers are itching to text Charlie and tell her to get the fuck out of there, but I can't do that. Not unless she asks me to. But damn it, I want to. I check our text thread for the twentieth time. Still nothing.

Charlie will be fine. She can do this. I told her as much, and I believe it. She doesn't take shit. She'll put Zach in his place if she needs to. I know that. I just really wanna be the one to do it for her.

I SWEAR the minutes tick by at an unbearable pace. By ten o'clock, I'm about to walk to Charlie's place like an obsessive creep to see if her lights are on. Is she home? Why didn't she text me back? I sent that apology twenty minutes before the date was supposed to start.

Fuck it. I'm texting her.

Yo, red, you still there?

Yo? No, I can't send that. Delete, delete, delete.

Good date, red?

Ugh, that's not right, either. Try again.

ME:

> Hey, Chuck. Hope you had (or are having) a good time.

I throw a smiley emoji in there for good measure and hit send. It still feels lame as fuck, but I can't overthink this any more than I already have.

CHARLIE:

> Hi

> I was just about to message you.

> I'm home.

> It was a great first date!

> Thanks again for setting this up.

Okay.

Okay, okay, okay.

She didn't go home with him. And she said *was*, so he's not at her place either.

Good. Good? Good. Yeah.

I'm not ready to let our conversation end, though.

ME:

Glad to hear it. What are you doing tomorrow?

Her reply comes right away, and the relief washes over me like a tropical rainstorm. Warm and unexpected.

CHARLIE:

I wanted to go to Ojai to see Maeve.

But I don't know how I feel about driving all that way.

Wrong side of the road, and all that...

ME:

Honey bun, it's quite literally the RIGHT side of the road.

I add an emoji with the tongue sticking out. I'm an emoji guy now, apparently.

CHARLIE:

Ha. Ha.

What are you doing tomorrow?

ME:

I'm driving up to see my family for the day.

Before the thought is fully formed, I'm typing the words.

ME:

> Ojai is on my way. Why don't you come with me? I can drop you off and pick you up on my way back.

The three little dots appear, then disappear, then they're back.

Come on, Charlie.

CHARLIE:

> Are you sure?

> Is it actually on the way?

> I don't want to impose.

> I do eventually have to get over this whole driving on the right side thing.

> I never drove in New York, but it seems inevitable here.

ME:

> I'm sure. I basically drive through Ojai to get there. And you can learn when you're comfortable. On calmer roads and not these unhinged LA streets. Cool?

CHARLIE:

> Thank you.

> What time are you leaving tomorrow?

> Please don't say some outrageously early hour.

> Anything before 8, specifically.

I laugh at the sequence of texts.

ME:

> I'm at your disposal. I just gotta be there for lunch or my grandmother will have my head.

CHARLIE:

> I need something so much more specific than this.

ME:

> How's ten o'clock?

CHARLIE:

> That's great.

> Thank you.

ME:

> Pick you up at 10. Goodnight, pumpkin.

Her first response is an eye-roll emoji, which I don't even try not to picture because I fucking like her eye rolls a whole lot.

CHARLIE:

> Goodnight.

———

I'M in front of Charlie's building at ten on the dot, an iced coffee waiting for her in the cupholder. Smitty most definitely gave me a sly look when I ordered it, and I most definitely flipped him the bird. That old guy thinks he knows everything.

I stand outside of my car, trying to look like I'm not insanely eager to see her. At 10:07 a.m. she steps out, shoving something into a bag, her phone in one hand as she tries to push her still-straight hair out of her face. I miss her curls.

Walking toward her, I reach out to take the bag from her, and her face snaps up.

"Blimey, you scared me!" She hands the bag over easily and blows a strand of hair away from her face, but it just flops right back down.

That's when I get stupid. I run my index finger along her forehead, then tangle my fingers through her silky, bright red tendrils as I tuck them back.

"Sorry," I say as I stuff my unruly, very bad hand into my jeans pocket. And I am sorry. For scaring her. For touching her.

"You're fine." Her blue eyes are so light in the sun that they're nearly silver. "Should we go?"

I open the back door and set her bag down, giving myself a moment to chill out. We have nearly two hours alone in this car ahead of us.

When I get in, Charlie is already in the passenger seat, buckling herself in. She freezes when she spots the iced coffee next to my hot one. "Is that for me?" I smile as her eyes widen, still locked on the cup.

"It sure is, carrot cake." I buckle my own belt, and her baby blues lock on mine for half a second. Then, she licks her lips and lifts the cup to her perfect, pouty mouth. And here comes those goddamn noises. I shift in my seat, mentally telling my dick to settle the fuck right down. Now!

She clutches the cup to her chest with both hands. "You are wonderful, and I love you so, so much." Her eyes are closed as she talks to her drink. It's adorable. So unlike the Charlie I'm used to seeing. I chuckle as she rocks side to side.

Wide eyes meet mine again, almost as if she'd forgotten I was here. Her gaze moves down to where I know my dimples are. I always know when people are looking at them. I was made fun of as a kid for having two deep dimples on one side of my face. Because kids fucking suck and will find anything to make fun of someone for. The way she is looking at that spot, though, is almost like she's in awe of them. But it's probably just the coffee-induced euphoria I'm seeing on her face.

I push the ignition button and put the car in drive. My playlist, which I picked out a little too carefully, consists of

Khalid, John Mayer, and some Brazilian songs. I hope she likes it.

"So, how was dinner last night? Give me the details." But not if those details include Zach putting his hands on you.

"I get why Adam and Lainey are obsessed with that place. Literally, every single thing looked amazing, and the lasagna was incredible. And homemade tiramisu?" She pinches her fingers together and brings them to her lips, mimicking a chef's kiss.

"I'm glad you liked the food, but tell me about the date." I feel the anger rise inside me, thinking about Zach's texts. I'm only asking because she said last night that things went well. I need to know what that means.

"Oh, right. The date. It was good." She pauses, looking down at her lap with a small smile on her lips. Is that smile for Zach? "Really good."

I don't like the way that answer makes me feel.

Really good? What does that mean?

"Go on," I manage to bite out.

"I don't know, I mean, you were right. He loves his family. Loves American football. Or *just* football. He wasn't rude to the waiter. Didn't get too handsy, and the kiss was nice." Cue the loud record scratch in my head.

"Kiss?" The question comes out a little screechy. Okay, a lot screechy.

"Mm-hmm. He walked me to my door, said he wanted to see more of me, and kissed me." She takes another sip of her coffee. "It wasn't like, earth-shattering or anything, but it also wasn't my worst kiss. Not all first kisses are super amazing, right? Not like in the books, anyway."

I hate the resigned tone in her voice. This was the first date she's gone on in a while, and she's already settling for not her *worst kiss*? Nah.

"I think first kisses *can* be earth-shattering. With the right person, I think *every* first could be. Not that I have any experience with the right person. I've never been in a long-term relationship. At the first sign of things not feeling right, I end it." How's that for an over-share? I hope that doesn't make me sound like an asshole.

Her eyebrows shoot up to her hairline. "Wow."

"I'm not always the one that ends it, but I mostly have been. I refuse to settle, and I refuse to string someone along if I don't see it being long-term." Yeah, I'm that guy.

"Oh. Yeah, that makes sense." She nods, looking down at her hands.

"So, you're going to go out with Zach again?" Yeah, I'm still fixated on that asshole.

"I think so." Her brows furrow as she pulls her lips in between her teeth—a move that tells me she's not sure. "I mean, if he wants to. Do you think he'll want to?" She looks up at me, and I grip the steering wheel so tightly that my fingers start to ache. Thinking about his texts last night won't do me any good, but I can't exactly tell Charlie about them, can I?

"He'd be an absolute dumbass not to, pumpkin pie!" I keep my voice as jovial as possible, despite the thoughts of how many ways I could break Zach's hands running through my mind.

"Ugh, you had to add the pie onto it, too?" Charlie shakes her head, but I don't miss the way her hands relax and her lips curl up slightly.

"I was gonna say pumpkin spice. Would that be better? You can be a little spicy sometimes with your eye rolls and that bit of sass you reserve for when I act like a real jackass." Maybe we can just do this for the rest of the drive. We can talk about all the things I notice about her. Make her almost smile at the dumb shit I say.

She giggles, but she's looking out of the window, and I don't turn my head fast enough to see it. Damn.

"If you're going to add to your already extensive list of

nicknames for me, let's make it spice and not pie, then. We already have enough food nicknames." A small smile stretches across her face, causing a fluttering sensation in my stomach. My muscles tighten and release as I feel the warmth of her expression.

"You got it, strawberry shortcake." I grip the steering wheel tightly again because my traitorous hand is itching to touch her.

Her head whips toward me. "That's only the second time you've used that one." She goes back to looking out the windshield, and I don't know what to say. She's right. The first time I thought of that nickname, I had been at the office doing nothing but looking forward to seeing her. Someone had brought in a strawberry shortcake for a birthday or something, and all I thought was about how it was sort of like Charlie with her creamy skin and her red hair.

Later that day, I was standing in front of her building waiting for her, looking up at the sky and smiling because the color was the exact shade of her eyes. I saw her and the nickname just slipped out, much like it did just now.

We sit in comfortable silence for a while, and I catch her bobbing her head along to the music a few times, making a mental note of the songs she seems to like.

She doesn't push for conversation, so I don't either. I notice that she perks up when she sees the sign for Ojai.

"Oh, I nearly forgot. Maeve is with the horses, do you mind dropping me there?" Her cheeks turn pink, and I hide my smile behind my hand.

"Of course. You got it."

Within a few minutes, we're pulling into Agape Stables. Owen and Maeve finally named it and have started to make things a little more official. There have been a few school groups brought in to learn about horses, and I think using the stables as some sort of rehab center for veterans is in the works.

As soon as we're out of the car, we can hear Maeve's voice. I've never seen a woman so pregnant and so nimble. I swear you wouldn't know she could be delivering a whole baby any day now. "Art, come on. They're *my* horses!"

"Yeah, Maeve, but it's *my* balls I'll lose if your husband catches wind of this." Arthur follows that up with a laugh, but I can tell he's actually a little scared of Owen.

"Hey, party people!" I don't know why that's the greeting I choose, but it's out there now, so whatever. "Maevey, look at you. You're so beautiful!"

Maeve looks up with a wide smile, and Charlie's shoulders slump slightly as her sister waddles toward us. Arthur mouths a *thank you*.

"Raffy! Charlie!" She hugs her sister first, rightly so, then tries to wrap her arms around my waist, but that belly gets in the way. "Ugh, I keep forgetting there's a whole baby in there. I mean, I know he's there, and I love our little bean so, so much. But I forget how much space he takes up, you know?"

"I so *don't* know, and I have no idea how you forget. That'd be like forgetting you have a watermelon attached to your stomach." I chuckle, and Maeve does, too. She's had a great pregnancy, unlike Elaina who basically threw up for nine months straight.

"Well, I hardly notice it. Hey, maybe you can convince your older and grumpier brother to let me see my girls?" She bats her eyelashes at me, and I raise a skeptical eyebrow.

"What does that mean, exactly?" I ask.

"It means she thinks she can ride her horses." Arthur scoffs, and I understand the comment about losing his balls. Owen would absolutely castrate him if he let Maeve ride while she's *this* pregnant.

"Uh," I start, but Maeve doesn't let me finish.

"Oh, forget it. Fine. I won't ride." She rolls her eyes, and the movement has me immediately looking at Charlie, who's quietly standing off to the side. "I'll just go say hello to Scout and Willow. Want to come, Char?" Maeve hooks her arm with her sister's, beaming with joy, the whole riding fiasco seemingly forgotten.

Seeing that they're about to take off, I clear my throat. "I'll pick you up in a few hours then, Chuck?" She gives me a quiet *yes*. "Text me when you're ready. I'm only twenty minutes away, okay?"

Maeve cocks her head to the side, squinting at me.

"Yep," Charlie answers. "See ya."

When I look back at Arthur, he's got his arms crossed and a shit-eating grin on his face. "Damn, brother. So that's the one, huh?"

"The one? What? What are you going on about?" I wave my arms around, and my brother laughs. Asshole.

"Charlie. Your Charlie. *The* Charlie. She's the one," he states blankly.

"Pfft. You don't know what you're saying." For some weird reason, my limbs feel tingly.

"All right. You deny it all you want." He raises his hands, palms up in surrender, but I know the motion is meaningless.

"Did you breathe in too much ammonia cleaning up horse shit?" I feel my brows tighten, and blood rushes to my face at his accusation.

"The hearts in your eyes are giving you away, little brother." He pats me on the shoulder and turns to walk into a stall.

"Art," I call out to him, "you're coming for lunch, right?" I shoot for nonchalance in my tone, but there's a hint of desperation there. He hasn't talked to our dad in months. No one knows what the hell happened.

"Nice try, bro." He waves at me without even looking back. It was worth a shot, I guess.

22 /
have you finally boned yet?

rafael

I WALK through the front door quietly, my presence not yet known because everyone is so loud they couldn't possibly hear anything outside of the kitchen, where I'm sure they're all gathered. I stand at the threshold, taking it in. My little sister, the youngest of us six, is in what looks to be a heated argument, but it's likely just a discussion about a soccer game with my dad.

My mom and Vó are at the island, prepping something. Marcelo, Gustavo, and Gabriel are just outside the door at the grill, munching on whatever they're cooking and laughing with beers in their hands.

Arthur should be here. I hate that he isn't, and I hate that he insinuated there's anything between me and Charlie. I don't know what the fuck he thinks he saw, but I'm not about to ask him, either.

The three idiots who were just at the grill walk into the kitchen, forcing the attention onto me. A chorus of cheers erupts in the room as they see me, arms thrown in the air in our family's typical dramatic fashion.

Shaking my head, I walk toward the two oldest women to

greet them first, because I know what's good for me. Then, I pull Daniela into a hug, lifting her off the floor as my dad laughs at her screeches.

My dad greets me with open arms. "Oi, filho." I kiss his cheek and take a few seconds to hug him before the three stooges are on me, throwing punches and handing me a beer.

"Fora!" Vó shoos us, telling us to take it outside. I blow her a kiss as she shakes her head, smiling down at the limes she's cutting.

"Kiss ass," Gustavo says under a fake cough, and the other two snicker like children. Gus ruffles up my hair as if I'm the younger brother. "Just messin' with ya, bro. You're everybody's favorite because you're so perfect. And rich." He laughs.

"Oh, shut up, Gus. You're the favorite because you're the baby." Marcelo smacks him in the back of the head then runs away.

"Shut up, asshole. Daniela is the baby!" Our two brothers chase one another into the backyard, eventually ending up tangled up on the ground just like they always have since we were children.

"Yeah, but you *act* like the baby," Marcelo yells as Gus gets him in a headlock. I love these dumbasses.

Gabriel, the quietest of all of us, chuckles into his beer bottle before taking a swig. "Idiots," he mumbles. "I'm the favorite, obviously." We both laugh, and I tap his beer bottle with mine. Cecilia is nowhere to be found, so she must be with her mom today. It's one of Gabriel's ex-wife's power moves, making sure their daughter is with her when we have family meals. Like she gets some weird joy out of keeping her away from us. She's the worst. My brother deserves so much better, and so does my sweet little niece. Our whole family does.

None of my siblings are adopted. Just me. And yet, you'd never know it. I've never been treated differently. It wasn't until Gus, at age nine, asked our parents why their skin was a bit darker than mine that they sat us down and finally talked about everything. I was fifteen the day my whole world changed. Nothing was different on the outside. Not the way my siblings wrestled with me, not the way my mom nagged me about leaving clothes on the floor, not the way my dad showed up to every soccer game. Nothing but the knowledge in my mind and in my heart that I wasn't theirs, and yet, they chose me and continue to choose me.

A lot fell into place for me, then, too. Why I was the only one with dyslexia and ADHD, why my siblings have some form of my mom's birthmark on their bodies, why the brown in their eyes were more hazel or green than my simply brown ones.

"Do you think he's ever going to come back?" Gabe asks. He misses Art the most. They're only a year apart, then there's another year between Gabe and me. People used to think that our parents didn't understand the concept of birth control because they had two kids under two when they "had" me. They always wanted a lot of kids, though, and somehow, they didn't hesitate when the opportunity to adopt me came up.

Gabe's eyes stay glued on the three different types of meat he's got on the grill, but I don't have to see them to know they're probably watery right now. We're a family of huggers, criers, and talkers. We were raised by strong women who taught us to be the adults we are now, and a soft dad who showed us that tears are not a weakness. They're not perfect people, but they know how to apologize, how to talk things out, and how to change for the ones they love. I couldn't have chosen better parents.

So, when one of us is missing, it's like a part of our bodies has been physically cut out. Arthur's absence is felt down to the bones, and every Sunday that he's not here makes that cut grow deeper.

"Yeah. I do." I'm not sure I believe my own words, but I'm hopeful my brother will come to his senses. "He has to, Gabe." My brother nods and wipes at his cheek, not hiding his tears. We watch the grill in silence for a few minutes, likely both thinking about how good it would be to have Art here.

The two idiots on the lawn stop fighting once they notice us walking inside with the trays of meat, and as if on cue, Vó steps through the door, brings both pinkies to her lips, and whistles so loudly I'm sure the neighbors a few acres over can hear. We've never needed a dinner bell.

Once inside, we all take our places at the table, which is whatever chair you're closest to. No assigned seats here. Daniela swats Gus and Marcelo's hands away from the food three times before our two matriarchs finally sit. The moment their bodies touch their chairs, we all dig in. They laugh at our impatience, as they always do.

During lunch, no more than three different conversations are happening at the same time. Sometimes, all this noise would agitate me, make me feel like I couldn't focus on anything because every conversation was so loud, and my brain would try to listen to them all. I'd get overstimulated easily. I wonder how Charlie would handle this. She would probably hate it? I mean, not that it matters, it's not like I'm going to bring her to a Sunday meal. I'm probably just thinking about her because I drove her to Ojai. I check my phone again and the motion does not go unnoticed by my mom.

"Everything okay, Rafa?" she asks, loudly enough for everyone to hear, stop what they're doing, and turn to me. *Great.*

"Uh, yeah. Why?" I take another bite of my picanha and pray for the voices to start back up around the table.

"You've checked your phone half a dozen times already."

She waves a finger across the table and pauses, waiting for my response.

"I'm picking up a friend on my way home today. Just making sure she hasn't messaged since we didn't set a time." It's stupid because I got here less than an hour ago. I know it's illogical, but I don't want Charlie to feel like I'm not paying attention if she's messaging me.

"She?" My mom's eyebrows raise as the clatter of forks being dropped on plates echoes around the room. All eyes are on me.

"Uh-huh." I take a sip of my Guaraná, but none of them move. "She's from England and not comfortable driving here yet. She's practically my neighbor, so I see her all the time. It's Maeve's sister, Charlie. I dropped her off on the way so she could spend time with her and her niece. You can all go back to eating now."

"Can we finally meet her?"

"You should bring her next Sunday."

"I never thought I'd see the day."

"Have you finally boned yet?"

That last one comes from Gus. At twenty-six, he still acts like a high school kid. Gabe, who hasn't said a word, smacks him on the back of the head for me.

Vó gives me a knowing look and chuckles. When she picks up her fork and resumes eating, everyone else does the same, continuing their conversations as if nothing has happened, and I let out a relieved breath.

My sister scooches closer to me, her voice quieter than anyone else's. "You know why they're all acting like this, don't you?" Dani might be twenty-five, but she's always been the voice of reason, so I'm curious.

"No?" I mean, should I?

"All you've ever said about Charlie is how much she hates you, and now you're spending time with her?" She widens her eyes.

I forgot that I accidentally let it slip that I'd met Maeve's sister and that we weren't getting along. They ate that shit up because, according to them, up until Charlie, no one had ever not liked me. "It's not like I talk about her all the time or anything. *Geez.*"

Daniela giggles, letting out a snort. "Oh my God, how delusional are you? Every time you see that woman, we hear about it." She shakes her head. "Charlie was in town for an event, and she ignored me the whole time. I'm going to London, and Charlie will be there, so it's probably gonna be weird. Charlie went to Vegas, and I think she actually had fun, though she didn't say a word to me." She mocks a deep male voice that sounds nothing like mine then laughs again.

"Shit," I mumble, and she only laughs harder.

Eventually, we move on to talk about other things, Charlie seemingly forgotten by everyone at the table—except me.

Once we're all finished, things are cleaned and leftovers are packed away, I start to make some coffee, needing the distraction.

"So, that's who was on your mind last week." Vó sneaks up beside me, checking on my technique with the traditional pour-over method we all prefer for our coffee.

"Hmm? Oh. No. It's nothing." I keep stirring slowly, methodically, not wanting to give anything away.

Vó flicks me on the nose and scoffs. "Don't bother lying to me." When I drop the spoon to rub my nose, because goddamn that hurt, she takes it over. "If you're friends now, maybe she can help with the recipe book. Bring her on Tuesday." Her gaze stays glued to the coffee, but I know the look in her eyes. She thinks she knows something. Well, maybe I'll ask Charlie and bring her just so Vó can see there's nothing like *that* going on. That ought to get her weird looks under control.

23 /
for the record, i
love surprises.

charlie

> ROBERT:
>
> Lottie, why aren't you picking up my calls? I miss you. I haven't even been going on any dates. I meant what I said. I'm ready now.

Robert's text comes through while Maeve is getting Julia from her afternoon nap, and it makes my stomach turn. He called yesterday, and I completely forgot about it. And though I sometimes forget to respond to people, I don't often forget about Robert because he's been such a constant in my life.

It's shocking how little I think about him these days. Is it an out-of-sight, out-of-mind thing? Is it more than that?

He misses me. He wants me there. He's ready to commit. I've wanted those things from him for years, so why doesn't this make me want to get on a plane to London right away like last time?

Maeve doesn't understand why I've waited for him for so long, but Robert and I have known each other for years. I know if I married him, I would be taken care of. *Safe*. I'd know exactly what to expect. It may not be the most romantic way to meet your life partner, but we're similar in so many ways. We work the same hours. We have the same friends. For someone who thrives on routine, it's sort of perfect. It makes sense. It's what my mum wanted for me—to have a normal life doing normal things. This is my chance to have that, and I don't want to mess it up, but there's a part of me that's resistant to the idea. As if I'm settling for less than I deserve.

It's probably just because I went on a date last night. Yes, that must be what's making me think there might be something else available to me than this plan I forged years ago with Robert.

My thoughts are interrupted by a happy giggle.

"Ah-tee, Ah-tee!" Julia's chubby hands reach for me as Maeve walks into the kitchen with her daughter perched on her belly. I happily take my niece, immediately pulling her in for a hug as she grabs at my hair. She's always fascinated by it. I'm not sure if it's the color or the texture, but she loves it.

"Yes, poppet, that's your Auntie Charlie!" Maeve looks on, absentmindedly rubbing at her ever-growing belly.

"Are you hungry, Julia?" Her brown eyes widen as she looks at me, bringing her hand to her mouth, signing for food. I giggle at her and lift her to place her in her highchair. Maeve is already grabbing fruit from the fridge as I get her bib on.

"Nack? Nack Mama? Nack Ah-tee?" She slaps her little hands on the tray in front of her, little legs kicking beneath it.

"Yes, Jules. You can have a snack." Maeve's patient tone is soothing. She was made to be a mother, and yet she used to question whether she would be capable of this. As she places down the tray with an array of foods for the child who's not biologically hers but hers in every way that matters, my heart expands with pride. Julia shimmies in her seat as she starts to eat what's in front of her slowly.

My phone vibrates in my pocket, and I check it immediately. I keep thinking Rafael is going to text that he's on his way back, and I don't want to make him wait.

"Oh." I smile down at the screen, seeing Zach's name lighting up the screen. We exchanged numbers last night, but I didn't expect to hear from him for a few days.

"What's that smile all about there, Char?" Maeve takes a bite of Julia's cracker and gags. "Oh. Gross. That's not... nope... yuck." The sweet baby between us repeats the word *yuck* over and over, giggling as she does. "Now, hand me the phone. Who's got you smiling like that?"

I pass her the phone, knowing that it's probably best that she be the one to see it first anyway. At least if he's texting to say he doesn't want to see me again, I'll see it on her face immediately.

Maeve taps the screen, and her eyes go as wide as saucers. "Blimey, that's a di-iiiiiifferent message than what I was expecting." She looks at Julia, who is unfazed and happy to be eating. "Char, you went out with this guy?"

"Last night, yeah. Why? What's he saying?" I try to look at the screen, but she hides it away. Maeve is smiling, so I know it can't be bad.

"And what exactly happened last night?" She looks at the screen again and snickers. What the bloody hell is in that message?

"We had dinner. Went for a walk. He took me home, kissed me, and we said goodbye. Why? Stop being weird and just tell me!" I reach for the phone again.

"It looks like he thought you wanted more than just a kiss, babe." She finally hands me the phone, a goofy grin still plastered on her face.

I nearly throw the phone across the room when I get a look at the screen. "Gah! That's a wank-uh-I don't know how to make this into a word that sounds like something other than wanker, and now I understand why you said *different* the way you did, and now I've just said that word in front of your daughter. I'm so sorry." Maeve breaks into a fit of giggles, and Julia joins her, even if she doesn't understand why. I look at the picture again. "Crikey, that's… is that… Why is it so angry-looking?" I can't see Zach's face, but I'm assuming this is his dick he's holding, or this message just got even weirder.

My sister continues, laughing until she nearly topples off her chair, tears springing in her eyes. I finally take a moment to read the text sent at the same time as the photo.

ZACH:

> Hey sweetheart. This is what you missed out on last night, but there's always next time, right?

Oof. This is not good. Zach had potential, but sadly he's just shit the bed.

"So, are you going to see what he can do with that?" I'm met with sparkling blue eyes and wiggly eyebrows.

"I don't think so. I would have gone on another date, but now? I know this is all he'll be thinking about, and I won't even be able to look at him." I close out of the text thread, checking that Rafael hasn't also sent anything.

He hasn't.

"What's wrong with that? If what you want is a good…" She puts a hand in front of her mouth and whispers *shag* to me. Between Owen and Elaina, this kid is going to grow up hearing every swear word known to man, but apparently, Maeve is going to make some sort of effort to stop that from happening. "Then just go for it!"

I feel the scowl take over my face. "I'm not sure that's all I want. If I'm supposed to be figuring out how to be in a relationship, I can already tell you this is not the guy to help me with that."

"Well, that's a great start. You know what you don't want. Move on, right?" My sister's right. I can just move on. No need to dwell on one date.

"Oh dun!" Julia waves her hands in the air, letting us know she's all done, so we clean her up and head outside for a walk.

The afternoon is spent in blissful chaos, and when I don't hear from Rafael, I settle on sending him a message letting him know he can come anytime he's ready but not to rush or anything.

RAFAEL:

See you soon.

Within thirty minutes, Rafael is coming through the gate, and I get a weird feeling in my stomach knowing that he's here. It's unwelcome but not unpleasant, if that makes sense.

"Teetee!" Julia screams and starts crawling toward the door when he comes inside.

"Hi, Juju." He rushes to her and scoops her up, covering her chubby cheeks with kisses as she giggles and squirms. *Damn.* That's a sight. Bronze muscles bulging everywhere, and yet this man is so delicate with this baby girl. I should make a note of this for a book.

The two finally finish their extended greeting, and Rafael makes his way into the kitchen, where we're all gathered. "Hello, James Family," he says easily to Owen, who is washing a sippy cup at the sink, and Maeve, who is practically inhaling another honey stick Owen just brought home for her. "Strawberry shortcake." He winks at me, and I nearly fall off my chair. I wonder if he was born with this charm or if this is something he had to work at, practice, and hone.

I wait for the feeling of disgust that usually bubbles up inside me, but it doesn't come. Getting to know Rafael has completely changed the way I react to him. Now, the only thing that doesn't sit well inside me is the knowledge that I was wrong about him for so long and whether I've been wrong before or since meeting him.

"Did you wanna go right away, or is it okay if I take a

minute to play with my favorite jellybean?" He tickles Julia's belly as he speaks but looks at me for an answer to his question.

"Oh. No rush." At my answer, Rafael beams, immediately holding Julia closer as he dances with her down the hall to music none of us can hear.

Maeve hums around her honey stick, looking wistfully in the direction of where her daughter was just whisked off to.

"Maevey, I swear, if you're swooning over Rafael dancing with Jules again, I might develop a complex." Owen's voice is deep, as it always is, but the way he chuckles at his wife indicates there's no sincerity in what he's just said.

"I can't help it. I just get all sentimental when I see how loved our little girl is. First, I got to watch Char with her all day, and now Raf? I—" A loud sob bursts out of my twin, and Owen is at her side before he can even turn off the kitchen tap. He quickly dries his hands and pulls her into him as she continues. "And our son gets to grow up with all these amazing aunts and uncles, too? It's just… We're just…" More sobbing overtakes her, and Owen rubs her back, attempting to soothe my seemingly inconsolable sister. "Stupid bloody hormones. Ugh!"

In an effort to help with the situation, I head to the sink and finish what Owen had started. It's not the first time Maeve has burst into tears during this pregnancy, though it is rare. By the time I'm setting the last bottle on the drying rack, Maeve has collected herself.

"Thanks, Char. I appreciate it." Owen squeezes my shoulder as I walk past. I had never imagined myself with a brother-in-law, so to find myself with one who loves my sister with a devotion I've never seen before and who simply lets me be feels like an enormous gift. From the moment I met Owen when I was nineteen, he has always been a calm presence. Even before he knew about my autism and ADHD— Maeve asked me if she could tell him—he never once made me feel like I couldn't be myself. Anytime I excused myself from something early or moved to a quieter space when things got too loud, he always understood that it was what I needed. No questions asked, no sideways glances, no commentary afterward. He occasionally throws me a thumbs-up from afar, his way of asking me if I'm all right, and as long as I send one back, he just carries on with what he was doing.

I've read a lot about found families. I've even written about them. And the more I pay attention, the more I realize that despite feeling like Elaina was my only family outside of Maeve, their partners have been worming their way into that world, too. I suppose Rafael is a part of that now. And Elaina and Owen's mom, of course. Eva is everyone's mom by this point. She's welcomed us all in from day one, and it's been really nice to have an example of a loving, supportive mother when ours is more concerned with which designer bag she's going to use to snag her next husband.

I shake away my thoughts as Rafael comes bouncing back into the kitchen with my giggling niece. "All right, jellybean, Titio is tired now. Time to go home, okay?" Julia rests her head on his shoulder for a moment, then straightens again, reaching for Owen, who takes her with the smile that seems to be permanently etched on his face since Julia and Maeve came into his life.

"Bye, Teetee!" She waves at Rafael, blowing him a kiss, and we all melt a little while he pretends to catch it and stuff it in his pocket.

"Bye, Juju. I love you." He blows a kiss back at her, and that feeling in the pit of my stomach comes back, catapulting me from where I stand.

"Right. We better go. Bye, Mae." I hug my sister. "Call me the moment this one decides it's time to make an appearance, yeah?" I give her belly a pat, and my nephew kicks me in response, making us laugh.

"You sound like Raffy with that *yeah*," she says, mimicking my question. "Careful, sissy. He'll rub off on you." She giggles, but I ignore her remark. And the little voice in my head that says that might not be such a bad thing.

Turning to Owen, I reach up to give him a half hug, and Julia takes a handful of my hair before plopping a sloppy kiss on my cheek. "Bye, sweet girl."

"Bye, Ah-tee."

I walk to Rafael's car with an enormous sense of gratitude that I got to have today with my sister and her family. The thought of staying in LA and making this a regular occurrence warms me.

As I'm buckling my seatbelt, a question pops into my head. "Do you want kids?"

"What?" Rafael chuckles, settling in and turning the volume down on the music.

"Sorry, you don't have to answer that." I feel the heat rush to my cheeks. Sometimes, the words just slip out, and the more comfortable I become with someone, the fewer filters I seem to have between my brain and my mouth.

"Oh no, it's fine. You just took me by surprise, Chuck." He starts to back out of the spot he parked in, his hand coming to rest on the back of my seat, ignoring the screen showing us what's behind the vehicle. Such a hot guy thing to do. Knowing he's focused on what's behind us, I let my eyes roam for a moment, and when they land on his face, he's already looking at me. "For the record, I love surprises." His right hand goes back to the steering wheel, and I'm still entranced with the way all of those muscles move. "To answer your question, I don't want kids of my own. I would rather help families trying to adopt and support the foster system in other ways. Plus, I kind of like being the cool uncle, you know?" He shrugs, completely unfazed by my far too personal question. He doesn't ask me to answer the same question, and I silently thank him. Despite my curiosity, now doesn't seem like the right time for me to defend my stance on not ever wanting to be a mum. Pregnancy is a hard no for me.

"Hmm. You're just so good with Julia. It seems to come so naturally to you." I pause, swallowing down the lump in my throat. "Everything seems to come naturally to you."

There's a beat of silence. "I think you know now that that's not true. I just had to embrace my strengths because my weaknesses were always pointed out. And kids are easy, you know? They're so pure and innocent. Plus, I get to hand them back and go home to snuggle my cat." He smiles widely at that, and I can't help but do the same.

"I thought your cat hated you," I say with a laugh.

His smile turns into an exaggerated pout that manages to be sort of cute on him. "Thanks for the reminder. She's probably going to be so pissed when she sees me come home tonight. I bet she's just hoping I'll leave and never come back. But guess what, Ginger Spice? I'm not a quitter! I'm just gonna keep loving that cute little fur ball until she loves me back!" His face is filled with determination, and I don't even have to question whether or not he's serious. I'm certain Rafael will not rest until this cat concedes.

24 /
stop saying dick pic.

charlie

WE'RE JUST ENTERING Santa Monica when Rafael shifts slightly in his seat, drawing my attention from the palm trees in front of us.

"Carrot cake?" I roll my eyes and turn to him in response, eliciting a smirk from the handsome man next to me. "If you're hungry, I have some chicken ready to be tossed on the grill at home and my grandmother's pavê in a cooler in the trunk. It's a dessert with ladyfingers—like the cookies, not actual fingers—and custard with chocolate on top."

"Oh. Um, I don't want to be a bother, it's—"

"Chuck, if you tell me right now that you don't want to come over because you need time alone or you simply don't want to, I will drop you off at your building and not ask any other questions." At a red light, he turns his head and looks at me as he says, "But you know I love to cook. I think you'd be very into this dessert, and I kind of want to ask for your help with something. So, if that sounds okay, please come have dinner with me?" The fact that it's a question softens something inside me.

"All right. I'll come." He pumps a fist into the air before

continuing with the flow of traffic, and I hate to admit how infectious his excitement is.

ONCE WE GET to his place, Rafael is quick to get things started for our meal. He moves around the kitchen effortlessly, gathering vegetables to grill along with the chicken. "Can I help with anything?" I'm not a big fan of feeling useless, but that's usually how it feels watching someone else do everything.

"Actually, would you mind grabbing us drinks? I'll take sparkling water with some ice. Grab whatever you'd like out of the fridge. I'm just gonna get these going. I'll be right back." Holding up the trays of meat and vegetables, he swings open the door with his hip and walks out.

Somehow, he always seems to know what to do to put me at ease, and I don't even think he's trying to. Something as simple as giving me a task and leaving me alone to do it. I look around his kitchen, thankful for the open shelves showcasing the glasses. I take two and open the fridge, eyeing the dessert he stashed away in there. It really does look delicious.

Once I've poured two glasses of sparkling water, I set them on the counter just in time for him to come back inside. He places a tray in the dishwasher, washes his hands, and turns back to me, clapping his hands.

"All right, so. About that thing I need your help with." He brings his hands to his chin for a moment, then looks at the floor. "It's kind of a personal project. Something I'm doing to pass along some family traditions, but no one in my family really knows about it. My grandmother and I have been putting together family recipes." He turns around, opens a drawer, pulls out a soft brown leather-bound notebook, and then twists to face me once again. "Normally, she writes the recipes while we do this, but it's getting harder for her to do that because of her arthritis. We get together once a week; we still have a few recipes left to add before this feels complete. I eventually need to get them typed up as well, and, well, that's where you hopefully come in."

He hands me the notebook, and I take it in both hands, running my finger along the embossed letters on the cover. *Machado Family Recipes.* "You'd like me to write the remaining recipes in here and then transfer them from this notebook into a digital file?" I look up and find Rafael toying with his watch, nervousness showing in his features for the first time. He nods and looks as if he's about to say more, but I continue instead. "And you'd need me to be there when you work on these recipes since she's struggling to write them down?"

His brows furrow, and he lowers his head so far that his chin touches his chest. "Yeah," he whispers, then quickly clears his throat. "Yes. I go there every Tuesday, and I guess I could type the recipes as I go, but my hands are usually pretty busy, and I don't trust dictating everything because if a mistake is made, I might not catch it right away, and the thought of multi-tasking all of this is already a little over-whelming, so I can't even imagine how it would feel if I actually had to—"

I reach out and place my hand on his forearm. The touch startles him enough to stop his run-on sentence, his eyes locking on where we're now connected as he takes a deep breath. I imagine this is what it must feel like to touch something with an electric current running through it. Instead of shying away, I grip a little tighter, and his eyes rise to meet mine.

"I'll be glad to help. Tuesdays are now for cooking with you and your grandmother. Done." I let my hand drop to my side, place the notebook on the counter, and immediately cross my arms over my chest to hide the shakiness I'm afraid is bound to be noticed by this far too perceptive man.

"Just like that?" With wide eyes, Rafael stands before me perfectly still.

"Yep." I step back and reach for my glass of water, washing away the sudden dryness in my throat. "Should we go check on dinner before everything's charred and we have to order takeout?" I motion to the back door, and he follows the movement, standing straighter. I pick up his glass of water, he grabs tongs from a nearby drawer, and we walk out together.

I set the glasses down on the bar next to the barbecue, and for reasons unbeknownst to me, I speak. "Zach messaged me today."

His jaw ticks, and I study the movement because this is romance novel gold. It's an actual thing. His jaw did an actual tick—like he clenched his jaw around nothing. How interesting.

"What did he have to say?" He continues moving things around the grill, adding corn and zucchini.

"Not much, actually. He had a lot to show, though." His eyebrows furrow as mine raise. "He seemed to think it'd be a good idea to send me a dick pic." I shrug, then jump as the clatter of the tongs crashing onto the metal of the barbecue startles me.

"He. Did. What?" Rafael picks up the tongs and slowly hangs them on the side of the barbecue, closing the lid and then placing both hands on his hips as he faces me. "Please tell me that was a joke."

I shake my head, taking in the serious look on his face. "I can't. He really did—" I stop short, feeling my phone vibrate with a call. I fear it's either my mum or Robert, but my eyes nearly pop out of my head when I pull the phone from the side pocket of my leggings and see Zach's name lighting up the screen. "Crikey, it's him." I turn the screen so Rafael can see it, and I swear his eyes look like they could shoot lasers out of them. "What do I do?

"May I?" Rafael extends his hand, reaching for my phone, and I practically throw it at him like it's a hot potato. With a swipe of his thumb, he brings the device to his ear. "Hey, Zach, it's Rafael." *A pause.* "Yeah, she's here, but you're not gonna talk to her." His eyes flick to me for a moment. "Listen, as your boss, I'm not gonna hold any of this against you because it would be unprofessional as fuck. But I am gonna tell you two things. You listening?" He pauses briefly, then continues, his tone almost even and relaxed. "One, don't send anyone unsolicited dick pics, man. It's not cool, especially when you're in your thirties."

He looks up at the sky, his jaw tight, and his voice now much more severe. "Two, lose this number. Erase the memory of Charlie's perfect face from your mind. From this moment forward, you've never met Charlie, do you understand me? And if you ever speak of your date with her, or this conversation, to anyone, ever, I will get really fucking unprofessional about it. Got me?" He finally takes a breath as he waits for an answer on the other side of this call. Seemingly pleased with what he hears, his shoulders relax, and his tone turns almost jovial. "Awesome. Glad we had this chat. Have a great night."

He hangs up and hands me back my phone, opening the barbecue again with a smile. "Dinner's ready," he announces. "Hang tight, I'm just gonna grab our plates." With that, he jogs back into the house, leaving me stunned and confused.

He said my name twice in that short conversation. That makes it seven times now.

Erase the memory of Charlie's perfect face from your mind.
Charlie's perfect face.

I snap out of my spiraling thoughts when Rafael comes back with his hands full. He sets two plates on the dining table, with napkins and cutlery, then comes back and places everything from the barbecue onto a clean platter. "Ready?" he asks casually. I'm still standing here, holding my phone. "Red?" The name registers, and I flinch. "Oh, shit." Placing the food down, he walks closer and stands in front of me, the same way he did in the alley. "Was that too far? I'm sorry. Did you like the dick pic? I just thought that was uncalled for. No grown man should be sending dick pics unless explicitly asked to, you know? I can call him back and say I was just joking. I'll tell him to send all the dick pics he wants. I shouldn't have overstepped, but, no, no, but. It's cool that you like dick pics. I shouldn't have overstepped, and I'm s—"

"Breathe, Rafael. And stop saying dick pic." The facts are clearly laid out in front of me. I've been seeing them for a while now, but this was the missing piece of the puzzle. "You didn't overstep. I didn't like him sending me that. You read the situation perfectly, as you seem to always do. And that's what I'm coming to terms with. I wanted to find someone I felt safe with, and I've found that person in the unlikeliest of places." I take another step closer to him, our toes nearly touching.

"I don't want to be set up on any more dates in the hopes that I'll meet someone I feel comfortable enough to try things with. Who knows how many more guys I'll have to date and kiss before I find someone else I feel safe with." He flinches at my words, seemingly as unhappy about that prospect as I am. "I've found my safe person. So, this is me formally asking if you'll be the one to teach me." I look up to find his chocolate eyes studying me.

"What does that mean? I need you to very explicitly tell me what you mean here, carrot cake." He stands so perfectly still it's as if he's hardly even breathing.

"I'm saying that I trust you. I trust that you have my best interest at heart and that you won't cross any lines with me." I take a deep breath, expecting to need to calm my nerves, but finding I'm not nervous about this at all.

"Okay," he says, body still unmoving. "Keep going."

"I'm going to tell you the real reason I came here. The reason I decided to start dating and experimenting. It's Robert. While we'd had an open relationship for a long time, we sort of agreed a long time ago that we'd eventually end up together. That we'd eventually commit to one another. Only one another. Well, he's spent the last several years dating while I've spent them not doing much of that. And I don't want to be completely inexperienced and dull, so I need to step it up. I want to be ready in case we follow through with this plan." Watching me intently, Rafael's jaw moves slightly, as if he's clenching and unclenching again. I've never noticed this little tick of his before. It must be new.

He takes a deep breath, closing his eyes as he exhales then locking those caramel and coffee eyes back on me. "What exactly are you asking me, then?"

Here we go. "I'm asking you to be my, I don't know, fuck buddy slash relationship tutor. In a very, uh, scientific method sort of way." Yeah, that sounds about right.

"What? No. You're not serious." Finally, he moves, bringing his hand to his face and slowly dragging it down. Then he takes a step back, away from me.

Realization slams into me, and I picture the ground opening to swallow me whole. Of course he doesn't want to. I've seen the women he dates. God, why didn't I think about this before blurting this out? "Oh. You… You're not attracted to me that way. Right. I suppose I read that wrong with the comments about my dress the other night. You're used to like supermodels or whatever. Yeah, well, this is awk—"

"Fuck that shit, Chuck. No. Nope. Do not continue. You are hotter than hot. Any guy would be lucky to be with you. To touch you. But that doesn't mean any guy should get to. Probably not even this Robert assho—" Cracking his knuckles, he shakes his head, eyes down. He's angry. I can feel it. "You're too good for just any guy. That's all I'm saying."

"You're not any guy." I could say more. It feels as though I should because this silence might actually kill me. "You get me. You see me, and you haven't run away yet. You have this incredible family, and everyone loves you. You're easy to be around. I want… I want those things, too. I want to know what it feels like to just be with someone without having to worry if I'm saying the right thing. I'm afraid that if my trial run is also with the guy I may end up married to, then I'm going to mess it up. It's too much pressure…" My voice fades as he remains quiet. He's probably thinking of ways to let me down nicely.

He takes a step forward again, and slowly, ever so slowly, he lifts his hand to my chin and tips it up until our eyes meet again. "Did you mean it? Everything you said about trusting me, feeling safe with me. Did you mean it?"

"I meant it," I answer truthfully, even if my brain is begging me to lie, to take it back, to make it easier for us to pretend this never happened.

"Okay. If this is what you need, then okay." Rafael lowers his hand, putting both in his pockets.

"It's what I need," I assure him. "I've been in the research and hypothesis parts of this method for too long. I need to get to experimenting and data analysis."

A slow, beautiful smile blooms on his face, and I swear the sun shines a little brighter, which seems impossible because this is Southern California. "Then call me Professor Machado, honey bun. Class is officially in session." He pumps his eyebrows up and down twice before turning back to the food, picking it up, and heading to the table. Unfazed and effectively taking the mood from tense to relaxed. How typically Rafael.

i'm the fucking guy.

rafael

I AM FREAKING the fuck out.

Don't drop the food. Don't drop the food. Don't drop the food.

I made it. I didn't drop the food, but I definitely set it down a little harder than I meant to. I pull in a deep breath and blow it out through my mouth before I pull out a chair and motion for Charlie to sit.

She's slack-jawed, eyeing me suspiciously, but when I point to the chair, she snaps her lips shut and walks over. "I'm not calling you that." She sits with a huff, and I push her chair in, laughing quietly, but inside, I really want to, I don't know… scream? Dance? Jump up and down? Call my best friend and tell him the hottest girl in the world just asked me to be her friend with benefits or relationship teacher or whatever the fuck this is? I don't even care because I'm the guy.

I'm the fucking guy.

I sit across from her and motion for Charlie to serve herself first. She doesn't fight me on it, thank God. I also notice she puts everything on her plate, so I guess this means she has no aversions to any of these foods. Good to know.

I'll have to save my thoughts for whatever the fuck is

going on with this British dickwad, Robert, later. What kind of guy makes a deal to end up with a woman—not just any woman, Charlie—but then proceeds to fuck around for years? And why would she agree to this?

"So, we're not going to make this weird, right? Because it's just research. I need to experience book boyfriend things first-hand and you happen to be somewhat of an expert, it seems. And this should get me well ready for whoever I end up married to." She takes a bite of zucchini, eyes widening as she hums. "Wow, this is good," she mumbles with a hand over her mouth.

"Thanks. And uh, no, we're not going to make this weird. But what do you mean I'm somewhat of an expert?" I love making her explain herself when she's accidentally complimenting me.

"Good. And I mean because you read romance, you know what I'm talking about when I say things like meet cute. You know what a door lean is, and you likely understand the importance of gray sweatpants." Her eyes fix on mine when she says *sweatpants,* and I laugh because, yeah, I do know all about the lean and the sweatpants, even if I don't get what the hype is. "And you're experienced. Physically. With women. I won't have to pull a Monica and draw you a diagram to explain where number seven is, will I? You'll know how to find my clit?" I nearly choke on my chicken and proceed to gulp down most of my glass of water.

"Jesus, Chuck. Can you wait until I'm finished swallowing before you—"

She laughs. Head thrown back, hand to the chest, lets out a little snort, laughs. Fuck me, I am not prepared for this. All the breath leaves my lungs in a whoosh, Charlie's skin flushes, and she wipes at her eye before settling down. Goddamn, this woman. *This woman.* She might just ruin me, and I might be willing to beg her to do exactly that.

"Whew. Thanks for the laugh, Machado." She lets out one

more chuckle before shaking her head and taking another bite of food. I make the decision to eat my dinner without saying another word. I don't trust myself not to say something stupid, or worse, do something incredibly impulsive like lay her on this table and show her just how well I could find her—

Nope. Do not go there, man. Eat your food and settle the fuck down.

"Can we agree on something, though?" There's just one thing I can't leave alone. She nods as she chews a bite of chicken. "Can we agree not to talk about this guy in London when we're together?"

She swallows, taking her time. "Robert? Oh. Yeah. Of course. I just, I didn't want to hide the whole truth from you."

"I appreciate that."

Without bringing our arrangement up again, we eat, talking briefly about her characters, who sound oddly familiar, but that's probably just because I've been reading a lot of romance lately. Charlie loves the dessert, like I knew she should, and when we're finished, we take everything back inside, moving easily around one another until a loud meow comes from the other side of the kitchen.

"Hey, Pumpkin!" I approach her, and she starts walking in the opposite direction, so I beeline for her food dish and pretend like I was just gonna do that instead of trying to pick her up. How fucking embarrassing that my cat won't even let me touch her.

Charlie gasps. "This is your cat! Oh, she's so cute." She crouches and starts making kissing noises. "Come here, sweet girl. It's all right."

"Yeah, good luck. She hates—" My traitorous cat walks over to Charlie and rubs her body all over her leg, purring. The little fucker purrs. I don't think I've ever heard that sound come from her. "What the fuck?" They look up at me, and I swear to fuck, they both shrug at the same time. After a few seconds, Pumpkin walks away from Charlie and struts to her food bowl, not even sparing me a glance.

"Your cat's name is Pumpkin?" Charlie narrows her eyes at me, hands on her hips.

"Uh… yeah. Well, her hair is orange, like…" Like yours, I want to say. Because the whole reason I got this cat over others was because of the color of her fur. And her eyes.

"Like a pumpkin. Right. Like my hair, too." She lifts a few stands of her hair as if I'm not keenly aware of the similarities between her and my cat. "Female orange tabby cats are rare, you know?" A small smile plays on Charlie's lips. I don't know how she knows this fact, but I appreciate that she does. "I had to research cats for a book once." Of course she did.

"Yeah, and she has blue eyes, which is also pretty rare. She's kind of unique. Exceptional, even." Charlie's eyes remain glued to my cat, who is sitting in front of her food bowl, happily eating and ignoring us.

"Hmm. Cool." She straightens, looking around the kitchen. "Well, looks like we're all cleaned up here. I should get home. I'll see you Tuesday, though, right?" I nod, unable to force any words out. "Great. Thanks for dinner. And for, you know, agreeing to help me." She smiles at me. It's a small, friendly smile, and it hits me that weeks ago, I hadn't seen her smile more than once or twice, and never at me, and now, I get to see her smile *and* hear her laugh. I get her unfiltered thoughts and her friendship, and soon, I'll get her kisses *and* her body.

When my dick twitches, I jolt up. "Yeah, no problem." We walk to the front door, and she gathers her purse, sliding her shoes on. She opens the front door and waves on her way out. "Later, *gata*."

The Brazilian nickname slips out so easily. The one I've only used once before.

by myself. with my hand.

rafael

A COUPLE OF HOURS LATER, as the sun is setting and I've finished all my laundry and deep cleaning the barbecue —thank you, hyper-fixation—I'm trying to coax Pumpkin into coming to snuggle with me on the couch, but she ignores me, as usual. My phone vibrates on the coffee table, and I consider ignoring it until it vibrates again, and again, and again. I smile as I unlock it to find a string of texts from the woman who's been running through my mind like she's training for a marathon.

> CHARLIE:
>
> Hi.
>
> I started a list.
>
> You know how much I like those :)
>
> And there are things I really want to experience firsthand from romance books, you know?

Still smiling like the idiot that I am, I start typing back.

ME:

Can I see the list?

CHARLIE:

Here you go.

1. Door lean. Is it really that hot?

2. Gray sweats. Need a visual.

3. Neck kisses. Pulse point kiss, are they really all that? What other spots feel good?

Want to learn this about myself and others.

4. Is it possible to fall asleep while cuddling? Never tried it. I think it would get too hot. This would require a sleepover, so if you're not into that, just let me know.

5. Techniques for giving good head. I don't personally love the idea of gagging, so I will have to experiment with this.

6. Dry humping. Never done it. Curious.

7. Making out in the car. Logistics, because the centre console seems like it would get annoying.

8. First kiss. Is it possible to have a great first kiss? Mine have all been lackluster.

9. Mutual masturbation. Sounds awkward?

10. Phone sex. What the hell does one say?

11. Sexting. Seems like less pressure than phone sex.

12. What's a day at home supposed to be like? I don't know how to just be around someone doing normal things.

13. Lingerie: do men really like it, and is it possible for it to be comfortable?

14. Hands tied during sex. Maybe a blindfold, too.

15. Sex in the shower.

16. Try as many sexual positions as possible.

17. Sex. Just sex. So much sex.

I'm sweating.

Reading this list is making me sweat. Goddamn it, I wanna do all of these things with her. Yesterday. Right now. I've always thought of Charlie as one of the sexiest women I've ever known, but getting to know her is waking something up inside me that I'm not sure I'll ever be able to put back to sleep.

Is this what she wants to do with that fuckface in London, though? Better not think about that. In fact, I'd like to forget about him entirely.

I read through the list again but find myself pausing and imagining how things will play out. Obviously, I'm taking too long because my phone vibrates in my hand.

CHARLIE:

You okay over there?

Having second thoughts?

ME:

No, I'm good. Just reading.

Let's maybe start with numbers 1, 2, 3, and maybe 12? We can work our way up to the other stuff. What do you say?

CHARLIE:

Cool.

I'm sure I'll have more to add.

Cool? I'm sitting here, harder than a freaking lead pipe, and she's just... cool?

I'm so fucked.

CHARLIE:

Can we start on Tuesday?

A pained groan escapes my mouth as I read her message. I'm gonna have to start right now. By myself. With my hand.

ME:

Yeah.

What the fuck am I doing?

———

I'VE HAD ROUGHLY fifty-five hours to prepare for this. I've jerked off three times. I've spent more time at the office than I usually do. I've gone for four runs. I've done skipping exercises twice. Today.

I texted Charlie ten minutes ago that I was on my way and that I was coming up to her apartment to show her something. Now, I'm leaning on her doorway like an absolute fucking moron waiting for her to let me in. My forearm is resting on the frame, I have one foot crossed over the other, and I'm about to forget about this stupid idea when she opens the door and takes me in from top to bottom, and I hear the little hitch in her breathing.

"Is this what you were thinking?" She steps back, letting her eyes roam over my body once more. "Or was it this?" I cross my arms over my chest, resting my tricep on the doorframe. Charlie swallows, still speechless, and a very cute pink blush appears on her cheeks. I push off the wall, kicking the door shut as I walk inside. She takes three steps backward, and before she trips on her shoes, I grab her around the waist and turn us both so her back hits the doorway into the kitchen. With our bodies nearly flush, I prop my arm above her head and lean down, making sure not to speak directly into her ear. "Or was it more like this?" Her chest heaves, her breasts pushed up against me, and then her head turns just ever so slightly, giving me access to her neck. God, I want to kiss her there, but it's too much. For her? Maybe, I don't know. But definitely too much for me. So, I settle for running my nose along her skin, watching goosebumps form in the wake of my touch. "You smell so fucking good, honey bun."

I physically feel the shiver run up her spine that ends with a moan. The blush on her cheeks is as pink as the flowers in my grandmother's garden. "Th-that's good. That'll do." She clears her throat of the hoarseness we both just heard in her voice, and I take a step back.

I hold back a chuckle, as she pulls in a deep breath, slowly collecting the little pieces of herself I scattered with our lesson on door leans. Fuck, I love me a flustered Charlie. "So, what did we learn today, Chuck?"

"Huh? Oh. Yeah. Good. All of those. Door leans. Very good. Indeed." She rushes to slip her white, low-top Chuck Taylors on and grabs her purse from the bench by the front door. "Ready?"

We make our way to my car in silence, but I can practically hear the gears turning in her head.

"Ginger Spice, what are you thinking about?" I ask as we both buckle our seatbelts.

"Oh, um, I just need to make some notes, I think. I don't want to forget these feelings when it's time to write, you know? Do you mind? I can just take some notes quickly on my phone. Would that be okay? Or is that rude?" She fiddles with a ring on her middle finger and grips her phone tightly in the other.

"Take all the notes you want, Chuck. I just wanted to make sure you're all right, and that I didn't cross any lines or anything. It's scary when you go silent on me, you know?" I chuckle, but I'm dead fucking serious.

"Sorry. I didn't mean to. And I'm fine. That was great. Top-notch, truly. You could actually teach a class on door leans, you're so good at them." She unlocks her phone and starts typing furiously, brows furrowed and thumbs moving at breakneck speed over the keyboard. Occasionally, she mumbles a few words, like biceps, ankles, and hot, but I can't make out what she's writing. It's adorable, the way she's so focused.

Eventually, she stops, pulling in a deep breath with a small smile on her lips.

"We're nearly there. All set?" I ask.

"I think so. I'm so sorry. I just got super focused on getting these thoughts down, and I lost track of time." She winces while looking out at the road ahead of us.

I was totally prepared to keep driving around if she needed more time. "No sweat, Chuck. Looked like you were having a solid hyperfocus moment."

She hums a response. "Was that awkward for you to do? The leaning?" Her eyes stay on me as I contemplate my answer.

"A little at first because I was just waiting for you to open the door while I stood there, but once we were inside, no. I definitely prefer leaning on a doorway when you're doing it with me." I smirk, and when I sneak a glance at her, her cheeks are flushed the same rosy color they had been when I told her how good she smelled. As if we're both remembering the same moment, she brings a hand to her neck. "Roses," I accidentally whisper. Maybe she didn't hear me.

After a few seconds of silence, I count myself in the clear. "What?"

Shit. She heard me.

I clear my throat, a sudden heat climbing its way to my

own cheeks now. "Your, uh, smell. You always smell like roses."

"Oh." She pulls her bottom lip in between her teeth, and I keep my eyes locked on the road for the remainder of our drive, which is about twenty-three seconds since I'm pulling into the driveway. "We're here?" I nod a response. "Wow, this is beautiful."

I look around, taking in the orange trees on one side, the old farmhouse ahead of us, and the mountains to the left. Yep. It's amazing here, but the best view is at the back of the house. I can't wait for Charlie to see it.

"Apologies in advance for my grandmother's inappropriate jokes," I say before getting out. She shoots me a confused look as I round the front of the car and open her door. "You'll see. Now, come on, strawberry shortcake. We have work to do." I bop her on the nose and take her hand, leading us both into the house, the smell of coffee floating out to greet us. "Vózinha?" Charlie tugs me back as she starts to slip her shoes off. "Oh, if you want to take your shoes off, I'll get you some slippers. They don't take their shoes off here." I roll my eyes, then scan the cubbies by the front door for slippers in case she does want them.

"Oh. Okay then." She slides her hand out of mine as she puts her shoe back on, and it's then that I realize we've been holding hands. I didn't register when the decision to take her hand happened, but I do notice that I miss the contact once it's no longer there.

I walk into the kitchen first and find my grandmother has an absolute feast laid out for us. Fruits, several different kinds of cheese, so much bread, and a ton of sliced meat. Then there are the cake, biscuits, and sweet preserves to be eaten with the cheese. She went *all* out.

"Bença, Vó." I reach for her, hugging her, then kissing her cheek loudly as she slaps my cheek in that way of hers. "This is my friend, Charlie. Chuck, this is my grandmother, Ana

Maria." I step back as the gorgeous redhead comes into view, her eyes a bit wide, and her lips parted. She's nervous.

"Prazer," Charlie says in a surprisingly proper Brazilian accent. Impressive as fuck, as always.

Charlie is frozen still, so Vó approaches her. The two women are nearly the same height, and when my grandmother reaches her hands up, her bright blue eyes widen further before softening. Seeing Charlie's face between Vó's wrinkled hands does something to my insides, a languid warmth leisurely making its way from my stomach to my chest.

"Linda. Muito linda," she says, smiling widely at Charlie, who smiles back, placing her hands over the older woman's. That warmth in my chest morphs into white-hot heat in a blink as I witness a moment I know I won't ever be able to relive again. The air shifts. The ground moves. The light seems to shine only on them, and in an instant, it's over. "Let's eat," Vó announces, and the three of us take a seat at the table.

27 /
bolo de laranja

charlie

I EXPECTED to feel overwhelmed by being somewhere new, meeting someone I know nothing about because, while I had intended to use the drive to ask Rafael about his grandmother and what I should expect, I ended up spending it writing down every thought and feeling that came over me from the moment I opened my door to find Rafael leaning on it, to the moment he told me I smelled good. I swear, I can still feel the press of his nose on my neck, like he branded me there. I worry that the mark is visible, and yet I want it there, so I'll never forget that feeling.

No doubt I'll be up until the early morning hours writing. So many ideas have started forming, the more I understood what it meant to experience someone standing like that, looking the way he looked, with anticipation and maybe a dash of nerves in his eyes. All of it transformed the second he pushed me against the kitchen doorway. Our bodies moved fluidly. I had never fully understood the appeal of a man who simply knows how to be sexy on a whim. It was as if every movement was intentional and rehearsed, but it felt like they were just for me.

Now we sit here, with more food than we could possibly eat in front of us, after his grandmother just called me beautiful while looking at me in a way that should have made me squirm. But her eyes are so kind, so full of love, that it was impossible to do anything but smile. It felt like some sort of understanding passed between us in that moment. In that silence. As if we already knew one another. It's impossible to explain it as anything other than just a pure and whole connection. Any of the apprehension and nervousness I'd felt had melted away.

"Charlie," Vó says, though it sounds more like Sharlie. I like it. She points to the food laid out before us, wordlessly asking me to serve myself first. I don't know where to start, though. Everything looks amazing, but I don't want to offend this lovely person by not eating something.

"This is bolo de fubá; it's a cornmeal cake. It's sort of like cornbread but sweeter. This cheese is a little soft and salty and pairs really well with the goiabada, which is a guava marmalade," Rafael continues, making his way around the table. "You've had pão de queijo, and this is a tapioca biscuit." As he finishes, he smiles at me, and I smile back in thanks. His face falls suddenly, and he stands. "I forgot to tell her you don't like hot coffee. Shit. Shoot. Desculpa, Vó."

I reach for his arm and wrap my fingers around his wrist. "Raf, it's fine. I'm good." He freezes, staring at me unblinkingly before sitting back down. I serve myself all of the things he just described, because they all sound amazing, as his grandmother pours the coffee into small cups for the three of us.

I take a bite of everything as Rafael and his grandmother chat about something that happened yesterday. He had told me they only speak Portuguese with her, but she's speaking English, and I assume that's due to my presence. I did attempt to learn a few words in Portuguese, but still, the guilt that they're having to change this for me doesn't sit well. I take a sip of the hot coffee without thinking and gasp, forcing the liquid to run down the wrong pipe. I cough, and Rafael's hand rests on my upper back, concern painted across his face.

"I'm fine. Sorry. I'm fine. Just surprised." I clear my throat and take another sip of the coffee, closing my eyes. "God, this is good. Mmm."

Rafael is the one coughing now, and Vó laughs. It's a lovely sound, her raspy laughter.

"I get it. I see why you do that to your afternoon coffee now. This is fantastic." I turn to the woman across from me. "Muito bom," I tell her, then take another sip as she smiles at me once again. "I was just about to say it's all right if you'd like to speak in Portuguese. I don't mind."

"No, you are a guest. But I like that you came prepared with a little Português. Did Rafa teach you?" The way she says his name is wonderful. It sounds like *haffa,* and her voice changes slightly when she says anything in her native tongue. That natural raspiness in her voice is more pronounced, and she can let her vocal cords do what they've always trained to do. When she speaks English, her voice is clearer, but it's almost unnatural. Not unpleasant, just slightly forced when she has to manipulate her mouth to create sounds it's not used to.

"I didn't teach her anything. This is kind of a surprise." His serious tone unsettles me, my mind immediately racing to wonder whether I'm mispronouncing things, if what I did is insulting, or if he thinks I'm a massive idiot. "A very thought-ful, very sweet surprise," he adds, yet again reading me with such ease. His hand comes to rest over mine on the table for only a second. In that time span, our eyes lock, and he mouths *thank you,* and squeezes my fingers in a way that reas-sures and completely settles me. I don't understand it, this capacity he has to scramble my every thought and then put them all back together again.

As we eat, we mostly chat about the food in front of us,

where it comes from, and the rich history behind so many of the ingredients. Brazilian culture is fascinating, and there's no amount of late-night internet reading that could ever duplicate the experience of learning about it from someone like Ana Maria.

"Why is the coffee in such a small cup?" I ask, immediately feeling my cheeks heat in embarrassment. I've been wanting to ask, but it sounded like such a stupid question in my brain.

"Fantastic question," Vó says. "Portion control. Imagine a huge cup of coffee with this much sugar? Ai ai ai."

My eyes snap to Rafael, remembering his coffee cup from the other day. He brings his index finger to his lips in a shushing motion, and I laugh, watching as he starts to do the same.

"Oh, I know all about how my neto drinks his cafezinho by the liter." She laughs with us, and I fear the coffee isn't the only thing making me feel warm and buzzed.

AFTER INSISTING that I was not allowed to help with clean-up, I walk out to Rafael's car to grab my laptop and the bag he forgot in the trunk. His car is impeccably clean, not unlike his house, and I wonder whether he's the type of person who organizes his closet by color. I love order but struggle to achieve it, and as a fellow ADHD'er, I guess I'm just waiting to find—holy mother of all doom piles. It's the trunk. I found it. This is where his mess lives. *Ha!*

"Wait, red, don't—" Rafael runs toward me, arms flailing. "Ah, fuck." His head falls, chin touching his chest as he raises a hand to scratch at the back of his neck. It's his biggest tell that he's uncomfortable in some way.

"Finally," I say as I wave a hand over the dumpster, also known as his trunk. "I found an imperfection!" I walk closer to him, close enough that I can feel his heat, and we're both standing in front of the evidence of his mess. "I was starting to think maybe you were one of those rare neurodivergent people to always be neat and tidy." I poke at his chest, and he raises his head, a playful grin now on his face. "But nooooo, you have messes too." I poke again. "Not so perfect, huh, Professor Machado?" Another poke.

He takes hold of my wrist and pushes me back, so my bum rests on the bumper, his thigh coming to rest between my legs. His other hand snakes around my waist, settling on my lower back and holding me close to him. "Careful, shorty. I like that nickname a little too much." He leans over me, bringing his lips just below my ear. "And I might be tempted to show you exactly how messy I like to get," he whispers. His warm breath caresses my neck, and I shiver, even if my skin feels as if it's on fire.

And then he's gone. He takes the bag he needed out of the trunk with the hand that was behind me and backs away, leaving me breathless. "Don't forget your laptop," he shouts with a wink, and he turns and struts away with all the confidence of a man who just left a woman completely turned on with a few words and a simple touch.

I want to hate how good he is at this, but I'm reaping all of the benefits, so can I really hate it all that much? At all?

This is exactly why I need practice. It can't be normal to react like this to a person. If this happens with Robert, I'm going to fumble my words or, worse, do something completely embarrassing. I must just be feeling things more extremely because this is so new, this kind of closeness with someone.

It takes a few minutes to collect myself and my laptop. Also, I take a second to take a photo of this trunk, because I never want to forget that he is just a regular neurospicy man who needs a doom pile in order to survive.

Walking back into the house, I hear quiet laughter from the kitchen, followed by a groan. A manly groan. A groan that definitely does not send a shiver up my spine because people making sounds with their throats can't possibly cause such a reaction, can it? Fact: it can.

"Any other one but this one, Vó. Por favor." Rafael's back is to me, but I can see he's got an apron draped over his front. I walk around to stand next to Ana Maria, and my laptop slips out of my hand when I take in the situation in front of us. Thankfully, I already had it hovering above the countertop, so it lands with a loud clatter, but without any damage. The lovely woman next to me laughs harder.

I take in the apron from top to bottom. The front is covered in a very realistic, very high-definition photo of a man. A naked man. With nothing but a hot dog bun covering the man's, uh, hot dog.

My hand flies to my lips as I try, but miserably fail, to hide the squeal making its way up my body and out of my mouth. I shake my head, unable to make eye contact with Rafael when he's wearing something so revealing. And yet not, because, of course, I know that's not his real body in that photo. It couldn't be. Could it? The man has a perfectly chiseled six-pack , a smattering of hair on his pecs, and the beginnings of a happy trail hiding behind the bun.

Sensing the multitude of thoughts and questions bumping around in my brain, he steps closer, tying the indecent cover-up at his back and whispering, "The real thing is definitely better." He walks away, taking ingredients out of the fridge as I do my best not to think about the possibility of that statement being true.

While lost in my thoughts, they set up their tools and ingredients, all while Rafael asks for a different apron several times. His requests are ignored every time.

I set up my laptop on the island, taking a seat for the front-row show I'm about to witness. If just being in the same room as these two is entertaining, I can't even imagine what watching them cook will be like.

"What are you making today?" I ask no one in particular.

Rafael answers, "Bolo de laranja, which is orange cake."

I'm supposed to respond with something. I know I am. But my brain is stuck on the way he said the words in Portuguese. He could be saying anything. He could tell me to piss off and I'd like it. I'd ask him to tell me again.

Damn it, what is going on with me? He smells my neck once, and suddenly, I'm like a dog in heat. Pathetic.

I survey the ingredients, of which there aren't many, and hum. "Sounds delicious." I open a new document and title it *Orange Cake*, then set up a spot for ingredients to be listed. The leather notebook I now recognize as one of Rafael's prized possessions slides into my sightline.

"I figured you might need this if you want to transcribe recipes while we're prepping or whatever. You don't have to; I just didn't want you to be bored or anything." He presses his lips together as if to keep himself from rambling further. His usual lightness and confidence are gone, and I have an innate need to get them back.

"How could I possibly be bored? I could stare at those abs and that wiener bun if I need something to do." I look over to Ana Maria, whose smile stretches from ear to ear. She gives me a thumbs-up, and I send one back to her.

Rafael groans again. "Fuck, what have I gotten myself into with you two?" He points at me before picking up a knife and an orange. "I hate that you said that with a perfectly straight face, by the way. That's bullshit." He twists his neck to look at his grandmother. "And I'm not apologizing for swearing anymore. Cece isn't here, and you have the filthiest mind *and* mouth of any of us." His face is serious, but there's no bite to his tone, and the juxtaposition mixed with the apron has a loud laugh bursting out of me. "Well, I suppose wearing the apron is worth it, if it gets me that." He casually points toward me, watching me with gentle eyes.

My face relaxes into a smile, and the one on his face is

brighter than the sun as he peels the orange in his hand deftly, his movements so fluid and natural. I suppose growing up next to orange groves would do that, though. But did he grow up here? Where did he grow up? What's his middle name?

"Did you grow up here? What's your middle name?" Damn it, here I go again.

His answering lopsided smirk morphs into a chuckle. "Yes, I did, and it's Guilherme. What's yours?"

It feels criminal to gloss over the name Guilherme because, bloody hell, that's a sexy name.

Are names sexy?

Yes, when they are Rafael Guilherme Machado, the answer is definitely yes.

Focusing back on the conversation, I ask, "You really don't know?" He frowns and shakes his head. "It's Maeve. My middle name is Maeve." I wait for the laughter and ridicule because it is ridiculous that my middle name is my twin's first name. I know it is. We both hate that Mum did that to us.

His brows furrow for a moment, then he asks, "Is Maeve's middle name Charlotte?" I pull my lips into a straight line and raise my eyebrows, indicating my yes. He smiles up at me. "That's really cute. I can't believe I didn't know that." He shakes his head lightly, a chuckle reverberating through him.

"You know what's not cute? The way you're peeling those oranges." Ana Maria takes the fruit and knife out of his hands, shaking her head with no malice in her tone. "Help Charlie get the recipe started. I'll do this." She winks at him, and before he can turn away, I catch the immediate blush that rises on his cheeks. An actual blush. From a man named Rafael Guilherme Machado. How is he real?

Rafael takes his time washing his hands and then settles on the stool next to me. "This is a really simple recipe, so I'll just measure everything as Vó goes along, and you can document it for us?" he asks. I shake my head, and he blanches. "No? Okay, yeah, that's fine. Uh, how do you wanna—" He stops himself, his eyes locking intently on my lips. I focus on the feeling there, noticing my bottom lip is trapped between my teeth, and I am definitely smiling. "Uh... what... uh..." The way he stumbles over his words is adorable. I release my lip and let my smile loose, watching Rafael's throat move as he swallows.

"You are such an anomaly, Machado." His curious brown eyes meet mine for a moment before I look away. "Of course I'll document it. It's why I'm here. Don't worry about me. I've got plenty to do here, and I like you better over there where I can see those abs staring at me." I wave him away with my hand and turn back to my laptop.

Before straightening, Rafael leans in, bringing his lips just behind my ear. "You ever wanna see the real thing; all you have to do is ask, shortcake." See what I mean? He blushes, stumbles through his words, and then this.

He walks away with a smug smile, clapping his hands together when he's next to his grandmother, who's clearly pretending not to watch whatever the hell is going on here.

you really know how to make traffic interesting.

charlie

I AM UNWELL. And it's from watching this man, who has been unabashedly taking up space in my mind and causing bodily reactions I did not realize were possible. He's making me sweat. The kind of sweat you get when you have a fever, so it's sticky and all over, and yet you feel like you can't wipe it away, you know? Like it's there, but it's not really there, it just *feels* like it's there. Just the ghost of sweat silently present and *very much* unwelcome.

I watched the adorable duo bake a cake that smells absolutely heavenly, all while they razzed one another, occasionally flicking orange peels when the other wasn't looking. At one point, Rafael threw an orange slice in the air and caught it between his teeth and then winked at me. I swear this man was written by a woman. He doesn't actually exist.

Now, we're packing the cake up to take home—because they both insisted this was for me all along.

"We have a birthday celebration happening in a couple of weeks. It would be lovely if you could come, Charlie. The Machados can be a little over the top, but I promise we're harmless. At least at first," Ana Maria says, laughing at her own joke. It's impossible not to join her. She is infectious in the most wonderful way.

"Oh, um—"

"Vó, don't pressure her. You don't have to answer now, red. And you don't have to come. But you would be more than welcome." Rafael looks at me with an apology in his eyes.

"It's really lovely of you to invite me." When I see the wall of muscle next to me step closer, I raise a hand, knowing he's likely going to tell me again that I don't have to come. "My only hesitation is that my sister is about to have a baby, and I want to make sure she's okay and doesn't need anything. Is that all right?"

Warm hands close around one of mine. "You're a good sister, Charlie. Of course that is all right. Just know you are welcome here anytime." She squeezes my hand and turns to her grandson, pulling him into a hug that has him closing his eyes. "See you Sunday, moleque." She pats his cheek in a borderline aggressive manner, and he smiles broadly at her.

As we walk out, I wonder how those hugs must feel. I also feel incredibly grateful that Ana Maria didn't make me feel like I needed to hug her as well. And then my mind wanders to whether Rafael told her about me. Warned her about my sensitivities. I hope he didn't, even if I would understand it if he did. I don't like to be treated differently based on someone's assumptions or whatever little knowledge they might have of me.

As we settle into the car, the cake safely stashed at my feet, Rafael exhales loudly while rubbing the back of his neck. "I'm sorry about her. If she was too touchy or pushy. I didn't get the chance to ask her to give you space or anything."

"She was lovely. She *is* lovely. And I had a great time, so thanks for bringing me here." I pause, gathering my thoughts. "I really would like to come and meet your family. I mean, I will most likely feel overwhelmed and overstimulated, but if they're anything like you, Arthur, and your grandmother, I think it would be okay. I think *I* would be okay." I shrug, keeping my eyes on the road because I'm not entirely convinced what I said is true, but I really want it to be.

"Well, you have time to decide what you want to do. No pressure, okay?" In my peripheral, I see his neck twist so he can look at me twice, but I keep my gaze locked ahead.

"Thanks," I whisper. And then we continue the journey in silence, neither of us feeling the need to add to it.

Once we get closer to LA, traffic is at a complete standstill, and I finally feel like I've caught up with my thoughts.

"Would *you* take me on a date?" It might seem like a random question, but I've been thinking about this. After an average—at best—time with Zach, I want a good, fun date without having to try so hard to be someone I'm not. Without worrying about getting unwanted dick pics.

"You really know how to make traffic interesting." He smiles, adjusting the temperature on his side of the car to a couple of degrees cooler.

"Are you going to answer my question?" I ask impatiently.

"Oh, my sweet pumpkin pie, I will definitely, definitely take you on a date." The *sweet* added ahead of the nickname has my cheeks heating up, and the double *definitely* makes me hold my breath, though I'm not sure why. "How's Friday night? As long as Maeve hasn't had or isn't having her baby, that is." He checks his blind spot and merges lanes while making room for the person ahead. While people are honking and driving far too close to other cars, Rafael is calmly moving along, letting others in front of him. So considerate.

"Friday is great, yeah. What should we do?" As much as I'd like him to take the reins, I'd plan the date if it meant getting to do what I wanted.

"Why don't you let me worry about that. I'll send you any

necessary menus and itineraries by Thursday morning?" He's very casual about it. Almost professional.

"Are you preparing for a date or a business meeting?" I try to force my tone to be playful. I have no idea if it's successful until he laughs. Success.

"Oh, definitely a date, shorty." He nods and then smiles completely to himself, and the residual feeling in me is akin to when someone says they have something to tell you, but they can't tell you until *later*. How can you think of anything else until that happens? How will I?

———

I DON'T.

I spent Wednesday writing and going for walks. Every word is filled with tension, with anticipation, and with all the feelings I'm currently experiencing. Jittery limbs, accelerated heart rate, this fluttery feeling deep in my belly, and the intense tightening of muscles when I dare imagine what this date might be like.

I fear Rafael is about to ruin me for all other men for no other reason than he is simply too thoughtful, too perceptive, too damn nice and good.

On Thursday morning at nine o'clock sharp, my phone vibrates on the coffee table next to my full cup of mint tea because the thought of adding caffeine to my already hyper-active body and mind is completely bananas.

RAFAEL:

> Hey, is it okay if we get going at around 3 tomorrow afternoon? If not, I can skip the first part I had planned, but I really think you'll like it.

He follows that up with a blushing smiley face, and I can picture it. I can picture the exact shade on his cheeks, the exact smile on his face, and it brings a ridiculously goofy grin to my own.

ME:

> Totally fine.

> Are you going to tell me anything else?

I fight the urge to send follow-up texts with more questions.

RAFAEL:

> Of course. Here's the menu for dinner.

He sends an image of a handwritten piece of paper with four options for entrées, four mains, and four desserts. All of it sounds amazing.

RAFAEL:

> No need to dress fancy or anything, but we'll be outside for a portion of the evening, so maybe bring a sweater? It's supposed to be a bit chilly tomorrow. Pack something comfortable to change into. Whatever you might wear to watch a movie with the girls. Sweat pants or something, I don't know. Just something to change into that's more comfortable than whatever you'll have on.

> I feel like I already said way too much.

> Since we're starting out early, do you want a coffee when I pick you up? A snack, maybe?

> You know what, never mind. I'll definitely have a coffee, but if you want a snack, too, just let me know.

Seriously? He wants to present me with coffee and a snack when he picks me up? I should be taking notes. Who wants flowers before a date when you can get coffee and snacks?

ME:

I'd never say no to a snack.

I'll pack some comfortable clothes, though I'm extremely curious as to why I would need them.

RAFAEL:

So... see you tomorrow at 3?

ME:

See you tomorrow at 3.

Great. I have thirty-one hours to prepare for this, which is completely fine because I should only need every single one to sort this out since I can't ask Lainey or my sister to help. It's fine. This is all good practice and prep.

At least, that's what I'll keep telling myself.

i was so right about those pants.

charlie

AT THREE O'CLOCK on the dot, there's a knock at my door. I didn't buzz him in, though, so it can't be Rafael, can it? When was the last time I buzzed him in?

I open the door to find the man himself, holding an iced coffee and a white paper bag, grinning from ear to ear. He has dark jeans and a light blue sweater on with a zipper at the collar that looks so soft, I'd like to snuggle it. His brown boots are scuffed but not dirty. Oh, and he's leaning on the doorframe, the jerk.

The moment his eyes take me in from head to toe, his grin falters, and he nearly drops the coffee. I reach for it, but he holds it up and away from me. "Turn around," he says.

"What?" I frown up at him, confused by the request. "No, hello, just *turn around*?"

"Yeah. I said what I said. Turn around, red. I need to see if I was right about something." He spins the coffee cup, making the ice rattle around inside, and my eyes track the movement. "You get the coffee when you turn around." I roll my eyes, turning around so he can't see me. "I saw that," he says softly before clearing his throat. Facing him again, I stick out my hand to fetch my reward. His smile is slow, like the dawn opening with the first rays of sunshine.

Eventually, the dimples pop, and I feel myself swallow, needing that coffee right now, at this very second. "Hey, shorty. You look gorgeous." He doesn't waver, he simply remains as he is, leaning and looking and smiling. It's unnerving.

Finally, he lowers the coffee so I can reach it, and I immediately bring it to my lips, needing the cold relief. The room suddenly feels too warm.

"Hi," I respond meekly. "Is that for me?" I point to the small paper bag he's holding in his other hand. "Oh, do you want to come in? Or should we go?"

"It's for you, and we can get going if you're okay eating this in the car." He holds out his hand to take my coffee from me, and I reluctantly hand it back so I can get my bags and lock the door.

In the elevator, he takes the tote bag I packed my trackies and jumper in, exchanging it for the iced coffee, and I realize something. "Did you ask me to turn around so you could look at my bum?"

"Yeah. I really did." He smirks proudly, without shame, as I gape at him, my jaw dropping to the floor. "I was so right about those pants."

I decided to go with one of the previously approved date outfits, the leather leggings and a sweater. I scoff my response, unable to find words for him. I like that he noticed. I like that he asked me to turn around. I like that he thinks my bum looks good.

This is exactly how a date should begin. With coffee, snacks, and the other person making you feel good about yourself. This is definitely it.

When we get to his car, he opens the door for me, waits for me to set my phone down, and then, he reaches over and buckles my seatbelt. I swear it's the sexiest thing to ever happen to me, watching him move over my body, feeling his hand push the seatbelt in, smelling his citrusy scent as he shifts to stand. It shouldn't be so effective, this simple movement, but it's more than enough to have the stomach flutters making a comeback. I'm thankful for the few seconds to calm down before he's in the car.

"You haven't even looked in the bag yet," he says as he starts the car and buckles his own seatbelt.

Can you really blame me for forgetting about the food when I have a whole other kind of snack sitting next to me?

I open the bag and find a container with a slice of cake with white icing on it and a small plastic fork neatly stashed in there. The cakey part is a bit orange, and I bring the now open container up to my nose to smell it, trying to discern the flavor.

"Is this carrot cake?" I scrunch up my nose, trying not to smile at the ridiculousness that is Rafael bringing me this particular dessert.

"Yeah," he smiles. "Seemed appropriate, you know? Plus, I couldn't find any pumpkin stuff this time of year, and strawberry shortcake looked a bit messy to be eaten in the car." He looks downright smug, jutting his chin, so proud of himself for what he's done. Shockingly it doesn't take away from the cuteness of the whole thing. I take a bite of the cake, and it's incredible. Perfect consistency and the icing tastes fresh.

"Mmm. Wow," I say around my bite. "That's so good. Where did you find this?" I take another bite and then close the container back up. I'm not actually hungry, but it was too tasty not to have another bite.

"Oh, I, uh, made it," he mumbles, and I nearly choke.

"You made me carrot cake?" I swing out my left arm, my hand landing on his thigh. His eyes bounce from my hand to my face to the road, lingering on the road, then back again to me. I snatch my hand back, sitting on it, lest it get any other funny ideas.

"I did. It's a Machado favorite, so I make it pretty regularly. It's no big deal." He shrugs, merging into traffic with the same composure as Tuesday. I'm thankful not to be the one driving. This would definitely stress me out.

"It's a big deal," I whisper, looking out of the window. There's no way he goes to this kind of effort for all his dates. I mean, there is. I suppose he could be this thoughtful all the time with everyone, and I'm actually not special at all. But I don't think that's true. I think he tried to make this special. I think he is trying to make this special because I told him I wanted to experience something exceptional.

Damn it. It's so bloody nice. If I think about this for too long, about how he bought ingredients and made a whole cake so he could bring me some to have as a snack for our date, I might cry. I don't want to cry. Crying on a first date is surely the sort of thing people avoid.

Robert would never.

Rafael blessedly interrupts my spiraling thoughts before they can take off. "Hey, red? Whenever you're done overthinking this, you should look in the backseat. I also packed other things in case you didn't like carrot cake." He points to the back with his thumb as I'm still processing the information.

"Oh. Thanks."

"It's gonna take about an hour to get to where we're going. Sorry about that." He looks over at me and then turns the volume up on the radio, so the car isn't completely silent. A familiar song is playing. I think it's the one from the first time I went to his house. "Do you, uh, want to know where we're going?"

"Yes!" I twist so fast in my seat I nearly give myself whiplash. "I mean, yes, please," I answer more calmly. I need the distraction from my thoughts and from the traffic, so yes, I need to know where we're going.

He chuckles, his fingers tapping lightly on the steering

wheel to the beat of the song. "We're going to a bookstore." His eyes find mine as he says that last word, and he watches intently for my reaction. "A really cool one." My eyes widen in wonder.

"Seriously?" Looking for something to do with my hands that doesn't include nearly groping my date again, I reach for my coffee. "This is top-notch book boyfriend stuff, Machado. Damn."

He laughs again. "I'm glad you think so. You wanted the book boyfriend experience, so let's go for it, right?" There's nothing but joy in his tone, and it sends a warm feeling through my veins, despite the ice-cold coffee in my hand.

The book boyfriend experience. Right. I just want the experience. Period. Not the actual boyfriend. Not yet.

I want to be prepared since I've never been in a relationship. I want to understand how this all works, how it feels, what it looks like. I want to be ready for this when I go back to London, because I am going back whether I end up with Robert or not. Sure, LA feels good right now, but it's not my home. This thing with Raf might feel good right now too, but it's not my forever. It's not what's been planned and agreed to.

This is the most I've thought about life after LA in quite some time, and I know I need to put a stop to it. Thinking about all of this while spending time with Rafael isn't going to help in any way. Not if I want to make this research as authentic as possible.

We spend the drive talking about the last two days. Rafael's been mostly working; I've been mostly writing and eating orange cake, which turned out to be absolutely delicious.

When we arrive at our destination, he parallel parks into a tight spot on a road I don't recognize and hops out of the car. He pays for parking, then opens my door for me.

"So, what's so special about this place?" I throw my purse

over my shoulder, always carrying the bare minimum with me. Glasses, lip balm, extra ADHD meds in case I forget to take them, wallet, phone, pen, fidget toy, tampons, and condoms. Essentials. I'll never understand how people lug around huge, heavy bags all the time.

"You'll see," he answers simply, taking my hand as we cross the busy street, jogging a little, which I don't mind this time.

When we get to the sidewalk, he drops my hand before moving to walk closest to the street. Fact: I really, really like that. We approach a storefront absolutely covered in plants, and Rafael announces that we've arrived.

That's right. This place has books *and* plants. There's a colorful bistro table and chairs set up outside and several full low bookcases next to them. As we walk in, there's a tunnel of plants with twinkly lights in between them. It's magical.

Instinctually, I reach for Rafael, taking hold of his arm as we walk through. I let him go as I clap my hands, a little squeal of joy slipping out of me as I take in the space. Further in, the ceiling is covered in moss and there are more plants among the thousands of books. The shelves in the middle of the store are low, so you can see over them, and the space feels airy, unlike typical bookstores. There are plants every-where, with cute pots lined up on some shelves.

"Should we just head straight to the romance section?" He looks down at me, not moving away from where I've gone back to holding onto his bicep.

"Yes, we should," I say, but we end up just walking around the store, browsing and wandering the aisles before we find the romance books. I notice my latest novel is front and center, which is nice but not something I can have much of a reaction to. Unfortunately, that doesn't stop Rafael.

"Oh, great, they have the new C.M. Howe. I've been meaning to get this." He reads the back of the book, a small smile playing on his lips. It's not a new book, just a special edition, so it surprises me to see him pick it up.

I reach for a dark romance about two contract killers who fall in love while looking for the same person. I let myself get lost in the books for a while, enjoying the peace that comes with discovering new stories. I only wonder once if Robert would ever take me to a bookstore for a date. If he would ever read one of my books.

Deep down, I know the answer.

i'm not going to kiss you.

rafael

CHARLIE IS COMPLETELY LOST in her own little world right now, and I'm okay with just being a spectator. I watch her face change with every book that she picks up as she rocks back and forth on her heels. I don't think she realizes it, but she's basically giving me a silent review of each one. Either her eyes light up and she smiles in appreciation, or she puts the book down with a frown.

I've picked up all of the books that have put a smile on her face. So far, I've got six books, one bookmark she giggled at, and a sticker that says *introverted, but willing to discuss books*, which she pointed at, saying, "True."

I had hoped she would like this place. It's less busy than the larger independent store in downtown LA, and the plants really do give a more calming vibe. I think it's a success, though I don't know if I should feel bad that we're not really talking to each other. This is supposed to be her dream first date, after all.

She picks up a notebook and clutches it to her chest as she continues to browse the shelves.

After about forty-five minutes, she lets out a slow breath

and turns to me. "All right, I think I'm done. I'm going to go pay for this, and we can go if you want." She turns to face me fully, and her brows jump up when she takes in the stack of books I'm holding. "Wow, you're getting a lot of books!"

She has no idea. This is just half of them. I had to unload the others at the cashier's desk because they were getting awkward to carry. I ended up deciding to get two of every book so that maybe, if she ever wants to, we can read these books together. Or I can just read them on my own. It'll be nice to know she's also reading them. I don't know. It seemed like a good idea when I thought of it.

"Here, let me get the notebook for you." I put out my hand to take it, but she continues to hug the gray and yellow journal. Her mouth opens, then closes, then opens again.

"Are you sure?" Her eyes dart from me to the person working the register, who is smiling kindly at us.

"Positive, pumpkin." Twisting to face the store employee, I pat the stack of books already on the desk. "These are ours, too."

"All of those?" When did you even—" Charlie's eyes rake over the spines, realization starting to sink in. "Those are all books I looked at. You're going to read all of those? Twice? Why do you have two of each book?" Okay, maybe she's not realizing what's happening here.

Withholding my laughter—because damn it, she's cute when she's sorting through something, but she will also snap me in half if she thinks I'm laughing at her—I tug at her chin, directing her to look at me. "They're for us, shorty. So, we can either read them together, or separately, or whatever. All right?"

Before Charlie can answer, the person across the desk makes a noise. "Aw, you two are so sweet! How long have you been together?"

The question makes me smile as Charlie stands motionless, big blue eyes begging me to answer. "This is our first date," I say, not breaking our contact or taking my eyes off her. "I'm just trying to make it so she wants a second."

"Oh. My. God. You're buying books to read with her and it's only your first date? This is the most romantic thing I've ever heard! I'm going to tell absolutely everyone I know about this. Will you two come back? I have to know if you keep dating. I mean, girl, how can you not keep this man—" They continue talking, but I block it out. All I see, all I hear is Charlie.

"You know I'm going to have to write about this, right?" She licks her bottom lip, and I drop my hand as she speaks low enough so only I can hear her. "I mean this is completely adorable and incredibly thoughtful. But please don't spend all this money if you're not going to read these books. And you don't have to read them with me. I mean, I would like that, and it would be fun to sort of have a little book club or whatever. I've never really done that before. But you don't have to. I totally get that you might not even want to read them at all—"

I place a finger over her lips to silence her. It's a bold move. One she might hate, but she doesn't bite me or push me away, so I keep it there. "Oh, I want to, red. I definitely want to." I lean in closer, not wanting the clerk to hear what I'm about to say next. "And who knows, we might just find some things to add to your list in these books." A rosy blush blooms on the apples of her cheeks.

"Right. Yeah. Okay." Her eyes dart sideways to the clerk who is still scanning items and pretending not to watch us closely. I can feel how uncomfortable it makes Charlie, so I step back and rest my elbow on the counter.

Charlie is busy looking at a small plant that has no leaves. She pets it gently with her index finger, smiling as she does. It sort of looks like it's just twigs, but it must be one of those succulents my sister likes because it's bright green.

"I'll take the plant, too, please."

The employee audibly sighs as they punch in some numbers. "The pot, too?"

"Please," I reply.

Two minutes later, we have all of our books in two separate bags, with Charlie's extras in hers. I take both, and when I step back from the desk, she looks up from the shelf she's been studying. "Don't forget your plant, honey bun." I lift up a hand, pointing to the little plant.

"You bought the plant? Wait, it's for me, isn't it?" She picks it up, shaking her head. "Really laying it on thick, eh, Machado?" Her lopsided smile brings us back to familiar territory where we can banter and tease.

"Yeah, well, I'm sort of trying to impress here." I look at her over my shoulder and see her smiling down at the weird little houseplant in her hands. She hums a response, and when we get to my car, I take the plant from her and pop the trunk, making sure Charlie doesn't come around to see all the shit I still have back here. I really need to clean this up. I grab a blanket that was trapped under a box of old DVDs I've been meaning to donate and create a little nest to prop the little pot into. *Perfect.*

Charlie is standing by the passenger door, looking pensive as she watches the cars roll by. I reach to open the passenger door, and she turns to face me. "Are you going to kiss me?" She crosses her arms in a protective way, almost like she's hugging herself rather than putting on a defiant stance.

I've thought about this. I've thought about kissing her, and not just because we're on a date. I've thought about kissing her just because I'm curious to know what she feels like, what she tastes like, and how she would fit against me. I've thought about how good it would feel to get Charlie out of her head for a minute or two, to watch her be consumed by something other than her thoughts or the things around her. The truth is, I want Charlie consumed by nothing but me. I do. I want to watch her let go, and I want to be the reason she can.

"No, shortcake. I'm not going to kiss you." I swallow as her face falls. "Not right now, anyway. Because I don't want to kiss you where anyone can see us. Where the thought of being seen might take away from the moment. I want to kiss you when it's just you and me. Just us." Her arms drop to her sides, shoulders relaxing. Her tongue darts out to wet her lips again, and it takes every ounce of self-control not to push her up against the car and steal her breath, steal her kiss.

"Oh," she breathes. "So, you will, then? You will kiss me?" She keeps her eyes locked on my mouth, and her breathing picks up, that adorable blush creeping up her cheeks again.

"As long as that's okay with you, yeah." I push a stray curl off her face, beaming from the inside out when she leans into the touch. *My* touch.

"Yeah," she whispers, nodding. Double confirmation. Fuck, yes.

I swipe my thumb across her lower lip, holding on to my self-control that hangs on a very thin fucking thread. "Good. Let's go eat."

31 /
we would never actually date.

rafael

WE ARRIVE IN AN INDUSTRIAL AREA, and I can practically hear the questions in Charlie's head. It does look shady as fuck, taking a woman to a place like this on a date, but Adam assured me this restaurant is legit. I'd never used his celebrity status to get me anything before, but he insisted. Of course, I didn't tell him who I was taking out, and he didn't pry too much, likely assuming it was someone I just met.

The thing is, that hasn't happened—meeting someone new—since Charlie walked into me. Actually, that's a lie. I haven't gone near a woman since I kissed that blonde last New Year's Eve and caught Charlie watching. Something about the anger in her eyes turned me on so fucking much. I feigned feeling unwell and didn't go home with anyone that night. The fact that her eyes on me turned me on more than the woman I was kissing was confusing as hell. That was a little over a year ago now, and I'm still confused.

Turns out, I'd rather be confused and on a date with Charlie than confused and without her. Now, there's a thought that feels far too deep to tackle in this moment.

"Uh, where are we?" She peers out of the window as I pull into the parking lot of an all-black building.

"I know it looks sketchy, but I promise it's a great spot. Trust me?" It's an innocent enough question, but she twists instantly to face me and, damn, those blue eyes knock the breath right out of my lungs.

After a long pause, she lowers her chin. "I trust you."

Every cell in my body comes alive with her admission. I know I've officially crossed a threshold not many people in her life get to, and it feels like an honor I'm not worthy of. One I'm not going to fuck up.

"K. Grab your sweater." I shoot her a smile and open my door, then jog to her side to open hers. In an attempt to bring the fun back into this date, I bow and extend my hand to her. "M'lady," I say in a deeper-than-normal voice.

Her answering giggle is like a warm breeze enveloping me. Her hand slides into mine, and I don't let go as we walk into the building that has one single sign with the words *The Patios* on it.

When we walk in at six o'clock on the dot, the hostess, dressed in all black with a name tag that matches the sign on the door, welcomes us with a smile. "Mr. Machado?" I smile back. "Right this way, please."

She leads us through an area with a few sofas on the left and the bustling kitchen on the right. At the back of the building, there are a series of black doors with small white numbers on them. She opens door number four and holds it for us to walk through.

We're on a patio. A completely private patio, complete with several heaters, a table set for two, a couch with pillows and blankets, and a fireplace already lit in front of it. There are string lights surrounding the space, and a view of the now fully illuminated city below us.

"You have this space to yourselves. Washrooms are back the way we came to your right. Morgan will be your server this evening and the only person to come into your space. Before he opens the door, he will ring the doorbell, wait a few seconds, and come in. If you need him, there's a call button on your table as well as on the side table next to the sofa. Do you have any questions for me?" I look at Charlie, and we both shake our heads. "Great. Have a lovely time." She backs up to the door and closes it, leaving us alone in our private patio.

"This is incredible," Charlie says as she walks to the glass railing, her hand slipping out of mine and leaving me feeling a little colder. Emptier. The view of her ass in those goddamn pants, though, that warms me right up.

We walk to the table and I pull out a chair for her. As she sits, the smell of roses hits my nostrils, and I force myself not to inhale a deep breath. Too obvious, Machado.

The doorbell dings, and after a beat, a tall, lanky guy with curly blond hair walks in with a friendly smile. We make small talk with Morgan and order our drinks.

When he leaves, I note she's already eyeing the hand-written menu. They don't normally release the menu ahead of time to anyone. There's no website for this place, either. I had to come here on Wednesday night and get creative with convincing the head chef, who turned out to be a very lovely woman in her fifties. She mentioned there were no guarantees she wouldn't change something, so I'm a little nervous to look down and find a completely new menu.

Of fucking course, the cursive writing on the menu might as well be written in Dothraki. Unfortunately, I am not Khal Drogo.

"Oh, they changed one of the desserts from crème brûlée to a lemon sorbet. Hmm." She scowls as she studies the piece of paper.

"Did anything else change?" I settle for just asking rather than reaching for my phone. Her brows relax as the realization of what I'm asking settles in.

"No. That's all." She sets the menu on the table. "Have you had a chance to read it already?" There's no pity, no condescension in her tone. This is just Charlie asking a question like any other. That trust she gifted me with? I'm realizing I've already gifted her with mine, too.

"Yeah, but honestly, everything sounds so good; I hadn't really decided on anything. I kind of just wanna get everything and try it all, you know?" The way her eyes light up at the idea is all the confirmation I need that this is exactly what we'll be doing tonight. "Wanna?"

"Yes!" She practically jumps out of her seat. "I'm so glad I didn't eat all that carrot cake in the car."

I laugh at her completely serious expression. "Me too." I take a sip of my water because seeing Charlie like this is cutting into that thin thread of self-control.

The doorbell rings, and Morgan walks in a few seconds later with our drinks. With a smile etched on his face, he sets our drinks down and tucks the tray under his arm. "Have you had a chance to decide what you'd like, or maybe you have questions for me?" His gaze swings between me and Charlie.

I smile at her before lifting my chin to look at our young server. "We're going to have one of everything, please."

Morgan's eyes widen, and his smile grows. "Oh, I like you two! Any changes to any of the dishes?"

I look to Charlie, who shakes her head. I realize she hasn't said much to Morgan. "No, thank you," I respond.

"Great. I'll be back in with your appetizers in about fifteen to twenty minutes, but please feel free to use the call button if you need me before then." He twists on his heel, and then it's just the two of us again.

I thought it was a great idea to book this place so there wouldn't be a busy restaurant for us to compete with or be overwhelmed by other patrons. But suddenly, it dawns on me that I'm nervous. The last time I was nervous on a date, I must have been seventeen.

"This is the most perfect date, Rafael." She eyes me carefully. "It's thoughtful and fun, and I really appreciate that you took the time to make this special. Even if it's not, you know, real."

I swallow the disappointment lodged in my throat. "What's not real about this date, Chuck?" The nickname slips out. This is the one I seem to use when I need some distance from her, from getting too caught up in her.

"Well, I just mean because you're helping me with research. It's not as if we like each other like that or anything. We would never *actually* date." I can't see her hands on her lap, but I would bet that she's clutching them together. I grab the bottom of her chair and pull it so she's next to me. She yelps at the sudden movement.

I hate to bring it up, but I have to make my point, so here goes. "You went on a date with Zach for research. That was *real*. You didn't know if you'd like each other *like that* either, but you kissed at the end of the night." I take her hands in mine, steadying her movements and hopefully whatever emotions are running through her. "What do we need to make *this* date real? Two people who want to spend time together? Who are physically attracted to one another? Because both of those boxes are checked off for me. If they're not for you, then we can end this right here, right now. No pressure. No hard feelings. No questions asked." I swallow again, but this time, it feels more like a giant cotton ball is stuck in my mouth.

charlie

BOTH OF THOSE *boxes are checked off for me.*

I shouldn't be surprised by this. And I'm not surprised that Rafael wants to spend time with me or that he finds me attractive. Not anymore. I'm surprised by his forthrightness. By the the truth of it all and where it could lead, which is to a place we absolutely cannot go.

I can't entertain the possibility of this being anything more than mutual attraction that is being explored for the sake of my research. For the sake of my future relationship. *With someone else.*

Actually dating Rafael for real wouldn't only affect the two of us. It would affect our best friends. Their children. That's why this is just research. I'm gathering data from someone who is an expert in dating. He does this all the time and he's completely unaffected by those relationships ending, so this will be no different. It's another reason he's the perfect person for this.

There. Dilemma resolved. I can state the facts and remain unattached like him. It's physical attraction and friendship. Robert and I had that, too when we met.

With my mind made up, I go on. "I like spending time with you. You are unfairly, obscenely attractive." The tension in his face eases until he senses what's coming next. "But..." I look at our hands on my lap, the way he steadies me. "But this can't go beyond this experiment. It can't be real. There's too much at stake with our friends, and I live in London."

There's a long pause as we both let the words sink in. "All right." His thumbs draw circles on my knuckles. "I got it. But there's nothing not *real* happening here. I *want* to be here with you, and I need you to want to be here, too. I need..." He takes a long breath in through his nose, releasing it slowly. "I need to know neither of us is doing anything we don't want to do. I won't do anything to cross lines with you, Charlie. I won't take that chance. So, I need to know that you want—"

"I do. I want to be here," I say quickly. "I'm not doing anything I don't want to do either. I'm sorry I made you feel like, I don't know, like I was just going through the motions or something." I bite down on my lower lip to give myself something else to focus on. Something other than the waves of emotions crashing inside me. Emotions I can't even name right now. "I'm sorry."

He squeezes my hands, then brings them to his face, placing my palms on his cheeks and keeping his hands over mine. I've never touched him like this. We've never touched each other like this. I look up to find him with his eyes closed, relief settling into his features. He pulls one of my hands to his lips and kisses my palm. The kiss lingers and seeps into my bones, as does the intimacy of this moment.

Our hands land back on my lap, then he's cradling my face in his soothing palms, his chocolate caramel eyes warm and soft. His fingers move to grip the back of my neck, and he pulls my face toward his.

This must be it. The moment he kisses me. The tip of his nose brushes mine, and my eyes instinctively close. His breath sweeps over my cheek, and he lays a lingering kiss there, then he moves to the other, and his lips touch down again, decisively not on my lips. He runs his nose along my jaw until it sits just below my ear.

"Not yet," he whispers, takes a deep breath, and pulls back, leaving me teetering. I have literal chills, and I'm more turned on than maybe ever before. *Definitely*. Definitely more than ever before. Never has a kiss caused any kind of throbbing at my core. Never have I felt this heady, intoxicating kind of arousal. I feel simultaneously wound up and taut, like I could snap at any moment. It's so much all at once. And yet with him, knowing how honest we have been with one another, how openly we just discussed this situation, the sense of security only grows.

The doorbell dings again, and I sit back in my chair, trying to get some air back into my lungs. Morgan sweeps into the space with a large tray, all four plates somehow balanced on it. I focus on his movements as he sets everything down. He says something I don't register, and then he's gone again.

"Hope you're hungry, shortcake." Rafael lays his napkin on his lap, that easy smile on his face. I lift my glass of prosecco to my lips and drink half of it in one gulp. The chilly bubbles help to cool the fire that's stoked inside me every time he smiles, calls me a sweet nickname, or looks at me in that way that tells me I'm in way over my head.

I start with the calamari because it's closest to me, knowing I'll try the tuna tartare next, then the tomato and burrata, and the mini pizza last.

Everything is delicious. Neither of us says much because we're both so focused on the food, but it's fine. We needed a reset.

"I want to keep eating, but we still have four mains coming and dessert. How are we going to do this?" Rafael lays a hand on his muscled stomach. Even through the cashmere sweater he's wearing, there's no hiding that he is solid muscle.

"You quitting on me already, Machado?" I raise an eyebrow, and he smirks at me.

"Never, red." He takes a sip of his sparkling water without breaking eye contact. Why the bloody hell is that hot?

Once again, the chime of the doorbell breaks whatever spell we find ourselves under.

Morgan wheels in a whole cart of food. It's obscene and also wonderful. "I hope you're both still hungry." He makes quick work of swapping a few empty plates and moving the half-eaten appetizers to the cart so that the entrées can be on the table. Chicken schnitzel, pot roast with mashed potatoes, macaroni and cheese, and fish and chips—which I will be judging most harshly.

There's a big focus on comfort foods at this place, and I am all for it.

Morgan places a clean plate in front of each of us. "I figured you could serve yourselves family style. Does that work?"

"That's perfect, Morgan. Thank you." Having warmed up to our server, I smile up at him, and he beams right back at me.

"You're so welcome. I can't wait to hear what you think about the fish and chips." He winks at me and clasps his hands across his chest again. "Anything else I can get you?"

We both shake our heads, taking in the enormous amount of food on the table. "I think we're all set. Thank you," Rafael adds.

"Bon appétit." Morgan closes the door behind him, and Rafael reaches for the pot roast.

We quietly serve ourselves, both starting with two dishes. "Ready?" he asks.

"You might have to roll me back to the car if this is anywhere near as delicious as the starters." I puff out my cheeks, but they quickly deflate when my handsome date's booming laugh fills the room. I wonder when it'll get old, making him laugh like this.

As we eat, we mostly chat about the food. There is still quite a bit left over when we both decide to call it quits.

"All right. Fuck, Marry, Kill: Dinner Edition." He wiggles his eyebrows at me, and my giggle breaks free. "Let's hear it."

"Oh, I have to go first, do I?" He nods, smile unwavering as he watches me closely. "Hmm. All right. I'd fuck the schnitzel," I say seriously. Rafael nearly spits out his water all over me; he starts laughing so hard. I join him because that's a sentence I never thought I'd say. When we both calm down, I continue, "I'd marry the macaroni and cheese, and I'd kill the fish and chips." I sit back, content with my answers.

"I knew you'd kill the fish and chips." A small, knowing smile plays across his lips. "My turn. I'd fuck the shit outta that pot roast and mashed potatoes." We both laugh again, though we recover much faster this time. "It's weird talking about fucking food." I respond with an *uh-huh.* "I'd also marry the macaroni and cheese. And I'd kill the schnitzel." He grimaces when he gives his last answer.

"No! How am I supposed to get shagged now if you kill my schnitzel?" I lift my hands and let them land loudly on my lap. His eyes narrow slightly, his tongue poking the inside of his cheek.

"You won't miss it, pumpkin. I'll make sure of that." His eyes lower when he catches the movement of my legs crossing, his lips lifting at the corner in a smug way that would have angered me weeks ago, but now, it only makes me curious for what my future holds.

I'll make sure of that.

That's a promise of a good time if I ever heard one.

Once all the plates are cleared, Morgan brings us coffee and tea, and we opt to take the desserts to go. The promise of dessert with Rafael later is, unsurprisingly, thrilling. Though I suppose we might just take them home. Separately. Hmm.

We take our mugs and set the biscuits Morgan insisted on bringing us—just in case we wanted something sweet now—on the table by the fire. We walk to the railing to enjoy our hot beverages as the city below shimmers with lights from cars on the streets, neon signs, and all of the Hollywood flair.

Rafael points out a few places he can make out below, like where there's another great bookstore and the general direction of Santa Monica.

When we finish our drinks, we take a seat on the sofa side by side, but he takes my calves, twisting my body to drape my legs over his lap.

"This was wonderful. Thank you." I reach out my left hand, resting my elbow on the back of the couch and letting my fingers run through his hair. He doesn't say anything; he just lets me explore this new dynamic between us, where we can touch one another more freely. "I've wanted to do that for a long time," I confess.

"What? Touch my hair?" He leans into my hand when I scratch his scalp.

"Mmhm. It's even softer than I imagined." Is it possible I'm drunk on too much delicious food?

"You imagined, huh?" He looks at me wide-eyed, a smile I recognize as playful by the way his lips press together, like he's holding back a wide grin. I feel the heat blazing in my cheeks and begin to pull my hand back, but Rafael wraps his fingers around my wrist, keeping my hand in place. With his other hand, he trails his fingers along my forehead, down to my temple, pushing some of my curls away from my face. "I've imagined things, too," he says as he tucks some hair behind my ear. His index finger presses on my cheek. "Like this perfect, rosy blush of yours." He drags his finger over my jaw, down the side of my neck, stopping at my pulse point. "And all the other places you might blush just like this." He trails his finger along my collarbone, and the touch sends a shiver through me. But I'm not cold. With all of the heaters out here, I haven't even needed my sweater.

He moves his hand to my waist, pulling me closer to him, and before I can miss his hand on my skin, he replaces it with his lips. I gasp when his tongue swirls on my collarbone; then his lips take the reverse path of his fingers. When he sucks on my pulse point, my fingers grip his hair more tightly, and he groans, the sound traveling like lightning through every nerve, landing on the spot where they all converge between my legs.

This time, however, rather than stopping at my cheek, he lets his lips hover over mine. Our eyes meet, and he whispers, "Now."

Then, his lips are finally, finally, *finally* on mine. Just a touch at first, then his tongue swipes over my bottom lip, and my lips part on a sigh. He brings a hand to my jaw, guiding me where he wants me, and when our tongues meet, a moan that is nothing short of indecent rolls through me. He tastes of coffee and shortbread, and God, I could taste nothing else for the rest of my life, and that would be perfectly okay.

When he slows our kiss and draws back, I whimper at the loss, having been so fully consumed by his mouth, his touch, and *him*, that I forgot we're in a public place.

"Fuck, red, we should have been doing this a lot sooner." He runs his thumb over my lower lip as I scowl.

"You're the one who's been holding off," I scold.

He chuckles, not taking his hands off me. "I meant a lot sooner than today. If I'd known kissing you would feel like this, I would have done it a long time ago. I can't believe I've lived this long without knowing what these lips taste like." He steals another chaste kiss, as if he just can't help himself.

"You say that as if I would have let you." I smile and try to smooth his hair, but it's probably a lost cause. He laughs almost silently, his chest shaking.

"You're right." His eyes glisten as he studies me more

closely than ever before, the attention making me feel wanted and precious. It's a completely new and foreign sensation, but with him, it feels safe.

"I like the way those words sound coming out of your mouth." I lower my hand to cradle his cheek.

His teasing smile makes his dimples pop, and I sigh, loving the sight of them so up close.

"I have a lot more things I'd like to say to you, short-cake." Before I can ask him what those might be, the door-bell rings again. I sit back to put a little bit of distance between us, but when I try to lower my legs to the floor, Rafael holds me in place. "Let's just, uh, stay like this a minute, okay?"

I flush as an understanding of what he's asking me lands. I fight back a smile, knowing that he's as turned on as I am. "Oh. Oh. Right. Yeah."

"Hi again. I have your desserts boxed up here. Is there anything else I can get for you two?" My back is to the door where Morgan is standing, and I'm thankful he can't see my reddened cheeks and surely swollen lips.

"I think we're all good, Morgan." Raf calls out. "I left a card on the table if you want to settle us up, please." He's completely unfazed by the situation, his hand casually running up and down my calf as if we had just been sitting here drinking our coffee and tea, talking about the weather.

I suppose we're going to have to leave now, drive back to Santa Monica, and go our separate ways. I'm not ready for the night to end, though. I want more. More kisses, yes, but also just more of *this*. Being close, learning this new side of Rafael—and of myself, too.

When Morgan leaves again, Rafael squeezes my calf, bringing my attention back to him. "You all right?" The concern in his voice brings guilt into the frenzy of emotions already weighing on my sternum.

"Yeah. Yeah, uh, I guess I was just feeling a little bit sad that the night is ending." I press a hand to my chest, trying to break up the heaviness there.

"Oh, my sweet strawberry shortcake, the night is not over yet." Well, I officially have a favorite nickname.

"It's not?" I smile, trying to stifle the bubbly feeling in my belly by biting my lower lip.

"It's not. And if that fact makes you smile like this, I'll promptly make sure the night doesn't end at all. *Ever*." He looks at me like he's trying to memorize every detail of my face.

"Is that so? You going to lasso the moon and make it so the sun doesn't rise?" I tease.

"If that's what I need to do, then hell yeah." Despite the playfulness of our conversation, he's serious.

"Just for a smile?"

"No, not for just any smile. For *your* smile."

33 /
blimey, i might be in trouble.

charlie

WE LEFT the restaurant the same way we walked in, hand-in-hand, and yet it now feels like two completely different people walked out of there. Rafael hasn't taken his hand off me since. Currently, it's resting on my knee. He squeezes lightly, pulling my attention to him.

"You still like old rom coms, right?" His focus remains on the road, eyes only flicking my way for a second.

"Yeah, I do. But how do you know I like them?" I know for a fact we have never talked about this.

"Um, you mentioned it once. About two years ago, I think. I mean, you were talking to Lainey, but I was sure I heard you say you liked romantic comedies, especially from the nineties and two-thousands." He pulls into a gravel driveway, only removing his hand from my knee to reach for his wallet in the center console.

He remembers a conversation we had two years ago. A conversation I can't even recall, but that he pulled this detail from.

The board in front of us says *10 Things I Hate About You* and *Love & Basketball*. Great movies.

"What is this place?" I look around at what looks like a wide-open parking lot, a few cars scattered around.

Rafael hands a man some cash and pushes the button to close his window. "A drive-in." His hand lands back on my knee.

"Like the ones in the movies?" I look around, taking in the giant screen that comes into view, the lights shining on the other side from the food trucks and snack stands.

"Like the ones in real life." He chuckles as he scans the place for a spot. "This one is a pop-up, but there are a few permanent ones around the city. Wait. *Wait*. Red, are you saying you've never been to a drive-in?" There's nothing but delight in his tone.

"That's what I'm saying, yes. When I lived in New York, we never went because we never had a car, and I guess no one has ever thought to take me to one in London." And I know Robert won't watch movies unless it's in his fancy home theater with pretentious leather recliners.

There aren't too many people here, but I notice that the crowd ranges from teenagers to people with mostly gray hair. I suppose between nostalgia and the sudden reemergence of all-things nineties and Y2K, this makes sense.

When I finish taking everything in, I turn to find Rafael already looking at me, that dimple-popping smile making my belly tighten. "Oh, honey bun, I'm so happy I get to be your first drive-in date."

It won't be my only first you get tonight.

His smile widens, and my cheeks heat. *Great.* Now I'm thinking out loud. Without missing a beat, he leans across the console, unbuckling my seatbelt and slowly releasing it into place. He tangles his fingers in my hair, holding me by the back of my neck. I don't know how he knows exactly how to touch me, but he does. Like he's been trained to know just how much pressure I like. "I'd like to have all your firsts, red, but since I can't, I'll take whichever I can get."

His lips touch mine, and immediately, I open up for him, needing to taste him again even though we were just making out thirty minutes ago. Sadly, this kiss doesn't last nearly as long. With his lips hovering over mine and his eyes still closed, he catches his breath, and I attempt to do the same. "I fucking *love* kissing you," he says softly against my skin. He presses his lips to mine again, then once more, and then his warmth is gone. The way he emphasized the word *love* plays over and over in my mind. The way he said it like he meant it, like I might be his favorite kiss, his favorite date, his favorite *everything*. No one has ever said they liked kissing me before, let alone that they loved it.

My body is tingling in so many places, my mind is racing through so many thoughts. I need a moment to process. I need a break from feeling so much all at once. Then my phone rings, and when I lift it, Robert's name lights up the screen. Rafael sees it, watches as I press on the side button, sending him to voicemail. I set my phone to *do not disturb*, knowing calls from Elaina and Maeve will still come through and shove the phone back into my purse.

I fight the urge to apologize, and I have a feeling Rafael wouldn't want me to, either. It's not my fault Robert has terrible timing.

"I'm going to go scope out the place, figure out where the washrooms are, and see what they have for food and drinks. You can get changed in the back seat. The windows are blacked out, so no one will see you. I'll come back in like ten or fifteen minutes and let you know what I find, then I can go get whatever you want, is that okay?" Those molten chocolate eyes are patient and kind as he yet again offers me exactly what I need. I nod, unable to let the words loose from the tightness in my throat, and a moment later, he's gone.

The car is quiet, except for the faint sound of music seeping in from outside and some faraway chatter. I settle into my seat, dropping my head back and taking a few calming breaths. Despite how wonderful this evening has been, I still find myself overwhelmed. In the past, if I'd had to ask to go somewhere else or excused myself for too long, my dates had either ended things immediately or appeared understanding in the moment, only to ghost me later or give some halfhearted excuse as to why we couldn't see one another again.

It's why I kept this part of myself mostly hidden from Robert. He described me as shy, introverted, sensitive to crowds and noises, never fully understanding the extent of things. I tried to explain it to him once, when he became a bit frustrated with me at Oxford because I was fidgeting too much during a study session. He told me everyone has a little ADHD and if autism was a spectrum, then everyone must be on it. I didn't push the issue. I'd heard all of that from my mother, too, when I received my diagnoses shortly before leaving for NYU. And then again, when I explained that the little pill I took every morning wasn't a cure or a fix, it was simply a tool to help me cope with ADHD, and that the same couldn't be done for autism.

And so, my mask was set more firmly in place. I could take it off at home, with my sister and with Elaina and nowhere else. And now I can take it off with Rafael, too.

After a few minutes of focusing on my breathing, my body starts to relax, and I find myself thinking of all my favorite moments from this evening, which turns into me essentially reliving the entire thing because it's all been amazing. I didn't know what to expect, but books, a completely private dinner, and a drive-in playing old-school romance movies were not it.

And then there's the kissing. Just thinking about Rafael kissing me makes my lips tingle. And other parts, too. I'd never experienced that all-consuming, full-body, I-think-I-forgot-my-name feeling. I was completely wrapped up in him, in us. And I think he was, too.

I get into the back seat and change into my comfy pants, a

tank top, and a zippered hoodie. I even packed my Birken-stocks and some socks because I am embracing at least some parts of living in sunny Southern California. It'll be a nice reminder of my time here when I'm back in London.

As I'm hopping over the console to get back into the front seat, I catch some movement outside of the car and see Rafael approaching. He opens the driver's door and slips back inside, placing two water bottles in the cup holders. "Woo, it got chilly out there. You look nice and cozy." He rubs his hands together and blows on them. "I managed to scope the whole place out for us."

Us. Not for me or because of me. For us.

"Thank you for doing that," I say, turning the vent, which is currently blowing warm air at my hands, toward him.

His lips turn up in a smile. "I got us some water, but I took pictures of all the menus in case you're hungry or you want anything else." Holding his phone up to his face, he unlocks it and hands it to me.

I put a hand out, indicating I don't need to take it. "I abso-lutely cannot right now, but thank you. Plus, we haven't had dessert yet."

His knowing smirk sends tingles down my spine as we both hear the innuendo in my words. "Right." He clears his throat. "I, uh, have a couple of blankets in the backseat, so if you want, we could get more, um, comfortable back there." His cheeks turn a peachy shade of pink I find absolutely fasci-nating. "Shit, there's no way to say that without sounding like I wanna feel you up in the backseat of my car, which I would love to do, obviously, because look at you, but that's not why I brought you here."

He rubs a hand down his face, looking up at the ceiling of the car like he's trying to find his next words there. I fight back a smile, thoroughly enjoying how flustered he is and offering no help.

"Okay, in all honesty, I hadn't really thought of the drive-in until I saw an ad for this pop-up today, and I didn't have time to clean my awful mess or go buy an air mattress so we could pop the trunk and be super comfortable, so I almost didn't do this at all, but when I saw the movies they were playing, I thought you might like it. Now, I wish I had planned this better because I don't want your first drive-in experience to be lame. I'll get the mattress for next time."

My eyebrows perk up, as if to question his statement, and he doesn't miss it.

"If there is a next time. If you want there to be one. Or whatever. Fuck." He whispers the last word, scratching the back of his neck, and I finally decide to put him out of his misery.

"I'm perfectly happy as we are, but I'm intrigued by the idea of an air mattress in the back. Is that what the people with their trunks raised are doing?" He looks out at the dozen or so cars around us and nods. "Hmm. Well, it probably would have been too cold to do that tonight anyway, so I think you made the right call." I offer him a smile, and I can almost see his nerves physically settle. "So, how does this work, anyway? How do we hear the movie?"

His grin widens, those side-by-side dimples causing my stomach to flutter. "Oh, pumpkin, I have so much to teach you." He licks his bottom lip, and I squeeze my thighs together.

Is everything an innuendo now? Will I ever be able to be around him again and not feel like this? Like everything we say and do is a lead-up to something else? I kind of like it, but I don't want it to feel like there's pressure for us to always be like this. Is that what being in a relationship is? Is it just constant sexual innuendos and trying to get each other naked? Shit, I hope not. There's no way I can keep up with that.

Rafael points to the screen in front of us, which is playing ads for local businesses, but I can't hear any sound. "In a couple of minutes, the screen will start playing the movie, and all we have to do is set the radio to the right frequency." He lifts the tickets the man at the gate handed him. With his tongue poking out of his lips, he plays with the radio buttons for a few seconds, then a jingle for a pizza place starts playing in the car.

"So, you're saying that we get to sit here while essentially wearing pajamas, in a private vehicle, eating all the snacks we want, where no one has to see us or talk to us, and we can control the volume of the movie?" He laughs, a proud *uh-huh* spilling out. "This is the best night of my life. Books. Private dinner. Private movie. Gourmet desserts. I might have to keep you forever, Machado." The weight of my thoughtless and hypocritical words, considering what I just said to him at the restaurant, hits like a bag of bricks straight to the chest. His smile falters, and he looks away, fiddling with the radio, then adjusting his seat, moving it back as far as it can go, and reclining it a bit. I do the same, attempting to fly past the awkwardness I caused.

The screen changes again as the movie starts and Rafael turns the volume up, not too loud. *10 Things I Hate About You* begins playing, and the parallels between the story and the screen and the one playing out in real-life between the two people in this car become impossible to ignore. I couldn't stand the sight of Rafael when we first met. I made so many assumptions about who he was. Look at us now.

About fifteen minutes in, he reaches back for the boxes of desserts. We got everything but the sorbet, for obvious reasons. He opens one up, offering it to me first with a plastic fork and spoon that Morgan must have packed for us. I take the plastic cutlery and cut into the cheesecake first. It's good. A true classic with fresh strawberries. I try the brownie next, which is delicious. It's when I try the chocolate chip cookie that my world changes. It's so chewy and soft, and there are three different types of chocolate chips in it—milk, dark, and white chocolate.

I keep the cookie but close the box, knowing I won't need any other desserts after I've had this one. On the last bite, I close my eyes and let out a satisfied moan. I let my head drop to the left, and when I open my eyes to thank Rafael for suggesting we get the desserts to go, I find him already looking at me, his eyes laser-focused on my lips.

"You can't be making noises like that when you're alone in a car with me, red." He puts his box of desserts away slowly, never taking his eyes off me.

"What do you mean?" I ask, confused and already a little turned on again simply from the way he's staring at me.

He props an elbow on the center console and reaches for me, his fingers finding their way into my hair again. "I mean, if you're gonna be making those noises when I'm with you, it better be because of me and not a damn cookie." His warm lips touch mine, and I inch my body closer to his, seeking out his warmth. When I taste the cheesecake on his tongue, I moan again because it definitely tastes better like this, when it also tastes like him.

He kisses me slowly, deliberately, like he enjoys tasting me as much as I enjoy him. And in the next instant, my thoughts get pulled to a dozen different places.

Can anyone see us?

My neck hurts.

I want to get closer to him, but I can't.

I decidedly do not like kissing in a car like this. Rafael must sense it, because he rears back suddenly. "You okay? What happened?" Every part of me knows he's asking out of honest concern, yet it still makes me feel like there's something wrong with me. Like I caused this rift, and now everything is awkward and weird. I've been here before, of course. I know the drill. "Red, talk to me. If I did something, I want to know." His hand moves from my neck to my shoulder, resting it there with a reassuring squeeze. I hate that he thinks he did something. I hate that I ruined the moment. So, I decide I might as well be honest about what's happening.

"It's not your fault; I was just uncomfortable. Because kissing in the car is kind of awkward when there's this whole thing between us, you know? With the armrest and cup holders and everything. My neck was sore, and I couldn't stop thinking about it all. I'm sorry. I always do this." I wrap my hoodie tighter around myself, trying to ward off the impending feelings I know are coming. Guilt, embarrassment, regret, insecurity.

His left hand moves down my arm as the right one tips my chin up, but I can't look at him. "You don't need to apologize. I want you to be comfortable in every way. And when we're kissing, I want us both to enjoy it, to be in the moment." His thumb moves along my chin, drawing little circles.

"You'd still want to kiss me? After that?" I do look up at him then, needing to see his response.

"I'll always want to kiss you, pumpkin." His earnest smile makes my eyes water. Apparently, it also makes me impulsive as I push him back into his seat and hop over the console to straddle him.

"I think I could be comfortable like this," I say as my breaths come faster, the adrenaline of simply doing without thinking pulsing through my veins. I watch as Rafael's eyes glide from my eyes to my nose, lingering on my lips before they continue down to my collarbone and my chest, where my hoodie's now gaping, exposing my tank top and the fact that I took the liberty of removing my bra earlier. "Is this okay?"

His answer is in the way his hands grab onto my hips, moving me closer to him. It's in the tip of his chin as he brings his lips to mine. In the way his lips part, asking mine to do the same.

My hands find their way to his hair again, and I love the

groan that reverberates through him when our chests press together, and my hips rock into him. This time, our kiss is hungry and urgent, and with every swipe of his tongue over mine, I grind harder onto him, reveling in the way his breaths grow more ragged and his grip on me tightens.

When I roll my hips again, feeling his hard length against my throbbing clit, I squeeze my eyes shut as a moan builds in my throat, forcing our lips apart. Rafael promptly latches onto my neck, his warm lips covering every inch of my skin.

"May I touch you?" I swear I feel my panties disintegrate.

I open my eyes for a brief moment, only to give him my answer so we can move forward with the certainty that he never has to ask me that question again.

"You can always touch me." I cradle his face in my hands and kiss him softly. "I want you to touch me," I say against his lips before tasting him again. Then his hands are every-where. Gripping my ass to align us better, around my waist, where his fingers graze my skin, up my back, where they massage and soothe, and finally around my torso, where his strong hands take hold of my breasts, his thumbs flicking my nipples back and forth over my top until I can't take it anymore and I'm gasping for air.

There's nothing but us in this moment, and when his hip thrusts up into me in time with my own movements, I teeter on the precipice of my orgasm. My back arches, bringing my chest closer to his face, and he yanks at my top, baring my breast to him where he licks and sucks my over-sensitive peak. I open my eyes to watch him and, as is usually the case, find his eyes already on me. This time, though, I see some-thing I've never seen before: desire.

My gaze flicks to the window, and my movements stiffen as I feel suddenly exposed. Rafael kisses up my chest, gingerly placing my shirt back in place. "It's just us, honey. No one can see us." He swirls his tongue on my pulse point, and I relax into him again. "I promise. I'd never let anyone else see you like this." His teeth graze my neck, the sharpness soothed by his tongue. "I've got you."

And knowing that I can believe him, I can trust him, I fall back into our rhythm, standing on the edge of that cliff again, but unable to jump.

With steady hands on my backside and my nipples brushing against his cashmere sweater, I close my eyes and focus on the sensations. Everything is heightened when he gently encourages me to keep going, not to stop. "You feel so fucking good." I feel his words against my skin and bring his hand back to my breast. "I've dreamed about you like this." The sweat gathers on my chest as I inch closer. "This is so much better than any dream." He matches my every thrust as I pick up speed. "That's it. That's my girl," he whispers as his grip tightens. "Fuck, Charlie."

And then I'm freefalling. Every muscle in my body tenses and relaxes simultaneously. Wave after wave of pleasure washes over every nerve ending, and when they finally subside, I collapse on a solid chest, arms wrapping tenderly around me. Rafael moves my unruly curls off my face, tucking some behind my ear and leaving kisses on my forehead as we try to catch our breaths.

He said my name. He said my name, and I came so hard I nearly passed out.

Blimey, I might be in trouble here.

34 /
i must be the biggest fucking moron on the planet.

rafael

I'VE NEVER GIVEN much thought to what heaven would look like, feel like, smell like. Now? Now, I know. It's this. It's Charlie's body tensing as she comes on my lap. It's the smoothness of her skin and her nipple on my tongue. It's the smell of roses and chocolate chip cookies.

It's *Charlie*.

She's relaxed now, hand sliding from my neck to my chest, where I'm sure she can feel my heart racing. Her face is tipped up, and I can't help but pepper her forehead with kisses. Seconds ago, she was the hottest thing I've ever seen, and now, she's adorably sated and limp, sighing as we both settle back into our regular rhythms. There's a small, relaxed smile on her face, and I'm thankful for the weight of her hand on my chest, because it aches heavily with the knowledge that this is temporary.

In a short time, Charlie has wormed her way into my every thought. And the weird thing is, it doesn't feel like effort. I always thought that Adam and Owen must be exhausted, always wondering how their partners are doing, always thinking of the next thing they want to do for them or when they'll get to see one another again. But it's the opposite of work. She fills a gap in my life I didn't even realize was there.

"Mmm. Dry humping. Big yes." Her eyes are still closed as she burrows deeper into me, that ache in my chest lifting as a chuckle is set loose. "I didn't take you for such an over-achiever, you know? We're really knocking things off the list." She giggles, lifting her chin to leave a kiss on my neck that sends a shiver through my whole body. It's the first time she's initiated a touch like this. Yeah, she jumped over the console and straddled me, but this is intimate. Sweet.

I tighten my hold on her, hoping to prolong the moment just a little while longer. She takes a deep breath and kisses my neck again. It's just a touch of her lips, but I'm not sure anything has ever felt so right. "You always smell so good," she whispers against my skin. "And this sweater is so soft." She fists my sweater like a blanket, and I chuckle in response. "I swear I feel that sound in my bones. Every time." She sighs again, her breath dancing across my skin. "This is kind of the perfect sensory experience. I could just…" She breaks off, and I wait for her to finish her sentence, but she never does. She's asleep.

I don't dare move. This is like that one time my cat fell asleep next to my leg. I didn't even want to breathe too hard because I was so scared she'd run off. So, I sit and enjoy every second I can get of Charlie letting her guard down and letting me in.

It lasts fifteen minutes. She wakes up and mumbles some-thing incoherent, moving her hips from side to side. I hold my breath and pray for my dick to keep it together and not make himself known. "Raf?" Her voice comes out raspy as she starts to untangle our bodies.

I loosen my grip on her to give her space. "Hi, gata."

"Hi." She sits up, stretching her arms. When she moves her hips again, I try to still her with my hands. She has no idea how much she's torturing me right now. "Ouch, my hips are going to feel this in the morning."

"Sorry, I didn't want to wake you. You looked so peaceful." I run my index finger along her cheek, moving the hair that's stuck there. She's a little disheveled, and it's so incredibly adorable that I can't help but smile.

She moves back on my lap, and I lift her and help her back into the passenger's seat. "I'm sorry I took a nap on you. Speaking of which, I think my legs are now asleep." She stretches them out, wiggling around in her seat the same way she had just done on my lap, and I miss it. I miss the feeling. "I should, um, find the loo."

"Do you want me to come with you?" The lot is well-lit, but I'd hate for her to get lost getting back here.

"I think I'm fine, but do you not need to go, too, and like… clean u—*Oh*. Oh. You didn't. Oh my God." Her cheeks turn a shade of red I don't think I've seen before. It's not the same as when I rile her up, and it's *definitely* not the same pink as when she's turned on. I've officially memorized that color. This is embarrassment. Her eyes dart to my lap, and it dawns on me that she's realizing I didn't come.

She reaches for the door, but I lean over her and stop her. She won't look at me, but I talk anyway. "I could have, believe me. I had to work very, *very* hard not to make a mess in my pants."

"You did?" Her voice is so small. I hate it. I hum a response, my words catching in my throat. "So, it's not because I did something wrong or—"

"No. God, no. You're perfect. I told you, red, a fucking dream. Better." I don't know who put this uncertainty in her head that she's anything but perfection. I wish I could undo it, make her see what I see.

"Okay," she whispers. "I should go." She sniffles, her eyes still on her lap.

"When you get to the end of the rows of cars, it'll be to

your left. It's pretty clearly marked. We're in section H, row 10." I release the door, and she nods, whispering *thanks*. And then, she's gone.

I pull at my hair, trying to calm down and remember that all I can do is reassure her, be a constant and steady source of safety for her.

By the time she returns, I'm so caught up in the movie that I don't register her being back until she shuts the door. Twisting my neck to look at her, I smile, seeing her bright orange-red hair piled on top of her head, her hoodie now zipped up to her neck. "Hey. Found everything okay?"

She answers me with a nod, tucking a stray strand of hair behind her ear.

"Oh, I love this part." She slips her shoes off and tucks her legs up on the seat, resting her chin on her knee. We watch the rest of the movie like that, and when *Love & Basketball* starts, she settles into the seat and falls asleep within ten minutes. She doesn't even stir when I buckle her seat belt, and I drive us home, reliving every perfect moment of the night.

Once I'm in the parking lot of her building, I start to wonder how I'll wake her up, but the second the engine shuts off, she stirs and stretches. "Blimey, I've done it again. Would you believe me if I said I've never fallen asleep on a date before?" Rubbing her eyes and stifling a yawn, she sits up straight, noticing we're no longer at the drive-in with wide eyes. "I'm home."

"I just figured you're obviously tired, so I didn't want to keep you out any later. I'll help you take your stuff up." I open my door and retrieve her books from the trunk while she gets the stuff from the back seat. When I walk around to her side, she's already waiting for me. Charlie in skin-tight pants is wildly sexy, but Charlie in sweat pants with her hair in a bun and sleepy eyes? Well, that's a sight I could live with every day.

We walk up to her apartment in silence, and just as I'm about to say I don't even know what, she speaks up. "I'm sorry I ruined our date." She takes off her shoes, but I leave mine on, standing just inside the door as it clicks shut.

I set her things down. "Why do you think you ruined our date?" Because she didn't. If anything, I'm the idiot who should have taken her home after dinner and ended the night on a high.

"Because I made things weird. And I fell asleep. Twice!" A groan rumbles out of her, and she shakes her head, staring at her socked feet.

I take two steps toward her and cup her face with my hands. "You didn't ruin anything, carrot cake. I liked you falling asleep on me. I liked you falling asleep in my car. You wouldn't do that unless you were comfortable enough to." I leave a kiss on her forehead, and she finally looks up at me.

"You're such a nice guy," she says, her brows furrowing. Then, she surprises the shit out of me when she winds her hands behind my neck and pulls me down for a scorching kiss. After the initial second of shock, I catch up and move my hands to her ass, picking her up and backing her against the door. Her legs wrap around my waist, pulling us impossibly closer as our kiss becomes feral, all tongues and teeth, a delicious push and pull of control.

I drag my mouth down her neck, sucking on her pulse point. When she gasps, I know I have to make a decision: drag her to the closest couch or bed and fuck her until she can't walk straight, or stop this now before we go any further. "I should go," I say against her skin. I guess I'm going with option two. It's the right thing to do.

"You should stay." Her fingers tangle in my hair, holding me in place as I kiss every inch of her skin I can reach.

"It's late." My fingers grip her a little tighter. "I should go," I repeat. She answers me with a moan that has me wanting to punch myself in the face for choosing to stop this. "As much as I want to stay and fuck you right here against this door…" She arches her back, her heat lining up perfectly with my painfully hard cock, and my eyes roll to the back of my head. "We should wait." I pull my lips away from her flushed chest, which she protests to with a whimper, and I rest my forehead on hers. "Fuck, I must be the biggest fucking moron on the planet." I set her on the floor gently as her hands settle on the nape of my neck.

"No, you're probably right. I'm sorry I'm walking away from this date with an orgasm and two naps, and all you get is blue balls." The direct way she recounts our date makes me laugh, and there's immediate relief that we can still be ourselves, even with this new dynamic, even with the promise of sex and whatever else Charlie has on that list of hers. "Text me when you get home, okay?" She touches her lips to mine one last time, and we reluctantly separate.

"Okay. I'll text you in a few minutes." I take a mental picture of her flushed skin, her swollen lips, and her bright eyes. "Goodnight, red."

"Goodnight." She steps away from the door so I can open it and let myself out. I hear the click of the lock behind me and walk down the hall.

I don't even remember the elevator ride down or the drive home. I step inside, check that Pumpkin ate her food, and head straight to my room, where I unlock my phone to text Charlie. There's already a text from her waiting for me.

CHARLIE:

> What would you have done if you had stayed?

Shit. Fuck. One question, and I'm already hard again, for, what? The fourth time tonight?

ME:

> I'm home.

CHARLIE:

Great.

Now tell me what you would have done.

Would you really have fucked me against the door?

ME:

Maybe with my mouth, or my hand, yes.

CHARLIE:

I need details.

Tell me where you'd put your mouth.

ME:

First, I would need you naked so I can see every perfect inch of that body, get a look at those gorgeous tits again. Then, I would slide my fingers over your pussy, feel just how wet you are for me. How wet are you, red?

CHARLIE:

You want me to touch myself and find out?

ME:

Fuck yes

CHARLIE:

Only if you touch yourself too and tell me how hard you are for me.

I don't even bother taking my pants off. I push them down with my boxer briefs and lay on the bed, so fucking ready for this.

ME:

> Honey, I've been hard for you all night. From the moment I saw your ass in those pants to when we kissed at the restaurant, then when you came on my lap. I couldn't think of anything else even if I tried. So yeah, I have my fist wrapped around my very hard dick right now. Now, tell me exactly how wet you are.

CHARLIE:

> I changed my panties after you left because they were still wet from earlier.

> I'm going to have to change them again.

> I'm soaked.

> Going to need a toy to help me.

ME:

> Fuck. I bet I could easily slide into that tight pussy right now.

Her response doesn't come right away, so I figure she must be caught up touching herself, which is so fucking hot. Though as the minutes tick by, I start to get nervous that I have gone too far.

ME:

> Red? Was that too much?

Nothing. I sit and watch the screen until three dots finally pop up. Then they disappear. A minute later, her text appears.

CHARLIE:

> No.

> I'm sorry. Sexting is hard.

> I can't actually touch myself because I need my hands to text.

And just typing words feels weird.

I just wanted you to get off tonight, too.

ME:

Forget about me. Are you turned on, or did you just say that because it's what you thought I wanted to hear?

CHARLIE:

I'm actually turned on.

I really do want to use my vibrator, but I can't do that and type at the same time.

And I feel like I can't get into it if I'm also thinking about what to say to you.

I don't know what to do.

ME:

Can I call you?

I don't wait for her response; I hit the call button, and she picks up after a few seconds. "Hi," she says softly.

"Let me help you, red. Let me tell you what to do. Put the phone on speaker and get your toy." I put mine on speaker, too, and set it on my chest. I can hear her rustling on the other end. "Turn your vibrator on." The faint buzzing comes on almost immediately. "Don't worry about saying anything to me, okay? I just want to hear you enjoying yourself. Can you let me hear you?"

"Okay. Yes."

"That's my girl." A soft whimper leaves her lips, and my dick very quickly comes back to life. "Take all your clothes off, shortcake. I want you naked for me." More rustling, then silence. "Good. Now, I want you to play with your nipples. Nice and slow. Give them a little tug and a pinch so they're nice and hard. Then, run your thumb back and forth over them, just like I did earlier tonight. I could tell how much you liked that. Imagine it's me flicking them, licking them. Fuck, you tasted so good, red."

Her breaths turn into pants, with tiny little moans in between.

"Move one of your hands lower. I want you to flick your clit the same way as your nipple." My own hand finds a rhythm, pumping up and down on my cock.

She moans a little louder this time. "Are you touching yourself?"

"Do you want me to touch myself, red?" As if I could help myself when I know what she's doing, naked, in her bed.

"Yes. I want you to touch yourself. I want you to think of me. Imagine me. I want—" She pauses to moan again.

"Tell me. Tell me what you want." I could come right fucking now.

"I want to hear you. When you come," she gasps through a ragged breath, and I grip my cock a little harder.

"Grab your toy, red. Get it nice and wet. Feel the vibration on your clit. Does it feel good?"

"Yes. Oh, God, I'm so close already." The sound of her moans has pre-cum dripping down my cock.

"Not yet, honey. I want it inside you when you come." Her breaths slow and a long moan leaves her mouth. "That's it, push it in. Imagine it's me filling you up. Goddamn, I wanna fuck you so bad. Wanna feel that cunt gripping me." I'm the one panting now, our breaths equally fast.

"Ah, yes! There." Shit. I'm not gonna be able to hold back much longer.

"Fuck, yes. I'm so fucking close. Say my name for me, red. Say I'm the one making you come. God, you're so fucking pretty when you come." Damn it, I'm going to lose my mind.

A strangled sound comes out of her, and I picture her writhing on the bed, eyes shut tightly. "It's you, Rafael. You're the one making me come."

"Fuck, fuck, fuck. I can't stop. I'm gonna come. Oh, Charlie." Shocks of pleasure shoot through me as I grunt out my release.

"Raf, mmm." She mumbles something else, but I can't hear anything through the roaring in my ears. I come so hard I see actual stars dancing in front of me. "Oh… my… God. Best night of my life." She moans again with a soft chuckle at the end.

I look down and see the mess I made. "Ruined my sweater," I pant. "Worth it."

"Oh no! I really like that one. I'm particularly fond of how it feels on my cheek when I'm napping." I can hear the smile in her voice, can picture her sated and relaxed with her eyes closed.

"I'll buy you a hundred more, shorty," I promise.

"No, I want that one. It's special." She laughs harder, likely imagining just how special it is now that I have come all over it.

"You're amazing, you know that?" She hums a non-committal response. "I'm serious, Charlie. You are. I know you're probably joking or whatever, but this was one of the best nights of *my* life. Thank you." We lay in silence, our breaths slowing.

"I don't really do jokes, so…" The admission hangs there, somewhere between where she is down the street and here, like a balloon about to pop, filled with something neither of us is ready for. "I should, um, get cleaned up."

"Yeah. Yeah, me too." I would throw this sweater straight in the trash, but I might just live with the humiliation of taking this to the dry cleaners if it means something to her.

"Okay. Goodnight again, Raf."

"Goodnight again, gata."

35 /
you really are the nicest human.

rafael

I'M SETTLING INTO BED, still thinking of Charlie when my phone starts vibrating on my nightstand. The continual buzzing makes me smile.

CHARLIE:

Can I ask you something?

Things, actually.

I'm going to ask anyway.

So just say yes.

ME:

It's always a yes for you, strawberry shortcake.

CHARLIE:

Yeah, that's what I need to ask about.

What's with all the nicknames?

And where did shorty come from?

ME:

At first, I liked seeing you blush whenever I came up with a new one. I still like that, actually. I like it when you blush for me.

Shorty is just short for strawberry shortcake.

CHARLIE:

So even my nickname has a nickname?

I laugh, picturing her brows furrowing. I wonder if she's cozied up in bed, too.

ME:

I guess so, yeah.

CHARLIE:

Okay.

Also, you called me Charlie tonight.

Several times.

That was ten times now.

And you did it during some intimate moments.

Why?

ME:

Because saying your name has always felt intimate for me. Nicknames have been a way to keep my distance, even though I never wanted to. I've been fascinated with you since the moment we met, red.

No sense in sugar coating it. She's so much more than the girl I've been curious about for years now. More than my friend's sister and the woman I love to rile up. So, so much more.

CHARLIE:

But you still use the nicknames.

What does that mean?

ME:

That they're a part of us now. And that I'm probably a little bit obsessed with the color of your hair. I mean, red, carrot cake, pumpkin (pie and spice), Ginger Spice, strawberry shortcake...

CHARLIE:

What about Chuck?

ME:

I think we can retire that one. What do you think?

That nickname was strictly to piss her off. And the first way I put distance between us.

CHARLIE:

I don't know. It's sort of grown on me.

If you really don't like it, you can stop.

But just know that I don't mind it.

Just never call me Charlotte.

Or Lottie.

ME:

Deal. Any other questions?

CHARLIE:

No. I'm good for now.

I guess I can stop counting how many times you say my name now.

> Thank you again for tonight. For being so thoughtful and understanding.
>
> And for the orgasms, too, of course.

ME:

> You can keep counting, but I bet that number will grow pretty quickly now.
>
> Of course. Can't forget the orgasms. Thank you for asking me to be the one to do this with you.

When she doesn't respond, I put my phone back on my nightstand and settle in, hoping I'll dream of this night so I can relive it all over again.

I wonder how long it'll be before she realizes this *practice* relationship isn't that at all. That what we're doing here is real and meaningful and... No. I can't let myself go there.

———

WHEN I OPEN my eyes on Saturday morning, I'm still thinking of Charlie saying my name when she came... seven hours ago. Am I ever going to be able to think of anything else? The jury's still out.

With a groan, I pick up my phone to find a message from Owen.

OWEN:

> SOS – Please come over. Maeve is officially over being pregnant, and I don't know what to do anymore.
>
> I'll give you anything you want if you also bring Charlie.

Well, okay, then. Twist my rubber arm.

I text the requested guest first so I know what to tell Owen.

ME:

> Morning, shorty. Are you available to visit your sister by any chance? Our presence has been requested by her husband.

CHARLIE:

> Morning!

> I was just about to text you!

> Mae says Owen is driving her crazy and can't do anything right.

> Can I come with you?

> I still haven't worked up the nerve to drive.

ME:

> Yeah, of course you're coming with me, red. Pick you up in an hour? We'll stop and get the donuts Maeve likes. Maybe grab her some flowers or something to cheer her up?

CHARLIE:

> You really are the nicest human.

> Wow.

> See you in an hour.

In exactly an hour, I'm at her apartment door.

My girl is in black leggings and a cropped blue crewneck sweatshirt with the words *Oxford University* printed on the front. I lift up my index finger, motioning for her to turn. She rolls her eyes but does a full spin for me as a small smile plays on her face. Mine breaks into a full grin as I step inside.

"How do you get in here without being buzzed in?" She gets that cute crease between her eyebrows

"Aegis handles the security for this building, and I know

all the people that work for me. Or, at the very least, they know me." I wince, realizing I never asked for permission to do this. Shit. "I can stop. I'll call up. I never asked you if you were okay with me coming up, and I'm sorry."

"I'm fine with it." She waves a hand in the air, dismissing the topic entirely. "Since when does your company do the security for this building?" She crosses her arms over her chest, eyes narrowing at me. Shit. I've been caught.

"Um. Would you believe me if I said always?" I scratch the back of my neck, and her eyes narrow further, giving me my answer. "Fine. Since I found out you moved here." I shove my hands into my jeans pockets to stop myself from fidgeting.

Her arms lower and her eyes widen. "Why? Why did you do that?"

I shrug as worry seeps in. She might think I've over-stepped. I have no idea. Here goes. "Because the company that was doing it before was absolute shit. I looked into them, and I didn't like what was going on, so I found a way to take over their contract and now here we are. No big deal. You ready to go?"

"No," she answers. "I have a question." My head shoots up, expecting to see anger, disappointment, or annoyance. Instead, I'm met with blue eyes that are ablaze. "Have you been tested for STDs lately, and if so were your results clear?"

I have no clue what's going through her head, but I answer. "After my last partner. All clear."

Charlie grabs at the lapels of my jacket and pulls me to her. "How dare you look this good at nine o'clock in the morning and be this thoughtful all the damn time." She all but climbs my body, then crushes her lips to mine. I don't miss a beat. My hands are on her, greedy for every inch of those delicious curves. Pulling her lips off mine, she stretches her neck, silently asking for my lips there. "Did you tell them a time? Are we going to be late if we—"

"No, I didn't," I answer quickly. "If we what?" Her skin is already that perfect pink; flushed and warm for me.

"If we have another lesson. There's something I want to cross off the list." Her hands roam over my back, nails scratching deliciously at the skin. Then, she lowers to her knees in front of me, and I whimper at the sight. I must be dreaming, so I don't stop her as she works the button on my jeans. Dropping my jacket to the floor, I pull my shirt off, watching those curious blue eyes as they map out my skin. "Blimey, it *is* better than the apron." Her hands continue working, and with her fingers wrapped around the waist-band of my boxer briefs, she looks up at me. "May I?"

"Fuck, yes." My voice is already strangled. Charlie is on her knees. For me. I'm so hard it hurts.

"Tell me what to do. I've never done this." Her eyes lock with mine, and slowly, so painfully and deliciously slowly, she lowers my pants and underwear at the same time.

With her eyes steady on mine, she rubs her hands up my thighs and continues her exploration, fingers skimming the ridges of my abs. When her gaze finally lowers, her eyes widen, her lips pursing as she swallows hard.

"Wow. Um. This is… you're so… big. Thick." The tip of her finger skims around the head of my cock, then she runs it down to the base, and I have to clench my hands into fists to keep my groan inside. Charlie is touching me. Fuck. Think about something else. Baseball. Puppies. Anything less sexy than this right now.

Her fingers wrap around me, and she gives me a slow, steady pump as if getting acquainted with my cock. "Raf?" I force my eyes open, not having realized I'd closed them. "What do you want me to do?"

"Lick it," I answer without hesitating. "Please." Can't forget my manners. Her tongue follows the same path as her finger, then she swirls it around the tip. "Again," I beg. She licks and licks until I'm completely coated in her spit. "Now, wrap those pretty pink lips around my cock."

She gasps but does exactly what's asked of her. With one hand wrapped around the base, she sticks out her tongue and takes me in her mouth little by little, adjusting to the invasion.

When she moans around me, my hands instinctively go to her head, holding her in place. She takes more of me in, panting as she tries to breathe around me. "If it's too much, you can stop," I tell her, moving my hand back to my side. She shakes her head and reaches for my hand, placing it back in her hair, and I nearly lose my fucking mind. She takes me deeper, moaning again. I pull back, and she lets me go with a pop. "Catch your breath, red. And when you take me back in your mouth, take slow breaths through your nose."

She catches her breath, spits on her hand, and starts to pump my cock in a slow rhythm. "Am I doing okay? You can tell me."

"Better than okay. You're perfect." Hearing my praise, she squeezes her thighs together. "That was so fucking hot. Now, work me faster." She picks up her pace and takes me back into her mouth, continuing to use her hand as well. "That's it. You're doing so well. And when you finish here, I'm gonna finally taste that pussy. Feel how wet you are for me. Would you like that?"

She nods, watery blue eyes connecting with mine.

"You look so gorgeous like this, with my cock in your mouth. Now, suck." Her cheeks hollow, and I nearly come right then. "S-so good. Ah, I'm close. Do you want me to pull out?" Furrowing her brows, she shakes her head no, then she shocks the hell out of me when she takes my balls in her other hand. She doesn't stop there. She slips a finger right behind them and presses down on a spot no one has ever touched before, and I come immediately. "Ohhhh shiiiiiiiiiiit, Charlie." She continues to suck as I come, and on my last shudder, she moves her mouth off me, then she's standing, eyes wide as saucers, cheeks puffed out. She runs to the kitchen sink and spits into it, then cups some water into her hand and brings it to her mouth to swish around.

I fight the urge to laugh at the scene playing out, but I know damn well that would do me no good. She washes and dries her hands then stands at the counter, facing away from me. Giving her a minute, I pull my pants back on, and walk the few steps to the kitchen. Placing my hands on her hips, I take it as a positive sign when she doesn't move away. I wrap my arms around her and rest my chin on her shoulder. "Talk to me, gata. What's going on?"

"I'm sorry. I thought I could, but then it was in there, and I... There was no way..." Her words are muffled as she brings her hands to her face, but she has to know there's no apology necessary here. I turn her to face me, gently moving her hands to my chest.

I take her face in my hands and start to gently massage around her jaw. "I'm honestly not sure I would enjoy semen being shot into my mouth, so I don't blame you. Not even a little bit. Is your jaw okay? Does it hurt?"

She lets out a low hum, not answering the question, and when I tip her face up to me, she lets me. "No, I'm okay. You're not disappointed?"

"Disa—no! No. That was... oh my God, I don't even have words for what that was. How did you know to slip your finger there? That's never... I've never... that was incredible. I'm gonna be thinking about this for the rest of my life, short-cake." She pulls her lower lip between her teeth, smiling around the movement.

She shrugs, inching her hands further up my chest, her fingers playing with the few hairs there since I didn't put my shirt back on. "I read a few articles. I wanted to be good at this."

"Oh, honey, you are. You're excellent. The very best." I

pepper her cheeks with kisses, and she giggles. "Now, take off those leggings. Let me see that soaked pussy."

Her answer is a gasp. "Oh. You still want to? But you don't have to. It's not on the list, I—"

"Fuck the list, Charlie, and let me fuck *you* with my mouth. You want to know what a relationship is like? This is how it should be. With your man desperate to taste you." I kiss her jaw, then her neck, sucking at that spot over her pulse that makes her squirm. "Please, pumpkin. I'm dying here." I squeeze her tighter against me, knowing I'll never want to let go now.

"So dramatic," she pants, and we both laugh. Goddamn, I love laughing with her. Especially like this. It just feels so right. She runs her fingers through my hair and kisses me lightly on the lips. "Okay," she whispers. "Yes. Fuck me with that filthy, glorious mouth." I don't need to be told twice. I shove her leggings and panties down to her knees and pick her up, setting her down on the countertop. She yelps at the shock of the cold.

"Shit. I should have thought about that." I set her feet back on the floor and quickly grab my discarded jacket, laying it on the countertop behind her before picking her up again. Then I yank at her bottoms, tossing them on the floor behind me.

Charlie eyes me for a moment, waiting for instructions. "Lie back for me. Let me see you." I lick my lips, anticipating my first taste of Charlie. Fuck, I hope it's not my last. She leans back on her elbows, still watching me as she lets her legs fall open. My eyes immediately go to the apex of her thighs. "Goddamn, shortcake. You're dripping. That's all for me?" Please say yes. Please say yes.

"Yes." Her voice is clear, but her chest is heaving with her quickened breaths. "Rafael?" I meet her eyes again. "Touch me." No preamble. No please. So very Charlie.

I start at her ankles and massage my way up her legs, kissing the insides of her knees. Her legs start to shake, so I grab hold of them, pulling her closer to me, kissing down her thighs. I take her in up close, the one strip of red hair leading down to the only place I want to be right now. Dragging my finger from her entrance to her clit, I move it around her sensitive spot, but never over it. Again and again, I tease her. "Beautiful," I say right before I move my finger over the tight nub, just once, making her groan. "Mine," I say, so quietly I'm not even sure she hears me. I repeat the movement as she writhes and whimpers. Then, I lick, and lick, and lick. I put my tongue and my lips everywhere except where she wants me most, until she's panting. Desperate. *Wild.* I take her clit into my mouth and suck gently, and she screams my name.

Fuck, yes.

I continue, alternating between flicks and a slower movement with the pad of my tongue, until I feel and hear what she likes best. "Mmmm, so good," she mumbles, fingers tangling in my hair, right where they belong. "Don't stop."

I don't ever want to stop. Nothing's ever tasted so good, so mine.

Mine.

That word plays in my head over and over.

Mine, mine, mine.

I push a finger into her, making her moan a little louder. Not enough, it tells me. I add another, and she gasps, her inner walls tightening around my fingers. "That's right, gata. Let me feel your tight pussy gripping my fingers. You take it so well. Like you're gonna take my cock." She tightens around me again, and I go back to lavishing her clit with my tongue, curling my fingers inside her.

"Fuuuuck. Raf!" She screams my name again and again, and I don't let up until her legs finally relax. I pull my fingers out, licking them clean, because Charlie is a taste I'll never have enough of. I know that now.

I wipe my mouth with the back of my hand, then pull her limp body into mine and hug her close, her head resting on my shoulder, her breath on my neck. I want to kiss her, but given her reaction earlier, I'm not sure if that's a deal breaker for her. But again. Charlie is full of surprises. She nips at my neck and kisses the same spot, then lifts her head to look at me, and our lips meet, her tongue swiping over mine as she moans into my mouth. Yeah, I've got the perfect woman.

Reluctantly, I pull back. "I know I said we wouldn't be late, but…"

"We should go," she finishes for me. "Yes. You're right. Let me go clean up." As she scurries away from me, clutching her leggings to her body, I already miss her.

36 /
you just like know all that?

rafael

WHEN WE'RE ABOUT to arrive at Owen and Maeve's house, donuts in tow, Charlie turns to me. "We have to… They can't know. No one can know. You know that, right?"

"About what, red?" She rolls her eyes at me, and yet again, my dick takes notice. "About how you had my dick in your mouth a couple of hours ago? Or how you came on my tongue?" Reaching over, she flicks me on the ear, and I wonder if she learned that from Vó or if she's also exceptionally good at inflicting pain with such a small movement. I take her hand and kiss her knuckles. "Or do you not want them to know how much I like kissing you? How you're my favorite taste in the world? Is that what you don't want them to know?"

Her answering blush travels from her cheeks to her neck. "Your filthy mouth is truly relentless."

"Yeah, but you like it, carrot cake." I wink at her, and she scoffs. Our old dynamic comes back easily, but now it's got a fresh foundation. One built on trust, understanding, friendship, and something I'm sure I'm not allowed to name.

Walking into the James household, Charlie is immediately whisked away by her sister. Owen steers me to a table outside, where Adam is nearly inhaling a cup of coffee.

"Hey, man. We brought donuts, but good luck prying them away from the girls." I give him a pat on the back and move to sit next to him.

"We?" He sets his cup down and gives me a knowing look. "You and Charlie are *we* now, huh? I guess the hate game you were playing has finally ended?"

"Well, we arrived together, if that's what you mean." I pour myself some coffee from the carafe someone must have brought out earlier. "And I never hated her. You know that."

Both of my friends hum a non-committal response, and when the conversation moves to Adam's latest project and Owen's expansion of the stables, my brain stays laser-focused on every minute I've spent with Charlie, which is probably why the question slips from my lips. "How did you guys know?" They both look at me, waiting for me to explain what the fuck I'm talking about. "That she was the one, how did you know?" Adam is about to start answering , but I cut him off. "Actually, never mind. You don't need to answer that. You fell in love with Lainey the second you saw her shaking her a—" I stop myself and glimpse at Owen, who is already shaking his head.

"Were you really just about to say my brother-in-law fell in love with my little sister when he saw her ass?" He rubs a hand down his face in exasperation. He had to watch Lainey and Adam fall in love, just like the rest of us did. But I don't feel bad.

"You know what, yeah. I was. And I'm not even sorry about it because you fuckers had to go and fall in love with women I was already friends with. Not my fault one of them is your little sister." I shrug, watching as both men rear back in surprise.

"Dude. You okay?" Adam asks. I don't know what's gotten into me. I don't actually give a shit that they fell in love with my friends. I love that we've built this little family. It just also feels like I don't belong here on my own anymore. Even with their wives in another room, they're not alone. They belong to a whole new family now.

Choosing not to dwell on my shit, I shake off the sadness that could surely bring me to tears right here and move on. "I'm fine. Owen, can you please answer my question?" The question I didn't mean to ask. The question that I can't stop thinking about now that I've kissed Charlie. Now that I've tasted her.

"All right. Well, I guess I knew when we started talking more. When she'd ask me to tell her something good. It was just this feeling, like I don't know, man, like I just felt better about everything, even while we were deployed. I don't know how to explain it." Owen and I both look at Adam, knowing he's got the answer sitting on the tip of his tongue.

"It's like some part of you that was always missing is there now. When I'm around her, I'm complete. The air is easier to breathe. The colors are brighter. Everything is better. Loving her isn't something I do; it's just part of who I am. It's automatic. Subconscious. Like breathing or blinking or closing your eyes when you sneeze. It just is." I watch as my best friend smiles, no doubt thinking about his wife.

Loving her isn't something I do; it's just part of who I am.

Owen nods, pointing at Adam. "Yeah. What he said."

I stare at Adam, wide-eyed. "Jesus, man. You just like *know* all that?"

His smug smile stays firmly in place. "Yeah. And if Charlie makes you feel any of those things, even just one of them, then this is worth exploring. Don't sell your feelings short."

Owen continues to nod, and I join him before realizing

what's just been said. "Wait. What? Who said anything about Charlie?"

My two best friends look at each other and then burst into laughter.

Assholes.

I fucking love these guys.

stop talking about my brother's dick!

charlie

MAEVE PULLS me into the living room, where Lainey is quietly breastfeeding her daughter. They both look tired, but different kinds of tired. Lainey looks happy, content, even as she yawns. Maeve looks a little crazed.

"You brought donuts? Oh, thank God. Owen keeps trying to feed me real food when all I want is donuts and french fries." She rolls her eyes, taking the box from my hands and setting it on the coffee table. She doesn't even take a moment to smell them as she normally would, just bites into one without wasting time.

"How rude of your husband to look out for the well-being of you and your unborn child," I say, pressing a hand to my chest, and Elaina giggles. "Was that the emergency, Mae? You needed donuts instead of fruits and vegetables?"

"No," she answers around a mouthful, then swallows. "Well, yes. I don't know. It's like everything he does is driving me bananas. I love Owen, obviously, but I kind of want to smother him with a pillow when he's sleeping. Because I'm *not* sleeping. And how dare he be able to simply lie down, close his eyes, and rest without having to toss and turn or get up to pee three hundred times a night. And don't get me started on the heartburn." She takes another bite of her donut as I stare at her with wide eyes.

I reach for the box of donuts. "You shouldn't be eating these—"

"Don't you dare!" She slaps my hand away. Obviously, pregnancy hasn't messed with her reflexes because that was unnaturally agile. I sit back, lifting my hands in surrender.

"Where's Jules?" I look around as if the tiny almost-toddler could be hiding somewhere.

"She's just out for a walk with Eva. My mother-in-law is a sweet angel sent from heaven. She's somehow juggling helping Bon and making time to be with Julia." Maeve sniffles, shoving another piece of donut into her mouth. She mumbles something that sounds like "she's amazing" and then starts sobbing.

Elaina looks on with sympathetic eyes, while I have no idea what to do. I settle for hugging my sister, who leans into me and continues to cry for a few minutes. Once she quiets down, I nudge her to lay her head on my lap, and I start to play with her hair like we used to do when we were kids. "Do you want to watch some episodes of *The Office* until they get back?" Even if I'd rather watch *Friends*, I know this is Maeve's favorite show.

She nods and pulls her legs up as far as her belly will let her. Within two minutes, she's fast asleep.

"She's so tired. This last stage of pregnancy is so hard." It's no surprise that Elaina sympathizes.

"You would know. Yours was tough the entire time. And yet here you are, looking like you've never been happier." I continue running my fingers through Maeve's soft, straight hair, so unlike my own, yet nearly as familiar to me.

"Yeah. You're right about that." She smiles at Agnes, now sleeping next to her, then looks back at me. "How are you doing, Char? I haven't forgotten that we need to talk about the little bomb you dropped on us, by the way. But first, tell me how you're doing." Of course she didn't forget I told her I'm the author of the romance series she and her husband are turning into movies. I've managed to have my agent attend every meeting on my behalf, and it seemed like everyone understood my need to remain anonymous since a lot of authors have pen names.

"I'm... um... things are good. Really good." Her eyebrows shoot up, and her smile widens. "I really like Santa Monica, and I've been writing a bit more lately. I feel like I'm finding my stride here, and... I'm happy."

"Happy enough to stay?" she asks hopefully.

"I'm not sure. It's only been a few weeks, and Robert keeps asking when I'll be back to get things moving with the CFO transition and with us." Just thinking about it has my stomach in knots.

Elaina's eyes are full of sympathy. "I understand. It's a lot to think about. But now that we know you're C.M. Howe, do you think you might like to be a bit more involved in the process of making the movies? I feel like we're always defaulting to your agent, and he's great and all, but he's not *you*, you know?" There's a hint of guilt in her demeanor. She told Adam. Of course she did; he's her husband. I'm not going to be upset about that, but...

"Does anyone else know?" I ask quietly. It's very possible Adam talked about it with Rafael, and he's been keeping it secret from me, even if we did agree to honesty at all times.

"I asked Adam not to say anything. I'm sorry I told him. I was just so excited that it's you." She fidgets nervously with the end of the baby blanket on her lap.

I wave away her concern. "Oh, it's fine. Don't worry about it. I just haven't told Raf yet. But I will." I know I have to.

"Raf, huh? Not Rafael?" Her hands relax, and a small smile tips the corners of her lips up.

"We've been friendlier with one another. He's really nice."

Nice. It's been my word of choice lately when I think about all the things Rafael actually is. Kind. Thoughtful. Safe. Perceptive. Irresistible. Hot. Sexy. *So damn sexy.* All. The. Time.

Like when he's making me come with his mouth. Or when he kisses me. When he looks at me like he wants me. Definitely when he says things like, *Fuck the list, Charlie, and let me fuck you with my mouth. You want to know what a relationship is like? This is how it should be. With your man desperate to taste you.*

But he's not that. He's not my man. He's just helping me, and he's doing a damn fine job of it.

Focusing back on the present, I noice Lainey's eyes are filled with tears, which is perfectly normal for her. "Thank you. Thank you for making an effort to get to know him." Her eyes widen, and she gasps. "Has he been helping you? With your book?"

Oh boy. I won't lie, but I can't tell her the whole truth. "Um, yeah, I've felt a bit more inspired lately." There. Not a lie.

She clasps her hands together, quietly clapping. "I can't wait to read it!"

We watch *The Office* in silence for a couple of episodes until Maeve stirs. "I smell donuts," she mumbles. "Oh, I love this episode." She's been awake for thirty seconds; how can she possibly know this is the episode when Pam and Jim finally kiss? Then again, she's probably watched this show a hundred times.

"Hey, how did you know that you were in love?" It's a question that's been on my mind a lot recently, with Robert suddenly feeling so sure about us and me feeling so not.

"Adam has always been so steady. He's my calm, and no offense to either of you because you're my bitches and I'd kill for you, but he's my best friend, too." She pauses in thought. "It took me a while to admit to myself that I was in love with him because I was scared, but when I saw him in Marblehead, there was no doubt in my mind. And, um…" She rubs at her chest, like she's applying a balm. "With Andy, it was the kind of love that grew from feeling like someone finally understood me, no judgment, no conditions. We were that for each other, and of course, it's like that now, too, but falling in love at eighteen is very different from at twenty-eight."

"Hmm. Yeah, I mean, I've only ever loved one man, but the love I feel for him now and the love I felt at nineteen? Totally different." Maeve pats her belly, her eyes glistening with unshed tears. "I knew I loved Owen at nineteen because his presence alone, even through a screen, was enough to make me feel alive. Seeing him, knowing he was safe, it was like oxygen to my air-deprived lungs." She shakes her head, a sad smile playing on her lips. I know how difficult those years without Owen were for her, even if she never talked about it. "And then last year, being around him again, seeing how he relentlessly loved me, I finally saw myself as worthy of that love too. Plus, he has a really great dick, and boy, does he know how to use—"

"I was just about to say how sweet that was." Eva's gentle voice comes from the other side of the room.

"What the fuck, Ma! Are you some kind of ninja, sneaking in here so quietly?" Lainey hisses as she rubs at her temples, then sets her eyes on Maeve. "And for the love of all that is good in this world, stop talking about my brother's dick!"

Maeve's first response is a laugh. "Never, Bon. Your reaction is just too good. Though, I am sorry you walked in on that, Ma. That was not for your ears." She shoots her mother-in-law an apologetic look, which Eva scoffs at.

"Oh, please. You're not even a little bit sorry." She laughs, and we all follow suit.

"How did you know, Eva? If that's not a totally inappropriate question, that is." I add that in quickly, not wanting to be insensitive to either Elaina or Eva.

"Not at all, sweetheart. Oh, I knew I loved Douglas when we went away together for the first time, and I got my period.

Instead of being totally grossed out or disappointed, he got me all my favorite snacks, movies, and a hot water bottle. We'd only been dating for a couple of months, and he told me he'd always take care of me. I believed him. And he never failed on that promise." She sniffles, and there isn't a dry eye in the room. Not even mine. Wiping away her tears, she looks me in the eye with so much kindness that it's impossible to look away. "There are lots of ways to know, Charlie. There isn't a right one, only a right one *for you*. A right moment, a right action, a right person. You'll know. Trust that. Trust your heart." Her smile is both reassuring and calming.

Trust my heart? But I've never done that before. I'm a logical person. I gather facts, weight them against one another and then make a decision. What does my heart have to do with that? What if my heart makes the wrong decision? Not that my brain has been any better at it lately.

You'll know. Trust that.

I let those words comfort me, and I hope with everything in me that Eva is right.

38 /
stop ignoring me,
charlotte.

charlie

WE ENDED up staying for lunch, and my sister seemed in better spirits by the time we all left, just in time for Julia's second nap. Maeve's, too.

We've just driven out of their neighborhood when Rafael turns to me. "Hey, do you want to practice driving? The roads are super calm here. No pressure, though." He sets a reassuring hand on my knee.

"Yeah, all right." My immediate answer surprises me because we didn't plan this, and I like plans. A lot. But I know that if I'm uncomfortable, he won't push me. I know I'll be able to stop and he'll take over without a fuss.

"Nice," he says happily. "Let's gooooo!" He jostles my leg, and as much as I want to roll my eyes, I simply laugh at his silliness.

When he pulls over, he's careful to adjust my seat, buckle me in, and make sure all of my mirrors are where I want them. Then he pecks me on the lips, as if it's the most natural thing, and jogs to the passenger side. "Whenever you're ready, pumpkin."

I pull onto the road, checking the mirrors and telling

myself over and over to stay on the right side. It's not as difficult as I expected, but Raf's silence makes me slightly anxious. "Can you please say something?" I chance a look at him, and of course, he's as cool as a cucumber. "Just talk to me."

"How do you think we did today at Maeve and Owen's?" It's a casual enough question, but there's apprehension in his voice.

"Great. I told the girls we've been making an effort to be friendlier, and they were well chuffed."

His chuckle is low and rumbly and I have to bite the inside of my cheeks to keep from having a *very* physical reaction to it.

"Well chuffed," he repeats. "God, you're adorable." He reaches over to touch my hair, and I feel my cheeks heat in a brand-new way. Adorable feels new. It feels warm and bubbly in my limbs. It feels affectionate. Personal.

I continue driving as he talks about something that happened at lunch, but I'm not listening. I feel a little guilty, but I can't focus on his words right now, though I'm also thankful he's not silent.

"Sorry, is it okay if I stop now? It looks like traffic is picking up."

"Yeah, of course." He directs me where to pull over, and within five minutes, the car is stopped again. He jogs over to my side and opens my door before I get to it. I turn my body to exit the car, but Raf wraps his arms around my waist and holds me in place, standing between my legs.

Steadying hands run up my back, rubbing my shoulders. How does he know exactly where I'm tense? I drop my head forward on a moan and rest my forehead on his. Our breaths mingle, and when he moves his hands down, I tilt my head, unthinkingly seeking out his lips. We kiss without hurry, without needing the kiss to lead to anything else. It's kissing simply for the sake of it.

When we finally break away, he kisses my jaw, my cheeks, my temples. He kisses as many spots as possible before he lingers on my lips for another few seconds. "You did so great. I'm proud of you."

"Why?" There's more bite to my question than intended, but he's unshaken, proven by the smile on his handsome face.

"Because you did something you had been nervous about. You did something hard today. So, I'm proud of you. I'm proud of you for showing up for your sister, too. I'm just proud of you for how amazing you are, even though I had nothing to do with it. I hope you're proud of yourself, too." He kisses me one more time and steps back.

He's proud of me.

When was the last time anyone told me that? My heart squeezes, and the ache left behind is wildly uncomfortable. It's an ache that fuels my guilt. An ache that tells me I need to talk to him about the books, about the CFO position that's waiting for me in London, about all of the details about Robert—that he wants to marry me and why I agreed to that once upon a time. We promised honesty, and here I am withholding information. It's not right.

With that knowledge, I allow the remainder of the drive to be a quiet one, and when Rafael drops me off at home, I kiss him goodbye. I kiss him, knowing that wanting to kiss him this much isn't part of fulfilling my list or practice for being in a relationship, but caring less and less about those facts.

Later at night, as I'm about to doze off, my phone vibrates. With thoughts of Rafael fresh in my mind, I pick it up, hoping it's him. It's not. And the four words on the screen bother me a lot less than they would have a few weeks ago.

ROBERT:

Stop ignoring me, Charlotte.

39 /
i will do unspeakable things.

charlie

THE THREE SOFT knocks at my door have the butterflies in my stomach fluttering like crazy.

We didn't see one another on Sunday or Monday, but now, Rafael's here to pick me up so we can go to Siesta. It's much earlier than last time, but I didn't bother questioning it. I'm glad to see him sooner.

I open the door and don't even get the chance to say hi before his arms are wrapped around me and he's pushing his way inside. I hear the door shut, but nothing else registers. Nothing but his lips on mine, the urgency of his touches, the desperation of his kisses down my neck. "I missed you, carrot cake. I missed you so fucking much. How the hell do you do that?" He tugs at the collar of my buttoned shirt, sucking on the soft flesh of my breast. "How do you make me miss you this much after only two days?"

I don't know. I don't know because whatever it is, he's doing it, too. I missed him.

Missed his laugh and his smell.

Missed these kisses and his sweet words.

I'm not sure if this is practice, and I can't bring myself to care because he feels so good. This whole thing, it feels so, so good.

He tugs at my bra, pulling it down, and just before his mouth latches onto my nipple, I stupidly stop him. "Raf, wait." Immediately, he puts my clothing back in place, adding some space between us.

"I'm sorry. Fuck, I'm sorry." He tugs at his hair with both hands as his typical self-deprecating thoughts are no doubt running through his mind.

"No, I quite enjoyed that greeting; I'm only worried about time. Don't we have to go?" I attempt to straighten my hair, despite how much I like it when Raf musses it up.

"No, I came early to spend time with you. Just you. But we don't have to—I can go and come back later." He's backing up toward the door, but I can't let him leave. I don't want him to leave. I want him to stay and do delicious things to me. *With me.*

"How long do we have?" I walk with him, not wanting the distance between us to grow.

"Uh, couple hours at least." He lifts his shoulders, and my heart starts hammering. I want him to stay. Surely, we can do something else from the list. Yes. The list. That's why he's here.

I start to unbutton my shirt, and his back hits the door. Wide-eyed, he watches the movement of my steady fingers and then his eyes move over my chest. I'm wearing a simple cotton bra, yet the way Rafael looks at me makes me feel like I'm wearing the most gorgeous lingerie.

Reluctantly, I turn and walk away, unclasping my bra and dropping it on the hall floor. That's when I hear his soft footsteps behind me. He must have taken his shoes off. Always so thoughtful.

As I walk into my bedroom, I shimmy out of my leggings, leaving my thong on. I hear the rustling of clothing and items dropping to the floor behind me. Just the thought of Rafael getting undressed has heat pooling between my legs. I stop at the foot of my bed, and he stops behind me, the warmth of his body sending a shiver through me.

"You're not cold, are you, shortcake?" I shake my head as his fingers trail a path from my wrist to my shoulder. He moves my hair to one side and lowers his lips to my neck. He nips and sucks, kisses, and licks until I'm melting into his hard body. "Are we knocking an item off the list today?"

"Yes," I pant, his hands touching all of my curves, my soft spots, and finally landing on my breasts.

He groans, pulling me tighter against him. "Get your toy. Toys. Whatever you want to use to get off while I watch you." His voice is soft but commanding, and before I can think too much about what he's just told me to do, I'm already at my nightstand, taking lube and the same vibrator I used the night we had phone sex. He takes both from my hand and tosses them on the bed, and then he takes me in for the first time. With enough distance between us for him to see all of me, I suddenly feel self-conscious. My arms cross over my abdomen, my skin heating from embarrassment as my eyes dart to the floor.

"Oh, Charlie, we can't have that." He steps closer, cupping my face in his hands. He tips my face up and kisses me gently, tenderly. "Your body is… Fuck, I don't even have the words for how perfect you are. Every curve, every dip, every rosy blush over your creamy skin… Goddamn, gata. I can't get enough." My arms drop to my sides, and his hands begin exploring once again. "These tits," he says as he rolls my nipples between his fingers. "I've daydreamed of these ever since the first time I saw them." He lowers his head, kissing and licking a slow, torturous trail until my nipple is in his mouth.

I moan as his tongue flicks back and forth slowly, my hands reaching for his hair to hold him there a little while longer.

His hands move lower, grabbing at my hips and lingering there, like he's testing the feel of them in his hands. Then, his fingers slip under my thong as he pulls them down as he drops to his knees. "These hips, this ass, this goddamn pussy that has me so fucking whipped. Fuck, Charlie, I will do unspeakable things if it means I can worship this body." He's eye-level with my very wet, very warm center. "Would you let me? Would you let me worship your body?" His eyes meet mine, and I've never felt as powerful as I do in this moment, with him on his knees for me, asking to worship me.

"Yes." Despite the intensely saturated desire coursing through every one of my veins, my voice comes out firm. He keeps his eyes on mine, but his mouth latches on to me, his tongue slipping in to toy with my clit. He moans, his hands gripping each of my ass cheeks as his eyes roll to the back of his head. With a final flick of his tongue, he moves his mouth over my body to my hips, trailing kisses across my soft belly, up my ribcage, over my breasts, and up my neck until he's standing at his full height again, lips brushing over mine.

"I know it doesn't matter what I think. It matters what you think. I want you to see what I see." Naked and clearly very comfortable that way, he walks away from me, picks up the large mirror propped up next to the closet, and brings it to the wall closest to the bed. Turning toward me, he sits on the bed and widens his legs, patting the spot between them.

"Come here." I move to sit, and he helps me, pulling me closer. We're not quite back to front as I lean on his left leg, my right shoulder resting on his chest. He wraps his arms around me, squeezing tightly and nuzzling my neck. "We won't do anything you don't want to do. You can tell me to stop anytime, and I will. All right?"

"Yeah. I trust you." Again, my voice is much steadier than I feel, but I mean it. I do trust him.

Loosening his hold on me, he soothes his hands over my

arms, then my legs, gently tugging them apart as his fingers graze over my inner thighs. "Tell me if you're wet, honey."

Keeping my face turned toward him, I let my fingers glide down my body until they're at the apex of my thighs. His presence is enough for me to be completely turned on, so I'm not surprised when I find myself soaking. I drag my wetness from my entrance to my clit, stroking and circling, my back arching with the movement.

"That's it," he encourages, reaching for the lube and squirting some on his hand before he begins to stroke himself. I gasp as I watch him pleasure himself. "Show me how wet you are." I dip two fingers into myself, then lift them to show him. "Can I taste you?" I nod, bringing my fingers to his mouth.

He rolls his tongue around and between my fingers, moaning as he tastes me, stroking himself faster. With his left hand, he reaches for the vibrator, turns it on then hands it to me.

I flick through the settings, finding the one I like, then I lower it to my clit, just like I did when we were on the phone. I alternate between watching his hand around his cock and his face. He watches my every move so intently, like he's committing me to memory.

His chin lifts, and his eyes lock on our reflection in the mirror. "Beautiful, Charlie. You're so beautiful." It's nearly enough to make me come, his awed words. I turn further into him, pushing the vibrator to my entrance slowly. Rafael groans, bringing his left hand to my breast. I clutch onto his leg for purchase as I push the toy inside. I focus on his quickening pulse, his breaths landing somewhere over my chest, and how it feels to have his body wrapped around mine.

"Raf," I pant as we find our rhythm. I'm so on edge already; I know it won't take much.

"Yeah, honey. I'm right here." He lowers his lips to my shoulder, biting lightly, then soothing the bite with kisses. "You look so good fucking yourself. You should see yourself, Charlie, dripping for me and so fucking needy for my cock that you probably use this toy every night, don't you?" Crap, how does he know?

"Yes. I use this every night and think of you." *Traitorous mouth.* I close my eyes and focus on the sensations.

"Good. Because I fuck my hand at least once a day thinking about you. The way it feels when I hold you. The noises you make when you come. The sound of your laugh." He takes my jaw in his hand and tips my chin up toward the mirror, but I keep my eyes closed. "The way you say my name when you're turned on. The way you roll your eyes at me when I annoy you, but you think it's cute anyway. Your tight pussy gripping my fingers. I can't get enough of you. I don't think I'll ever have enough, Charlie." He keeps his hold on my jaw, gentle but unrelenting. Just like his words. "Look at yourself. Look at us."

I swallow and pull in a deep breath, and then I open my eyes. And I see it. I see what he sees. I look nothing like the woman I've always been told I am. I look free, blissful, sexy. My skin is flushed and glowing.

"I see it," I whisper.

"That's right. Now you see what I dream about. You see the woman I've seen all along. You see what you do to me. You see all of that?" The pace of his hand picks up to match mine, and I've never wished so badly that it was him inside me.

"Yes. I see all of that. And I see you, too. All of you." Our eyes lock in the mirror, and Rafael's body tightens beneath me. He doesn't say anything as he comes, but our eyes remain locked on one another's.

My orgasm hits me intensely, a tingling sensation that travels from the top of my head to the tips of my toes, like warm water being poured over me. I come, and I come, and I come until tears trickle down my cheeks and I gasp for breath.

I toss the vibrator aside and curl my legs up as my core still throbs. Rafael pulls me into him, my cheek resting on his chest, holding me close with one arm, his right hand wrapped around his still semi-hard cock.

"Here, lie down. I'll be right back." He covers me with the blanket at the foot of the bed and moves swiftly to the bathroom. When he comes back, he has tissues, which he offers to me, and I'm thankful he lets me do this on my own after having felt so exposed. Then, he climbs into the bed behind me, urging me to rest my head on his bicep. "Thank you for trusting me." He kisses my shoulder. "Are you okay?"

"I'm great." I lock my leg between his muscular ones and rest my hand over his, linking our fingers. "Thank you for…" I don't know what. How do I even begin to articulate this? "Thank you." He nods a response into my skin, his lips kissing the same spot over and over.

I've never done anything as intimate as what we just did. I keep having that thought. And not only after every item we cross off the list, but anytime I'm with him for any reason. I find myself noticing that they're the most intimate experiences I've shared with a person. And the more these encounters happen with him, the more I wonder if I *could* experience them this intensely with anyone else.

i'm honestly going to lose my ever-loving mind.

charlie

BY THE TIME we start the drive to Siesta, I feel as if I'm floating. We got coffee on the way out of the city, and Rafael has been telling me a bit more about his siblings as he drives.

He's mentioned his niece, Cecilia, a few times as well, but never with anything that highlighted her autism. I tuck away the bits of information he shares, like how she is in kindergarten and is fascinated with animals.

That his parents have been married for nearly forty years.

That Gabriel is the responsible one, Arthur is the eldest, Marcelo and Gustavo are the silliest, and Daniela is the youngest but probably more mature than all of them.

He speaks about them with so much love and affection that it nearly hurts my heart.

"I need to tell you something." I break a brief lull in our conversation with the ominous words. He must feel it because he swallows, tipping his chin for me to continue. "I'm C.M. Howe."

There, I said it.

"What do you mean?" He glances at me briefly, his grip tightening on the steering wheel.

"I mean, I'm the author. C.M. Howe is my pen name. I've been writing romance novels since I was a teenager, then I self-published one a few years ago, and it sort of blew up, and now I have an agent and a multi-book deal and a movie deal and all that." I'm rambling, but I'd really like to be very clear so he doesn't hit me with any more ambiguous questions.

Seconds tick by, but they feel like minutes. Then, Rafael turns onto a quiet road and stops the car on the shoulder. He gets out of the car and walks to my side of it, pulling open the door. He reaches in slowly and unbuckles my seatbelt. Gosh, I love it when he does that. But I'm nervous about his reaction.

Holding out both hands silently, he beckons me to step out of his SUV, and I do as my insides practically vibrate with anxiety.

"I couldn't say this in a moving vehicle, hence pulling over. I'm sorry if that made you nervous. I just had to tell you that I've always thought you were the smartest, most inter-esting person in any room. In every room. But now? Damn, carrot cake. You've been writing books while running a whole-ass finance department? Fuck, I—" He takes my hand and brings it to his chest, pressing down so I can feel his fero-cious heartbeat. "That's what that does to me. I'm so fucking amazed by that beautiful mind of yours. By the fact that you created some of my favorite book characters ever." I bring a hand to his cheek, running my thumb over his lower lip for no other reason than simply needing to touch him. His hands come to rest on the car as if he's holding himself up, caging me in the process and my hand on his chest lowers to his abdomen, slipping under his shirt. I don't mean for it to be sexual, but I can't help my moan when his muscles flex beneath my fingers. The low groan that comes out of him has me tipping my chin up to see his face. I love seeing how his lids lower and his lips part, as if his always-expressive face completely relaxes when he's under this lusty haze.

"So, you're not angry, then." It's not a question; the

answer is very obvious. "Because I kept a secret, and we promised honesty."

"Not angry. Never angry at you. But I'm *honestly* going to lose my ever-loving mind and any semblance of gentlemanliness or self-control if you keep touching me like that." He rests his forehead on mine, and when I pull my hands away, he lets out a slow breath. "You've told me now. That is being honest." Lifting his head, he places a gentle kiss on my forehead. "Is there anything you *can't* do?" He asks, almost to himself.

"I don't know how to whistle." It's a fact. I just can't make my lips twist the right way, and all that comes out is air, no whistling sound.

He rears back. "What, like..." He whistles a tune so easily that it's almost annoying. I want to hate it. I want to hate the way that his lips pursed like that makes my stomach do a little backflip. I want to hate that Rafael whistling is both somehow adorable *and* sexy all wrapped into one hot, muscular package. I want to hate that I'm now thinking about his *package*. But I'm very much thinking about it and how much I don't seem to hate anything about him anymore. Quite the contrary, actually.

"Red? You okay?" He cups my cheeks in his hands, his thumb caressing the spots where I am most certainly blushing.

"Mm-hmm." I anchor myself to him with my hands around his wrists.

"Hey, will you sign my copies of your books?" He blushes. Actually bloody blushes. Again! And I nearly can't take it. "I have all of them. Special editions, and everything." His smile is so warm, as are his hands that have little calluses on them, just rough enough to tease my skin. I love the feel of them on me.

"Of course I will. That's... It's so..." Tears prick the backs of my eyes, and the words don't come.

He leans down and kisses me softly, tenderly. "Thank you," he whispers against my lips.

I don't know what he's thanking me for when I should be the one thanking him for the most perfect reaction. One completely opposite of the one Robert had, which was essentially full of condescension and dismissal. I hate that my brain always chooses to compare these two men. I get it. They're complete opposites.

There's more I want to confess, but fear stops me. I don't want to completely erase this perfect moment where Rafael has just told me that he loves my brain, that he has *all* of my books. And selfishly, I want to keep this memory just as it is. Perfect and happy. Mine.

So, when he takes my hand and kisses it before buckling me back into my seat, I say nothing.

I promise myself I'll tell him another time.

Soon.

it's okay, she knows i'm crazy about you.

charlie

AFTER A SLIGHTLY SMALLER FEAST THAN the last time we were here, Ana Maria starts getting things prepped for today's recipe: farofa. She explained that it's a staple in their household and Brazilian culture, but how she makes it has always been a mystery. Until today.

"All right, Char, this one is a side dish, but it's got a lot going on, so I might be at the stove more than I'm here, okay?" Rafael is resting his forearms on the island countertop across from me, but I hardly notice his muscles or the apron he has on that says *Hot stuff coming through (and I don't mean the food)*.

"You just called me Char." My eyebrows are suddenly very well acquainted with my hairline.

"I call you a lot of things, pretty girl." He winks and steps off to the side, giving his grandmother room to stand next to him. Where the bloody hell does this charm come from? And how was I immune to it for so long? With his hands on his hips, he smiles widely. "Put me to work, Vózinha!"

For the next twenty minutes, they chop and prep. And

now, Raf is standing with his back to me at the stove, working two pans at the same time.

Is it hot in here? Why is that making me feel warm and tingly?

It smells amazing, and I've got my work cut out for me with this one as they both hover over the stove, occasionally shouting ingredients or instructions at me, like "add the onions into the bacon grease" and "a mix of green and black olives." I do my best to make it all make sense, and whenever there's a lull as they wait for something to cook, I either just watch them joking with one another in that easy way they have, or I type out another recipe that was already in the notebook.

In the end, I find that I very much enjoy farofa—despite being skeptical of some of the ingredients going into it. It's soft yet crunchy, savory, and incredibly flavorful.

I help with the clean-up this time, since I get to reap the benefits of their hard work, and as I'm wiping down the countertop, Ana Maria places her warm hand over mine, stopping my movements. "Thank you for what you're doing here. I'm so glad he has you in his life. You know, Rafa truly is the best of us all, with the kindest heart. He's never been anything other than ours in every way that matters, but I know that he sometimes still feels like he needs to prove his worth. As if he needs to work harder than anyone else to be a part of this family." She squeezes my hand. "He doesn't, of course. I hope you know that. I hope you'll see that."

"Oh, dona Ana, I know he doesn't need to. The way you love him is written all over everything you do. It's obvious, even to someone like me." I stop, wondering how I can backpedal. "Someone coming in as an outsider, that is, that you mean the world to one another. He's lucky to have you, yes, but you're equally lucky to have him." I don't know if I've said too much, or maybe not enough, but she smiles brightly.

When her grip on my hand loosens, I expect her to walk away, but instead, she palms my cheek in the same way she does to Rafael when she greets him. "I knew you could see it too. How special he is. Now stop calling me dona. It's Vó." Her touch is gentler with me but no less full of affection. It makes my chest tighten with a longing for my own loving grandmother. The one I never got to have.

Just as she lets me go, Rafael walks back into the kitchen. "All right, the garbage is taken care of. Should we head outside for a bit before we go? I bet Charlie will love your garden, Vó." Standing between us, he wraps us both up in his arms, laying a kiss on his grandmother's head, then turning to do the same to me. Receiving this kind of affection sends tingles right down to my toes. I know he gives it away easily, freely, but with him, that doesn't make it any less special. Not one bit.

As we step onto the back deck, the orange grove I could see from the kitchen comes fully into view, and it's far larger than I thought. But it's the backyard itself that takes my breath away. Just below us is a vast expanse of green grass. The size of a football field, at least. On one side, there's a large sitting area with several chairs circling a fire pit. The small pond next to it is perfectly still. On the other side, there are several rows of raised garden beds with a large greenhouse next to them.

With her hand tucked into the crook of his arm, Rafael helps Vó as we walk down together into the greenhouse. Despite the chill in the air, it's toasty warm in here. There are flowers everywhere. Each more beautiful than the last.

"This is gorgeous." I run my fingers through some leaves, close my eyes, and smell the literal roses growing in here.

Warm fingers wrap around mine. "Careful of the thorns, gata," Rafael whispers as he brings my hand to his lips. I twist quickly to find Vó is pruning a plant, blissfully unaware of her cheeky grandson's actions. He chuckles, letting his lips linger over my fingers. "It's okay, she knows I'm crazy about you. It's impossible to hide anything from her." She might know that, but do I? He's never so bluntly said that before. Sure, he's attracted to me, and he likes spending time with me, but *that*? It sounds awfully close to something real.

It's a large greenhouse, so we step away a bit further, hidden behind some of the larger plants where we have more privacy, which is wonderful. I mean, no, it's terrible because then Raf's lips are on my neck, his whispered words making me shiver. "I used to come in here sometimes just so I could smell the roses. So I could feel closer to you."

Every part of me wants to lean into him, to let those words wash over me, but I'm so terrified of what will happen if I leave LA. *When* I leave LA. *When*. That thought alone has me stepping away from him, moving on to look at other flowers. If he's disappointed, he doesn't show it. Not for the rest of the day.

———

ON WEDNESDAY MORNING, Rafael texts me to let me know he's thinking of me.

ME:

I've been thinking of you too.

I've been thinking I'd like to try that pasta recipe.

The one you made for me?

I bought all the ingredients.

Even the veggies to hide in the sauce, like you recommended.

Would you like to have some with me?

RAFAEL:

> I would love to have dinner with you, carrot cake. Why don't you come make it at my place? The kitchen at yours is tiny, and I doubt Taylor even owned pots and pans when he lived there.

> I'll send you the door code. Come over anytime. I won't be home until about six, but you're welcome to whatever you want.

ME:

> Okay.

> I'll come make it at your place.

> Thanks, by the way.

RAFAEL:

> Really? You're gonna be here in my house when I get home tonight?

ME:

> Well, yes.

> That's what we just agreed to.

His next response is a GIF of Joey and Chandler from *Friends* doing a happy dance.

ME:

> See you for dinner.

RAFAEL:

> I like this way too much.

I like it way too much, too. It's dangerous, how much I like the idea of being in his house, having dinner with him, that he trusts me to be in his home when he explicitly told me he doesn't have women there.

But it's also what a couple might do, right? This is the

'normal relationship stuff' I've needed to try. This is what I need to understand and practice just as much as the naked stuff. Not that there will be any of that tonight. Will there? Does anybody want to have sex after a plateful of pasta?

I guess we'll find out later.

———

BY FIVE O'CLOCK, I've got the sauce made and everything cleaned up. I had no idea how long this would actually take, so I've been here for two hours already.

It feels good being in this house. It's warm and inviting, and it smells like Rafael, which I like very, very much.

The only thing left to do is boil the spaghetti, but I'll do that when he's here so we can have it fresh. Pumpkin—the cat, of course, because I would never refer to myself in the third person or by one of Raf's nicknames for me—has been in and out of the kitchen since I got here, and she's been inching closer and closer each time.

Since I have nothing to do but wait, I go to the living room and look through his books. Sure enough, every single one of mine is there, including the new one he just bought. I dig through my bag for the Sharpie I always keep on-hand to sign copies when I see them at bookstores and pull out all my books. Without messing with the order he had them shelved in—chronological, by series, because he's the perfect man—I open them up to the cover page.

Rather than just signing my name, I decide to leave him a personal message in each one. It's surprisingly easy to come up with things to write to him, which I suppose makes sense since we know one another so well.

With fifteen minutes to spare, I finish signing and place everything back as it was. When I sit back on the sofa, Pumpkin jumps up next to me. She had been cautiously watching from the other side of the room, and as I wrote my messages, I said them out loud, sharing them with her as I went.

She purrs into the side of my leg and looks up at me with those striking blue eyes. Looks like we're both starting to feel a bit more comfortable here.

42 /
i want to taste you before anything else.

rafael

I WALK into my house full of excited jitters. It smells amazing in here. "Hello," I call out.

"In here." Charlie's voice comes from the living room. She's sitting on the couch, feet propped up on the ottoman, and when I walk around the corner, I see Pumpkin is asleep on her lap.

"Holyyyyyyyy shit. How did you… When did she—" I've lost the ability to speak. The sight of Charlie on my couch with my cat has killed any brain cells I had left.

And then she goes and giggles. I'm a goner.

Standing behind her, I place my hands on her shoulders, and she rolls her head back to look at me, red hair fanning around her like a fiery halo. "Hey, firecracker." I lean down to kiss her and feel her lips smiling against mine.

"Another nickname? Really?" She rolls her eyes, and I have to work overtime on not throwing her over my shoulder and taking her to my bed.

Instead, I lower my mouth to her neck and my hands to sit over hers where Pumpkin is still contently sleeping. "Admit it, you've grown to love my nicknames." I nip at the spot below her earlobe, and her breath hitches. "You probably even have a favorite." I leave a trail of kisses all along her neck.

Her giggle is music to my ears. A song I'll never tire of. "Even if I did." She turns so we're nose-to-nose. "I'd never tell."

"Brat." I kiss her nose, and she laughs, startling Pumpkin from her nap. "Well, the snuggle was good while it lasted, I'm sure. But now it's my turn." I flip myself over the couch, my head landing on her lap as she squeals.

"You are insane!" She's still laughing, hands lowering as the shock of my lunging onto her lap wears off.

"Nah. I just really, really like you." I nuzzle into her, wrapping my arms around her waist. Her left hand lands on my hair, fingers combing it gently back and off my forehead. Her stomach chooses that moment to growl at me, and I shake with laughter. "Hungry, shortcake?"

"Well, I was so preoccupied with dinner that I forgot to eat lunch."

"Hmm. Yep. Been there." I lift my head, very reluctantly might I add, and kiss her stomach. "Let's get you fed, then." I jump off the couch and extend my hand to her. I don't let her go until we get to the kitchen, and she beelines for the large pot on the stove, opening it up to stir it. It smells incredible.

"I just need to boil the pasta, so we can start with the salad while we wait if you'd like?" She twists to open the fridge door, but I take her by the waist and haul her to me.

"I think I'd like to eat something else while we wait, if that's okay," I say into her neck.

"Oh. W-what did you have in mind? What about the pasta?" She melts into my body, her head rolling back to rest on my shoulder.

"You're gonna play coy?" I chuckle and watch as the

goosebumps rise on her skin. She's wearing a long skirt, and her T-shirt is knotted loosely at her waist. I slip my hand easily under the hem, and she gasps. "You, gata. I want to taste you before anything else. And I promise I'll cook that pasta as soon as I'm done making you come." I move my fingers under the waistband of her skirt, and she squirms against me.

Not willing to waste any more time, I flip her around, pick her up, and place her on the counter. I'll take all my meals at the kitchen counter if they include Charlie.

FIFTEEN MINUTES LATER, Charlie's had two orgasms, and my dick is doing its damnedest to break out of my pants. While she gets cleaned up, I get the pasta going, but I can't resist having a taste of the sauce. All right, so I have more than just a taste; I have several. Whatever vegetables she put in this severely improved the flavor.

I've just finished sneaking another spoonful of sauce when I hear a *tsk-tsk* coming from behind me. "Patience, Machado." Her tone is soft, that gorgeous afterglow making her skin look flushed. I love that I did that. She smiles widely at me as she walks closer and takes the spoon out of my hand, setting it down. "Based on the sounds you were making, the sauce is good?" Running her fingers from my chest to my abs and back again, she waits for an answer.

"It's delicious, honey bun." I clear my throat, which suddenly feels a little tight. "I think it's better than mine." Her nose scrunches, pure joy etched on her beautiful face, and I can't help but run the pad of my thumb over those pink lips. I suck in a sharp breath that doesn't seem to pull in enough air and clear my throat again, feeling a twinge of anxious energy making its way through my chest. "What, uh, what did you put in the sauce?" I can feel the sweat starting to build on my forehead, a familiar dread now climbing its way up my throat.

Charlie's excitement is obvious as she starts going on about how she would normally never eat this thing because she hates the texture, and alarm bells start firing in my brain. I barely register any of the words, but one stands out among the others. *Mushrooms.* She's still talking when I step aside and rush to the front closet, flipping a bin upside down to find what I need. I think she's calling out to me from the kitchen, maybe closer, but I can't hear anything over the roaring in my ears.

When I turn, she's there, confusion written all over her features. I show her the contraption in my hand, but she doesn't take it. Too fatigued to stand, I slide my back down the wall and sit on the floor. When I open my mouth to speak, nothing comes out. I push my hand as close to Charlie as I can get it, and when she takes the EpiPen in my hand, understanding kicks in.

She's still talking, but it's all jumbled, and I'm going to pass out soon from lack of oxygen. I place my index finger on my thigh, near the spot where she should insert it, silently begging her to understand.

Finally, I feel the pressure followed by the sharp sting of the EpiPen connecting with my leg. I wait. And I wait. I know it's only seconds, but they feel like minutes. Then, I pull in a deep breath of air, relief washing over me like a bucket of ice water.

"Thank you," I whisper. The usual side effects start to take over as my heart rate shoots up and my energy comes back.

By the time I stand, Charlie is handing me my shoes. "Put these on. Do you have your wallet?"

"Yes. What?"

"I'm taking you to the hospital. Is the one a few minutes away from here okay? Or should I go to another one?" She's moving so fast, getting her shoes on, taking her purse from one of the hooks on the wall.

"What's happening?" My body might feel energized, but my brain is still working at a snail's pace.

"I'm driving you to the hospital. You could go into anaphylactic shock again." She looks at my shoes, still in my hands. "Do you need help with those?" I shake my head and slide the white sneakers on my feet. They don't go with this outfit, but I'm not about to tell her that.

Charlie ushers me out, locking the front door on her way, and gets into the driver's seat of my car. As her hand comes down with the seatbelt, I stop her. "Charlie. I can drive myself. It's okay. You're not comfortable driving in this kind of traffic."

Shimmying away from me, she turns the car on. "Yes, I am. Not here, but I drive in London all the time. And you're not driving yourself to the hospital." She pulls onto the road as I'm about to argue with her, but I see the set of her jaw, and I know I won't win this argument. She's switched into crisis management mode, so I can tell nothing will deter her, and it's probably safer if I don't drive anyway.

We arrive at the hospital in less than ten minutes, and Charlie pulls into the first parking spot, practically getting out of the car before she's even turned it off. She's next to me as we walk through the doors and beelining for the nurse behind a desk.

"He's just had an allergic reaction to mushrooms. EpiPen was administered less than twenty minutes ago. His throat swelled up, and he wasn't able to speak. He was struggling to pull in air, and I don't think he went without oxygen, but it would be worth testing his brain function as well." I've never seen her like this before, so completely hyper-focused on a single task. The fact that taking care of me is that task feels pretty fucking awesome.

The nurse starts asking me a bunch of questions as Charlie

steps aside, silently watching and listening. I'm taken into a room, and Charlie stays back. Where is she? I'm so jittery, but my head is starting to pound, the hammering pain quickly becoming unbearable. I want to ask for her, but instead, I run to the washroom and empty the contents of my stomach.

Great. Here we go again.

you. i need you.

charlie

A DIFFERENT NURSE comes to me fifteen minutes after Rafael has been taken back. "Hi. You came in with Mr. Machado, right?" I nod once. "Are you his partner or significant other?"

"N-no. I'm not. I'm just a friend." I swallow down the disappointment that I didn't think to lie and say I'm his partner so I can see him.

Is that all this disappointment is about?

"All right, well, unless he asks for you and authorizes it, we can't take you back to his room or give you any updates. I'm sorry." She smiles kindly at me.

"Right. Thank you. I'll just be here, then." I sit on the hard waiting room chair and replay the last hour.

How did I not know he was allergic to mushrooms? I pull the fidget toy I have in my purse and focus on the movements as I stand and pace the small room, trying not to spiral into a pit of guilt and shame.

Maybe I should leave? No. I should stay. No one even knows he's here. I don't have any contact information for his family. If this were Robert, I'd be able to call his dad. If this were Robert, this never would have happened. He doesn't have any food allergies. We've talked about that before because we used to see one another nearly every day. For years. Because that's what it takes to really know someone, isn't it? It takes more than just a few weeks and orgasms, but actual time together, getting to know important facts. I don't know anything about Rafael. Not really.

After the first hour passes, I feel like I may throw up.

Ninety minutes after I drove us here, it feels like every organ in my body is tied in knots. I've managed to keep my meltdown at bay by running through all the strategies I've developed with my therapist. I know I'm only prolonging the inevitable, but I don't have it in me to meltdown here, in the middle of a hospital. I'd much rather do it at home. Alone.

I have to go. He hasn't asked for me. He must be so upset. Of course he's upset. I poisoned him!

I'm going. I'll get a cab back to my place. No, back to his. I should clean up the sauce.

I'm halfway to the door when I hear someone. "Miss Howard?"

"Yes?" I turn back to find the same nurse from earlier.

"He's asking for you. Urgently. He's a bit agitated, actually, so can you please come with me?" She extends her arm, indicating the hallway we should go down.

I follow her, all the while preparing myself for him to tell me he never wants to see me again.

When we get to the room I'm assuming Rafael's in, the nurse opens the door but doesn't follow me inside. As it shuts behind me, I find myself unable to move. My feet are glued to the floor, and I feel the need to stay as close to the door as possible so I can run out when he dismisses me. Hot tears roll down my cheeks as I take in the scene in front of me, as I see the consequence of my mistake.

He's hooked up to an IV, his strong body tense and rigid on the bed that looks too small for him. His eyes are closed, and the lights are dimmed, so I clear my throat to announce my presence. His lids barely part, and he's squinting as if he's in pain. "Red?"

"Yeah," I answer, wiping at the tears on my face.

"Why are you so far away?" I don't say anything. "Short-cake, can you please come here? I need…"

Those two words have me practically sprinting to his side. "What do you need?" I scan his body for I don't know what.

"You. I need *you*. Come here." He reaches for my hand, pulling me to the bed. "Please?" He whines as he pulls me closer. So close that I'm practically toppling onto him.

"Rafael, I—"

"*Please*, Charlie," He pleads with eyes still closed.

"All right," I whisper. His shoulders visibly relax, and I settle on the bed next to him. On him, really, because it's a tiny bed. I lay my hand over his heart, my head on his shoulder. "Are you okay?"

"No," he answers plainly. "Not yet. But I'm much better now. Thank you." He kisses the top of my head, holding on to me tightly. The pressure is like a weighted blanket, easing me toward calm.

"I didn't know you—"

"Shhh. I know. Is it okay if we do this later?" His voice is so quiet, I hardly hear him. This is a version of Rafael I've never seen before, and I have a feeling most people would say the same. There's no joy in his voice, no playfulness.

"Okay," I answer quietly. "Anything I can do to help?"

"Would you read to me? I don't care what it is. The ticking clock and the beeping from the hallway are driving me crazy. And I love the sound of your voice." He kisses the top of my head again, then whispers into my hair. "Please, Charlie?"

New level of intimacy unlocked. I try not to read too much into it. He's probably doped up, but aren't people more honest when they're in this kind of state?

My heart wants desperately to believe this is special, but

my head is telling me it's nothing, that I can be here for him now and then go back to whatever we were before we asked for each other's help.

Without answering him, I take out my phone and lower the screen brightness as much as I can. Then, I continue reading the book I had started, certain there are no sex scenes I'll come across since it's a closed-door romance. It's hard to say whether it's being this close to Rafael or reading having the effect on me, but within minutes, I feel calmer, and I feel him relax as well, his breaths growing steadier.

I'm not sure how much time passes, but we lay together until someone knocks lightly and then comes in. With my back to the door, I try to move away from Rafael, but he holds me in place.

"Hi," the nurse whispers. "Mr. Machado, how are you doing?"

"Better now that you let my girlfriend in here." He opens his eyes to look at her, and my body goes completely stiff at the word *girlfriend*. He must have told them that so that they'd let me come. "Can I go home yet? I'm pretty sure I expelled any trace of mushrooms that had been in my stomach, and I don't need to be hospitalized for a migraine. I deal with those pretty regularly." His voice is calm, but there's pain etched into it. I don't like knowing I put it there.

The dimmed lights and his quiet voice make sense now, knowing he's dealing with such pain. I wonder how often he has migraines, how they affect his everyday life. I can't imagine it's easy.

The nurse checks a few things in his chart and nods. "It'll probably be at least a couple more hours before you can go home, but we're okay to give you something for the migraine now." She shifts her kind eyes to me. "Miss, are you going to take Mr. Machado home? It's possible that the medication will make him quite drowsy."

"Yes, of course," I say, trying to sit up, but again, Rafael will not let me. The nurse, whose name tag I can't see because of the dimmed lights, hides a smile behind her hand. She lets us know she'll be right back, and as I shift to lay my head on his chest again, he pulls in a long breath and holds it.

"Shit," he mumbles. This time when I move to get off the bed, he lets me, and then he's up, dragging his IV pole and taking long strides to the bathroom on the other side of the room. He slams the door shut, and I can hear him dry heaving. I wince, because I feel awful for him and also because, well, vomit is gross.

I give him his privacy and look around the room to find a bottle of water. There's one on a nearby table, and I pour some into a cup for him. He stumbles out of the bathroom a minute later, wincing, eyes nearly shut. I go to him to offer him some support to get back to the bed, helping him sit on the edge. I get the cup of water and hand it to him, but his eyes are closed. I stand between his legs, and, holding the cup to his lips, I whisper, "Open your mouth and tip your head back."

He groans in pain, so I support the back of his head with my other hand. I have no idea if anything I'm doing is helping, but I know I can't sit here and do nothing. When he's finished, I set the cup on the table and bring my other hand to the back of his head, massaging gently. He groans again, but this time, it seems like it's a happier sound. Resting his forehead on mine, he wraps his arms around my waist and pulls me closer. "Thank you," he whispers.

Again, I feel tears prick at my eyes, and before I can think of a way to respond, the nurse is back.

"Hi." She hands him the little cup with pills and some water, and I step away from the bed. "I'll be back to check on you soon, but call me if you throw up again or feel anything unusual."

Rafael nods, making no mention of the fact that he just threw up. Before she reaches the door, I catch up to her.

"Sorry, nurse… I didn't catch your name. My apologies. I'm Charlie, by the way. He did just throw up, but I take it you'd like to know if it happens again, after the medication?"

"I'm Lisa. Nice to meet you, Charlie. And yes, if he continues to throw up, we'll need to know. This medication should help with the nausea as well as the pain."

"Thank you. He's…" I look down at the floor, and Lisa simply waits for me to continue. "He's okay, right? I mean, other than the migraine now?"

She lays a gentle hand on my forearm. "He's doing great. Showing no signs of anaphylaxis coming back, and he's been much calmer since you got here. We'll keep him a bit longer, just in case, but you should both be able to go home soon. You're doing great." She squeezes my arm, and I nod, incapable of telling her just how wrong she is since I'm the whole reason he's here. "If you need anything, call for me or come find me out there, okay?"

"Yeah. Thank you."

"Carrot cake? Where are you?" Raf's lying back down, and his arms feel around the bed, looking for me. Even in a world of pain, he manages to be sweet.

"I'm right here." I curl back into him on the tall but narrow hospital bed. "I'm right here," I repeat, because, despite the fact that I caused this mess, there's nowhere else I'd rather be.

charlie? raf's charlie?

charlie

RAFAEL FELL asleep about an hour ago, but now, his phone keeps ringing. I don't want to overstep, but I take a look at the screen anyway, assuming it's someone who obviously really needs something. The photo on the screen is of Rafael and a woman I can only assume is his mother—also, the name says Mãe, which I know is Portuguese for Mom.

I clear my throat and walk into the bathroom, not wanting to wake Raf up. "Hi, Mrs. Machado? This is Charlie."

"Charlie? Rafa's Charlie? Oh, thank goodness you're with him. Is he okay?" Her voice is a little panicked; that much is clear.

"Yes, sorry. I should have led with that. He's all right. I... I'm so sorry. This is all my fault. I didn't know he was allergic to mushrooms, and I wanted to make him dinner." God, I can't believe I'm telling his mum I nearly killed him today.

"Ah, the pasta recipe you liked. Yes, he told me you were going to make it."

"He told you?" My voice comes out all screechy, because, um, what?

She laughs lightly. "Yes, we talk pretty regularly. Are you still at the hospital?"

I feel so stupid focusing on the bloody pasta when I haven't properly updated her on his well-being. "Yes, sorry. We're here. He just fell asleep a little while ago. The migraine meds seem to have kicked in. I'm so, so sorry. This is all my fault—"

"Oh, Charlie, it was an accident." Her voice is much more soothing now, and I recognize the gentle tone of her voice. It's so much like Raf's. "You know, when I was pregnant with Daniela, I was craving fettuccini Alfredo, and I put mushrooms in it, completely not thinking. We already knew Rafael was allergic by that point, but my pregnant brain simply forgot. I felt very guilty about that for a very long time, and I don't want you to carry that same guilt. You didn't know."

"I see where Rafael gets his nurturing demeanor from now. You haven't even met me, and you're consoling me after I put your son in hospital." I let out a humorless chuckle that sounds completely hollow.

"He is pretty special, but from what I hear, so are you. I can't wait to meet you on Sunday." She hums, almost as if to herself. "Will you please call me if anything changes with him? At least I know I don't have to worry now, knowing you're there." My chest fills with an ineffable feeling that I know is significant. Her words, her reaction, the way she called me Raf's Charlie... They all nestle into my heart. No, more like burrow. Deep.

"Yes, I definitely will, Mrs. Machado. I'm so sorry again, and that I didn't call sooner." I'm never ever going to let myself live this down.

"Don't mention it. Thank you for picking up and for taking care of our boy. We'll talk soon."

"Of course. Have a good night."

"Bye, honey." Her kindness has left me a bit shaken up. She's so sincere. And I knew Rafael's mom probably would be, but the circumstances of our first conversation have just solidified that.

THREE HOURS LATER, Rafael is finally allowed to go home. I'm not sure if it's the migraine medication they gave him or the mix of that and the epinephrine, but he is definitely a little woozy at the moment. He's been trying to bop me on the nose with his finger, but he keeps missing and hitting my eyes, cheeks, mouth, and even ear.

Lisa walks in as I'm gathering our things to leave. "Hi, I just need one more form signed, and you're free to go." She comes over to me with the clipboard, noticing the look of surprise on my face. "It's just to make sure he's getting home safely."

"Got it." I start to read over everything, but Rafael is basically hanging off me, trying to touch my nose again. I shoo him off like a fly, but he's relentless.

"Isn't my girlfriend soooo pretty, Lisa?" I close my eyes briefly, shaking off the butterflies attempting to take flight in my stomach at hearing him say that word again. "She is," he continues. "She's the most pretty. I like her so much, I would eat mushrooms again for her."

"Please don't," I say sincerely, and Lisa laughs.

"He really is completely smitten with you. It's very sweet." Lisa looks from Rafael to me, her tired eyes swimming with delight.

"I really am. All I ever think about is Charlie. Charlie, Charlie, Charlie." He sighs dramatically. "I think about her smiles and her laugh. I think about how smart she is and how great her boobs are. She has really, *really* nice ti—"

"All signed. We can leave now. Let's go, Casanova. Thank you so much for everything, Lisa." I take him by the hand, practically dragging him to the door.

"You're welcome. You'll be okay with him?" She shoots me a sympathetic smile, and I scoff at the man next to me.

"He's a lot, but I can handle him."

"Yeah, you can, baby." Raf's eyebrows jump around, and I pull him faster toward the exit.

"Oh my god. You've lost it. Bye, Lisa!" I wave a hand toward her as we make our way through the hallway, chuckling at the complete lunacy of this evening.

"Bye, lovebirds," Lisa says back.

RAF IS quiet on the drive home. The bright lights and the movement of the car make him a bit queasy, so we're both glad it's a short drive. I send him upstairs with a bottle of water immediately, then get to work on cleaning the kitchen.

It doesn't take long, since I had cleared all of the prep things away, and I made sure to get all the remnants into garbage bags and into the bin outside. No traces of mushrooms in this house.

It's late, and as I walk upstairs to check on Rafael, I notice that most of the lights are off. I wonder if it's because they're still bothering him or if he forgot to turn them on in his hazy state. I don't know which room is his, so I wander quietly until I hear him call my name.

His bedroom is the furthest down the hall, and his citrusy smell is even stronger here. I love it.

"Hi. I just wanted to check on you. Feeling okay?" I stand at the foot of his large wooden bed, which is covered in a linen duvet in a neutral color. The walls are painted something dark, and there's a soft rug beneath my feet. It's nice. It feels like the kind of room you could sleep all night and all day in.

"Not okay. I miss you." Only his head is out of the covers, and I can't see his face.

"I'm right here," I repeat for the third time tonight. "I was going to stay downstairs, in case you need anything, so I'll be close by. All right?"

"No," he answers immediately. "I mean, can you please stay here? With me?" He sticks his arms out, making grabby hands in my direction.

"Oh. Uh, I'm—"

"Please, shortcake." That same desperation from when I walked into his hospital room is back in his voice. "Go through my stuff and find some comfy clothes to change into. I have new toothbrushes in the bathroom cabinet. You can use whatever you want."

"Okay." I mean, he's hard to say no to. And again, I poisoned him. I can handle whatever this is for one night. "I'll be right back."

"Yessssssss." I see him kicking up his feet under the blankets, and I can't help but smile as I walk downstairs to get my purse. I'll need my phone and my glasses up here with me.

I end up finding a huge T-shirt with the Marine Corps logo on it in the softest, most worn-out cotton. It's perfect. I also find a toothbrush, as Rafael said. I use his face wash, remove my contacts, and when I get to the other side of the bed where I suppose I'll be sleeping tonight, he's so still that I wonder if he's fallen asleep.

I get in as gently as I can, and once I settle my head on the pillow, a big, strong arm wraps around me and pulls me into a hard body. A hard body with very little clothing on. He must have stripped down to his underwear. "You're too far away. I need you closer." He nuzzles into my neck, taking a deep breath. "Mmm. Roses. My favorite." With our bodies perfectly lined up, he lets out a low hum. I'm keenly aware of all the parts of our bodies touching with nothing between us. As he usually does, Rafael senses my thoughts before they're even fully formed in my head. "No funny business tonight. I just need you close, okay?"

My brain is still stuck on the three words he's said, and not for the first time tonight. *I need you.*

Usually, when people need me, it's to solve a problem. When Robert needs me, it's always because of something going on with the company or his dad or both. It's because he needs something *from* me. But Rafael doesn't want a thing or a solution to a problem. He just wants *me*. I don't even have to do anything.

How wonderful to be needed by someone like this, right? Wrong. Because he's not the one I'm going to wake up to every morning for the rest of my life, is he? He's not the one I'm preparing to marry. And while I know that person isn't going to be Robert either, it's also not Rafael, who is currently hopped up on meds and saying things he probably doesn't mean.

I sometimes wonder if this thing with us has gone too far, or perhaps he's just playing into it because he knows now that the goal is for me to be comfortable in a committed relationship with someone.

My thoughts are a mess. I'm tired, and with everything that's happened, I need to decompress and come back to all of this with a fresh mind. I'm all over the place right now.

"I can hear your brain working, red. I know you're tired, so for now, let's rest. We'll talk about it tomorrow, all right? I promise." He kisses my shoulder once, twice, three times on the same spot. Something about that repetitive motion soothes me. I don't know if he knows it, but every time he does this, leaving these series of kisses on one spot, everything in me calms.

His slow steady breaths eventually become my own, and I very quickly fall into a deep sleep.

45 /
it's time to face the
music.

charlie

I WAKE up in an empty bed, in a darkened room. I don't remember the curtains being closed last night, but they are now, and it's perfectly cozy in here, and my goodness, these sheets are amazing.

Giving myself a few minutes to luxuriate in this gigantic bed and the fact that it smells like Rafael, I finally make the decision to get up. I quickly brush my teeth, throw my hair in a messy bun, and put my glasses on before grabbing a pair of socks from Raf's drawer. I hate bare feet.

As I make my way down the stairs, I hear muffled talking and the front door closing. Just as I make it to the last step, Rafael turns around, a tray of drinks in his hand and a paper bag between his teeth. He does a slow perusal of my body from top to bottom, his mouth falling open and the paper bag crashing to the floor. I allow myself to do the same, starting at his bare feet, his absolutely pornographic gray sweatpants, his naked chest, and the thick, black-rimmed glasses on his face. All the man needs now is a backward baseball cap, and he'd be a romance reader's wet dream.

My wet dream.

Well, too late for that, really.

I realize I've gotten caught up in my thoughts when he bends to retrieve the bag and sets it and the tray of drinks on the entryway table. "G-good morning," he mutters, running a hand through his perfect waves. I'm still frozen on my spot. I don't want to move. I don't want to erase this image from my memory. *Somebody take a bloody photo!*

When he takes a step closer, I snap out of it, physically shaking my head to clear the lust-filled haze I'm in. "Gray sweats *and* glasses? Really? You didn't have anything less slutty?" Apparently lust makes me say what I'm thinking, so that's cool.

His answering grin makes my skin break out in goose-bumps everywhere. "I could say the same about you, gata. Wearing my clothes *and* glasses? What's next? You're gonna read to me and play with my hair? Jesus, woman tone down the sex, would ya?" My face must show my confusion because he runs a hand down his face, muttering an apology. "I mean you're incredibly sexy. This is the sexiest thing I've ever seen. You, in my clothes, after waking up in my bed. And if this were a real-life fantasy playing out, you'd play with my hair while you read to me. After we'd had incredi-ble, mutually mind-blowing sex, of course. Goddamnit, I'm gonna shut up now." He pinches the bridge of his nose and mutters, "What the fuck was in those migraine meds?"

I pull my lips between my teeth to keep myself from smil-ing. His rambling soothes the nervousness I'd been feeling when I walked down here. "What have you got there?" I point to the tray of coffee and paper bag next to him.

"Oh, uh, I had breakfast delivered. I wasn't sure if you'd want hot coffee or cold, so I got you both. And a tea. And Schmidt packed a bunch of stuff for us to eat. He said he made you a grilled cheese. Would you believe he wanted to come in here and give it to you himself?" He huffs out a laugh. "That fucking guy loves you." I watch his throat bob as he swallows, looking down at his feet. "I would have made us something, but I haven't been in the kitchen yet, and this just seemed safer."

My stomach drops to my feet. Of course he didn't go into the kitchen. For all he knows, it's covered in the one food that could kill him. This moment of normalcy between us was lovely, but this is the reality. I fucked up. Badly. In the worst way.

Last night, he said he needed me because he was so high on whatever meds he was given, but now, it's daylight. And the sun is shining brightly on the mistake I made. The one that will probably cost me any chance of being friends or anything else with the one person outside of my sister and best friend who actually gets me.

It's time to face the music.

46 /
i like messy. you've seen my trunk.

rafael

WHEN I LOOK UP, Charlie's eyes are watery, and her lips are trembling, the corners pulling down into the saddest, cutest frown I've ever seen. God, I want to keep her and never let her go. And the sight of a single tear rolling down her cheek has me nearly falling to my knees.

Before I can rush to her and pull her into me, she raises both hands and takes a step back, the backs of her ankles hitting the bottom step of the staircase. "I-I-I-I'm s-so s-s-s-sorry. I-I didn't m-mean to. I'm—" She's shaking now, and I can't keep my hands to myself any longer. I hug her tightly, her arms trapped between us, hands resting on my chest.

The sobbing wracks her body as I try to pull her closer. "Charlie, no, of course you didn't. It wasn't your fault." I feel my own tears gather, but they don't fall.

She yanks herself away from me, taking several steps away. "Yes, it was!" she practically screams. "It was all my fault. All of this." She waves her arms in the air before curling in on herself. Her voice lowers as more tears roll down her face. "I made this huge mess, and now I have to live with it."

"No." I keep my tone even. "I *know* you wouldn't intentionally hurt me. I trust that. I trust *you*."

"You shouldn't." A quiet sob leaves her as she starts pacing, hitting her forehead with the heel of her hand.

"Too bad. I do anyway." I take two steps closer, and she doesn't back away. "Whatever mess you think you've made, I want it. I like messy. You've seen my trunk." I take another step, and this time, her sob is a half-laugh.

She's still pacing back and forth, so I gently take her hand and place it on my chest. I inhale and hold my breath, then inhale again, fully filling my lungs, and then I blow out my breath through my mouth. She catches on and does the next cycle with me. We repeat this several more times, and I take her face in my hands, wiping away the tears that have stopped flowing. I hug her again, holding on to her tightly, letting the embrace settle both of us.

After a while, she sniffles, keeping her eyes down. "Do you think you can forgive me?"

"Nothing to forgive, pumpkin." I kiss her forehead, hoping she can let this go and let me in.

"I'm asking you to. Please. Or this guilt will—"

"Done. Forgiven. Forgotten about." I kiss her head again, but she pulls back.

"Rafael, be serious." Her adorably furrowed brows make me want to smile, but instead, I clear my throat and nod thoughtfully.

"I am serious." I take her glasses off since they're all fogged up and wet with tears. Pulling up the hem of her shirt —my shirt—I wipe the lenses clean, taking my time and lifting the shirt just a little higher than necessary so I can take in the red booty shorts she's got on under there.

"You're ridiculous," she says, with a roll of her eyes. But I see the little smile playing at the corners of her lips.

I place the glasses back on her face, pouting when the hem of my shirt swoops down just above her knees. "You mean ridiculously handsome?" I snake my hands around her waist, nuzzling her neck—my favorite spot. "Ridiculously funny?" I bite her neck lightly, eliciting a gasp from her. "Ridiculously sexy?"

She giggles then, and like tectonic plates moving into place, we shift back into just being us again. "Your coffee is probably cold," she taunts. But I know she's enjoying this. Her little whimpers give her away every time I kiss or suck somewhere new.

"You're right." I straighten my body, and she whimpers for a whole other reason. "Let's drink those coffees and see what Smitty made you." I take her hand in mine, grabbing the drink tray in my other hand and leaning down to bite the top of the paper bag. I lead us into the living room, and we both plop on the sofa. She huffs in feigned annoyance and takes the iced coffee from the tray, taking a long pull from the cup before setting it on a coaster.

"Um, the kitchen is cleaned up, by the way." There's so much uncertainty in Charlie's voice. Her hands rest on her lap, fingers entwined. "I got rid of everything last night," she whispers. I look up from the obscenely large bag of food on my lap to find her eyes welling up again. She shakes them off, blinking a few times.

"When? You must have been exhausted after being at the hospital for hours waiting on me. Shit. I'm sorry." I rub at a spot on my forehead, but I drop my hand when I hear Charlie's laugh. "What's so funny?"

"You. Apologizing to me. Stop. I was fine. I needed to get it done and make sure your home wasn't a hazard to your health." She takes another sip of coffee, seeming much more relaxed.

"Thanks for doing that. And staying with me. I don't remember much, but I'm pretty sure I was being a whiny little bitch." Like I always am when I get migraines. But I mean, they're fucking awful.

She laughs again. "No, you were actually quite adorable. Mostly. A little needy, but I didn't hate that part." Her lips twist to the side, and she shrugs.

"Oh, ho ho ho. You liked it!" I set the bag of food on the coffee table, twisting to face her. I'm met with narrowed eyes and a *very* fake frown. "You did. You liked me being needy." I pull her legs toward me, and she topples over, laying on her back. I lean over her, pushing one knee between her legs, a flash of red drawing my attention as the T-shirt she's wearing pools at her waist. "You liked me asking for you." I run my hands from her knees, up her thighs, along the edge of her panties. "Tell me it's true." She rolls her eyes again, and this time, my dick eagerly responds. "You like me begging for you. I didn't know this about you, shorty."

Her lust-filled eyes clear, and she scoots back, propping herself up on her elbows. "There's a lot we still don't know about each other." Her words are clipped, and I can tell that, despite me wanting to bring levity to this situation, she's not ready for that yet.

I sit back up, giving her space to do the same. "You're right. But that's kind of how these things work. You'll probably never know everything about someone because we're always changing, learning, and hopefully experiencing new things, right?" I don't wait for an answer. "You know more about me than most people in my life." I take the grilled cheese sandwiches and napkins out, noticing there are also two cookies at the bottom of the bag. "But I get that there are some details I've maybe left out, like my allergy to mushrooms. I'm not allergic to anything else, by the way. Are you? Allergic to anything, I mean?"

Charlie shakes her head. "No, no allergies that I know of. Have you always worn glasses?"

I smile at the question. "Yeah, since I was a little kid. I started squinting at the cereal box, and Vó took me to the doctor the next week. You?" I peek into each wrapper to see if they're different. They're not.

"Since I was little, too." One side of her lips tip up. "Once I got over touching my eyes, I found contacts easier than having something hanging on my face all day." Her head tips to the side as she studies my face. "I like glasses on you." Those pink lips stretch into a smile, but just as quickly as it appears, it's gone. I hand her a sandwich, which she takes from me, and when our fingers touch, she lingers there. "I'm sorry I'm so all over the place, I just—"

"I know. Yesterday was a lot. I understand if you want some space." I don't want it myself, but I'm always going to give Charlie what she needs.

"It's not that; I don't think I need space. I think I'd just like to spend time together without thinking about the list, or practicing, or whatever. It's okay if you have things to do, though. I can go home after this." She opens the sandwich slowly, almost as if she's unsure whether or not she should.

"I'd love for you to stay. I'm not going into the office today, though I have to sit in on a call later if that's all right." We both take a bite of the sandwiches. "Damn," I say after I swallow. "That's a good grilled cheese. Even cold."

"Smitty might be my favorite man." She moans around her bite, completely unaware of the effect that sound has on me.

I wait for her eyes to open and connect with mine. "I'm gonna have to change that, firecracker." I take another large bite and watch the blush creep up her cheeks. I don't push it any further, though.

ONCE WE FINISH EATING, Charlie insists on going home to shower and get a few things, like her laptop. I do much of the same. Shower, feed Pumpkin, make the bed, and fold the shirt Charlie wore to bed last night. I might never wash it again, and I don't care if that's a stupid thought.

She lets herself in through the side door, and I smile like the absolute lovesick fool that I am. "Hey, did you know that Pumpkin is outside?" Her eyes are wide with concern.

"Yeah, she likes to sit in the sun sometimes. She'll meow very loudly and paw the door when she's ready to come back in." I chuckle at my temperamental cat, and Charlie visibly relaxes. I like that she cares about my cat. I like that she cares about me. I like that she's here and that she let herself in. I like that one of my pillows smells like roses. I like it all. A lot.

"She just does what she wants, doesn't she?" She giggles as she unloads a water bottle from her backpack.

"Pumpkin is an independent woman." I pause. "Even if she can't feed herself and has very particular living requirements I need to adjust to. I wouldn't change a thing about her."

"Hmm. She really is a lot like me," Charlie responds absentmindedly.

Yeah. And I wouldn't change a thing about you, either.

i like you honest but inappropriate.

rafael

WE SPEND Thursday morning working side by side at the dining room table; Charlie writing, and me answering emails and checking in with the team at Aegis. Though she's put her contacts back in, I kept my glasses on. Contacts post-migraine are a big no for me.

When I take my call, I find Charlie peering over her laptop a few times. I pipe in with a few comments here and there, but I mostly listen to the call until the end, when someone asks if I have anything to add. "Yeah, thanks for asking, Miguel. I'd love to see if we can add a few more scholarships to the Dream Big Foundation fund. I'll match whatever amount you think we can manage." I see a few nods and continue, "Thanks, everybody. I know I sound like a broken record, but I appreciate the work you're putting into this. I couldn't do it without you all. I hope you know that." I smile at the faces on the screen and find Charlie watching me with wide eyes. "And remember: Never play hide and seek with Asha and Sam. You can't hide anything from the finance department." I laugh and watch as most of them give me a pitiful laugh. "Have a great day, everyone." I leave the call and close my laptop, finding blue eyes still fixed on me.

"Did you just make a finance joke?" She tips her head, and I instantly feel dumb for what I said. An accounting joke while sitting across from Charlie, of all people?

"Ugh. It was bad, I know. I just always like to close on a good note, and I couldn't think of anything else." I scratch the back of my neck.

"So, you always thank your team profusely and make jokes when you meet with them?" Her eyebrows raise in curiosity.

"Uh, yeah. I guess. Owen is the serious CEO, and I'm the one who makes jokes. It's a good balance, I think." My shoulders rise on a shrug, and I feel the self-consciousness creep in when she doesn't respond. "Is that bad?"

"Oh, no. No, it's just different. No executive at my firm has ever made a joke or said thank you during a meeting. It just—" She pauses, her brows furrowing in thought. "It doesn't surprise me that you do, and it's nice. You're nice. To everyone." With a small smile, she goes back to whatever she was doing on her laptop.

Nice.

She's told me I'm nice before, and I don't know what exactly that means. I don't know if he's trying to tell me something with this word, but I do know I don't want to ask her right now.

"You hungry?" I settle on making lunch plans instead.

She places a hand on her stomach and looks up at me. "I am, actually."

"How does a Greek salad with some grilled chicken sound? I checked the fridge, and I have everything I need for that." She doesn't seem repulsed by the idea, but I can tell there's a debate happening in her head. "Or I can do literally anything else."

She shakes her head and stands, her lips fixed in a straight line. "I just don't want you to feel like you always have to cook for me."

I walk to the other side of the table and watch as she paces back and forth for a few seconds.

"And I also don't like red onions. But I feel badly telling you that because I don't want to seem ungrateful." She winces. Before she can say anything else, apologize or whatever it is she's about to do because she thinks this is some kind of inconvenience for me, I stop her pacing with my hands on her arms.

I rub a few circles on her biceps. "I like cooking. I like cooking for *you*." Giving my words a moment to sink in, I lower my face to hers. "And I don't like red onions either. Especially raw. Gross." I make a face, and her smile lifts her cheeks.

"You're not just saying that?" Her eyes finally meet mine.

"I would never. You can check my pantry if you want. Not a single red onion in there." I challenge her with raised brows.

She shakes her head. "All right then. But I'd like to help."

"Yeah? Okay. Let's do this, carrot cake. Let's cut up some veggies!" I give her a little shake, and she responds with a giggle. Making Charlie giggle is my favorite thing to do.

"Okay, weirdo." She rolls her eyes, and fuck, it's nearly impossible not to throw her over my shoulder and show her what that eye-roll does to me. But we're just hanging out today. As friends? I don't know.

IT TURNS out that just spending time with Charlie and keeping my hands off her is exactly as excruciating as I assumed it would be. I've thought about kissing her about as often as I've blinked these last few hours. I don't know if she can sense my struggle because she doesn't seem to be suffering from the same withdrawals. Of course not, though. This isn't anything more than a practice run for her. At least that's what she keeps telling me, and no doubt herself. But I'm not sure I'm buying it anymore.

By mid-afternoon, I'm finished with any work things I needed to accomplish, so I leave Charlie to concentrate on whatever she's doing and excuse myself to get a workout in. I'm antsy as fuck, and I need to move my body.

After a warm-up and a very intense upper body workout, I decide I haven't had enough and pull the skipping rope from the wall, using my usual playlist with mostly upbeat songs I can skip to. This and running are the two guaranteed ways to shut my brain off and exhaust my body enough to get rid of the constant fidgety feelings.

I don't realize my eyes are closed until I hear her voice. "You've got to be bloody joking me." It looks like she's standing with her arms crossed, but I can't see shit because I took my glasses off before starting my workout.

Just as I place them back on my face, she raises her hands, which are holding her phone, and snaps a photo. "I need proof of this. No one would ever believe you exist otherwise."

"What do you mean?" I chuckle at her expression, not missing the slight blush on her cheeks and neck. "How long were you standing there?"

She hesitates, swallowing before lowering her hands, her eyes quickly raking over my body. "I mean, look at you. Backward baseball cap—I called it, by the way. I just knew you'd pull that shit off. You're all sweaty, shirtless—*again*—and now you've just put those damn glasses on. Were you written by a very horny woman?" Her lips turn up in a cheeky smile as I walk closer to her. I don't even realize I'm doing it until she tips her chin up to look at me. "And you've been back here just working out for over an hour? No wonder you're made of solid muscle. Aren't you tired?"

I can't help it. I lean in to her and bring my lips just below her ear. "I've got more stamina than you're giving me credit for, gata." Her breath hitches, though she tries to hide it by clearing her throat. "I can go for as long as you need me to." I straighten and, with one finger, push her chin up, forcing her mouth to close. "I'm gonna have a quick shower. If you need anything, you know where to find me." With a wink, I walk away, adjusting myself in my shorts because, goddamn it, I'm always turned on around her.

I spend my shower fluctuating between feeling guilty for pushing the boundaries of what Charlie asked for today and feeling pretty damn proud of myself because if this were all just practice for her, she wouldn't be having physical reactions to me like blushing and gasping. There's no way.

WE SPEND the rest of the afternoon watching only our favorite episodes of *Friends* on the couch, then we order dinner in and decide to watch season three because it's definitely the funniest one.

At one point, Charlie asks me to pause it so she can go take out her contacts. It's so completely mundane, and at no point in the evening do either of us touch one another, but I feel more connected to her than I have ever felt to a woman. Even sitting in silence two feet away from each other, the sense of contentment is entirely enough. And every time we laugh, we look at each other, and for a second, I wonder if she likes seeing me laugh as much as I like it on her.

Sometime just before midnight, I notice Charlie's fallen asleep. I was hoping she wasn't going to try to leave tonight, and she didn't. I love that she was comfortable enough to stay, to fall asleep, even.

I try to pick her up without jostling her too much. I figure I can take her to my room, and I'll sleep on a guest bed. I'm not about to make this weird by spending the night in the same bed as her again when she's asked me for space.

She nuzzles into my chest and opens one eye to look at

me. I kiss her forehead because, again, I can't help myself. "You can go back to sleep. I'm just gonna take you to bed."

"Mmm. Yes, please." Her arm wraps around my neck, and she runs her fingers through the hair at the nape before her breathing slows again. Fuck. She's not gonna make this easy.

Not bothering to turn on any bedroom lights, I lay her down on one side of the bed while I pull the covers down on the other, then pick her back up to tuck her in on her side.

Her side.

Damn, I like the sound of that. But it's really just the side of the bed she slept in last night. That's all it is.

Shaking my head at my stupid thoughts, I take her phone from my pocket and place it on the nightstand, then carefully remove her glasses and do the same with those. She put my shirt on again when she washed her face, but with leggings this time, which is a terrible shame.

Knowing I'm about to leave and not see her until morning, I take my time gazing at her, drinking her in. There's a light on in the bathroom, and it's just enough to illuminate her face. "Raf?" she whispers as I drape the duvet over her. "Where are you going? Come to bed."

Fuck the guest bed.

I have never moved as fucking fast as I do now. I practically rip my shirt off and throw my glasses on the nightstand. The second I'm in the bed, she turns toward me, opening her eyes.

She starts to shimmy under the covers and then tosses something over the side. "Can't sleep in pants," she mumbles with a scowl that makes me laugh. She keeps moving before throwing something else. "Or a bra." She sighs, seemingly content, and I nearly choke on air. And just when I was doing so well at not thinking about her naked.

Still coughing, I respond, "That's okay. I can't sleep with a shirt on."

"I can see that," she says as her eyes rake over my chest

before she closes them again. "I actually thought of you more as the kind of guy who would sleep naked."

"I normally do," I admit, and her eyes open widely for only a second before she shuts them tightly. "You think about me naked, shortcake?" I wouldn't have asked, but she brought it up.

"Far too often." Her confession takes me off-guard, and I don't respond. "Sorry, that was... well, it was honest but inappropriate."

"I like you honest but inappropriate," I say in a low voice that makes her laugh. It's one I haven't heard before, a little husky, and a lot sleepy. "In fact, I think we should amend our agreement to say we have to *always* be honest *and* inappropriate."

"Of course you do." She blows out a breath, opening her eyes, but just barely. "Can I be honest again?"

"You can always be honest with me, honey bun." I bop her nose, attempting to ease her mind. Her giggle tells me it's working.

"You did that while you were hopped up on meds, do you remember?" she asks and I shake my head no. "You nearly poked my eyeball out." A smile overtakes her face when I laugh. But then her features turn serious again, and I brace myself.

"I really liked today. A lot. Being with you feels easy and fun." Her brows furrow and I feel the *but* coming before she even says it. "But..." There it is. I hold my breath, not even wanting to make noise as she potentially ends whatever this is. "But I'm confused. I just... I don't know what to do anymore." She yawns, and I slowly let out my breath. "I'm sorry. I've been thinking about this all day, but I don't think the words are coming out right." Rubbing at her eyes, she sinks a little further into the pillow.

"It's all right. You're tired. Why don't we talk about it tomorrow?" For the second night in a row, I prepare myself to sleep next to the woman I've fallen completely head over heels for. And for the morning to come so we can have a conversation I really don't want to have.

She yawns again, nodding and letting her eyes remain closed this time. "Mmkay." Her breathing slows almost immediately, but then she shifts again, snuggling into me, and after a few seconds of both of us shuffling around, her head is on my chest, her left leg draped over mine. It's the sweetest torture.

"Goodnight, Charlie." I kiss the top of her head, letting the smell of roses fill my nostrils.

She runs her hand over my chest and up to the back of my head, pulling me down as she reaches up. Her mouth covers mine, our lips fitting perfectly together as they always do. When we separate, she lets out a satisfied hum. "Goodnight, Raf." She kisses my chin and lowers her head back down to my chest, which is suddenly feeling very tight. If she breaks this off tomorrow, I don't know what I'm going to do.

48 /
i only dream
about you.

charlie

THERE'S a something heavy draped across my back. A weighted blanket? No. This is much warmer. And breathing? I inhale the scent of oranges and remember where I am. Who I'm with.

Rafael's large hand is under my T-shirt, his grip firm yet gentle on my breast, and his leg is draped over one of mine, his thigh nestled at my core. He shifts, and the friction of his leg and my underwear has me biting down on my tongue to stifle a moan.

His nose burrows into my neck, and his sleepy morning voice is nothing short of delicious. "I hope I never wake up from this dream." My now-hardened nipples are sensitive, and when his thumb flicks across one, I do moan. That only seems to spur him on. His leg shifts again, and I feel him behind me. Hard. So hard. And I know I'm slick when his thick thigh moves again, causing the seam of my panties to perfectly rub against my clit. I rock into it, and he groans.

I let out another moan, louder this time, but when I turn my head back slightly to see him, I note his eyes are closed.

Is he sleeping?

I can't find it in me to care when his hips pump again, seeking the same pleasure I am. I rock my hips again, and he pinches my nipple, making me nearly cry out. "That's it. That's my girl. Ride me until you come all over me." And I do. I writhe and roll my hips on his thigh until my muscles start to tense up, and my orgasm is nearly at my fingertips. "Goddamn it, you're perfect for me, Charlie. I'll never want anyone the way I want you. Never." He bites down on my neck, and I gasp. Loudly. Too loudly. And my orgasm hits so intensely that all I can do is keep riding his leg until both of us are panting. Until I feel a wetness both on my lower back and between my legs. Until I turn my head to see wide, chocolate eyes on me. He kisses me, and I melt further into the bed, into his body.

I should hate that we both have morning breath. I should be bothered by the way my neck is turned back to reach him. But post-orgasm Charlie doesn't seem to notice anything but the perfection of this moment. The way our mouths know one another so intimately. The way our bodies are starting to, as well. The way my heart swells every time he says my name or shares a tidbit of the way he feels about me.

Needing a full breath, I pull back, and our eyes meet again, his hand slipping out of my shirt in one swift motion. "Shit. Fuck. Shit." He must see the confusion on my face at his reaction to our kiss and whatever that was before. "I'm sorry, pumpkin. You wanted space and none of this, and I—fuck. I was dreaming, and—"

"You were dreaming about me." I don't ask. I know it was me. It was my name on his lips.

"I always dream about you. I *only* dream about you." His steady gaze makes my breath hitch, but I nod in under-standing of what he's just said.

"I think I need, I should..." I shift my body farther from his, and he lets me go, moving his leg off mine. Awkwardness sets in, and it feels like a first for us since we started this strange little agreement of ours. An agreement that feels like it happened so long ago now. An agreement that feels so different from whatever has been growing between us. And that has me rushing out of his bed. "I need to go. I need some time to... I don't know. I just need to go."

He nods. His bare chest heaving as he blinks rapidly. "Whatever you need. Will you... will you still come with me on Sunday?"

The birthday.

His family.

"I don't know," I answer honestly and Rafael nods again, looking away from me this time, and as I turn away to pick up the leggings I tossed off the bed last night, I'm sure I see him wipe at his cheek. But I can't look back to confirm. I need to move. I need to leave and get my thoughts straight, gather my reckless, illicit feelings, and make some sense of it all.

I gather my things and go. I walk back to my flat, clutching my bag to me like a security blanket. I walk in and sit on the sofa that isn't mine, watching the sun shining through the balcony doors. And when my phone vibrates next to me, my first thought is that I hope it's Rafael asking me to come back. Telling me he needs me again.

But no.

As the phone continues vibrating, showing me another man's name on the screen, I let a tear fall down my face.

It stops.

Then the humming is back, but only once.

I glance down to see five words I wish I could instantly forget.

ROBERT:

I'm coming to Los Angeles.

———

THE LITTLE SLEEP I got was filled with vivid dreams. In the last one, I was standing in my kitchen back in London; Robert's arms were wrapped around me as he kissed my neck. I flinched and turned around to find Rafael standing there. The one before that was similar. I was in LA, in Rafael's bed, much like yesterday morning, with his body keeping me warm. When he flipped me over to kiss me good morning, it was Robert's face I saw.

So now, I probably can't ever go to sleep again.

I thought about responding to Robert, asking him when he's coming, but the truth is, I don't care. He probably has my address because I had my assistant at the firm mail me a couple of things. But it doesn't matter. Even if he shows up here, I know what I need to say to him.

I spent most of yesterday writing down what I was thinking and feeling, and all I could make sense of in the end was that things between Rafael and I got too muddled.

In the end I concluded that I think Rafael could be treating me the way he is out of obligation as my relationship coach. I think he could simply be an overly affectionate person who can handle this kind of attachment to someone and then can let them go. I also think it's difficult for me to discern between liking something versus liking it specifically with him.

But what I feel is his sincerity in everything he does. I feel myself falling for a man I never expected to need in my life so thoroughly. I feel incredibly confused about what this all means.

Since I couldn't tell who was right—my brain or my heart—I decided to at least give Rafael an answer about Sunday.

ME:

If you still want me there, I'd really like to meet your family.

We don't even have to do any of the relationship practice.

> I can just be there as your friend.

It will probably be the only time I ever see them all, and I'd really like to apologize to his parents in person about putting their son in the hospital, maybe get a hug from Vó before I mess everything up.

After a few minutes of staring at my phone, I'm about to go distract myself with something else when his message comes through.

RAFAEL:

> Of course I want you there. In whatever capacity you want.

I think it's relief I'm feeling, based on the way I just let out the breath that was lodged in my chest. I don't know if I want to keep up the practicing. I don't think we should. Things feel too muddy.

ME:

> Whose birthday is it? I'd like to bring something for them.

RAFAEL:

> Don't worry about that, please. No gifts.

ME:

> Come on.

> This is me we're talking about.

> I absolutely will worry about it.

> Just tell me what they like at least?

> Promise it'll be something small.

> Don't make me show up empty-handed.

RAFAEL:

> Fine. Reading. Same taste in books as me.

> And thank you. That's very thoughtful of you.

I briefly wonder if it's one of his brothers, but there's no way, statistically speaking, that more than one Machado man reads romance, is there? Must be his mum or his sister, and given they like what Rafael likes, I know just what to get them, because it's what I would get for Rafael himself if it were his birthday.

My mind wanders to how I'm getting to Siesta tomorrow. I drove that little bit with Rafael and then to and from the hospital. I'm perfectly capable of driving myself, so that's what I'll do.

RAFAEL:

> Pick you up at eleven tomorrow. See you then, shorty.

Oh. Well, never mind then.

49 /
which us?

charlie

AT ELEVEN O'CLOCK on the dot, the buzzer goes off on the intercom that was updated throughout the building approximately a week after I ran into Rafael.

Huh.

I buzz him in, wishing he had just let himself up as he usually does while I gather my things. When he knocks, I'm ready. My black skirt flows out over my knees, the old leather boots that nearly meet the hem of the skirt already on. My emerald green long-sleeved top is tucked into the skirt to accentuate my waist. I'm ready.

Until I open the door.

Rafael is standing there with a bouquet of flowers in his hand, looking down at his feet, wearing a black button-up shirt with sleeves rolled to the elbows and black pants.

And those bloody glasses.

His hair is styled in perfect curls and waves that touch the frames. But he's looking down at his feet rather than at me. His eyes shift to my feet, then slowly rise, gliding over every part of my body until he reaches my eyes. This time, I'm the one waiting for him to look at me.

We haven't said a word yet; we're just staring at each other.

"Hi, Charlie." He swallows, shifting one of his hands into his pocket. "You look beautiful."

The fact that he hasn't touched me, mixed with the emotion I can see in his eyes, has tears immediately building up, and I feel the heat of one trailing down my cheek. Before I can catch it, Rafael's gentle touch is there, my tear trapped beneath his thumb.

He steps into my space and brings his forehead down to mine as the door shuts behind him. "Why?" He breathes out the question.

Why what, I wonder? Why am I crying? Why did I leave yesterday? Why does this feel like the beginning of the end?

I don't have any of the answers, and he seems to know it.

"If this isn't real… If this has to end, can it just not be today? Please? Not yet?" I feel his desperate questions on my lips as he inches closer. He must set the flowers down because I feel his other hand on my lower back, pressing us together until I can't take any more.

My lips reach for his, and the kiss is a chaste press, but I swear I feel him tremble before we pull away. "Okay," I whisper. "Not today."

We both let out a long breath, and after I place the roses he brought me in a vase, we silently make our way out to his car.

———

IF THIS ISN'T REAL. *If this has to end.*

I may not be an expert at relationships, but I do believe myself to be as close as one can get to being a Rafael expert, and he's emotional whenever we talk about me leaving or ending our agreement. And I'm starting to become emotional over it, too, because I don't want this to be over. Yet? I don't know. But I can't think about this any longer.

By the time we're settled in the car and on our way to his family home, I wonder if we can take it a day at a time. One normal day at a time. Then, we can see what happens.

"Can we just be… us?" My question must pull him out of whatever deep thoughts were running through his mind.

"Which us, Charlie? The us that bickers? The us where we avoid each other as much as possible because things are awkward? Or the us where I can touch you without asking permission and kiss you whenever I want?" His words are pained. The way he said my name—it's different. It's laced with hurt.

"Th-the third one. I want the third one." And I do. I want that version of us. Maybe always. He lets out a sigh that almost sounds relieved.

"For now, right?" he clarifies, and there's a small voice inside me that is begging me to just commit to being with him. But my brain won't allow it, and the knowledge that I need to tie up loose ends with everything and everyone— well, Robert— in London nags at me.

"For now," I whisper back, because I can't say otherwise for certain.

He swallows twice, and his grip on the steering wheel tightens to the point that his knuckles whiten. "Okay," he says.

Rafael reaches over and places a warm hand on my knee, and, just like he knew it would, the action soothes my nerves and makes me feel more at ease. I don't chance looking up at him. I'm nearly certain that his eyes will be too sad. Too full of whatever he's feeling, and I'd really like to not cry again today.

50 /
geez. we're in my
family home.

rafael

NOT TODAY. *For now.*

Fuck.

She's going to end it.

Charlie is going to end whatever this is, and it might just end *me* because I'm so fucking in love with her, I'm not sure I'll ever be able to recover.

Well, fuck thinking about that. It's not over, so I'm taking every second she'll give me. Every smile. Every kiss. Every chance to soothe her obvious nerves over meeting my family and this whole situation. I'm going to keep giving her all of me. I just hope it's enough in the end.

If there's anything I'm good at, it's covering up how I actually feel and pretending everything is okay. Though I had stopped doing that with Charlie. She saw me at my most vulnerable. Took care of me. The only women who have ever done that before are the two who raised me. The two who prepared my requested cake today and who are, without a doubt, anxiously waiting for us to get out of the car and greet them.

The rest of our friends not being here today is intentional.

Maeve, Owen, and Jules sent a very sweet video, and Adam, Elaina and Agnes surprised me on the morning of my actual birthday a few days ago with muffins and a gift. The baby snuggles were also awesome. I just figured, even with people she knows, this might feel too overwhelming for Charlie. They all agreed, and the girls thought it was nice that she would get to meet my family. Because, you know, we're friends.

And now, here we are.

I keep my hold on her knee a moment longer before I squeeze and let go. "Ready?" I'm not sure that I am, but we're here. When I see her nod, I open my door and walk around to open hers. She's carrying the bag with whatever gift she's brought for today. I didn't even remember to ask about it.

My hand remains on her lower back as we approach the house, and she relaxes into the touch. When I open the front door, reluctantly letting her go, the place isn't as noisy as it usually is on a Sunday. "Hello?" I hear the patter of little feet, and then I see a head of brown hair rounding the corner.

"Tio Rafa! Finally!" I barely have time to crouch down before Cecilia's little body crashes into mine. Her short arms wrap around my neck so tightly it nearly hurts, and I squeeze her right back, picking her up and swaying us so her little legs dangle around me.

"Hey, if it isn't my favorite niece. How are you, my brilliant girl?" I lower us so her feet touch the floor again as she giggles.

"I'm your only niece, you silly goose." Cece's green eyes are full of joy, and I'm immediately more at ease, knowing that today is going to be incredible no matter what. Charlie is quiet behind me, and I sense the tension the moment my niece notices the stranger in the room.

"Cece, I brought my friend Charlie with me today. She's very nice. Do you remember when I told you about her?" She nods, moving closer to me. Meeting new people is hard for

Cece, but I'm glad Gabriel was able to have her here today. In my peripheral vision, I see Charlie lowering to her knees next to me, setting her things on the floor.

"Hi, Cecilia. You have a beautiful name. What does it mean?" Charlie keeps her hands close to her body and gives my niece, who doesn't look up, space.

"It's from the Latin name Caecilia, which comes from the word caecus, which means blind or hidden. But my whole name is Ana Cecilia, so I have part of Bisa's name too. Ana means gracious." Cece shrugs, still holding on to my arm tightly as Charlie hums.

"That's very interesting. Thank you for sharing all of that with me. My name is Charlotte, but I like to be called Charlie." There's a beat of silence, then she continues, "I'm pretty nervous about going in there today, Cecilia. Meeting new people is really hard for me."

Cece's head pops up, and she takes Charlie—whose eyes are down on the floor—in for the first time. "It's hard for me to meet new people, too."

"Well, you're doing a great job with me. I can already tell I'm going to like you very much." She does look up then and offers my niece a genuine smile. "I might need to ask your uncle for one of his special hugs later if I get a little…"

"Overwhelmed?" Cece finishes for her. No one bats an eyelash at the five-year-old saying a word like that because that's just Cece. "That's what my daddy calls it when I need time out."

"That's exactly right. Overwhelmed. I usually need a little time out, too, when I'm in a new place or if it gets a little too loud." Charlie winces, showing my niece what they have in common.

"Our family can be loud, but I promise they're nice. So, if it gets too loud, I have a special spot I go to. And special headphones. I could share them with you if you need them." Cece's grip on me loosens, and she stands a little straighter.

The tears in my eyes are immediate as I reach out to touch Charlie's arm, lowering my hand until our fingers are linked.

"That's—" Charlie clears her throat of the emotion lodged inside it. "That's really kind of you, Cecilia. I really appreciate that. Actually," she pauses, "it's very *gracious* of you to share things that are so special to you. Thank you."

"Cece?" My brother's deep voice sounds from down the hall. Gabriel stops when he takes in the scene, not missing the tears I don't bother hiding. "You made Titio cry already? And on his birthday?" There's no actual mockery in his tone, but I sense Charlie tense next to me. I guess she might as well know now.

"He cries a lot. But he's so productive, right Titio?" She gives me a loud kiss on the cheek then, and I laugh, not understanding whatever little inside joke she just told herself. Squeezing Charlie's fingers, we both move to stand. Cece lets go of me and takes her dad's hand. "Daddy, this is Tio Rafa's friend, Charlie. She gets overwhelmed like me, so be nice to her, k?" My heart squeezes almost painfully with all of the emotions inside it.

Gabe brushes Cece's hair off her forehead, then extends the same hand to Charlie. "Hi, Charlie. I'm Gabriel. It's great to meet you." He gives her an apologetic look for his daughter's comment, but Charlie smiles down at her, mouthing *thank you*.

"Nice to meet you too," Charlie says as she shakes his hand. "Your daughter just quoted Taylor Swift. Did you know that?"

Gabe groans and rubs the bridge of his nose with his thumb and forefinger. "Excuse me, I need to go find my little sister and have a chat about age-appropriate music." My brother and niece turn back the way they came, and I'm left alone in the front entry, holding Charlie's hand.

"It's *your* birthday?" Her tone tells me what I already

knew: she's not super happy about this little surprise. But she hasn't let go of my hand, so I'm calling it a win.

I don't get a chance to say anything, though, because my parents come around the corner with big, wide smiles on their faces. My mom immediately reaches for me, giving my cheek a kiss and wrapping me in a warm hug. "Oi, meu filho." When she lets go, my dad repeats the same motions, but I don't let go of Charlie's hand.

"Mãe, Pai, I'd like you to officially meet Charlie." I free up her right hand but keep a firm hold on her, moving my hand up her spine to her neck with a gentle squeeze. "Charlie, these are my parents, Andrea and Ivan."

She relaxes and reaches out to my mom first, taking me by surprise when she doesn't reach for a handshake, but rather touches my mom's shoulders and kisses her left cheek, then the right. It's a traditional Brazilian greeting, but I never expected it. My mom, however, doesn't seem the least bit fazed, and neither does my dad when she greets him in the same way.

"Thank you so much for having me today." She steps back, a little closer to me this time, linking out fingers together again. Her voice is a little shaky, a little unsure. "I'm so sorry about—"

"We're so glad to finally meet you, Charlie. We're happy you're here, and we're so grateful to you for the way you took care of our boy. Please. No apologies." Dad's voice is gentle despite the interruption. "We hope our son hasn't been giving you too hard of a time?"

"Other than having me show up to a birthday party I didn't know was for him, no. He's been perfect." Her voice softens at the end, and my mom's eyes fill with tears before she blinks them away, that huge smile still on her face. Then, she turns to me and purses her lips.

"Rafa, why did you not tell her?" Mom's hands go to her hips as she scolds me, but I smile.

"Because I wanted to make sure she would come." I play on the old dynamic with me and Charlie, the one where we bicker like an old married couple, and I'm glad she goes along with it for the moment.

"Good call," she says, looking at me. Her face is so serious, I wouldn't know she was joking if it weren't for the twinkle in her sky-blue eyes.

Both of my parents break into laughter, and we join them. "I knew I'd like you," my dad says. "Now, let's go before our nosy children burst from the anticipation of meeting you, Charlie girl."

My parents take off ahead of us, and Charlie tugs on my hand, so I twist to face her. "They're lovely," she whispers, smiling.

With my hand on her chin, I rub our noses together. "*You're* lovely, shortcake." And then I kiss her. I kiss her until her body sags into mine. She lets out a little whimper and grabs my shirt. I nuzzle into her neck and leave a kiss there, and then another, and another, because how can I not? How can I not kiss her after the way she just met my niece, my brother, *and* my parents? Charlie moans when I suck lightly on her pulse, and I smile into her skin. "Shhh. Not now, gata. Geez. We're in my family home."

She gasps, and the hand that was grabbing my shirt pinches lightly at my side. Her rebuttal gets lodged in her throat when Gustavo's voice comes from the kitchen. "Stop making out and come introduce us already!"

51 /
i think tio rafa is your pickle.

charlie

WE STEP INTO THE KITCHEN, and everyone is busy with something, eyes lowered to their tasks, except for one man. His hazel eyes are bright, and his smirk is all mischief. There's no doubt in my mind he's the one who shouted for us to come in here.

"Hey there, lovebirds," the man I assume is one of Raf's younger brothers says. He might not be biologically related to Rafael, but his teasing tone is identical to the man's next to me.

"Gus." Raf's tone is more of a warning, and his brother raises both hands, palms up, then walks a few steps toward us.

"Great to finally meet you, Charlie. I'm Gustavo, the good-looking brother." Rather than give me his hand to shake, he starts to point across the room. "That's Marcelo." A man who looks nearly identical to Gustavo other than the eye color waves to me. "You met Gabe and Cece." The pair look up at me with matching smiles and go back to folding napkins. "And our baby sister, Daniela." A girl with long, dark curls, who is setting up a charcuterie board, smiles brightly at me and mouths what I think is *I love your skirt.*

I raise a hand in my own awkward wave as all of the Machados welcome me as quietly as I'm sure they can manage. Simultaneously, Rafael and I walk toward Ana Maria, who is drying her hands at the sink.

"Bença, Vó," Rafael says as he reaches for her in the same way as he did with his parents, still holding onto me. Once she's responded and patted his cheeks, she turns to me, brows high in the air as if expecting me to say or do something.

I clear my throat and say the only thing I can think of. "Bença, Vó." I kiss her cheeks and pull back, feeling like I did the right thing when her smile grows.

"Deus te abençoe, minha filha." She pats my cheeks, slightly more gently than she did with her grandson, and lingers on me for a few seconds before looking lovingly at Rafael and stepping away from us.

"Can I get you a drink, Charlie?" Andrea is walking to the fridge before I have an answer fully formed.

"I got it, Mãe." Rafael kisses the top of my head and walks away from me. I guess after Gustavo's comment about us making out, it's okay for them to assume we're together? Or was that a friendly head kiss? He's done this to his grand-mother. To Lainey, even. So, I suppose this is just Raf being Raf.

I feel oddly comfortable in this kitchen. Perhaps because I've been in it when there are just three of us, so I don't hesi-tate to ask, "Can I help with anything?"

"No way. You're the guest of honor. You're literally the one person we've been waiting for since Mãe made us all get here early to prep," Daniela says.

"I would take offense to that, Dani." Raf walks up behind me, setting a drink on the island countertop where I have been normally perched during our Tuesday visits, and wraps his arms around my middle. "But I'm not even mad because Charlie is always the most important person in the room to me."

I melt. Andrea swoons. Daniela clutches her chest. Marcelo makes a loud gagging noise. And then we all laugh, easing the tension I had started to feel with Rafael's sincere proclamation. He didn't even have to think about it; he just came out and said it so naturally.

SHORTLY AFTER INTRODUCTIONS, Andrea and Vó asked to be left alone in the kitchen, so the rest of us headed outside with drinks and snacks. They ask me about London, whether I'm liking California, and how Raf and I met—though Gus admitted that they already knew, they just wanted my version of the story.

"And you work in finance, right? Rafa told us you're very good at what you do." Ivan smiles kindly at me. When I look at Rafael on the other side of the patio, he's blushing.

"You've been talking about me?" I ask the question teasingly, grinning at Raf before answering his father. "I do work in finance. And he's right. I am *very* good at it."

"I like you," Daniela points at me. "You're badass."

I shake my head. "Well, I might be good at my job, but I don't like it very much." The admission sends tingles over my skin.

Ivan clicks his tongue. "You should love whatever you do, Charlie girl. Life is both too long and too short for you not to do what makes you happy, you know?" There's a sadness that comes over Ivan's features then, but he covers it quickly. "And I have a feeling your current job isn't the only thing you're good at." His eyes crinkle kindly at me.

"Pfft, this is nothing," Raf says. "She also writes books. And she smiles when she writes them. It's incredible, to watch her create an entire world full of people and places no one has ever seen before. Charlie's stories are amazing." He's positively beaming with pride as he tells his family about me. My entire body is taught, and he must see it. His smile fades and he mutters a curse, mouthing the word *sorry* to me. But there's nothing to be sorry for. I only tensed at the initial shock of his words. I know he's proud of me. I can feel it. I can hear it in the way he's excited to share pieces of me with his family, and they're excited to know me. It's... wonderful. *He's* wonderful.

"Really? You're a writer?" The youngest sister's question rips me out of my spiral.

I breathe out a laugh. "Okay, yes, but let's not go down that rabbit hole right now. I'd love to know more about you all. I'm fascinated by the fact that your backyard is an orange grove. And I'm going to need to see some Brazilian skills put on display on that football pitch." I lift my chin in the direction of the nets set up on the grassy field.

"Ai," Ivan clutches his chest. "You know it's a grove *and* you call it football, not *soccer*." He emphasizes the last word with an exaggerated American accent. Looking pointedly at Rafael, he continues, "Better not let this one go, filho."

Raf's eyes lower, a tight smile pulling at his cheeks. I wish he would look at me so I could see the emotion in his eyes. From here, with his head down, I can't get a read on him.

"Get ready, Charlie," Marcelo says on a laugh. "Now you'll have Pai talking about oranges and The Beautiful Game for the rest of the day." He winks at his dad and everyone laughs.

Ivan does talk about both oranges and football, and I try to remain engaged. But after an hour of conversation with so many people and my first official admission of being an author, I'm starting to feel my social battery start to drain.

"Daddy, can I show Charlie my quiet place?" Cece approaches her dad cautiously, careful not to get too close to the hot grill he's cooking part of our meal on. Gabriel closes it, turning to give her his full attention.

"Only if she wants to, sweets. And if she says no, another grown-up needs to go with y—"

"I know, Daddy. I know the rules." She shakes her head, and based on the way her dad's eyebrows rise, she probably just rolled her eyes at him, too. I look away, stifling a smile. I didn't expect to like a five-year-old so much, but here we are.

I watch as her little shoulders rise on a deep inhale. She's probably psyching herself up to ask me to go with her. It's a big deal. For her to approach me, for her to share such a special place with me, so I decide not to cause her any further stress. When she turns around, however, with determination written all over her sweet face, I have to change my mind. Because this little girl isn't in any kind of distress over this, she's simply finding her courage.

"Hi, Charlie," she says when she approaches me. Rafael is deep in conversation about a football match—the kind you play with your feet, not the American kind—with his dad, but he looks over as his niece approaches me.

"Hey, Cece." I pretend that I didn't just hear her whole conversation with her father.

"I want to go to my quiet place, and I was wondering if you'd like to come with me. We won't be long since it'll be time to eat soon, and my dad has a rule that a grown-up has to come with me, so if you don't come, I'll have to ask someone else." She states the facts and then waits for my answer, all while looking over my shoulder. Cece hasn't made eye contact with anyone but her dad since I got here, and no one has tried to force her into it during any interactions either. I've never experienced anything like this.

"I'd really like to come with you. Thank you for asking me." I start to stand, setting the glass of prosecco Rafael had gotten me earlier on the table.

When I walk past him, he snakes an arm around my waist,

squeezing gently as he kisses my temple. "Take your time," he whispers.

"Let's go, Charlie." My little green-eyed friend skips away from me, crossing to the other side of the backyard toward the pond. When she gets close to the water, she stops and waits for me to catch up, then walks to a wooden bench where she sits and looks at the calm water.

"Vovô made this bench for me, and Titia painted it." She pats the seat next to her like the bench is precious. I'm sure it is to her.

I know from listening to her interact with her family members for a little while that Vovô is her grandfather and Titia is Dani, her aunt. Vovó is Grandma, and Bisa is short for Bisavó, which means great-grandmother.

"You can sit here if you want." Cece's hands go to her lap as she looks our at the water.

I walk closer to her and take a seat on the simple but beautiful bench, which has tiny flowers painted along the back of it. The letters "ilia" are visible among the florals, so I can safely assume her name is what's written there in the beautiful cursive.

"Thank you." I don't say anything else. This is a quiet place, after all. So, we sit in peaceful silence, enjoying the way the trees sway and the reflection of the sky on the water's surface.

Several minutes pass, and though I can't say how long it's been, I know I feel much more at peace now, and I can tell Cece does too. My thoughts have quieted. My emotions, too.

"Are you going to marry Tio Rafa?" Her tone is perfectly calm as I nearly choke on the air caught in my throat. "It's okay if you're not. I know sometimes grown-ups look at each other like that, but they don't get married. Tio Gustavo is like that with his friend, too, and he says he would never ever marry her. And Mommy and Daddy used to sort of look at each other like that, but they don't anymore. That's why they got divorced."

"Oh," is all I can think to say. "H-how do we look at each other, your Tio Rafa and me?" I'm not sure I should be asking, but she's five. It's fine, right?

"Just like I look at my favorite stuffy." Okay, yeah, this is fine. "Mommy said she forgot to pack her today, so you'll have to meet her next time." *Next time.* My heart breaks a little. She gets a sad look in her eyes before continuing. "I like all of my stuffies, but Pickle is special. I look at Pickle like she's the one I treasure the most. Like I feel safe with her, and she makes everything good even better, and everything sad a little happier. I never ever want to be away from her. And when I am away from her, I feel sad and I cry, like I did today when Mommy dropped me off. I think Tio Rafa is your Pickle, and you are most definitely *definitely* his." She raises her chin, confirming these so-called facts to the open air.

"Oh," I repeat. That double definitely sends me into a déjà vu of when I asked Rafael if he would take me on a date. "I'm really glad that you have Pickle. She sounds like the best sort of stuffy."

"She is. She's my best friend, too." Her brows scrunch together as she thinks about her next words. "My best not-human friend. Daddy is my best human friend, and Tio Rafa and Tia Dani and everybody who's here. You can be one of my best human friends, too, if you want." She doesn't give me time to respond to that incredibly sweet and heartfelt offer. "But with Pickle, it's just easy because I can tell her everything. I don't have to try to explain myself; she just knows me."

I sit with that for a moment, completely in awe, and yet not at all surprised that the same little girl who offered me her quiet place would offer up this kind of insight.

He's the one I treasure the most. I feel safe with him. He makes everything good better, and everything sad happier. I never want to be away from him. It's easy because I can tell him everything; he just knows me.

I think it. My head tells me these are facts.

I feel it. My heart tells me these are truths.

I don't need anything else. Head and heart are in perfect harmony. I thought this would be scary. I thought giving in to this kind of love would be turbulent and disruptive. But it's as peaceful as the glassy water on this pond.

A loud whistle sounds from the back of the house, and we both look back to see Ana Maria at the kitchen door with both pinkies at the corners of her mouth.

"Wow." I can't hide my surprise.

"Yeah. Bisa is awesome." With that last bit of truth, Cecilia stands, and we start our quiet walk back to the house. My heart trots along to a steady beat, so completely content to simply be here with these wonderful people.

When we walk in, the youngest brothers are already at the table. Gabriel waits for Cece and helps her into her chair, speaking quietly to her as she points at what she wants to eat. Rafael saddles up beside me, pulling me into him with an arm around my waist.

"Hi, gata." His smile is full of tenderness, his brown eyes shining on every inch of my face, until a scoff sounds from the table.

"You call your girlfriend gata? That's like the most basic shit ever." Marcelo's smirk turns into a wince.

"That's five dollars, Tio. You owe the most today." Cecilia doesn't even look up from the little puzzle she's working on.

"Cece, at this rate, I might as well just buy you the book." Marcelo takes out a bill and hands it to his niece, who pockets it quietly.

"What's happening?" I ask Raf.

"Cece gets a dollar for every swear word any of us say. She's saving up the money for a really expensive version of a book about wizards with pop-ups and sh—" He eyes his niece quickly. "Stuff. Anyway, she usually waits until the end of the day or until we get to at least five because she doesn't want a bunch of dollar bills." He lets out a small laugh, not because his niece amuses him in a comical way, but like he's truly impressed by how smart she is.

"Anywayyyyy," Marcelo drags out the word. "Back to the fact that you chose this pet name, Raf. You couldn't be a little more original?" He attempts to steal a piece of a shoestring chip off the table, and Daniela smacks him on the back of the head as she walks by on the way to her seat.

"Why is it not original? Doesn't it mean cat? I mean, I don't know why you call me that, but maybe it's because I'm sort of temperamental like a cat?" I ask, looking up at Raf, then back at Marcelo, but I find no answers in his satisfied smirk. Raf takes my hand, leading me out of the room until we're in the same hallway where he kissed me earlier.

"It does mean cat." Raf reaches up to grab the back of his neck. "It also means…" His voice lowers to a whisper like he's worried his family will hear. "Hot. Or sexy." His eyes are laser-focused on the small space between our feet on the floor, and his cheeks are the color of a ripe peach. It makes me want to kiss him again. It makes me want to hug him and never let him go. And, of course, my brain pinpoints a detail that probably doesn't need to be mentioned right now.

"You called me that for the first time last year. In Ojai. The day you switched sandwiches with me because mine had…" I shift my feet, so I'm facing Raf, watching as his face softens.

"Mushrooms, yeah. I remember, pretty girl." He pushes a strand of hair behind my ear as we stand nearly chest to chest, the sound of people moving around the kitchen now even more muffled thanks to the questions sounding off in my head. As if he can hear them too, he says, "Lainey probably forgot to ask for no mushrooms. She was newly pregnant, and we didn't even know it yet. Honest mistake." He shrugs. "And yeah, that was months ago. I may not have great vision, but I have eyes. I can see you. I've always seen you, Charlie. It was just a little fuzzier before. A little out of focus. But then it was like one day, I put my glasses on, and everything was so clear. You became so clear. You became my *only* focus. The only thing I even wanted to look at anymore."

Raf blows out a heavy breath and sniffles. This man and his emotions. They're all always out here, out in the open. I take his face in my hands as he blinks back the tears that have welled in his eyes.

"No tears on your birthday, all right?" I kiss him lightly, and he nods into the kiss, wrapping both of his arms around me. He lowers his face to my neck and kisses the same spot so many times I lose count.

"Roses. My favorite." He leaves one final kiss on my nose, smiling down at me. "Let's go eat?"

"Let's go," I answer and begin to make my way toward the kitchen. He smacks my bum lightly as I walk away, and I yelp. By the time we come into view of everyone else, we're both giggling as if we had just been doing far naughtier things in that hallway, and now it's my turn to have rosy cheeks.

he deserves this happiness. more than anyone.

charlie

THERE'S soft music coming from the kitchen where post-dinner clean-up is happening. After sitting at the table for at least three hours, I don't know that I've ever eaten so much, but it was all delicious.

When I step into the kitchen, Ivan is shimmying to Andrea. He spins her around the middle of the kitchen, pulling her into a dance as she laughs. Their eyes immediately soften as they take one another in, falling into what must be a familiar rhythm, swaying to a song with lyrics I can't understand but with a beautifully soft melody.

Marcelo reaches for Ana Maria, and they start to dance, then, to my absolute shock, Gustavo bows, extending his left hand to me, and for the second time today, I think of a past moment with Rafael. Without thought, I place my hand in his and Gustavo spins me quickly onto the makeshift dance floor in the middle of the kitchen.

"I have no clue what I'm doing," I say on a laugh.

His smile is wide when he asks, "Raf hasn't taught you yet?" He cocks his head to the side, and I shake my head. He's taught me a lot of things, but dancing isn't one of them.

"Well, no big deal. You'll get the hang of it." He shrugs and pulls me a little closer, keeping his hand in the middle of my back. Right when I feel like I might be getting the steps, Gustavo spins me again, and I land against Gabriel's chest who immediately huffs at his brother.

"Sorry about that. He probably didn't prepare you for that spin or the partner change, right?" His voice is deep but not loud—the deepest of all the brothers—and it suits him perfectly.

"He did not. And as you can see, I'm not much of a dancer." I wince, and he smiles kindly back at me.

"You're fine. Just follow our lead." He looks up momentarily, and I follow his gaze to Rafael, who's watching us with intensity in his eyes. "I'm sure by the next family dinner, you'll have it down." His calm and confident tone is reassuring. "Thanks for being so great with Cece today, by the way. I really appreciate your patience with her."

"Well, she's wonderful. But you already know that." I sway a little more confidently, not thinking about the steps as I go.

Gabriel smiles, pride for his daughter beaming out of his eyes as he watches her dancing with her grandfather. "She really is. Now, are you ready? To your left. Pai's got you now."

And then Ivan is there with a warm smile.

"Oh, I'm sorry, I'm not a very good—" I start, but for the second time today he interrupts me to stop me from apologizing. How is it possible to feel so seen by people you don't even really know?

"Nonsense. You're doing great." The song changes, but the beat is similar, which I'm thankful for. "I hope today hasn't been too overwhelming. I know my family is a lot." He chuckles, looking around at the group, who are mostly being silly as they dance together.

I shake my head because, yes, they're a little loud, a lot

affectionate, but they're all so wonderful. "Your family is beautiful.I feel really lucky to be here."

"Good. Good. Because you're stuck with us now, Charlie!" He doesn't explain; he just pulls away from me and tucks himself under our joined hands, and I'm met with Marcelo as my next dance partner.

"I bet you were hoping I'd be Raf, but we're trying to see how angry he gets that we're all getting to dance with you first." His smile, so similar to Gustavo's, makes me believe these brothers are nothing but mischief.

"Rafael? Angry? He doesn't get angry over anything." I chance a look at him as he dances with his mom. They're laughing, and I wish I could take a photo.

"I'm pretty sure you're the exception, Charlie. To just about everything for him." Marcelo is looking at me when I meet his gaze, and that's when I see the silliness in his face fade away. "Be good to him, yeah? He deserves this. He deserves this happiness. More than anyone." His eyes shine with tears, and my God, I have to hold my breath to keep my own eyes from welling up. These Machado men…oof.

Marcelo stops, takes a step back, and lowers into a bow before placing my hand in another's.

Rafael.

"Finally," he whispers into my hair, pulling me in much closer than any of my previous dance partners, letting his hand settle a little lower on my back. "I missed you."

I giggle at his seriousness. "I've been here the whole time."

"Not close enough unless you're right here, firecracker." He lets go of my hand and pulls me into him with both hands until my cheek is resting on his chest and my hands are on the back of his neck. "That's better."

"Yeah, it is," I agree. We stay like that for a couple of minutes, and when I let out a contented sigh, he puts a little space between us.

"Ready to see how it's really done?" His eyebrows dance on his forehead, and the moment my hands slip down his chest, he takes them both and starts to move us around. I spin one way, then another, and nearly crash into him, but he catches me smoothly at the last second. Somehow, he moves my body exactly the way he wants, and I hardly even need to do anything but let him.

My laughter is uncontrollable and as soon as I hear Raf laughing with me, I swear I float up into the air. It's magical. It's wonderful.

When we finally stop, we sway nose-to-nose, and as our giggles start to die down, I take notice that the music has stopped and a new song has started. Raf's whole family is singing Happy Birthday to him in Portuguese, his mom holding a cake in her hands topped with candles as she walks toward us. There's clapping and cheering, and then Rafael pauses, looks at me for a long moment, then closes his eyes and blows out the candles.

Andrea gets to work on cutting the cake, and Rafael hands out the plates, with the first going to Cece, which is apparently a big deal. I get the second and hear a few *oohs* and *aahs* from the younger brothers.

I look at the slice of white cake with whipped cream and strawberries. "Is this—"

"Strawberry shortcake… cake." Rafael kisses my cheek. "My favorite." He winks and returns to his task, making sure everyone has a slice. Yet again, I find my face heating as I keep my eyes on my plate. I smile at the thought that either this really is his favorite, or this is the flavor he chose especially for this year.

Just as Rafael is walking toward me with his own piece of cake, both of our phones start ringing loudly. Mine is somewhere in the house, but Raf has his in his back pocket, so he sets his plate down to look at it. He gives nothing away, his face unchanging. Then he reaches for me, takes my plate, and sets it next to his.

With gentle hands cradling my face, he smiles down at me. "Everything's okay. It's Maeve. Her water broke, and they're on their way to the hospital." Time comes to a complete standstill as I momentarily forget how to breathe. I watch as Rafael's expression turns to worry. "Breathe for me, Charlie. Just like me." He pulls in a deep breath, and I attempt to do the same, though my lungs won't let me just yet. On the next breath, I get a little more, and he smiles at me. "That's my girl. You got this."

By the fifth breath, I'm back to normal, and the severity of the situation hits. "I have to go. But you should stay. It's your birthday party. Stay. I'll get a taxi or—"

"I'm taking you. No question. You're about to be an aunt, shortcake. For the third time!" His smile widens, and he kisses my lips three times in quick succession, in that way that soothes every nervous feeling in my body and has my hands automatically grabbing at his shirt for purchase. "You ready?"

I'm not, but I nod anyway because we have a couple of hours in the car before we get to the very fancy LA hospital where Maeve is giving birth. Rafael takes my hand and guides me out of the house. When we get to his car, Andrea is there, tucking something into the back seat while Ivan shuts the trunk.

"There are snacks and leftovers packed and enough cake for everyone in a cooler. I put some extra blankets in the back seat because hospitals are always too cold." Andrea joins her husband beside the SUV. I have no idea when she had time to do all of this.

The rest of the family is out there, too, waiting to say goodbye to us. My heart is so full of emotions that I'm not sure what to do with them all. Raf's family didn't even bat an eye at this sudden change in plans, at this disruption to the party they were throwing for their son. They look happy. Completely unbothered. Just like Raf.

Without letting go of my hand, he starts to kiss his parents goodbye. Andrea's voice is calming, just like the day I spoke to her on the phone. "It's going to be all right, Charlie. Maeve is strong and she's going to have her very best friend right there next to her. She'll be so happy to have your support." She kisses my cheek and pulls me in for a hug. I let go of Raf's hand then so that I can hug her back.

"Thank you," I whisper. "Thank you for your kindness. For raising the most exceptional man I've ever known. For welcoming me here."

"This is your home now, too, Charlie. You are always welcome," she says into my hair, giving me one last squeeze before letting go.

With tears in my eyes, I hug Ivan, whispering another *thank you* to him. Then, I hug the entire Machado family, thanking every one of them. I don't say what for, but it feels like they all know.

I wipe away the last tear as I step into Raf's car. He's already inside, ready and waiting to take us to the hospital. He honks as he drives away from his family, who are all standing on the driveway waving us off like we're newly-weds going on our honeymoon, and the image feels so real, so vivid, that I have to shake my head to rattle it away, forcing myself back into the present.

"Thank you, Raf." I twist so I can look at him and watch as the wide grin blooms on his handsome face. He takes my hand in his, bringing it up to his lips for three quick kisses, then sets it back on my lap. We drive to the hospital like that, holding hands and listening to the sounds of the tires on the road. He drives calmly and safely, as always, while my mind spins, wondering what my sister is feeling, what tonight is going to be like, whether everything will be okay.

When we arrive, he parks in a short-term spot and walks

inside with me, my hand still in his. He seems to know exactly where to go and who to talk to, and I'm thankful for that because I haven't done anything other than text Maeve to let her know I'm on the way.

We stop in front of a room, and Raf faces me, taking my other hand in his. He opens his mouth to speak, but I get to it first. "Childbirth makes me really nervous. I researched it extensively as a kid, and I just remember it being so scary. So much can go wrong, you know?"

"I get it." He squeezes my hands. "Maeve is in good hands. Owen will be right there, and you know he's not going to let anything happen without asking questions. And you'll be there advocating for her. I won't tell you everything is going to be okay because I can't see the future, but I know that Maeve and that baby are going to be well taken care of. That no matter what happens, you'll be okay because you have family who's going to be here for you always. I'm here for you. *Always*. Okay?"

I wrap my arms around his neck and kiss him. I kiss him with everything I've got. I kiss him in a way that I hope tells him everything I haven't said out loud yet.

I love you, this kiss says. *I'm helplessly in love with you, and I never want to leave you*, my hands say as they caress his neck. *You're the only man I'll ever love*, my body screams as it presses against his.

"Holy fucking shit!"

"Bloody hell!"

I step back, tears running down my cheeks and heart beating in my throat, to look at my sister and my best friend standing side by side with their mouths wide open. Owen is behind them, but his eyes aren't on me. They're on Raf, and he doesn't look surprised; he looks pleased. He raises a hand and gives Raf a thumbs-up. Yep, definitely pleased.

"Uh, it's not what it looks like. I mean, it is. We were kissing, but it's not like that. It's not what you think, I—"

Maeve keels over then, something between a groan and a growl leaving her body, and I know deep in my bones that I can't think about whatever this is. I need to focus on my sister and this baby.

Owen is there, holding her hand and massaging her back.

"We need to get you back into that bed, Maevey." His deep voice is calm, but I can see the slight panic in his eyes.

"Yep. We sure do, darling. Looks like your giant baby is ready to rip apart my minge. Let's do this." Maeve takes a few short steps toward the door, and I step into action, holding it open for them.

"I'll be at your place with Adam and the kids so your mom can be here," Rafael says to Owen.

"Thanks, man." Owen lowers his chin and follows Maeve in. Lainey takes my hand and pulls me into the room with them. Raf doesn't follow. I look back twice, hoping he'll come through so I can... I don't know, exactly. But he doesn't.

53 /
put me in, coach.

rafael

IT'S NOT *what it looks like. It's not what you think.*

Well, at least now I know that this was never real for her. To me, it looked like the fucking love of my life and I were kissing, and like she was trying to tell me something with that kiss, but I guess not.

I keep misreading the situation, which is really frustrating. I thought we could read one another so well.

I ARRIVE at Owen and Maeve's in a shit mood, but I reel it in because I'm not about to take any of this out on undeserving people.

When I step in, Eva is already at the door, putting something into a duffle bag.

"Hi, Raffy. Thank you so much for coming to stay with Adam and the girls. Their nanny is sick, so the timing is just a little chaotic." She hugs me tightly, and I let that soothe a little of the hurt in my chest.

"Of course. Sorry, I couldn't get here any sooner." I pick her bag up to take over to the car Owen has waiting for her.

"Nonsense. You're here. And we're grateful Charlie happened to be with you so you could take her to the hospital." She winks at me, and I force a smile back.

"Go meet your third grandbaby, Yia Yia." I open the car door for her and drop the duffle into the back seat. Tapping the top of the car twice, I wave her off and head inside, rolling my shoulders to soothe the tension currently making its home there.

I'M DOWNING a glass of water when Adam strolls into the kitchen. "Hey, Raf. Sorry, I didn't hear you come in. Agnes decided to fight a nap for the first time in her life." He rounds the island and comes to me for a hug. "Thanks for being here. I'm sure I would have figured it out on my own, but I'm really glad I don't have to. Plus, it feels like it's been a while since we've hung out."

"Yeah, of course. And I miss you, too, buddy." I pat him on the shoulder as he smiles at me.

"Good. You ready to pull some major uncle duty? I don't think we're going to see anyone until at least tomorrow, even if everything goes quickly." He grimaces, but I can tell he's not actually worried. It won't be the first time he takes care of Jules, and he's latched on to this whole dad thing like an absolute pro, anyway.

"Put me in, coach." This time, my grin is genuine, and I set aside my own bullshit to take care of this family of ours.

————

TWELVE HOURS LATER, I've just finished my shift with the girls while Adam sleeps for a few hours. We decided we'd be a better team if we're well-rested, so he's just had a solid four-hour sleep, and now, it's my turn. I'll be up again just in time for breakfast.

Before letting my head hit the pillow, I text Charlie. She hasn't sent any updates, so we only know that things are moving slowly because of Eva and Lainey, who have been busy in the group text with updates.

ME:

> Hey, shorty. Hope you're doing okay. Do you need anything?

When she doesn't respond after ten minutes, I decide to just go to sleep. We'll talk tomorrow.

———

IT'S BEEN over twenty-four hours. She hasn't responded to any of my messages, but she also hasn't written anything in the group text, so I try not to take it personally.

———

FORTY-EIGHT HOURS. That's how long it's been since I kissed Charlie. Since I saw her. Since I had any form of contact from her.

I've gone home to get clothes, and Adam's done the same. Owen has assured us none of them need anything because Eva packed absolutely everything they could want, and the hospital also has everything. They each have their own beds, too, so they've taken shifts being with Maeve and resting.

———

ANOTHER SIX HOURS LATER, Douglas James came into the world. Little man didn't wanna leave his mama, it seems. But he's here now, and they're both healthy and on their way home after spending a little time at the hospital.

While the girls had their morning naps, I cleaned up

around the house and made a fresh batch of cookies with what was in Owen and Maeve's very well-stocked pantry. They're not Elaina's muffins, but they'll do.

Not wanting to overwhelm Maeve and the baby, I left a few minutes after they arrived, and so did Adam and Elaina, both no doubt exhausted and wanting to get back home for a bit.

Just as I open my front door, my phone buzzes in my hand.

CHARLIE:

I'm sorry I didn't reply. I didn't even look at my phone the entire time.

Thank you for checking in on me.

I'm at home now, just going to have a shower, and then I was hoping I could see you?

I need to talk to you.

If you're not exhausted or whatever.

My cheeks hurt, I'm smiling so damn hard at all the texts coming in. But then the words *I need to talk to you* land like a bag of bricks to my gut.

ME:

Never too exhausted for you, carrot cake. I'll come over in like an hour?

The sooner, the better, right? Might as well get this over with.

CHARLIE:

That's great.

See you then.

Fuck. This is gonna suck.

54 /
fucking robert

charlie

I'VE JUST COME out of the shower when I hear the intercom. I should have told Rafael to just come up, let himself into my apartment, and come straight to my bed.

No, that would have been a bad idea. We do still need to actually talk. I need to make my feelings known and also figure out when I'll talk to Robert.

Fucking Robert.

Two minutes later, with my hair still sopping wet and my body wrapped in nothing but a towel, I skip to the front door as I hear the soft knocks. I open it, not bothering to fight the smile breaking free on my face, and I'm met with...

Fucking Robert.

"Hey, Lottie. Miss me?" With his hands in his khaki pants, he smirks as he regards my lack of clothing. If I could kick myself for making it so easy for him to get my address, I would. He probably told my assistant he wanted to surprise me or some bullshit. "I hope you don't always answer the door in your towel, Charlotte." His tone is scolding, as if I'm a child. "Obviously, you were expecting me." He walks past me and into the apartment as I roll my eyes out of his sight.

"I wasn't, actually. What are you doing here?" Maybe it's my lack of sleep. Maybe it's the time I've spent with Rafael, feeling like I can speak my mind. All I know is I don't feel like holding back right now.

"I told you I was coming. So, here I am. It's time to come home. It's clear that this is what you wanted, right? Some grand gesture for me to get you back to London? Well, I'm here. Now you can stop fishing for attention." He walks around my space as he talks, hands still in his pockets as if he doesn't want to touch anything in here. Like he's too good for this place. God, I'm so angry at myself for wasting so much of my time on this tosser.

"No," is my simple response. He turns to look at me, then. I expect to see shock on his face, but the bastard is smiling.

"No? And you're going to, what? Stay here? In *this* place? I can make it so you never find another job in finance again, Charlotte. You *will* come back to London to work for me. To marry me. We had a plan." He takes his hand out of his pocket to inspect his nails, the pompous asshole.

I can feel the anger rising in my body, making my blood boil. I want to hit him. I want to kick him out of here and straight back to London so I can be sure to never see him again.

"I'd rather not have this conversation with you when I'm so undressed. I'll be right back." Without giving him time to respond, I walk into the hall and to my room, closing *and* locking the door. Not because I feel unsafe, but because I just need a moment to know no one is going to come in here while I gather my thoughts.

I take my time getting dressed, brushing my hair, and tidying a few things before I pick up my phone to text Rafael. He's supposed to be here in twenty minutes, so I'm sure he hasn't left his house yet.

ME:

Hi. So sorry, but something's just come up.

I'm not sure how long it'll take.

Can we meet in a few hours?

It's vague, I know, but once Robert is gone, I can explain everything to him, and hopefully—finally—get him naked in one of our beds.

———

rafael

I'm super early, but I don't care. I can't fucking wait anymore. I need to see her and hear her say the damn words to my face.

As I enter the building, Carla greets me with a smile at the front desk. My hands tremble as I step into the elevator, and I shake my arms out to calm myself. The jitters intensify as the elevator rises to Charlie's floor. When I stand in front of her door, my nerves feel like sharp claws tearing at my insides. I knock three times, and heavy footsteps sound from the other side of the door.

Weird.

The door swings open too quickly, and a pair of blue eyes I don't recognize greet me.

"May I help you?" The guy's hair is slicked back, and his khakis are definitely too tight, even for a dude this slim. When I don't answer, he widens his arm, which is a stupid move, because if I wanted to break in, he just made it easier. But that's not why I'm here. "Hello? Are you a delivery man or something? Perhaps you're at the wrong flat? We didn't hear the intercom."

His British accent registers. His use of the word *we*. I know who this fucker is.

Fucking Robert.

Fuck this guy.

"I'm looking for Charlie, actually." I step a little closer, trying to look over him. We're about the same height, but I'm still nearly double his size.

"Charlotte's occupied. She's just getting ready for our date. You know how women are." His tone is so condescending as he rolls his eyes; it makes me want to punch his stupid face and make sure his eyeballs get stuck back there so he can never lay eyes on my girl again.

"I see. Well, you can tell her that Rafael came by, and I'm ready for that talk whenever she is." I pat him on the shoulder and wink at the man as he scoffs at me. "Thanks, mate." Turning on my heels, I whistle all the way to the elevator, keeping my gait nice and relaxed while my heart fucking breaks inside my chest.

As I get to the front door of the building, I see a text message come through from Charlie, and then another, and another. When I read the third message, all the air is sucked out of my lungs.

Something came up all right.

Fucking. Robert.

———

charlie

Rafael doesn't respond right away, and I leave my phone in my bedroom, not wanting to be distracted by it while I tell Robert to hop back on a plane.

Without me.

He's sitting on the sofa when I come into the open living space, and it pisses me off. He doesn't need to sit for this conversation. It won't last long enough to warrant a sit-down.

"Did I hear someone at the door?" Walking around the

sofa to stand in front of him, I plant my feet firmly on the floor.

"Yeah. Wrong flat," he says dismissively.

"I'm not going back to London, Robert." I remain standing and watch him, arms spread wide on the sofa, looking far too comfortable and carefree.

"How much longer do you need here? I'd like to be married in the next month, so if you're okay with my assistant planning it all, you can have another four, five weeks tops." His arrogant tone has my skin prickling with rage.

"You can get married whenever you want. But it won't be to me." I know he's about to ask me why, like the absolute moron that he is.

"What do you mean? Why not?"

Called it.

"You only want to marry me because it's what your daddy needs for you to become CEO. You want to marry me because you think I'll turn a blind eye to your infidelities since we were in an open relationship—if you can even call it that—for so long, and because I'll always make you look good. Tell me I'm wrong." I cross my arms, the irritation coursing in my veins enough to power me through this conversation despite my exhaustion.

"You want monogamy? Fine. Whatever." He flicks his wrist like I'm one of the clients he's trying to appease.

"So, I'm not wrong then? This marriage is basically just a business deal to you, isn't it?" He better answer the damn question.

"That's what we agreed to, right? I get the position, the company. And you get the title you want, a husband and a very comfortable life." He turns down his lips, as if I couldn't possibly ask for anything more.

"And what about love? Joy? Family?" *Everything* I've had these last few weeks.

"I mean, we love each other, right? We've known one

another for years, and we still get along. We could be happy. You can pop out as many kids as you want. We could start practicing now." He makes a move to stand, but I take a step back, shoving my hand in the air toward him, asking him to stop.

"I don't want children. You know that." My face scrunches with disgust at what he just insinuated.

"That was in our twenties. *All* women say that in their twenties. Then they hit thirty, and boom. They want babies." He sets his hands on his lap so confidently. God, I want to kick him in the shin with one of those pointy heels Maeve has.

"Not *all* women. Not me. I don't want children, and I don't want to marry you. In fact, I'd like to have as little as humanly possible to do with you, so you can leave now. I don't want to see you ever again." My jaw is clenched so tightly that I'm practically talking through my teeth.

"Lottie. You don't mean that." He does stand this time, despite me taking another step away from him. "Come on, we're so good together, babe."

"No." I'm running out of room as he keeps stepping into my space. "And if you take another step toward me, I'll call the owners of the security company at this building. One is my brother-in-law, and the other is the man I'm in love with, so I think they'd be rather interested in knowing there's an unwanted guest here." The truth is Owen would probably not answer his phone right now, what with two babies and a recovering wife at home, but at least Rafael would handle the situation. I'm confident in that.

"So, you came to LA and fell in love, did you? That's cute. His name wouldn't happen to be Rafael, would it?" He stops moving, but his eyes flick to the front door when he says Raf's name.

"Who was at the door earlier, Robert?" The blood in my veins runs cold. If Rafael came here and saw Robert, why did he leave? Why wouldn't he stay and demand to see me? Did he figure I wanted Robert here? Did he see this as his way out of our arrangement? No, no, that's stupid. Rafael cares about me. I know this. "Answer me." Robert remains quiet. "Fine. Don't. Now, get the hell out before I make that call."

"You *will* regret this, Charlotte. And when you come back to London, begging for a job and to get me back, I'll be there. It was always you and me, babe."

This time, I don't bother hiding my eye-roll. "Goodbye, Robert."

Once he's out of the door, I lock it and start gathering my things. I'll wait a few minutes to make sure Robert isn't hanging around, and then I can go and make things right. Because Robert is so wrong. I won't regret this. Even if Rafael turns me down, I won't regret telling him how I feel.

55 /
please choose me.

rafael

I'VE PACED around my backyard so much in the past twenty minutes, I'm starting to get a little concerned that I'm going to leave a mark on the patio. That's a lie. I'm not concerned at all. The only thing I'm concerned with is Charlie, because in the time I've been pacing, I made a decision. I'm not letting her go back to London until she knows exactly how I feel. No more beating around the bush and only giving her pieces of me. She already owns me anyway. She might as well know it.

Still, my skin feels too tight, knowing I shouldn't have come home. I should have demanded to see her. But demanding is just not who I am, and and I don't always make the best decisions in the moment. I need time to think about everything I should do before I get it right. And I've had time to think about Charlie. Lots of time. Not just today.

So, I hope I get it right.

But now, she's out with that greasy plate of fish and chips, and there's nothing I can do about it except pace. And think. And hope to fuck that she chooses me. Because God, I want her to choose me.

I need her to choose me, and I'm not ashamed to admit that.

———

charlie

I hit send on the email to Robert's father ten minutes ago, and the lightness I felt was immediate. I locked all the doors. I watered the little plant Rafael got me on our first date. I even checked for any food that might spoil while I'm gone. Because I'm prepared to sit on his front porch until he listens to me. Until he believes me. Until he loves me back.

Yeah, it's giving Zach Braff in *The Last Kiss* vibes, minus the cheating, but whatever.

Walking to Rafael's front door, I knock. Loudly.

Please, please, please be home.

No answer. I try again, and still nothing.

I'm about to get really crazy here…

The gate opens when I try it, so either he's home, or he left it unlocked. Unlikely, given what he does for a living. I close it softly behind me and walk into the yard, intent on going for the kitchen door, hoping he either can't hear me or that I'll catch him ignoring me.

Instead, Rafael's back comes into view. He's standing with his hands in his hair, looking up at the sky, when he turns abruptly, saying "fuck it" under his breath.

———

rafael

I stumble back when I see her. "Charlie. What… I was just about to go back to your place. What are you doing here? I thought you and… You know what, that doesn't matter. Why are you here?"

She's here, standing in front of me, hands fisted at her sides, unmoving. I shake my head, not waiting for her to answer me because it doesn't matter why. "That doesn't matter either. I need to say some things to you, and I can't wait anymore, so I'm glad you came." I blow out a breath, tasting the words on my tongue before they're out there and I can't take them back.

"No." She steps forward. Well, fuck, I don't know that I've ever been turned down *that* fast before. She licks her lips and shakes her head, mumbling something to herself. "I need you to hear me first." Now I'm the one shaking my head, because I don't think I can. "Yes," she demands firmly. Her brows furrow tightly, fists tightening at her sides.

We're in a full standoff now, and when her mouth opens to speak again, I do the same. "Please choose me," I beg.

"I'm in love with you," she shouts over me. "What?"

"Wait. What?" I step toward her, needing to be closer, needing those words again; to hear them, to taste them.

"No," she says, taking a step back. "You first. What did you just say? Because I shouted my thing, so I didn't hear you."

"I said—" I clear my throat, swallowing down the lump that has been lodged there for far too long. "I said, please choose me." I take another step, and she stays put. Her blue eyes glisten as they fill with tears, and mine do the same.

A watery laugh shakes her. "Choose you?" She laughs again, moving closer to me, but we're still too far apart. I can't reach her. "Wh—How can you ask me to do that when you're the only bloody option? Do you really think anyone else ever even stood a chance against your dimples? That smile? Or your hugs? And the sound of your voice in the morning? How about the way my whole body lights up when you're close? How my heart beats harder just at the sight of you? You really think there's anyone else who can do that?

"I miss you the second you're not around. I can't wait to hear what you say next, to learn one more thing about you until I know everything. And I know I can't know *every*thing, but I want to.

"I want to soak up every detail of you, every thought you have, every opinion, every joke you tell. I want to be your best friend and the person you come home to. I want to cook with you and Vó, and watch you wrestle with your brothers. I want to dance with you and your family until they're my family too. I want to embed myself so deeply in your life, in your skin, in your bed, in your everything until I can't see where I end and you begin. I want it all with you in a way I never thought I could.

"There is no one else to choose from, Rafael. There never will be. You are and will always be my only choice. So, you can't ask me to choose. And I'm sorry. I'm sorry it took me this long to see it, to see *you*. I'm so—"

I'm finally close enough to reach her, so I effectively stop her apology with my mouth on hers. Her hands find their home around my neck, in my hair, scratching lightly at my back as we both moan into each other's mouths. We pull apart with sniffles, our cheeks stained with both of our tears.

"Please don't apologize. That was the most amazing thing I've ever heard. I was prepared to spend the rest of my life pining for you, missing you, begging you to love me the way I love you." I sniffle again as a soft sob leaves her lips. I wipe at her tears, kissing them when they refuse to stop falling. "So, don't apologize because you have just given me everything I've ever wanted. *You*. You're everything, Charlie. I love you. I've wanted you for so long, and that want grew into love so fast I didn't even see it happen. Like that little seed sat dormant for years and then bloomed overnight. And then I saw it, and I couldn't unsee it. Couldn't ignore it. But I was so scared to tell you, to not be chosen by you, because that would have broken me, carrot cake. I can handle the rest of the world not choosing me, but you?" I touch my forehead to hers, shaking my head as I swallow down the sadness I was prepared to feel today.

"I'm not going back to London," she whispers. With another sniffle, she straightens. "Well, I am, but just to get my things. I've already sent my resignation in. And I told Robert to go fuck himself. Well, no, I didn't say that, exactly. Bollocks, I should have told him to go fuck himself, shouldn't I? But I told him I didn't want to see him ever again. Those exact words. I made myself very clear. I think. I hope. Have I made myself clear? To you?" Her lips turn down into that adorable pout like she's about to start crying again, and I can't help my smile. She's so fucking cute.

"I think what you're saying is that you're desperately in love with me." Her lips purse, as if she's fighting back a smile. "And that you sent that asshole in the tight khakis packing." I bring my nose to her neck. "Because you couldn't resist me." Kissing along the column of her neck, I pull her closer, and her grip on me tightens. "Because you're kind of obsessed with me." She scoffs at my teasing tone, then gasps when I bite down on her shoulder. Looking at her beautiful face, I smile down at her. "How did I do, Chuck?" I test the old nickname, and she rolls her eyes as a cheeky grin spreads over her face, and I groan. "Careful, that eye-roll doesn't have the effect you think it has." I shift my hips, making sure she can feel the *exact* effect it has. Her cheeks take on a different blush. The one that I know travels down to her neck, her chest, coloring her skin in my favorite shade of pink.

"Show me, then." Her eyes lock on my lips before meeting my own.

"Show you what, gata?" I want her words.

"What I do to you." She runs her fingers over my cheeks, tracing the shape of my jaw and my nose. "How much you love me. That you're *mine*." She kisses me, soft and slow. "Show me with your hands, with your tongue, with your cock. Show me *everything*," the woman I love whispers onto my lips, giving me the words I pissed her off with when we first met. Now they have new meaning.

Without another word, I squeeze her ass with both hands and pull her up, her legs instantly wrapping around me. We're about to spend the rest of the day in bed. The rest of the week, maybe.

i should let you make all the decisions.

charlie

HE MOVES SO QUICKLY through the house that everything moves around me in a blur. There's no time to react, to giggle, nothing. I just hold on tightly until he sets me down more gently than I expect him to.

He stands in front of me, flexing his fingers, looking me up and down like he's trying to decide something. "What is it?" I ask.

"I can't decide if I want to undress you slowly or if I just want you to be naked already." His eyes lock on my heaving chest, and they don't leave that spot when I make the decision for him by pulling my shirt over my head. I work on my leggings next and then my bra and panties join my discarded clothes on the floor as Rafael watches me intently. "Okay, yeah, watching you get naked was definitely the better choice. I should let you make all the decisions."

"Can I get that in writing?" I tip my head to the side teasingly, smirking.

He narrows his eyes at me and steps forward. "You're such a brat, red. Do you know what brats get?" I shake my head as his chest brushes against my perked nipples. "Brats get eaten out until they come so many times they have to beg for mercy." Raf licks at my pulse point, and I push his shirt up, feeling his abs flex beneath my palms. "Brats get tied up and don't get to touch," he whispers and takes hold of my wrists. My eyes widen, my breath hitching as my fingers desperately reach for him. "But not today. Today, I want your hands on me. I want you pulling my hair when you come on my cock. Because you will, Charlie. You're gonna come all over my cock. Now, say it."

Placing my hands on his stomach, I bunch his shirt up until he takes over and pulls it over his head, tossing it on the bed. My touch is light over his pecs, his abs, my fingers trailing over the button of his jeans as I undo it. When the zipper is down, I grip him through his boxer briefs. "I'm going to come all over your cock while I pull your hair, Rafael." My grip tightens, and he hisses at the mix of pleasure and pain. Then, he pushes his pants and underwear down with one hand while the other reaches for an unopened box of condoms in his nightstand. He rips at it with his teeth and tosses the box on the bed before doing the same to me.

My shocked giggle fills the room as I bounce on the bed, but it quickly dies on my lips when I see him hovering over me. His intense stare makes my skin heat and the dampness between my thighs intensify.

"Number one," he says as he nuzzles into my neck. "Honesty and transparency. I haven't been with anyone in over a year, and you know I've been tested since." *Over a year?*

"It's been—"

"You don't have to tell me." I can feel his brows move together on my skin, so I take his face in my hands to look him in the eyes.

"I want to. It's been two years." His expression relaxes, and he nods. "And I have an IUD, but I'd like to use a condom anyway." He nods again, and I know he understands. He doesn't need an explanation or justification. "I'm probably very wet right now because I really, *really* want you to fuck me, but sometimes, I struggle to stay that way, and I need lube." Seemingly unfazed by my admission and my requests, Rafael goes back to kissing my neck. But then he bites me, and I gasp with the shock of it.

"You can't just say things like how much you want me to fuck you when I'm trying to have a serious conversation, firecracker." He shakes his head, looking up at me. "I'm already struggling to keep it together here. Give me a damn break." The pained look on his face would be convincing if it wasn't for the lust in his eyes and the mirth in his voice. I giggle at his silliness, and his eyes soften, focusing on my mouth. "I love you," he says on an exhale. "And I love the sound of your laughter. The way your freckles move when you smile." Well, my insides are officially jelly. Going back to his ministrations and leaving me no chance to respond, he leaves a trail of kisses over my collarbone. "Contract item number four, ask for what you need."

"I remember." In the same way he knows I need to feel safe, I know he needs me to feel that way, too. "I just told you what I need. What do *you* need, *meu amor*?"

His answering groan and how his hips thrust lightly against my center make it difficult to concentrate on this conversation, but I wait for his response rather than arching into him, which is what I *really* want to do. "I have everything I need. Right here." His lips hover over my chest, and he lowers his lips to leave three consecutive kisses directly over my heart. Tears prick at my eyes.

How is he real? Why did it take me so long to see what was right in front of me?

"Doesn't matter. We only look forward now, carrot cake." His eyes flit to mine with the crooked smirk that used to piss me off and now sends shivers down my spine. "Yeah?"

"Yeah. Forward." My back does arch then as his mouth latches to my nipple, his tongue flicking the hardened peak the way he knows I like. My fingers tangle into his hair as his hand lowers between us.

He releases my nipple with a pop, moving on to the other with a groan as his fingers discover just how turned on I am. He teases my clit, spreading my wetness around it, then I feel two fingers slide into me. I don't understand how he can focus on kissing me, holding himself up, *and* working his fingers inside me. I can barely concentrate on just lying here.

Shit. No. Get out of your head, Charlie. Now's not the time.

He nudges my nose with his. "You with me, Char?" His hand is resting on my stomach, and I was so caught up in my thoughts that I didn't even realize.

I swallow, feeling myself start to recoil. "I'm here. I'm sorry. I'm with you. I want to be here."

The shake of his head is minuscule, but I know he's telling me that I don't need to apologize. "What can I do?"

"Take control. Consume me. Put that filthy mouth to use." It's what I need when I get like this—for the other person to take over, then maybe I can do the same when I'm more grounded. I need the back and forth, and we have always been good at that.

His response is immediate. His mouth covers mine, and his tongue demands entry, which I readily give. I moan into the kiss, immediately feeling my muscles relax into the mattress. His fingers grip my inner thigh, massaging their way to where I need his touch the most. His fingers match the tempo of his tongue, flitting over my clit until I'm writhing beneath him. I'm on the edge, my orgasm cresting as I'm ready to crash. And that's when he stops, but then his fingers are plunging inside me, curling and stroking, driving me so wild there are no thoughts left inside my head.

My hands reach for him everywhere, and when I wrap my fingers around his hardness, he moans into my mouth. The sound alone has me seeing stars. I stroke him, and he curls his fingers inside me. And I'm right there, ready to beg him to make me come, but he pulls back again.

My whimper is more of a whine, and he knows I'm frustrated. Those twin dimples on his cheek give away his intentions. Rafael sucks on the two fingers that just drove me to near insanity, and I reach for the condom box, take out a wrapper, and rip it open.

He watches with widened eyes as I slip the condom over his cock slowly, deliberately. When he lowers himself again, I anticipate feeling him at my core, but he wraps an arm around my middle and flips us over so I'm straddling his thighs. With superhuman strength, he sits up and shuffles so his back is resting on the headboard, taking me with him on his lap.

Reaching into his nightstand drawer, he takes out a bottle of lube and casually squirts some on his erection, stroking himself twice, and then wiping his hand on his discarded shirt. All I can do is watch, my lips parted as I'm nearly panting with want.

"Sit on my cock, red." He grabs the backs of my knees, pulling me closer until I'm sitting on the base of his cock. "Just like at the drive-in. Ride me and make yourself come. Fuck me." His tone is serious, bossy, even. And yet, he's handing me so much control. It's the perfect balance.

I raise onto my knees, moving forward until I'm hovering over him as he lines himself up. I take my time, needing to feel every inch of him. Bracing my hands on his shoulders, I lower about halfway, then lift so he's almost all the way out again. I repeat this a few more times, reveling in that initial stretch. His hips thrust up, seeking me out, and I tsk, rising on my knees.

"Stay still. I'm the one doing the fucking right now, remember?" My legs are starting to get tired, but I hardly feel it when I see the fire in Rafael's eyes, and it only urges me on to be bossy right back to him.

He nods, his hands loosening around my waist. "May I touch you?" He licks his lips, his touch now feather-light.

"I told you, you don't need to ask me that anymore. I always want your hands on me." I trail my hands down his chest, over his abs, and then I take one of his hands and bring it to my breast. "And your mouth," I add. "Now, are you going to be a good boy and let me fuck you?"

Rafael's gasp is immediately followed by a whimper. An honest to goodness whimper. "Goddamn it, Charlie." He throws his head back against the headboard, blowing out a breath. I'm only giving him back every ounce of frustration he caused me earlier, waiting for his answer. "Yes. Yeah. I'll stay still. I'll be good." His cheeks are flushed, so I run my fingers over them, feeling the warmth as I start my movements again.

He watches everything. My face. The way my body moves. The place where we're connected. When his eyes move back up to mine, I lower myself completely, and we both moan in relief. "Raf," I whisper, rolling my hips. "I feel so full." Another moan slips free. Who it belongs to, I don't know; it could be us both.

His grip tightens on me again as he holds back from moving beneath me. Picking up the pace, I take his face in my hands and kiss him deeply. My nails dig into his shoulders, and I come up for air.

"Fuck, look at you riding my cock. Fucking perfection." His umber eyes shine with lust, love, admiration. I grind harder, leaning back until he hits the perfect spot inside me. "You take me so well, red. I knew you would."

I'm right on that precipice again, completely consumed by the feel of him inside me and his words. "More," I cry, begging shamelessly.

He chuckles, and the vibration sends a shiver up my spine. "You look so perfect fucking me. Taking what you want." Strong hands caress my curves, his breath on my skin setting me on fire. "So gorgeous with your pussy dripping for me." My moans are loud, my movements erratic as I jerkily wrap my fingers around the back of his head, tugging on his hair, our foreheads coming together.

"I love you, Charlie," he says in the clearest voice, just before he kisses me, and I detonate. My whole body is vibrating, shaking with the force of my orgasm. He holds me through it, his strong arms hugged around my waist as his hands caress my back.

And he still hasn't moved his hips. He also hasn't come, obviously holding back, so focused on his task.

"You've been a very good boy," I say as I catch my breath. "So good, meu amor." He tenses everywhere when I use the term of endearment again. "You can fuck me now." Before I complete the sentence, I'm on my back, and Rafael is on top of me, our connection unbroken.

Holy shit.

fucking finally.

rafael

GOOD BOY. Jesus, fuck. Leave it to the romance author to hit me with that shit. My entire body feels like it's been doused in gasoline and set ablaze, and Charlie is the one lighting the damn match.

I flip us both over, and her eyes widen in shock as her back hits the bed, but there's excitement when her lips part, curling at the corners on a gasp. My movements are instant, and I thrust into her hard and fast, her tits trapped against my chest and her fingers digging into my biceps. Pulling almost all the way out, I slam into her, my eyes rolling to the back of my head with how tight and perfect she is.

"So deep," she mumbles on a moan. Her eyes tightly shut as she moans again.

I hold myself up on one arm, running my right hand up her torso, between her breasts, until I'm holding her jaw. I close my eyes and kiss her soft and slow, completely unlike the way my cock is still driving into her. She whimpers as her body melts beneath mine, and her grip on me loosens. I move to take her hand in mine, setting our linked fingers above her head. Breathing one another's air, we open our eyes.

"There you are," I whisper, and she fucking smiles. A bright, beaming smile that could light up all of LA at night. God, I love this woman so fucking much. "Touch yourself, Charlie. Play with your clit."

Still smiling, she reaches between us, her smile falling as her mouth gapes open on a pant when her finger grazes my dick. I groan, resting my forehead on hers. She rolls her hips in time with my thrusts, holding our connection a few moments longer before moving to her clit.

"Raf," she moans. "It's… This feels… You feel so—"

"I know," I say, kissing her jaw. "I know, shortcake. Now, pull your knees up for me." I move back to give her room to adjust, and she does as I ask. "Higher," I demand, and she listens. My eyes flick down to where she is still playing with her clit, then to her tits that are shining with sweat, bouncing in time with my thrusts. She squeezes my hand, and we lock eyes.

"Harder. Harder. Harder," she whines. And that's when I let loose. I give her what she wants, because I always will. A shudder starts at my neck, traveling down my spine, and straight to my cock. "I'm coming." Charlie thrashes below me, and when her clit can't take anymore, she moves her fingers back to my cock. "I want to feel you," she pants. "I want to feel you come."

And I do. Immediately. With her pussy gripping me and her finger grazing the side of my cock, I come so hard I stop breathing, every muscle in my body tensing at the same time. I grunt into her neck, holding myself up on one arm, trying not to crush her as I feel her arm trapped between our hips.

"I love you." She grips my hand tighter still, and I squeeze my eyes shut, committing this moment to memory forever.

"Tell me again," I say, lifting up to look at her shining blue eyes. "Tell me again while I'm still inside you."

"I love you." She doesn't hesitate. "I love you, Rafael Guilherme Machado. I love you." Her smile is small, but it's full of emotion. *Love.*

"Fucking finally," I breathe out. I heard her earlier. She said she's in love with me, but I needed these words. Relief washes over me, easing an ache that has been deep in my bones for my whole life. I don't have to ache anymore. I don't have to wish anymore. I don't have to wonder if my turn will ever come. "I love you, Charlie. Do you feel loved? Because I want you to feel loved every day. Every single day. Forever. I want you to feel my love."

"I feel *very* loved." She brushes the hair off my forehead. "In fact, I'll probably be feeling your love in my knees and thighs for a couple of days." Her teasing smile is followed by a wince as she stretches her legs out, and I finally slip out of her. Her knee pops, and she groans then bursts into laughter. I can't help but follow her.

Sex with Charlie, ten out of ten. Cuddling with Charlie, ten out of ten. Pretty much anything with her is a ten.

But laughing with her?

Off the charts.

"I never want my love to hurt you." I slip the condom off, but I don't move off the bed just yet.

She shakes her head, still smiling. "It doesn't hurt. And I would take the delicious ache of having you between my legs every day over the anguish of not having you." The crease between her brows makes an appearance, like she's thinking about something unpleasant.

"You never have to worry about not having me. I'm yours, carrot cake." I kiss that little worry crease three times, lingering on the third, and when I look down, it's gone. *That's better.* "I'm just gonna clean up real quick and get us some water, then I'm gonna come back here and snuggle you so hard." Her giggle makes my skin tingle, but I force myself off the bed and into the bathroom, not bothering to put any clothes back on because I need to know what naked snuggles with Charlie are like. "Oh, and you better still be naked when I get back," I say from the hallway. She answers with a laugh, but I'm so fucking serious.

————

AFTER SNUGGLING, falling asleep, and then waking up to a still-naked Charlie in my bed, I decide that this is my favorite place in the whole world. She snuggles deeper into me, still sleeping, and I keep my breathing even as I take in the small but satisfied smile on her face.

"You better not be watching me sleep, Machado. That's weird." Her smile grows, and she buries her nose into my neck, throwing her leg over both of mine. "You're hard," she says matter-of-factly.

"You're naked in my bed, Chuck. I'd be worried if I *weren't* hard." As if on command, my dick twitches, and she giggles into my skin.

"I need to go home and shower." She sighs, like the thought of it makes her tired.

"You're welcome to do that here," I say, combing my fingers through her hair. She stiffens in my arms. "No pressure, red." I hope that's clear by now.

"I know. I just… I'm particular with well… everything, I suppose? I tend to stick to a very specific routine, and I'm not sure I should subject you to that. At least, not yet." She still hasn't moved. Not closer to me, but not further away either.

"You're not subjecting me to anything, you're letting me into your world. And I want in, Charlie. All the way in." Keeping my movements steady, I give her time to let my words sink in, but she starts laughing. It's quiet, but her whole body vibrates with it.

"That sounds—" She's laughing so much that she can't finish the sentence, and catching on that she's laughing because what I said sounded sexual, I laugh too.

Once she settles down, she places a hand in the middle of my chest, scratching lightly at the hair there. "If it's far enough from my usual routine and I can be distracted, I could make showering here work." Her little shrug is followed by a sigh, and I can tell she's nervous about it, but she's letting me in. Emotionally, of course, but she's also about to let me *in* in. Again. And I can't fucking wait.

"I'm gonna turn the water on and get our toothbrushes ready. You grab a condom and the lube. Meet me in there." I kiss her on the head and extract my body from underneath her limbs. She doesn't say anything, but I catch the way her breath hitches into a gasp when I smack her ass lightly.

While the water heats, I set towels on the warmer, making sure there are three, so Charlie can have one for her hair and her body. When I finish putting toothpaste onto our brushes, she walks in completely naked still, condom and lube in hand. I smile as she sets them down and we get to work brushing our teeth.

It doesn't sound sexy, but like so many other moments with Charlie, it's the simplicity of something, the intimacy of it that makes it so hot. Her eyes on my body, the way she leans on the vanity facing me, the fact that we're hiding nothing from one another.

58 /
just spell chuck.

charlie

STANDING in his bathroom as the steam billows around us, we brush our teeth together. He's still hard, watching me as I lean on the vanity, letting my eyes roam over his body. The tattoos I've never asked him about on his arms. The clearly defined muscles beneath his dark leg hair. The thick cock I already miss being inside me.

When my eyes make their way back up to his, his gaze is hot, laser-focused on my face. He spits, rinses and pops his toothbrush back in the cupholder, takes the condom and lube, then turns away, giving me privacy. Because if he assumed I didn't want to have him watch me spit toothpaste into a sink, he was correct.

He is checking the temperature when I turn, and I sigh as I stare at his naked bum. It's a really good bum.

"Are you staring at my ass, red?" He looks over his shoulder, smirking at me as my cheeks heat. I don't know why my body forgets that we don't need to do that anymore. But maybe that's just the effect he has on me. "Coming?" His brows raise on his forehead, and he smiles so wide the dimples pop.

"That remains to be seen," I taunt, and his eyes narrow as he shakes his head. The shiver that runs down my spine is a thrilling mixture of excitement and reluctance. Like the moment you're about to get on a roller coaster, and you wonder whether it's a great idea or the worst idea, but you also know that you really, *really* want to just try it anyway.

I want to try showering with him. Because I've never done it with anyone, because he's my person. And because, I mean, look at him. *Crikey.*

My feet move me toward the shower without checking in with my brain, and I'm glad for it when I reach him and he takes my hand, walking me into the massive shower. The water is a perfect temperature as it touches my back, and I lean back to soak my hair. I turn into the stream, letting it hit my chest, and then Rafael is behind me—his body close and his hands gently massaging my scalp. It takes me a few seconds to realize that he's lathering it, making sure every strand is covered. He's washing my hair. And I want to cry, except I don't want to actually *cry*.

The feel of his erection at my back pulls me out of the nearly tearful disaster, and I lean back into his chest.

"Turn around, please, my love." The deep timbre of his voice and the sweetness of his words both hit me straight in the chest.

God, I love it when he says please.

His chuckle startles me as I rotate to face him. "I'm happy to ask nicely anytime you want, Ginger Spice." He rinses the shampoo out of my hair, focused on the task as I process what the hell is even happening.

He applies and rinses the conditioner with the same level of patience and care, then he lathers his hands with body wash and starts massaging my body. He doesn't say anything else, and the water hitting the tile is all I hear as he works.

I'm already turned on, so when his strong hands work over my back, arms, and shoulders, then slip and slide over my breasts, I'm practically panting. His fingers flick my already hard nipples over and over. I moan, and immediately, his hands are gone as Rafael lowers to his knees. He washes my legs, massaging my ass, but completely avoids going anywhere near where I want him most.

When he rises to his feet again, he reaches behind me and pulls a handheld showerhead, rinsing the soap off my body. He moves my arms, making sure to get all of the suds. When he's finished, he maneuvers us so I'm facing the bench and he's standing behind me, then he pulls my knee up onto the bench, and I watch as he lowers the showerhead over my stomach. When the water hits my center, my knees nearly give out, but he is there with an arm around my waist. He loosens his hold when I brace my hand on the wall.

"Feel okay?" His nose brushes my shoulder as he aims the water perfectly at my clit.

"Feels s-so, oh, shit. So good. So good. So good." My eyes are about to roll into the back of my head as I moan, my fingertips pushing against the smooth tile.

"Is this not how you normally wash your pussy when you're alone, red?" He's relentless, and I'm powerless to this sweet torture. I could lower my leg, but I don't want to. It feels too good. "Hmm?" he asks.

"N-no. Never like this," I answer.

"Never?" he asks, his mouth hovering over my neck.

"Never," I admit, and he groans. I'm about to come; I can feel it. The heat building in my stomach, the tingling all over my skin, the way my hips are already bucking into the pressure of the water. "Raf," I moan, throwing my head back and closing my eyes. I hear a crinkling sound, but my brain doesn't register what it is.

"I know." He moves the wand closer, the pressure intensifying. I move a hand to my breast, my nipples aching for his touch. "That's it. That's my girl. Come for me so I can finally slide inside you." I gasp, my orgasm now at my fingertips. So close. "You want that, Charlie? You want me to bottom out inside your tight pussy again?" I nod frantically. *I need it right the fuck now.* He chuckles, as again, my thoughts slip out of my mouth. "Not until you come. When you come, I'll let you take every inch. I'll fuck you as soft or as hard as you want. Tell me how you want me."

"Hard. I want you to fuck me hard. I want you to make me come. Oh God, Raf, please. Please." I'm prepared to beg, then he drops the showerhead, and I feel a scream of frustration building in my throat.

He places a gentle hand between my shoulder blades, urging me to bend at the waist and he thrusts into me. Deep. Hard. His rhythm is steady, hitting that perfect spot inside me. Neither of us says a word. We don't need to.

When I straighten, needing more of his warm body against mine, he wraps an arm around me. His hands roam over my stomach, my breast, my neck, until he takes hold of my chin, turning my face towards his. Our lips meet in a bruising, needy kiss as he fucks me exactly the way I asked. And when his finger touches down on my clit, I come so hard I scream into his mouth.

He joins me, groaning into my neck, his thrusts punishing, erratic, delicious, as he pulls me tighter against him. He stills inside me, lips on my skin, kissing my neck once, twice, three times. How this man can fuck me the way he just did, then kiss me so sweetly is beyond me.

I whimper when he pulls out of me, loosening his hold, but not letting me go as I lower my foot to the floor. After taking a deep breath, he tosses the condom on the floor as I turn to face him. His gaze roams over my face, filled with affection, and his hand reaches out to gently brush a strand of hair behind my ear in that way I love. His fingers linger on my jaw.

I finally break the silence, even if it is a comfortable, soothing one. "Can we order breakfast, eat it in bed, and then have a nap?" I'm still exhausted from the lack of sleep from being at the hospital with Maeve, and I'm not used to this level of, shall we say, physical activity.

His smile is wide as he chuckles. "We can do anything you want, shortcake. Why don't you order whatever you're hungry for on one of the apps on my phone while I get my body clean? The passcode is 24825. Just spell Chuck." He kisses me on the nose, and I blink slowly, letting that piece of information sink in.

"Your passcode is Chuck?"

"Yep," he answers simply. "Been that way for at least two years now." He presses his lips to mine. "Don't overthink it. I told you I've wanted you for a long time. And even though I would never have admitted it to anyone, you were never not on my mind, Charlie. That's how it's been, and that's how it'll stay."

I let out a laugh. "I'll never need to research anything for book boyfriends ever again now that I have you."

"That's right, shorty. No more experiments, no more practicing. Because you have me." His eyes turn serious, and his smile falters. "But you know I'm not perfect, right? I'll make mistakes. I'm gonna mess up."

"Oh, I know." I smile, but he doesn't join me. "So will I. I'll make mistakes too." I cradle his face in my hands, attempting to soothe his insecurities.

He nods. "But I'll never hurt you. I'll never disrespect you." He swallows hard, as if just the thought of doing those things to me causes him pain.

"I know that, too, Raf. You're not perfect, but you're a wonderful man with a beautiful heart. I trust you." I kiss him slowly, whispering *I love you* when he rests his forehead on mine, and his smile grows until the two little dimples appear.

Extracting myself from his hold, I dry myself quickly with

a perfectly warm towel, wrapping the wet one around my hair and using a fresh one to wrap around my body. It's heavenly.

And by the time Raf is out of the shower, I've ordered us a feast to be enjoyed in his huge bed.

holy forking shirtballs! how? when?

rafael

THE GATE at Owen and Maeve's house closes behind us, and as we approach the house, Charlie's hands twist on her lap. I take one in mine, kissing her knuckles.

Walking to the front door, we don't bother knocking. They know we're here. Owen rounds the corner, some sort of baby blanket draped on his shoulder. "Hey, you two. Fancy seeing you not sucking each other's faces." He smiles, waving a finger between us.

I chuckle, and Charlie groans. "I'm ignoring that. Where are the babies?"

Owen points toward the living room at the back of the house, and when I think Charlie is going to let me go to take off that way, she turns into me and pulls my face down to hers, pressing her lips to mine. She doesn't do more than that, but the small action is enough to warm my chest.

I watch her go as Owen chuckles and brings a hand to my shoulder, squeezing. "Congrats, brother. I'm happy for you. For both of you."

"Isn't that what I'm supposed to be saying to you right

now?" I pull him in for a hug as he shrugs. "We're happy for each other, I guess."

"That we are," he says as we follow Charlie into the room where Eva has a sleeping Agnes on her shoulder while talking to Lainey and Arthur. Adam is playing with Julia on the floor and Maeve is holding her brand new son on an armchair.

Before I have a chance to greet anyone, Maeve's voice booms across the room. "Well, well, well. You stopped sucking my sister's face long enough to come meet your godson, did you?" Her blue eyes are tired but shining with love, and a little mischief, too, because these Howard women have some sass.

"First of all, we were not sucking faces, and your husband just said the same thing. Second of all... what?" I know I heard her say godson, but we've never talked about that before.

"Oh, bollocks. I bungled it, didn't I?" Maeve's eyes flick to Owen, who's yet again laughing next to me.

"I think that was kind of perfect, sunshine. Except we didn't really ask them." Owen strides over to his wife, kissing the top of her head and looking down at his son in her arms, sleeping peacefully. He takes him from her and kisses his head, too, before walking back toward me. "You don't have to answer now. It's a lot. I mean, you'd be responsible for two kids if anything ever happened—"

"Yes. Of course. Yes. Oh my God are you fucking serious? You want me to—" With slightly shaky hands, I take the baby Owen is now placing in my arms. A big, fat tear splashes onto his blond hair. "Shit. Sorry, little buddy." I sniffle, more tears already gathering as I look down at his chubby little face. "Owen. Dude. I... I don't know what to say. This feels like the biggest honor I've ever been given. You know I would do anything for these kids. For all of you."

"We know. We know you both would." His head twists

toward Charlie, whose eyes are shining with tears as she watches me holding her nephew. Then her eyes go to Owen and quickly to Maeve, who's also crying.

"Yeah, sissy. We'd like you to be godmother." Before she finishes, Charlie is on her, hugging her awkwardly so Maeve doesn't have to stand.

Charlie straightens, wiping her cheeks before turning toward me. Her eyes flick to baby Douglas in my arms, and then those baby blues are back on me.

"Well, honey bun, we're really stuck together now, yeah?" I smile brightly at her, watching as her eyes go from watery to warm with affection.

"Yeah, Machado. *Now,* we're stuck together. Because our best friends marrying each other or the fact that I'm in love with you definitely weren't sufficient." She rolls her eyes as she approaches me, placing a gentle hand on the little baby in my arms, the other wiping at the tears still on my cheek. Then she reaches up on her tiptoes and kisses me. Again. She kisses me in front of our friends and family, and I don't know what to do with myself, with all the love threatening to burst out of my chest.

"Called it," Arthur says. "That'll be fifty dollars." He points to Adam and then Owen, who are both smiling, despite clearly losing some kind of bet.

"In love? Holy forking shirtballs! No. That's not right. Holy fucking shit, you two! How? When?" Adam chuckles at his wife's attempt not to swear. "In love?" she repeats, and takes a breath, sniffling.

"Yeah, I mean, we wanted you to like each other so you could be godparents without bickering all the time, but I did not see this coming." Maeve shifts in her seat, tears wiped away as she watches us.

"How did you two not see this? Raf's been obsessed with Charlie for a long-ass time." Owen shakes his head, still smiling as he places a bill in Arthur's hand. "I just didn't think they'd figure it out so fast."

"Yeah, well, don't underestimate the Machado charm." Arthur smirks. "Not that I possess any of it myself, but my little brothers sure do." His eyes meet mine for a moment, and he lowers his chin in a very *told you so* way.

I shrug, looking down at my girl kissing our godson with a sweet smile on her face. I don't care about them betting on how long this would take, that Arthur called it, or that Vó assumed it. All I care about is that she's here. We're here. Together. And that's how it'll stay.

epilogue

charlie

two months later

"HONEY BUN?" Raf calls out from somewhere in the house as I walk into the kitchen with my hands full of groceries. There's a bag of chips between my teeth, however—because screw taking anymore than one trip from the car—so I can't answer. "Do you need help? I'm in the living room." He knows me too well. I've hardly made a sound, and yet he knows I have my arms full of something.

I drop the chips on the counter as I set the bags on the floor. "Nope, I'm good. Be right there." Picking the bag of chips back up—with my hand—I head into the room and come to a halt when I see all of the books spread out on the coffee table, Pumpkin laying on some of them without a care in the world and not sparing me a glance. I love this cat.

Rafael is smiling as he opens one to the front cover. I'd forgotten about this. That I wrote in all of his books before I knew I was falling in love with him. I have no recollection of what's written in those pages.

"Uh, hi." The snack in my hand crinkles loudly, and my favorite pair of brown eyes meet mine.

"Get over here, red." He pats the spot next to him on the couch, and I take slow steps, willing my brain to recall what I wrote. "When did you do this?" His brows crinkle as he reads another message.

"Mushroom night." He doesn't like it when I refer to that event as anything having to do with the hospital or me poisoning him, so I just call it that.

He nods, as if my answer somehow clarifies something. I do remember that I neatly printed everything, not using my usual swoopy handwriting. I wanted him to be able to read it easily.

"Will you read this one to me?" This is not an unusual request for him. I read aloud to him often. Scenes I'm working on, a book we're reading together, little sticky notes I leave to myself on my laptop. And it's not because he can't read most of it himself; he just likes it when I read to him. And I like doing it. He hands me a book opened on the cover page, and I set the bag down on the floor.

I begin reading slowly.

> *Raf,*
> *I feel I should confess that the villain in this book was based on what I knew about you at the time, which wasn't very much. I'm sorry,*
> *-Chuck*

I wince, closing the book and setting it on my lap. Before I can say anything else, he hands me another.

Rafael,
In my mind, the hero of this book laughs just like you. Deeply, sincerely, with his whole body.
-Carrot cake

As I finish, he takes the book I've just read from and hands me another.

Raf,
Do you remember the reference I made to Friends in this story? I thought of you when I wrote it.
-Ginger Spice

My chest feels tight as I remember sitting here, with Pumpkin watching me, reading these out loud to her as I wrote, wondering if he would ever find them.

Machado,
When I wrote the first kiss in this story, I thought it was unrealistic because there was no way anyone could ever actually experience something so wonderful. You proved me wrong. Thank you for that.
-Red

"You were kind of obsessed with me, huh?" His tone is sweet when he breaks the silence, but still, I roll my eyes at his comment. The look he sends me is both a warning and a promise, and I have to shift on the sofa as my insides warm. "It's nice to know I wasn't the only one." He tucks a strand of hair behind my ear and then pushes my curls off my shoulder.

"I suppose you made a small impression on me." I shrug, feigning indifference, simply to push his buttons.

"I'm about to make a very big impression on you now if you don't quit that sass." He leans into me, kissing my neck, and my breath hitches on contact. It's not new. In fact, I feel his lips on me every day now, and still, I get goosebumps every time.

"We can't," I whine. "We need to clean this up and get all of that food ready." I cradle his smooth cheeks in my hands and kiss him softly, pulling back quickly so as not to be tempted for more. I wish I'd come home sooner.

Home.

It's where I am now. It's where he is always.

And it's where our families are about to be in thirty minutes to celebrate me officially moving in.

———

rafael

I had been putting away the copy of the book Charlie got for my birthday when something nagged at me to open one of the other books up. Once I started, I couldn't stop. Every single one had something sweet or funny written inside. Every single one was signed by a nickname I'd given her. I'm going to have to request a personalized message to be written in all of her future books.

With a raging hard-on, I eventually put all of Charlie's books back on our bookshelf and then helped her get food and drinks set out. After we went to London to get her things packed up a few weeks ago, I suggested she have her things brought here because there was no room in the small apartment she was subletting. Two weeks after that, she realized she was keeping more of her everyday things here also, and without preamble, asked if I thought I could handle her staying over being a full-time thing.

I cried because I'd been wanting her here every day since she walked into me with her eyes closed. Then, I finally fucked her on the couch. Our couch. Figures she would be the first and only.

Now, nearly everyone we love is here. My mom is holding a baby, my brothers are acting somewhat normal, and Vó is chatting with Eva, who spends more time here in California than in Massachusetts. I turn toward the kitchen door to grab another tray of food and spot a familiar head of brown hair coming in through the gate. I didn't think he'd come.

"Hey, little brother." Arthur pulls me into a hug, and when I don't say anything, he continues, "I wasn't gonna come, but I wanted to be here for you and Charlie. I don't want any drama. I just wanted to come and say hello, and I can take off." He scans the backyard quickly, likely looking for our dad, who just happened to run out to grab some more ice, something he insisted on doing since a host shouldn't leave his own party.

"I'm happy you're here, man. Really. Thank you for coming." I hold his eyes for a moment. "Pai just stepped out, but he'll be back soon." I leave it at that. He can do with this information what he will. I'm just glad he felt comfortable enough to come.

Arthur blows out a relieved breath. "I'll just say hi to Charlie and everyone. I won't stay long."

I nod, understanding but also not, because we still don't know what the fuck happened between him and our dad.

"I'm really happy for you, Raf. For Charlie, too." He squeezes my shoulder, a small smile on his lips. Arthur is the least emotional of us all, but he has his moments.

"I know you are, brother. And I appreciate the hand you had in helping me figure this out, you know? Thank you." I pull him in for another hug, holding on a second longer this time. "Go find my girl. Mãe and Vó will be really happy to see you too."

ARTHUR DIDN'T STAY LONG, like he said. I don't even know if he and my dad saw each other, and no one really mentioned it, likely not wanting to bring it up. Seeing him here today, though, gave me hope that they'll sort this out soon.

I've just finished loading the dishwasher when I hear soft footsteps behind me. I look over my shoulder to find the most beautiful woman I've ever seen. Her red hair is piled on top of her head, she doesn't have any makeup on, she's wearing one of my hoodies that reach her mid-thigh and bright orange knee-high socks on her feet. Her hands are behind her back, and she's biting her lower lip like she has something to say.

Setting the dishwasher, I give her my full attention.

"I have something for you. It was supposed to be a birthday gift, but I didn't know it was your birthday on your actual birthday, and I thought I'd have more time, and then we went to London and then the moving, and now we're here, and it's finally ready, and I can't wait any longer to give it to you, so here, please just take it." She sticks her hand out, a black box with a bright green bow on it. Her cheeks are pink, and her breathing is quickened from the run-on sentence.

Taking the box from her, I run my finger over the silky ribbon, tugging one end to undo the bow. I tuck the piece of green satin into the pocket of my sweatpants, taking a deep breath before lifting one end of the box. Whatever is in here is important to Charlie.

Once I've flipped the lid and put the box inside it, I move the white tissue paper to reveal a brown leather book with the words "Machado Family Recipes" in gold lettering. It looks similar to the notebook Vó had been writing in, but I know that's not it. As I open it, I'm met with family photos, all taken around the kitchen or table, some from when we were kids, others as recently as the day of my birthday festivities a couple of months ago. Every recipe that had been written in the notebook is typed up in a font I know is meant to be easy to read for dyslexics. They're all here. Every dish I've made with Vó so far. I swallow hard past the tightness in my throat.

"You got these photos from my family?" I meet Charlie's wide blue eyes, and she nods. "And the recent ones of me cooking with Vó, you took those?" I know she did, yet I feel my muscles relax when she gives me another affirmative. "These rings on the inside; do these mean that we can add more pages to this cookbook?" I can hardly keep my eyes open, I'm squinting so hard, trying to keep my tears controlled. A whispered *yes* is her answer. "You didn't have to do this, shortcake."

"I wanted to. I wanted to from the moment you asked me to help you, and I knew I needed to that first Tuesday afternoon in your family's kitchen." She licks her lips, fingers fidgeting with the hem of the old sweatshirt.

"Thank you, Charlie. Thank you for this, and thank you for loving me the way you do. You love me in the way I've always wanted to be loved, you know? You pay attention to the things I say, to what's important to me. You see me, and you choose me anyway." There's no holding them back now. The tears roll down my cheeks in quick, hot streams.

"I love you the only way I know how. I see you, and I choose you because you're the best person I know." Her voice is clear, sure. I set the box down and reach for her, my arms wrapping around her waist. "Because you've always seen me, and even in my hardest moments, you've always chosen me." Her delicate fingers wipe away my tears as I hold on to her as if she's my anchor, keeping me steady on the ground. "I love you because I don't know any other way to live now, and I never will. However long my life might be, I will spend the rest of it loving you and only you."

"If I ask you one day, would you marry me? I don't have a ring yet, and this isn't an official proposal or anything, but would you want that? With me?" I can't believe I just fucking asked her to marry me. I mean, I want that. I want that so fucking badly, but it's too soon. I know it is.

She opens her mouth to speak then closes it again, thinking through her answer. "Could we do the ceremony in your parents' backyard and have our first dance in their kitchen? Because I think that's the only way I want to do it." Her nose scrunches, and her freckles dance across her creamy skin. "And we'll drive away with the little cans dragging behind the car while everyone waves us off outside." A laugh bursts out of me as more tears come.

"Yeah, carrot cake. We can do that. We can do whatever you want." Somehow, my love for her grows even stronger, my heart expands to make more room for all the ways I love this incredible woman.

She smiles brightly up at me. "Then, I'll definitely, *definitely* say yes when you ask me. One day."

THE END

acknowledgments

I've said it several times during the last year—definitely over the last six months—because it's true. This book was HARD to write. It challenged me in so many ways. It pushed me, it made me dig deep, it made me cry, it made me laugh. Charlie and Rafael have become my favourite characters not because I spent the most time with them, or even because they required the most amount of research. They're made of some of the deepest, truest parts of me and I love them so, so dearly. I hope you do, too.

To my husband, who heard me gripe on and on and on about how I didn't know how to continue the story, or about how I sat at the computer for hours and wrote next to nothing. You encouraged me to take breaks and pushed me to keep going. You keep believing in me and this wild dream, even when it makes no sense. Thank you. Forever and always.

To my kiddos, who wanted so badly to contribute to the book by naming characters and understanding where they were from. You asked me how many words I had written, and how many I had left, and if I met my goal for the day. You cheered me on and held me accountable. You made lists of Brazilian foods for me. My little angels. I love you endlessly.

FamJam - thanks for asking me about my books, for cheering me on, for encouraging me and for wanting to read my books even when I beg you not to. You have no idea just how much it all means.

Now, in no particular order, here goes.

Megan McSpadden. How the fuck did I get so lucky? Thank you for letting me send you endless voice notes while I verbally processed this story. And for letting me send you snippets that made no sense, but that you celebrated with me anyway.

Meg and Julie - I don't know that this book would have happened without you. Remember all those times when I was like, "I don't know what I'm doing." And you were all like, "Keep going, you've got this!" And then I did, and now there's a whole ass book here, with a beginning, middle and end? Same, because it was literally every 2 weeks for months! Thanks for your feedback, your encouragement, your excitement and your friendship. I don't think I want to write any books without you now, so please never ever leave me!

Kristen, you make this process so seamless and enjoyable, I almost don't even hate editing, because your comments light me up. I'm so thankful for you!

Katie, I'm so sorry for all the tears with this book. I promise not to make you sad with the next one. Thank you for all you do, for believing in my stories, and for endlessly encouraging me to keep going.

Beta readers: whether you finished your copy or not, your comments helped me shape this story into what it is now. Your feedback helps me see the gaps, and also helps me to know that I can sometimes write funny, sweet, sexy things. You are an invaluable part of my process.

Lisa. Oof. I don't know how to even begin. Charlie would not be the dynamic, layered, authentic, beautiful character she is without you. She simply wouldn't. Raf wouldn't be the perfectly sensitive and intuitive book boyfriend without you either. I was so nervous to ask for your help with this project, and when you so enthusiastically said yes, I cried. I cried reading your comments. Thank you for every single call, text, comment, email and whatever other way we communicated during this process. I am so in awe of you.

Megan G. - sensitivity reader extraordinaire! You probably had no clue what you were getting yourself into when you said yes to me. Multiple voice notes, panicky messages letting you know I made changes, and a 3-part epilogue (I'm still sorry about that). Autism shower logistics (TM pending) make sense because of you, and I'm not sure I have enough ways to thank you for the work you put into this story with me.

Lemmy @ Luna Literary Management - you're my rock. I'm so thankful I have you in my corner. Good luck getting rid of me. Ever!

Now it's your turn. Yep. You. Reading this right now. You literally make it all possible. Thank you times a million for giving my book a chance. If you enjoyed this story, would you please let me know? DM me! I love hearing from you! Leave a review and let other people know what you liked! Seriously, those things make a world of difference.

Thank you for letting me be a part of your world for a little while.

xoxo,
-Cristina

about the author

Cristina Santos is a mom of two little boys who hopefully will never read this book. She is married to the man of her dreams and lives lakeside with all her wild boys (pup included) in Nova Scotia, Canada. She loves a good sunset and will forever and ever and ever believe in the power of playlists, 90's romantic comedies and love stories.

This is Cristina's third book.

cristinasantosauthor.com

instagram.com/cristinasantosauthor
tiktok.com/@cristinasantosauthor

also by cristina santos

LOVE IN LA SERIES

Lost Love Found (Adam and Elaina)

Sparks Still Fly (Owen and Maeve)

Out of Focus (Raf and Charlie)

———

SOUTHERN SHORE SERIES

Untitled Holiday Book - Coming October 25, 2024

MACHADO BROTHERS SERIES

Untitled (Arthur and ?) - Coming Spring 2025

Please note that though these are interconnected, they can all be read as standalones. Remember to check content warnings.

there's more...

Want to keep in touch? Learn more about Cristina's books?

Head to cristinasantosauthor.com!

———

Flip the page to read chapter 1 of *Lost Love Found*

lost love found

book 1 in the love in la series

1 / did i really just write that down?

elaina

The upside of living in LA is that it's seventy degrees on December 23rd. The downside of living in LA is that it's seventy fucking degrees on December 23rd! I feel the sweat collecting under my boobs as I pack up my shit. I curse myself for choosing a blouse that feels as though it's made of velvet and wide-legged pants I keep nearly tripping over.

This almost makes me miss Massachusetts and New York winters. Almost.

It's my last day at the studio and we've just wrapped shooting on a movie I'm super stinking proud of, despite the fact that it was supposed to wrap four weeks ago. I was so looking forward to seeing Mom and Owen, but the shooting delays have forced me to cancel my plans. While I'm relieved to be staying put, a deep pang of guilt lingers within me for how I must have disappointed them.

Owen, my older brother by four years, has been living in Marblehead for eighteen months after retiring from the Marines and has yet to come and see me. We'd been close as kids, but since Dad passed away, Owen and I haven't talked.

I know Ma has been stressing about it too, and I feel such

guilt about that. I haven't been able to bring myself to make the trip back to Marblehead. It was hard enough after Andy and impossible after Dad. But I know I need to go back. I know I won't heal until I go back to the place that hurt me the most.

The thought causes my stomach to roll and I'm thankful for the breeze sweeping through the air as I walk to my car. When I reach the trunk, dropping my bags in, I realize I didn't say bye to Manny, my favorite security guard at this studio. It's become such a part of my routine to stop and chat with him before going home, and I've been meaning to ask how his wife is doing. Poor Jen was so sick a few days ago, so I sent over some chicken noodle soup and muffins. Is cooking and baking for people a love language? If so, that's how I choose to show my love for people. Forever and ever.

I sit in the driver's seat and turn my car on, but I don't drive away just yet. I'm too busy basking in the icky feelings building up inside me. This year has been so... much. My normally optimistic and glass-half-full personality has been seriously slacking off lately. I don't know what to do to change it, but I know I need a plan.

Make Ma's Moussaka recipe and take Frankie for a long walk at Runyon Canyon? Or maybe go to the wrap party? Neither. Pick up ice cream and wine, put on comfies and have a solo dance party in the kitchen. YES!

The almost smile on my face turns into a full-blown grin when I see my BFF's name pop up on my phone screen.

MAEVEY

Bonnie! Are you going to the wrap party?

I hope you are. You need some fun to get out of this funk!

More than a best friend and much like a sister (though she already has a twin of her own), Maeve can always put a smile on my face. Ever the Brit, she's called me Bonnie, meaning *beautiful*, since the day we met and she proclaimed my emerald green eyes, plump ass and perky tits should be illegal all on one person. Her words, not mine. I'm about to respond when I see the three little dots flashing.

> MAEVEY
>
> And if you don't go tonight and decide to go home and dance around the kitchen, I'm coming and we're having ice cream for dinner. No need for fancy meals since we have that all covered between Christmas and NYE! EEK!

I purposely ignore her mention of the New Year's Eve party she's throwing. I'm having eye surgery on the 31st and I hope, against all odds, that I can still somewhat enjoy the night. I need to end this year on a higher note than how it started, which was with removing all proof of my last relationship from my life.

> It's really eerie how well you know me, you know that? Come over. Lizzo surely has something we can shake our asses to and I'm picking up enough Ben & Jerry's to feed a small village of hormonal PMS-ing women.

> You goddess. See you in an hour. I have wine.

An hour later Bruno Mars' "That's What I Like" is coming through the kitchen speakers. I hear the door shut and Maeve's "yoohoo" as she's making her way down the hall. She is a natural-born star. You know when you see someone, and you can tell they're meant to be Hollywood famous? That's Maeve Howard.

When she speaks, everyone in the room hangs on her

every word. She enthralls us all with her radiant smile and contagious laughter. Her vivacious energy and enthusiasm fill the air, and no matter the company, she is the life of the party. Her straight blonde hair always seems to fall perfectly around her shoulders, and she's got a charming smattering of freckles on her button nose. If she was a season, she would be summer: bright, warm, eternally sunny. She's singing along to the lyrics and casually grinding into my ass before I can even turn around to greet her. Man, I love this girl.

Over my shoulders, I see her aggressively biting her bottom lip, a bottle of wine in each hand, eyes closed tight. I can tell she's holding back a big smile, trying to be serious as she pushes her crotch into my hip.

"Baaaaaabe! You did it! Our first movie together with you as production designer extraordinaire and you killed it! I'm so proud! Let's celebrate the shit out of how awesome you are!" She drops the wine on the countertop and hugs me, jumping up and down. I take in the scent of her lavender shampoo and yes, I really do feel better now.

I swear this girl saved my life on more than one occasion. When I moved away from home after Andy died. When my dad got so sick, I didn't even have time to go see him before *he* died. When that douche canoe Ben ended up cheating on me repeatedly during our three-year relationship. Maeve was there for all of it. She's a constant in my life and I know how lucky I am that I found my soulmate in this woman.

The kiss she leaves on my cheek is loud and proud, but when I take in her face, I can see she likely feels as tired as I do. Her eyes look more like a stormy sea than their usual sky blue. She's been working hard, too. She was the lead actress in the movie we just wrapped today. Yep, it was kind of a dream come true to have my best friend on the same set as me for four entire months.

"Why aren't you going to the wrap party? You should

celebrate!" I say this to her as I pour us each a generous glass of wine. Wine first, then ice cream.

"I'd much rather spend time with my brilliant BFF. We haven't been able to see one another much outside of the set and I've been looking forward to just being with you." She brings her glass of wine to her lips, swaying her hips. Even tired, Maeve exudes energy.

I smile softly at her. "I've missed you too, Maevey. And you were right earlier. You know how much I hate being in a bad mood. I don't know what it is." I take a sip of wine and she looks at me intently, taking in every word.

"Ugh. Is it because I'm not going to see Mamá for the holidays?" I pause, looking out over the backyard where my dog Frankie (a.k.a. Frank Lloyd Wright) is miserably failing at chasing a bird who is taunting my little labradoodle.

I look back at Maeve. She's waiting for me to process everything out loud, as I always do.

"Do I even have any right to be in a funk? My life is kind of great, isn't it? I bought this house. I've worked on some amazing movies. My career completely took off. What the fuck do I have to be in a damn funk about?"

As I say this, I point to the massive kitchen and look out the window again.

West Hollywood Hills is where I live. I knew I needed to stay in Los Angeles with my job, and I love it here. I'm never over nine miles from any of the major studios. Thanks to some early investing in real estate after my dad passed and left me some money, I get to live in the house of my dreams. Though I'd trade just one more day with my dad for this house, my job, and all my other earthly possessions. Fuck, I'd give it all up for one more minute. Just to hear his laugh.

Maeve doesn't answer any of my questions. She just keeps sipping and swaying, watching me with eyebrows slightly arched as I have my freak-out. She knows I need time to process either out loud or in my head or both before I make sense of things.

"You're right," I say, even though she hasn't said a word. "This is stupid. I should just let it go. Must be my period or Mercury is in retrograde again or something. I'm sure after this wine and some ass shaking I'll be just fi–"

I'm interrupted by the sound of her wine glass coming down hard on the countertop.

"Oh, helllll, no, Elaina James! No, you do not."

Oh shit, she used my full name. That's not good.

"No more of this '*it could be worse*' bullshit. Take your emotions seriously, just not literally, do you hear me? If you're in a funk, be in a funk. I know it doesn't happen to you often because you don't let it, but it's OK to just feel shitty sometimes and not have a name for it. Feel your feelings, girl! Also, maybe get some REAL dick in you sometime soon? That ought to help."

She wiggles her eyebrows at me when she says the words '*real dick*' because she knows all too well I gave up trying to date or have sex with men after I walked away from that dumpster fire of a relationship last year.

"I know you haven't been with anyone since leaving *he who shall not be named*." Her voice deepens a little. Her disdain for Ben runs deep. She never liked him. "And I'm not saying you need a man to make yourself happy, but an orgasm or two from something other than your collection of sex toys might feel good!"

I scoff at that.

"Oh, please. As if I'm guaranteed even a single orgasm from a man. No, thanks. I got it handled." I shoot her a smile that I know doesn't reach my eyes.

She looks at me, places a gentle hand on my shoulder and says,

"Time to get serious. You know what I think, babe? I think you need a break to focus on yourself. Just you. You haven't stopped working since we moved here six years ago. I think you've forgotten how to do things just for you. I think you've focused on your career as a way to avoid other things, too."

She squeezes my shoulder knowingly. It's no secret that my best coping tactic is avoidance.

"But before we get too deep into your coping mechanism, let me ask you… when's the last time you read a book? Or went on a non-work trip? I'm talking about no research, just for f-u-n?"

She arches her eyebrows so far up her forehead that I'm afraid she's going to lose them in that beautiful head of blonde hair.

By now, we've both emptied our first glasses of wine and I pour some more, realizing we need to open the next bottle because those were REALLY generous pours. Lizzo is showering us with some essential lyrics as "Good as Hell" comes on. Answering no questions, I dance and sing around the kitchen and Maeve joins me. By the end of the song, I'm feeling *almost* good as hell. And that feels like enough for now.

Maeve and I eat three different kinds of ice cream, finish both bottles of wine, and are both tucked into our own beds by 10 p.m. She basically has her own room at my house, and I have one at hers. It makes BFF sleepovers way more fun when I don't have to share a bed with her. She's a human popsicle who also steals all the covers in her sleep, so I'll pass on the bed-sharing!

———

I wake at nine a.m., which is early for me when I'm not on set. Mornings are *not* my thing. Maeve's words from last night keep repeating themselves in my head. When *was* the last time I read a book? Or went on a trip just for fun? When did I do something just for me, other than cook meals? I honestly don't remember. So, I make a list of all the things I want to do just because *I* want to do them. Here we go.

- Get a manicure and pedicure - this will make me feel pretty and even if no one sees my toes, I'll know they look nice.
- Have more dance parties in the kitchen. Alone, With other people. Just generally dance more.
- Host a dinner party. Make an extravagant meal. Enjoy every second of the chaos. This is for me because being around people brings me joy.
- Visit Mamá in Marblehead. Tell her I love her. Hug her tightly. Lots.
- Make a new friend? Just at least try. But only if it feels right and good and the vibes are impeccable.

Fuck, I feel lame writing that last one, but all of Ben's friends took his lying, cheating side. I'm also not very good at meeting new people unless they're on the set design team, and then it's hard to be friends with them because I'm their boss and no one wants to be friendly with the boss. Ugh. OK, moving along.

- Go on a trip just for fun. Pick somewhere I haven't been, or somewhere I have been and loved. Go and eat all the delicious things, see all the beautiful things and do whatever the hell I want.
- Kiss someone. Make it someone really kissable. If they suck at it, stop and find someone new. Kiss because I love kissing and because it's fun.
- Buy (and wear) sexy lingerie. Try to make it comfortable. Don't look at the price tags. Feel good about your little secret no one else can see.
- Wax my lady parts. Just because I've always wanted to try it. Because it's new. Because I want to know what it feels like.

Because Lord knows my girly bits haven't gotten any kind of TLC for more days than I care to count!

Alright, well, that's a solid start to a super-duper lame list of things normal women do fairly regularly. Great! I put my notebook down on my nightstand and head to the kitchen for some coffee. The machine isn't programmed to brew it for another forty minutes since I'm not usually up this early on a day off.

Ohhh, maybe I should go for a walk to that cute coffee stand on Santa Monica Blvd. Frankie will love that!

I turn off the coffee timer and notice a piece of paper sitting on the island. It's a note from Maeve.

Bon,

I hope you enjoy your sleep in! I'm off to see Charlie and get things ready for the NYE party, which you are most definitely, absolutely coming to. I don't care if your eye surgery makes you groggy or whatever. You're coming. Also, who books a surgery on New Year's Eve?

I love you. See you tomorrow night for prezzies!

-M

I totally forgot that Charlie, Maeve's twin, landed in LA today. She's coming to spend the holidays with us since Maeve couldn't fly home to London thanks to this movie being so delayed.

A wave of optimism washes over me as I think about coming home and snuggling on the couch with a cup of hot cocoa to listen to classic Christmas carols while wrapping presents and seeing my best friends tomorrow.

Nope. No, no no no no. I am NOT feeling better about everything anymore.

Christmas isn't the problem. It was a wonderful Christmas. For dinner, I ended up making a traditional Greek meal, all with my mom's recipes, which the girls loved. Charlie was in charge of dessert, and she made a Strawberry Fool, which is a delicious combination of strawberries, cream, and custard. Maeve was the bartender for the night, and served up delicious cocktails to keep everyone hydrated.

I spent the week preparing to check off items from my list. To satisfy my love of reading, I purchased two books - one murder/mystery and a romance novel - both of which were highly recommended by our resident bookworm, Charlie. As a treat for myself, I also made an appointment for a mani-pedi. Even though my toes are highly ticklish, I thoroughly enjoyed it!

So why the negativity? Well, I just found out I basically won't be able to see after my eye surgery for twelve to twenty-four hours because apparently, my eyes are extra sensitive to light. That's right. I'll be all sober and half-blind tonight, New Year's Eve, and likely unable and/or unwilling to be around a large group of drunk people. Did I mention I also can't drink? Yeah… whose brilliant idea was this, anyway?

Maeve's driver, Gary, picked me up and we're headed back to her house where the partying will begin in exactly three hours.

"How you doing, Miss Elaina?" Gary's gravelly voice is cheery in a way I simply cannot appreciate at the moment.

"Other than the current fucked up state of my eyeballs, pretty great! How have you been, G? It's been a while."

Gary has been Maeve's driver here in LA for years. He's a gentleman, no taller than my 5'7" frame, and laughs at everything I say, which makes me feel great. Also, he doesn't bat an eyelash at my colorful language.

"I've been well. Thank you for asking. Miss Maeve told me about your plan to get this surgery before year-end no matter what. Any regrets?" I would bet money that he's looking at me through the rear-view mirror with a quipped eyebrow and a little glisten in his brown eyes. I've seen it enough times by now.

"Not yet, but the night is young, right?" I feel my face for the giant sunglasses Dr. Blau insisted I wear. They are huge! And feel more like safety goggles than anything I would ever actually wear in public. "Actually, these glasses. These might be a regret. You can see them, so tell me your honest opinion, Gary. How bad are they?"

His deep chuckle makes my lips quirk up.

"If anyone can pull them off, it's you, Miss. Elaina." I can hear both the lie and the smile in his voice.

The car comes to a gentle stop, and I thank Gary, wishing him a very happy new year before I try to leave and remember I can't see. Gary takes me by the elbow and gently guides me to the front door, letting me know where each step is. I give him a hug that lasts a little too long, but I'm groggy still and maybe these drugs make me more affectionate than usual.

Ha! Not possible.

"Thanks so much, Gary. What would we do without you?" He chuckles as he knocks on the door. "I hope you have the best New Year's Eve ever. Drink some bubbly for me. Give your husband a big, juicy kiss at midnight, OK?"

Ugh, I guess this will be one more year I go without a midnight kiss.

Charlie comes to the door and takes my hand.

"Thanks, Gary. I've got her. Happy New Year!" I hear the front door close, and Charlie wraps an arm around my back. "Well, hey there, pretty girl. Lovely to see your face."

Charlie is making a joke in the most Charlie way possible, meaning it isn't obvious and I think it's hilarious. My giggling makes her snort, and my heart does a happy little somersault. I miss having her around.

"Oh, you've got jokes, Char! I know these glasses cover at least half of my face, but the doc said I need to wear them because of the light sensitivity." She takes me into the kitchen and helps me onto a stool. I hear her moving around the room quietly for a few seconds, then she's back next to me.

"I'll be right back, Lainey. I need to check on something with the caterers. I have some water here for you." I nod and run my finger down the bottle. I SO wish it was vodka. My eyes definitely hurt a little and I have to keep putting eye drops in them, so they don't dry up. Charlie looks at me… or I think Charlie looks at me.

"Remember, no looking at your phone. I dimmed the lights for you." She pats my hand lightly. "Back in a few." I nod as I hear her walk away.

I'm not supposed to do anything too strenuous, and I have to be very careful about light, so I guess I'm stuck with these crazy-looking sunglasses even inside. At least there's music. Maeve has one of my playlists on. I can tell because I hear "Let Me Love You" by Mario on the speakers, and '90s to early '00s music is kind of my thing. I stand up, needing a little kitchen dance. Just a little one. I take off my shoes and start to move my hips, singing along to the sexy lyrics.

———

Lost Love Found is available on e-book, Kindle Unlimited and paperback.

Made in the USA
Columbia, SC
21 August 2024

40761572R00274